**Daisy Wood** worked as an editor in publishing before she started writing her own books. She has a degree in English Literature and an MA in Creative Writing from City University, London. She divides her time between London and Dorset, and when not lurking in the London Library, can often be found chasing a rescue Pointer through various parks with a Basset Hound and a French Bulldog in tow.

By the same author:

*The Clockmaker's Wife*
*The Forgotten Bookshop in Paris*
*The Royal Librarian*

Under the name of Jennie Walters:

*What We Did in the War*

# *The* Banned Books *of* Berlin

Daisy Wood

avon.

Published by AVON
A division of HarperCollins*Publishers* Ltd
1 London Bridge Street
London SE1 9GF

www.harpercollins.co.uk

HarperCollins*Publishers*
Macken House, 39/40 Mayor Street Upper
Dublin 1, D01 C9W8, Ireland

A Paperback Original 2025
25 26 27 28 29 LBC 6 5 4 3 2
First published in Great Britain by HarperCollins*Publishers* 2025



A catalogue copy of this book is available from the British Library.

ISBN: 978-0-00-869918-5



Set in Sabon LT Std by HarperCollins*Publishers* India

Printed and bound in the United States

*For Amy Mae Baxter*

# Author's Note

This novel is set partly in 1930s Germany, several years before the outbreak of the Second World War in 1939, as Adolf Hitler and the Nazi party were gaining power. A few months after Hitler was made Chancellor at the beginning of 1933, the Nazi Student Association proclaimed a nationwide 'Action against the un-German spirit'. The students drew up a list of so-called 'un-German' authors, whose works were not only to be banned, but also thrown on to ceremonial bonfires across the country. On the evening of 10 May, 1933, Nazi students marched in torchlight processions through most university cities, and more than 25,000 books were burned while speeches were made about purifying German culture and thousands of onlookers cheered.

Hitler's propaganda minister, Joseph Goebbels, wrote in his diary the next day: 'I gave a speech outside the [Berlin] opera house, in front of the bonfire, while the filthy, trashy books were being burned by the students. I was at the top of my form. Huge crowds.'

I have tried to make the historical background of

this story as accurate as I can, although the characters and smaller scale events are mostly invented. Only one person who actually existed makes a brief appearance: Sir Horace Rumbold, the British ambassador to Germany from 1928–33. He was well aware of the dangers posed by Adolf Hitler, writing a report for the British government on his departure which ended with the words: 'I have the impression that the persons directing the policy of the Hitler government are not normal.'

Hitler's appearance at the Kaiserhof hotel, which I describe in the book, was also rooted in fact. I read about his visit in *Blood and Banquets*, the secret diary of Bella Fromm that was published in 1943. As far as I'm aware, no threat to Hitler's life was made on that occasion, although there was a possible plot to poison him on another occasion at the Kaiserhof. Several of his party were taken ill but Hitler was the least affected – possibly because of his vegetarian diet. There were other assassination attempts in the years to come – some of which only narrowly failed.

Steps to ban books have increased massively across the world in the past few years. The charity PEN America counted more than 10,000 book bans in public schools in the academic year 2023–24. It seems extraordinary that, given what we know about the past, there are calls today for books not only to be banned, but also burned. In my opinion, this is not a road we should be going down; we've seen where it leads.

# Prologue

*Oxfordshire, November 1946*

She is standing at the window, looking out into the park. Tawny deer are grazing on the other side of the ditch, mist pooling around their hooves like soft grey smoke. Mating season is nearly over and the stags only occasionally rear up to clash antlers – half-heartedly, as though they can't really be bothered. Mid-afternoon, and the sky is already darkening. How many times have you seen that view on a dreary winter's day, misery clenching your body in its iron fist?

She turns around as you walk towards her and gives you that old dazzling smile. 'Hello, stranger. Been a while, hasn't it?' And she holds out her hand for you to shake. You exchange pleasantries about the weather, and the journey you've taken to get here. By unspoken agreement, you're both talking in English.

'Have a seat,' she says, indicating a chair by the fire. 'It must feel a little strange, getting a taste of life on this side of the house. I'll ring for tea in a minute and that will really give you the heebie jeebies. I'm afraid things have gone sadly downhill since your day. Rationing, you know. It's worse than the war. If it wasn't for the chickens and the kitchen garden, we'd be sunk.'

'We heard things were tough over here,' you say, perching on the edge of the chair.

She's so thin! Not lithe and slender in the way she used to be, but shrunken, desiccated, as though she's being eaten up from inside. Her eyes look bigger than ever and her cheekbones stand out like razor shells.

'Thank you for coming,' she says. 'I wasn't sure whether you would.'

'Of course I came,' you reply. 'How could I refuse you anything?'

'We'll see about that,' she says, and smiles again.

The tea tray is delivered by a slatternly maid in wrinkled woollen stockings and no cap, and it's disappointing. Fish-paste sandwiches and leaden, grey crumpets with marrow jam that hasn't set.

She pours the tea and passes you a cup. 'So how are you?' she asks. 'You look well. Bonny, even, which I'd never have guessed. You must find me sadly diminished.'

You tell her that you're glad to see her, and it's true. She knows you better than anyone else in the world and being with her reminds you of the old days. Days that were so glamorous and painful, brighter and sharper than any that have passed since then.

She lights a cigarette, which makes her cough, and an ancient Pekinese waddles out of its basket by the fire and heaves itself on to her lap. Stroking the creature, she says, 'I invited you here because I have a request to make. I have several things to tell you which may come as a shock, but will you hear me out?' And she looks at you with an expression you've never seen on her face before: pleading, vulnerable.

'Of course,' you say.

'Promise?' she asks, like a small child, and you nod.

'Promise.'

And so she begins to speak, and the world stops turning. Stop talking! you want to shout, but you've given her your word and have to listen. On and on she talks, and her voice drips like acid, eating its way through your heart.

# Chapter One

*Berlin, June 1930*

They seemed to have been waiting for an eternity. The apartment lay hushed and still, with only the curtains sighing and billowing in the breeze like the sails of a ship. Opening the windows to let in some fresh air, Freya had been startled by the sharp, sweet smell of linden blossom. It seemed extraordinary the outside world should still exist, so focused had she been on her mother's laboured breathing and stifled groans as Ingrid tossed and turned in bed – for weeks, it seemed, rather than days. Yet a couple of streets away, the river Spree would be flowing steadily towards the centre of Berlin, past the Reichstag parliament building and on through Tiergarten park towards the magnificent Charlottenburg Palace before heading for open country and finally, the sea. Across the city, people would be lifting their faces to take deep, heady breaths of the intoxicating scent that spoke of summers gone by, of dappled sunlight falling through heart-shaped leaves and bees thrumming among the sticky yellow flowers.

'Come outside,' the trees called to Freya, their branches rustling, and she closed her eyes for a moment as she stood by the living-room window, folding her arms over her chest. She had been named after Freya, the goddess of love and truth who inhabited the lindens. 'You can never tell a lie under a linden tree,' her mother used to say, and now finally Freya had to admit the story she'd been telling herself for months – that Ingrid would recover and their family would survive, battered but intact – was merely wishful thinking. The doctor had called that day and warned them Frau Amsel didn't have long. Ingrid's time had come, and Freya would never again smell linden blossom with innocent pleasure. Her mother was calmer now, heavily dosed with morphine and sleeping for long periods with intervals of lucidity. The pauses between her irregular breaths were sometimes so lengthy that Freya would lean forward from her chair by the bed, watching with her heart in her mouth until her mother's chest rose again. She couldn't bear to let Ingrid go and yet at the same time, she wanted this torture to end. Her mother had suffered long enough; she deserved some peace.

And now Freya was waiting while her brother Otto sat with Ingrid – saying goodbye, presumably, though she couldn't imagine that. Emotion made Otto uncomfortable. She took another breath of the scented air and closed her eyes, prolonging the moment, until the sound of the bedroom door opening made her turn around.

'She wants to see you,' Otto muttered, his eyes downcast, avoiding Freya's enquiring gaze as he strode past. If they'd had a different kind of relationship, she might have made a move to comfort him, but she knew he'd resent her sympathy. She'd be allowed to cry because she was a girl and two years younger, but he couldn't be seen as vulnerable. Strength, that was what he valued: the ability to withstand one blow after another and come back for more. Freya admired her brother and probably loved him, too, but he also made her a little afraid. So she merely nodded, pretending not to notice his distress. The whole family had become used to pretending over the past few weeks. If they'd been able to face the possibility Ingrid would not recover, they might have had time to talk while she was still able to speak, to share emotions that were too overwhelming to bear alone, and make plans for the future. But that moment had passed and now they were making their way through a strange land as best they could, inarticulate and alone.

The few steps it took Freya to reach her mother's side felt endless. Her legs had suddenly become weak, and she had to wipe her damp palms down the frowsty dress she'd been wearing for the past three days. Ingrid was propped up in bed, her eyes closed. Freya laid her head gently beside her mother's on the pillow. Ingrid no longer smelt of clean laundry, fresh bread or spiced biscuits warm from the oven; now she gave off an odour of disinfectant and stale sheets. She was already slipping out of reach.

'*Mein Schätzelein,*' she murmured, opening her eyes and stroking Freya's hair. 'My little treasure. How much joy . . . you have brought me.' Every word was an effort.

'I love you, Mutti.' The phrase sounded so banal! Yet maybe language didn't matter after all. Freya and her mother had always been close, attuned to each other's moods; Ingrid would know how she was feeling. It was enough to lie here, just the two of them, their hearts beating in time.

'I'm going to miss you so much,' Freya murmured, although she hadn't meant to say anything at all.

Ingrid sighed. 'I'm sorry, *Liebling*. But you are . . .' Her voice tailed away and she motioned towards a glass of water on the bedside table. Freya helped her take a sip, which induced a paroxysm of coughing that left Ingrid exhausted. She lay back, letting Freya wipe her face with a lavender-scented cloth as she knelt by the bed. Neither of them spoke for some time. Freya had assumed her mother had gone to sleep when Ingrid suddenly opened her eyes and gazed intently into hers. What was she thinking? Was she afraid of what was to come?

They stared at each other in silence for a moment before Ingrid murmured, 'You must be . . . strong.'

'Of course.' Freya squeezed her mother's thin, cold hand. 'Don't worry about us. I'll look after Otto and Vati.'

'No!' Ingrid struggled to sit up, fighting for breath before falling back on the pillow. 'You have to . . . get away. Find your voice . . . and use it.'

Freya didn't answer for a moment, uncertain how to respond.

'Promise me!' Ingrid said, gripping Freya's fingers so tightly that she winced.

'I promise,' she replied hastily.

Ingrid nodded, closing her eyes and turning her face away. 'Fetch Ernst,' she whispered, so quietly Freya could hardly hear.

'Of course.' She kissed her mother on the cheek, lingering for a moment at the bedside until Ingrid raised her hand in an unmistakeable gesture of dismissal. Freya opened her mouth to speak, but there was nothing more to be said. Her eyes blurred with tears, she stumbled towards the door and through the apartment, snatching a shawl from the hook.

She stood for a moment outside, scanning the street for trouble. Fights were always breaking out between the various gangs: Nazis and Communists, who hated each other, Reichsbanner veterans from the war who seemed to hate everyone, and local thugs, looking for any excuse to settle old scores. The police waded in with relish, armed with rubber truncheons and guns they were liable to turn on anyone who happened to pass by. Prostitutes were gathering on street corners and lamps were starting to be lit in the various bars that would stay open till late at night. Freya had lost track of time but the shops were closed now, their shutters drawn. Her father was bound to be drinking in one of them; he spent as little time at home as possible these days. Freya understood his need to stay away: Ingrid's suffering was hard for anyone to bear, let alone her husband. Ernst was on the grumpy side of taciturn, but Freya had never doubted her parents' devotion to each other.

She found him in the third bar she tried, sitting in a dark corner near the back of the room. He was staring into the empty beer mug in front of him, his shoulders slumped in an attitude of despair. Freya paused for a moment, looking at her father as though he were a stranger. He wore a cap, as usual, and hadn't bothered to change out of his paint-stained overalls. He'd been working – when work was available – as a decorator for the past seven years, ever since his paint and wallpaper shop had shut down: a casualty of those terrible times when people couldn't afford to eat, let alone decorate their homes. The country had been crippled by debt, forced to pay huge sums to the Allies after losing the war, and prices had shot up by the day until the mark had become virtually worthless. The money Ernst had been so careful to save over the years shrank to nothing. The government printed more and more money, first million-mark notes and then billion-mark notes; the amount of cash you'd need to buy a loaf of bread would fill a wheelbarrow. The only way to get Ernst talking was to mention the Treaty of Versailles, signed at the end of the war, and then you'd be in for a lecture. Germany could never get back on her feet, that was the gist of it: the rest of Europe and America were bleeding the country dry, getting rich on the sweat of honest German workers and laughing behind their backs in the process.

Freya's earliest memories of her father were of him standing behind the counter in a shirt and tie and spotless white coat, directing his assistants up ladders to fetch tins of paint or rolls of paper, advising customers and negotiating discounts before ringing up their purchases with a flourish on the imposing cash till. That man and Ernst the house painter seemed two entirely different people. Losing the business had been a blow from which he hadn't seemed able to recover, and now it looked as though he was about to lose his wife. Freya's heart ached for him.

He didn't look up until she was standing directly in front of him, his bloodshot eyes instantly alert and fearful.

'She's asking for you,' Freya said briefly. 'Better hurry.'

Ernst nodded, draining his glass of the last precious drops before shambling out of the bar with his cap pulled low. Freya let him go; he wouldn't want her tagging at his heels and she needed some fresh air to clear her head. So, closing the door on a room that reeked of alcohol, fried sausage and cigarette smoke, she headed for the riverbank and walked along it for a while: briskly, so she wouldn't be taken for a tart. A barge passed by, carrying coal to the huge Klingenberg power station downriver.

Why had her mother told her to get away, and how was that even possible? Freya had passed all her exams with excellent grades and in September she'd be going to teacher-training college. Her mother had been the driving force behind that idea. Ernst had originally said there was no point carrying on educating a girl who was only going to get married and raise a family, but Ingrid had insisted the world was changing and their daughter was far too clever to change nappies and wash dishes for the rest of her life.

'God has blessed you with a talent, *Liebling,*' she would tell Freya. 'You mustn't waste it!'

Freya's talent was her imagination. Her mother would read to both children every night when they were small, and while Otto lost interest in stories at the age of seven or eight, Freya never tired of listening to Ingrid's soft voice in a circle of lamplight. They graduated from *Grimms' Fairy Tales* to the adventures of Heidi, the little girl who was sent to live with her grandfather in his mountain home. For months, Freya would go to sleep dreaming she was Heidi, snug in the hayloft of a wooden chalet, blanketed in snow. Ingrid also shared her love of poetry; in particular the works of Heinrich Heine, which she recited reverently from an edition bound in turquoise cloth with gold lettering on the spine that lived in a glass-fronted cabinet. Heine could be lyrical, Ingrid said, but he was radical too, brave enough to embrace new ways of thinking that challenged the status quo. By the age of twelve, Freya was taking out six books a week from the public library.

Freya's literature teacher, Fräulein Schneider, took a special interest in her star pupil – the most gifted to have come her way for years, she told Ingrid – and encouraged her to think of university. That was a step too far for Ernst, although Otto had paved the way to higher education by then. Ingrid wore her husband down. She had been putting aside some money over the past few years to help with Freya's studies and was determined her daughter should stay an extra two years at school to prepare for college entrance. It was an investment, really, as Freya would earn higher wages with some sort of qualification. In the end, Ernst grudgingly agreed that if Freya passed the necessary exams, she could train as a teacher.

'It's not what we planned, though,' he grumbled. 'She was meant to be taking over the business from you.'

Ingrid was a well-established dressmaker with a circle of regular customers. She'd taught her daughter how to sew, and Freya had been helping at evenings and weekends as soon as her stitching was up to it. Yet her heart wasn't in the work. Her mind might have been free to wander but she'd far sooner have been reading a book than squinting over a piece of cloth, and boredom made her slapdash and irritable. The only part of the process she enjoyed was watching her mother's clients fall for the vision of themselves in silk or velvet that Ingrid sketched with a few deft strokes of her pencil. Once the sketch had been approved, a toile of the pattern pieces was made from calico and adjusted for a perfect fit before the final garment was put together. There was something unbearably poignant about the gleam in Frau Bloch's eye as she stood before the mirror, admiring her squat, barrel-shaped body swathed in pale-yellow chiffon, or Frau Weber's timidly produced picture of a willowy mannequin in a ballgown, torn from *Elegante Welt* magazine.

'Freya hasn't the knack for dressmaking,' her mother told Ernst. 'I shall find an apprentice and train her up instead.' And that was that: once Ingrid put her foot down, there was no shifting her. Elisabeth came to join the household, and Freya only helped in the workroom when there was an emergency.

As Ingrid's illness (no one ever used the word 'cancer') advanced, she stopped sewing and concentrated on supervising Elisabeth – until she was feeling better, that was the message for clients. She'd become too tired for shopping and housework, which Freya did her best to tackle when she wasn't at school or cramming at home. A local girl came once a week to do the laundry and some dusting but apart from that, running the household was now seen as Freya's responsibility – even though Ernst spent days at a stretch without work, and Otto had plenty of free time during his long university vacations. This situation is only temporary, she told herself, without daring to imagine how it might end.

Freya had always been conscientious. She'd learned from her parents the sense of achievement that comes from a job well done and had worked hard at school, besides doing her chores at home. Both children had their duties, with Otto helping Ernst in the shop at the weekend in the good old days. He was always drawing and making things: tiny houses out of matches, clay or cardboard, which he would paint or decorate with scraps of wallpaper from the shop. He loved woodwork classes at school and could soon turn timber offcuts or packing crates into functional furniture.

'He might become a carpenter,' Ernst said, seeing the tray Otto made for his mother, 'and there's no shame in that. Good honest work, when you can get it.' The boy became obsessed with buildings, though, and carpentry fell by the wayside. He would cycle for an hour south of the city to watch the Horseshoe Estate taking shape: a huge ring of apartments and houses built around gardens in the centre, commissioned by a housing cooperative and designed by Bruno Taut.

'This is the future,' he told Freya, overflowing with enthusiasm. 'Modern homes with bathrooms, combining the best of the city and country. Berlin is bursting at the seams – we should knock down the slums to make way for developments like these, clean and full of light. Taut is a genius.'

It came as no surprise to anyone when Otto announced he wanted to become an architect, though his father took some time to come around to the idea. His best friend at school, Leon Kohl, was hoping to become a lawyer and must have encouraged Otto to aim so high. Clever Leon, with whom Freya had been hopelessly, thrillingly, agonisingly in love since she was thirteen. She hugged her feelings close and most of the time they were manageable, although she was often tongue-tied and blushing in his company. While he and Otto were busy talking about football teams or summer camp, she would snatch covert glances at the dark hair curling at the nape of his neck, or the dimples in his cheek when he laughed, or the stubble along his angular jaw. In bed at night, she would go over everything he'd said, thinking of all the witty or insightful remarks she could have made that would have had him turning to her with new respect. She didn't merely love him for his looks, but for the way he thought; he was so clever, and funny, and kind. Otto might have been his closest friend but Leon was nice to everyone, even the one-legged veteran who talked to himself on the street corner and growled at passers-by.

Unlike the Kohls, no one in the Amsel family had ever dreamed of university, and where would they find the money? Otto was determined, though, and his teachers told Ingrid and Ernst their son was right to be ambitious; scholarships were available for clever boys. Besides, as

Ingrid pointed out, unemployment was so rife that Otto might as well study for a while in the hope more jobs would be available by the time he qualified. So he spent Saturdays making himself useful at an architectural practice, applied for and duly won a scholarship, and had now been studying at the Technical University in Berlin for nearly two years. It was accepted that he was destined for higher things and could no longer be expected to help around the apartment. His education came first.

Freya, on the other hand, knew she could only study once she'd finished her chores. There had never been any question of her neglecting the shopping or cleaning because she had an exam the next day. That was just how things were; Otto and Ernst would have laughed in her face if she'd asked them to help. That evening, she finally faced up to the reality of her situation. She would be run ragged with housework on top of her studies, and if she complained or fell short, she'd have to give up any idea of a career. There would be no ally to speak up for her, with her mother gone.

Her mother gone. Freya stared into the falling dusk, trying to absorb the impact of those words. She couldn't bear to go back to the apartment and face the news she was dreading. If she could just stay sitting on this bench, gazing into the dark water, maybe she could keep Ingrid alive by the sheer force of her will.

# Chapter Two

*Berlin, June 1930*

Ingrid died the next morning, with her husband beside her. Those left behind were felled by grief, each retreating into his or her own bubble of misery. The days passed in a blur. Freya distracted herself with practical tasks: deciding which of her mother's clothes she could bear to give away and which she might remodel for herself, because fabric was expensive, after all, and her own wardrobe wasn't extensive; receiving visitors who'd come to pay their respects; planning the catering for Ingrid's funeral, held in the nearby Lutheran church, with cake and sandwiches in their apartment afterwards. The place was packed, with mourners overflowing on to the stairwell outside. Ingrid had been loved and respected, the recipient of many confidences which were never shared; she'd be sorely missed.

Freya's head ached from the effort of absorbing so much sympathy. She was leaning against the kitchen door for a moment with her eyes closed when she felt the tray in her hands being taken from her – and there was Leon, his dark eyes concerned.

'Let me help,' he said. 'You look exhausted.'

For the first time that day, Freya was in danger of breaking down. She drove her fingernails into her palms, knowing that if she started to cry, she might not stop, and that wouldn't be a pretty sight. 'I'm fine,' she said, summoning a watery smile. 'Thanks for coming, Leon.'

'Of course,' he replied. 'You know how much I loved your mother. She was always so good to me.'

Leon's own mother was a scientist who worked long hours in a lab, so he was often at the Amsels' apartment for meals and sometimes to stay the night. They all liked having him around: he was easy-going and funny, and Otto was more relaxed in his company. In fact, the whole family seemed to function better when Leon was there.

'Sit down, have a drink and talk to me,' he told Freya, filling one of the empty glasses with schnapps. 'You can spare five minutes.'

Talking to Leon alone was a delicious torture. Freya was usually tongue-tied and awkward, afraid of revealing the feelings which must surely be written all over her face, yet at the same time, longing to confide in him when she had the chance – or at least, make an impression.

'You won't always feel like this,' he said, passing her the glass and pulling out a chair opposite her at the table. 'When my father died, I couldn't bear to carry on at first. The simplest tasks seemed impossible and I couldn't stop thinking about him, missing him so much it was hard to put one foot in front of the other. With time, though, the burden becomes a little easier to carry.'

Of course: Leon's father had died suddenly of a heart attack a couple of years before. Freya took a sip of the fiery brandy. 'I'm so sorry. I had no idea what you were going through.' She hadn't known what to say when Leon had reappeared in their home, pale and sad, so she'd left her mother to console him, telling herself she didn't have the right.

He shrugged. 'Hard to imagine until it happens to you.' He covered her hand with his own, warm and comforting.

'But I should have tried,' Freya said, agonised. 'You must have thought I didn't care.'

Leon smiled. 'Not for a minute. No one could ever accuse you of that, *kleine* Freya.' She felt her cheeks grow hot and he added quickly, 'I mean, you care so much about everything. Perhaps you should be easier on yourself. You don't have to be perfect all the time. Now sit here for a while and let the world carry on without you.'

He got up, squeezing her shoulder as he left. Freya finished her schnapps, torn as usual between longing and despair. Would Leon always see her as nothing more than *kleine* Freya, Otto's kid sister?

At the end of the evening, when the last mourners had finally gone home and Otto was bringing through countless cups and plates for Freya to wash, her father asked them to stop for a moment because he had something important to say. They sat at the living-room table, where he told them that life for the Amsels would be changing. There was no money left in the bank or under the bed: every last mark had been spent on drugs and doctors' bills. Otto would have to work longer hours for the firm of architects which sponsored his training, and there could be no question of Freya going to college. She would have to carry on her mother's business with the help of Elisabeth, who was fully trained now.

'But I don't like dressmaking,' Freya blurted, horrified.

Ernst laughed mirthlessly. 'What difference does that make? Do you think I like painting and decorating? We need to earn money somehow, all of us, or we shall end up on the streets. I'm sorry, but there it is.' He couldn't look at either of his children. 'And Mutti always wanted you to carry on the business,' he added.

But that wasn't what Ingrid had wanted at all. Freya remembered what her mother had said, the night before she died: 'You have to get away.' She must have known her savings had gone and her daughter would be trapped.

Ernst cleared his throat. 'We shall have to make the best of things – sink or swim together.' He was humiliated, grey with exhaustion.

'Of course, Vati,' Otto said, clapping his father on the back. 'You can rely on us.'

Freya nodded without speaking. There was no point making a scene, today of all days; she would think everything over and come up with a plan when her head was clearer. Yet this was a double blow: not only had she lost her mother, now her hopes for the future were shattered, too. She couldn't blame her father for their financial predicament, but she would be making the greatest sacrifice and it stung that neither he nor Otto could acknowledge that. Although self-pity would get her nowhere, she allowed herself a moment to indulge.

The next few weeks were an ordeal. Every fibre of her being rebelled at the tedium of this new daily routine: appointments with customers for measuring and fitting, costing outfits, ordering fabric, endless cutting, shaping, seaming and hemming, as well as keeping Elisabeth up to the mark – not to mention cleaning and cooking at home.

Was this to be her life from now on, or at least until she married and swapped her father and brother for a different man to care for? It wasn't so much the loss of a teaching career she mourned, but those vital years to study, expand her mind and decide the kind of person she wanted to be. She did her best not to resent Otto, but it was hard to see him continuing much as before, apart from the fact he had to work longer hours at Meyer und Söhne and study in the evening. He still had time to go drinking with Leon, and for long hikes on a Sunday. Passing the mirror one day, Freya was shocked by the bitterness of her downturned mouth and the frown lines etched between her eyes. She looked at least ten years older than she was, a sour and disappointed creature. Ingrid would have been horrified.

As Freya sat at Ingrid's worktable, using Ingrid's scissors and tape measure, she found herself thinking more and more about this quiet, self-contained woman whom they had all taken so much for granted. Had she been disappointed with her lot? Had she ever wanted to travel, or write her own poetry, or live in a house with a garden, rather than a cramped apartment overlooking a noisy street? It was too late now for all the questions circling around Freya's head. There had been a desperation in the way her mother had gripped her hand and urged her to get away. It was the last thing Freya had expected her to say. 'I'll try, Mutti,' she promised silently. 'It might take me a while, that's all.'

Ingrid's presence still hung over the apartment, as though she had just slipped out and might return at any moment. Maybe that was partly why Freya felt so trapped. Sometimes she would have to down tools and hurry downstairs to stand in the fresh air, or at least put her head out of the sitting-room window. In the evenings, she went for long walks through the city, no matter the weather – either escaping from her mother or searching for her, Freya wasn't sure. She was lonely, with Otto shut in his bedroom or out with Leon, and Ernst off drinking somewhere. She'd lost touch with most of her school friends after staying on to take extra qualifications; by now they'd been settled in jobs for a couple of years and she didn't know how to talk to them. Charlotta was a copy typist, Greta worked in a factory producing turbines, and Anne was married with a baby. Her assistant Elisabeth wasn't much company, either. She was a year older than Freya and resented being told what to do or reprimanded for being late, which happened increasingly often. They'd never been close, and the fact Freya was now Elisabeth's boss made for added tension.

Eventually Freya gave herself a good talking-to, since her mother wasn't around to do it. Her father was right: pining for their old life was a waste of energy. She would have to play the game with the cards she'd been dealt. At least dressmaking didn't occupy her mind completely, and she liked hearing about the lives of her clientele: bored wives, ambitious mothers, secretive mistresses, jealous sisters, frustrated daughters; all yearning for love, or freedom, or security, or money, or – like Freya herself – escape. Perhaps if she found some new clients, she could take on another girl to help with the endless sewing that she found so soul-destroying and concentrate on building up the business. After a couple of years, surely the pain of Ingrid's death wouldn't feel so raw and she'd have the energy and finances to make a change. Otto might have a girlfriend by then, and maybe Ernst would have found a widow who could run the household. Freya could pass her mother's business on to someone else and move on.

She dreamed of a room of her own where she could live on her own terms: meeting interesting people, wearing unconventional clothes and eating only bread and cheese, or fried sausages from that stall under the U-Bahn that shook when the trains roared by. She would write – short stories or newspaper articles, perhaps even plays – and take a part-time job to get by. For the time being, she would work as a seamstress, but at some point in the future she was determined to express herself with words, rather than lengths of cloth. Despite Freya's best intentions, however, the business was steadily declining. Ingrid's former clients were drifting away, no doubt missing her mother's touch, and she found it hard to replace them. She wasn't a natural saleswoman, being reluctant to sing her own praises, and her taste was different from that of these matronly women; they were tightly corseted and liked to be upholstered in frills, swags and ruffles, whereas the fashion now was for loose, simple clothes to reveal a slender figure. They also wanted a confidante who understood their lives and would listen to their troubles. Freya and Elisabeth were part of a different generation. Why, they could hardly remember the war! And most important of all was the fact that times were getting harder by the day; people didn't have the money to pay for food and rent, let alone splash out on new clothes. Soup kitchens had sprung up across Berlin and the streets were full of people hungry for work as well as food.

Freya had never paid much attention to the family finances but she came to realise that her mother's business had been keeping them all afloat. Now the income from Mode von Ingrid had halved and she was having to make drastic economies in the household budget; they could only afford meat once a week and lived mostly off potato dumplings and rye bread. Ernst spent hours going through her accounts, seeing where she might save a few pfennigs and urging her to put up prices. She wanted to tell him he might have been more usefully employed finding work himself, but he was still her father, and she didn't want to hurt his pride. Matters came to a head one day when Elisabeth informed Freya as she was collecting her wages that she wouldn't be turning up the following week. She'd managed to find a job in the hat factory at Spittelmarkt, in the heart of the city.

'You could have given me some notice,' Freya said, although her first reaction had been one of relief. The joy of not having to listen to Elisabeth sighing and snivelling (she had a perpetual cold in winter and trouble with her sinuses in summer) was almost worth the pain of having to finish their outstanding orders by herself. That wouldn't take long, though. She had to face the uncomfortable truth: there wasn't enough new business coming in to justify two employees. Elisabeth had jumped before she was pushed, and who could blame her.

'Sorry, Mutti,' Freya said, during one of those one-sided conversations she was always having with her mother. 'Looks like you were right: I'm not a born dressmaker.'

After a sleepless night, pondering her options, she got up early the next day. Walking always helped her think, and the glimmer of an idea was already taking shape in her mind. Summer was long since over and it was a cold, raw day. The massive trees in Tiergarten park were leafless, and there were opaque patches of ice on the river that ran through it. Plunging her hands in her coat pockets, Freya headed deeper into the city, letting her legs take her wherever they chose. She ended up in the vibrant Schöneberg district, home to scores of clubs and bars but deserted at this time of the morning, except for a couple of women in furs and long evening gowns that trailed on the pavement, arm in arm with a champagne bottle tucked between them.

Shivering, Freya was rubbing her arms for warmth when her eye was suddenly caught by a flash of colour: a billboard poster showing a line of dancing girls kicking up their legs amid a froth of vivid tulle. 'Forget your cares at the Zaubergarten!' read the caption. Freya stared at the image for several minutes, transfixed, as the thoughts she'd been trying to pin down wove themselves into a plan. It was as though her mother had been leading her to this very spot. The main door to the building was locked but Freya banged on it anyway and after a few minutes was rewarded by signs of movement inside. A very old man in a cloth cap unbolted the door, opened it a crack and asked her what she wanted.

'I'm early for an appointment with the wardrobe mistress,' she replied, her teeth chattering. 'Will you let me wait inside?'

The old man squinted at her doubtfully.

'Please? It's freezing out here.' Freya smiled as winsomely as she could manage. Not saying a word, he opened the door wider and motioned her to come in with a jerk of his head.

She walked into a small foyer, carpeted in threadbare crimson with a crystal chandelier in the centre which looked as though it could do with dusting. A zinc-topped bar stood at one side, complete with a line of stools, and beyond that was a circular dance floor. The caretaker led her across it, and Freya caught a glimpse of a curtained stage in the next room, with a piano directly beneath and ten or fifteen round tables dotted about in front. The harsh light of day revealed every cigarette burn on the carpet, every chip out of the Bakelite table tops and every crack in the windowpanes, but she could imagine how the place would look when the curtains were drawn, the lights dimmed and the Zaubergarten girls sashayed onstage.

The caretaker opened a side door on to a narrow, winding staircase. 'You can wait down there,' he said, and shuffled off.

Freya descended cautiously, feeling her way, down to a corridor with doors on either side. They were all locked, except for one door at the end which stood ajar. Pushing it fully open, she found herself in a large, low-ceilinged dressing room, even shabbier than the theatre upstairs. Cobwebs clung to the cracked walls, and the various pots and potions among overflowing ashtrays on the dressing tables were coated with dust. The place smelt of face powder, grease paint and musty clothes. Endless pairs of stockings were draped over a makeshift washing line stretching across the room, and there were costumes hanging from hooks across the wall and ranged along a wheeled rack. Freya wandered about, trying lipsticks on the back of her hand and dabbing her cheeks with rouge. She sat on a stool for a while, gazing around, and then had a furtive rummage through a heap of clothes on the floor: black-and-white Pierrot outfits with ruffles around the neck, lying muddled together with the laced corsets and dirndls of traditional peasant dress, and some strange, oversized romper suits in blue and pink seersucker. It must have been a mending pile, since every garment had a trailing ruffle or hem, missing buttons or a torn seam.

The sound of voices raised in a furious argument made

her straighten quickly before the door was flung open and two people burst into the room: a stout, dark-haired woman in an astrakhan coat, and a younger man of thirty or so, wearing a black opera cloak lined with crimson silk.

'All I'm asking for,' he was saying, 'is a modicum of—'

'Ha!' the woman declared, pulling off a glove. She was about to continue when the sight of Freya pulled her up short. 'And who the hell are you?'

'My name is Fräulein Amsel,' Freya replied, wondering whether to hold out a hand or curtsey, and settling instead for an awkward nod of her head. 'The doorman said I could wait in here till you came.'

'What for?' the young man asked, looking her up and down. 'Are you planning to attack us? I warn you, we'll put up a fight.'

'I'm sorry to arrive unannounced, but I've come to offer my services,' Freya said. 'I'm a dressmaker, you see, and I've always wanted to work in the theatre.'

'Have you indeed?' the woman said drily. 'And has this passion suddenly become so overwhelming that you've had to rush here first thing on a Friday morning and share it with us?'

The young man sniggered, prompting her to glare at him.

'Something like that.' Freya drew herself up. 'My circumstances have changed, and now seems the right time for a new direction.'

'Well, you've had a wasted journey,' the woman replied, pulling off her other glove as she gazed coolly at Freya.

'Yes, Frau Brodsky has a positive army of helpers beavering away behind the scenes,' the young man declared, 'and yet she still finds it impossible to fulfil a simple order for nine sailor suits by the end of the month.'

Frau Brodsky tore off her hat and threw it at him. 'Because I'd been told Rhinemaidens, Herr Schwartz, as you very well know,' she cried, her husky voice rising. 'We'd already started work! You're constantly changing your mind, and who pays the price? I do!'

Herr Schwartz skipped nimbly out of range with a swirl of his cloak. 'You are a simple woman with no understanding of the creative soul,' he said. 'Fräulein Amsel, wouldn't you prefer to work for an artistic director? I shall need an assistant in my new role.'

'You?' Frau Brodsky shot him a look of withering contempt. 'All you do is spout airy-fairy nonsense and scribble childish drawings. What help do you need with that? Someone to carry the pencil and paper?'

'Perhaps I could assist you both,' Freya suggested, trying to sound professional. 'I'm skilled in all aspects of tailoring, from design to hand-finishing. And maybe I could improve channels of communication.'

'Excellent,' said Herr Schwartz. 'You can become my right-hand woman. I shall have a word with the owner immediately.'

'You will not.' Frau Brodsky was quivering with rage. 'And even if you do, it won't get you anywhere because he'll never agree. If this young woman is to work for anyone, it will be me. Now get out of this room before I lose my temper completely.'

'Leave your card with the doorman, Fräulein Amsel,' Herr Schwartz called from the safety of the doorway. 'I shall be in touch on Monday.'

Frau Brodsky let out a roar and cast around for a suitable missile, seizing a nearby tap shoe, which bounced off the closing door as Herr Schwartz retreated. 'Idiot,' she muttered when he'd gone, smoothing her hair. 'Calls himself artistic director but the owner's only taken him on out of pity.'

She took off her coat and draped it over a chair. Beneath it, she wore a black crêpe-de-chine frock with a white lace jabot at the throat, and a mass of gold jewellery. She always wore black, Freya was soon to learn. Her thick hair was cut in a simple bob that followed the line of her cheek, with a streak of pure white at the front. She looked like a plump-breasted, beady-eyed magpie. Gazing at Freya, she took a cigarette out of a mother-of-pearl case and lit it, her bracelets jangling.

'Well?' she said. 'What are you waiting for? Off you go.'

'But I thought you said I could work for you?' Freya replied, disconcerted.

'No I didn't. I said if you were to work for anyone, it would be me – that's not the same thing at all. There are hundreds of people looking for jobs at the moment. Why should I employ some girl who's wandered in off the street, even if I had the opportunity? I don't know the first thing about you.'

'My mother was a dressmaker for years. Have you heard of Mode von Ingrid?' Frau Brodsky shook her head, drawing on the cigarette. 'Well, she died a few months ago,' Freya continued. 'I've been carrying on the business but her clients are leaving. I need to earn some money and it's true, I do love the theatre. I could make myself useful, Frau Brodsky. You wouldn't have to pay so much for piece workers and I could suggest other economies. I'd sooner work for you than Herr Schwartz.'

'Of course you would. The man's an imbecile.'

'All the same, if he's prepared to offer me a job, I couldn't turn it down,' Freya replied. 'Although I can see how annoying that might be for you. I mean, you clearly have far more on your plate.'

'Herr Goldstein would never give that fool an assistant,' Frau Brodsky declared, though with less certainty than before.

'He might find it hard to refuse,' Freya said. 'I imagine Herr Schwartz can be quite persuasive.'

Frau Brodsky stubbed out her cigarette in an empty face-cream pot, narrowing her eyes.

'I'd be so much more useful here, though,' Freya went on. 'Why don't I show you what I can do? I could spend a couple of hours tackling your mending.' She nodded towards the pile of clothes in the corner. 'No obligation. You wouldn't have to pay me if you weren't satisfied.'

'Mending? That's a bit of a comedown for a *bona fide* dressmaker, isn't it?' Frau Brodsky remarked. 'If you are what you claim.'

'Well, I doubt you'll let me loose on anything more demanding,' Freya replied.

Frau Brodsky put her head on one side and looked at Freya for a long moment. 'Come with me,' she said, apparently reaching a decision. 'Let's see what you're really made of.'

She walked through the dressing room to a door at the far end which opened on to a smaller workroom, furnished with a sewing machine on a large table, an ironing board and iron, a chest of drawers and a couple of dressmaker's forms. Rolls of fabric and pattern-cutting paper were stacked along the wall, and a window high above let in some light.

'Our costumes are made up elsewhere,' she told Freya, 'but this is where we design them. Why don't you put together a sailor suit for me? Doesn't have to be finished: a toile will do. You can look at Herr Schwartz's sketch, for what that's worth, or draw your own.' She nodded towards sheets of paper on the table. 'Now, what will you need? Here's paper and calico,' she said, selecting rolls of the squared paper and cream-coloured fabric, 'and scissors – my own, so treat them with respect.' Taking a pair from the top drawer of the chest, she continued, 'And pins, needle and thread, tape measure, pencil and dressmaker's chalk,' placing each item beside the sewing machine as she spoke. 'I've called your bluff. Show me what you can do, Fräulein Amsel. I'll be right outside, so don't think of running off with anything.'

Freya was initially daunted. Herr Schwartz's drawing was little help: the figure he'd sketched was completely out of proportion so she had no idea where the waist was meant to be, whether darts should shape the bust or which trims might be appropriate. There was no suggestion of a hat, either, which she'd have thought was essential for a sailor – even one on stage at the Zaubergarten. Flipping the paper over, she began to draw on the other side, hearing her mother's voice in her ear: line down the centre of the body for balance, divide into nine equal sections, neck half the length of the head, legs four times the length of the head. Once she had the proportions right, she could start to design the outfit: a fitted bodice with short cap sleeves and a sailor's shawl collar attached to a short, flared skirt, with contrasting satin ribbon for a belt at the waist and stripes around the hem. She also sketched a jaunty nautical cap with an anchor on the front to be cut from gold card. Then, taking a deep breath, she unrolled lengths of paper and calico, picked up her scissors and got to work.

# Chapter Three

*Berlin, November 1930*

A random act of fate had brought Freya to this small cabaret club in the Schöneberg district, she reflected as she cut and stitched on that cold winter's morning: the place she hadn't realised she'd been looking for. All she'd known was that if she didn't get out of the apartment, and soon, she would suffocate. Working and living at home was stifling, whereas here in Schöneberg she felt part of the world again. She could hear the place gradually coming to life: footsteps overhead and whistling down the corridor, someone playing scales on the piano above, Frau Brodsky muttering to herself in the next room – and then a sudden bang followed by an alarming crash, which made her jump up, throw down her scissors and rush to the door.

Frau Brodsky was embracing a girl with a shock of ginger hair falling over her face, the pair of them swaying together in the centre of the room beside an overturned chair. The girl was groaning, while Frau Brodsky struggled to keep her upright. When she saw Freya, she called, 'Grab the chair – quick!'

Freya rushed forward to do as she was told, and together

they lowered the girl on to it. She sat with her head slumped to one side. Her skin was chalk white and a chemical smell overlaid the reek of alcohol on her breath.

Frau Brodsky shook her head. 'Oh, Perle,' she sighed. 'Not again.'

The girl opened one sooty eye, looked at her sideways and laughed. Then her stomach heaved and she put her hand to her mouth. Frau Brodsky lunged for a nearby wastepaper basket and just managed to catch a stream of foul-smelling vomit that splattered into it.

'Here,' she said, passing the basket to Freya once Perle had stopped retching. 'Make yourself useful. There's a lavatory down the passage.'

Holding the receptacle at arm's length and turning her face away, Freya ventured into the corridor to find it. She hadn't gone far before a door opened and Herr Schwartz's head appeared.

'Fräulein Amsel!' he hissed. 'Come and talk to me about chiffon and sequins. I know you are the one to turn my dreams into reality.'

'I can't at the moment,' Freya replied, indicating the basket. 'Perhaps another time?'

'Is that ogre sending you on errands?' he asked, leaning forward to peer into it.

'Don't!' Freya cried – but too late. He recoiled, staring at her in mute horror before closing the door in her face. She couldn't help but smile.

By the time she'd found the lavatory, done her best with the wastepaper basket and returned to the dressing room, all that could be seen of Perle was a mop of red hair falling over a blanket on a mattress in the corner.

'Is she all right?' she asked.

'She'd better be,' Frau Brodsky replied. 'We've a matinée this afternoon. Once the drugs are out of her system she can usually manage, just about. She might need some more pills to rev her up but one of the other girls will no doubt oblige.'

'Well, I'd better get back to work,' Freya said.

'I had a look at your toile,' Frau Brodsky told her, and Freya stiffened, wondering what was coming next. 'Not bad,' she went on. 'A little rough around the edges but you obviously know what you're doing. Your mother taught you well.'

Freya had to blink away the tears which Frau Brodsky either didn't notice, or pretended not to. 'Carry on,' she said briskly. 'At least attach that bodice to a skirt. I don't expect you to hem it.'

For the next however long – time seemed to fly past without Freya noticing – she worked on the sailor suit: shaping, pinning and stitching with a focus and enthusiasm she couldn't summon for the pile of half-finished outfits waiting for her attention back at the apartment. In this extraordinary place, people might fall down drunk, shout or throw things at each other, but they were also interesting and funny (if unintentionally). They expressed their emotions rather than brooding over them in silence. She felt at ease here; liberated. As she worked, she devised a plan for the future that seemed so obvious and so practical, she couldn't imagine why it hadn't occurred to her before.

Eventually she emerged, the garment over her arm, to find red-haired Perle sitting against the wall with her head thrown back and her eyes closed. Her face was chalk white, streaked with black rivulets where her make-up had run. Frau Brodsky cracked an egg into a glass and threw its shell into the wastepaper basket Freya had emptied and rinsed.

'Finished?' she asked, whisking the egg with the handle of a tortoiseshell comb. 'Hold it up and let's have a look.'

Freya displayed the dress from both the front and the back, turning it around slowly so that every detail was visible.

'Well done,' Frau Brodsky commented, producing a hip flask from her pocket and pouring a slosh of what smelt like brandy into the glass. 'I think we have a workable pattern there.'

'So have I passed the test?' Freya asked.

'Yes, I'd say so.' Frau Brodsky pushed the concoction into Perle's hand. The girl opened her eyes, took one look at the glass and closed them again. 'I'd be happy to have you making up costumes for me.'

'That's not what I want,' Freya said, because she was tired and angry now, and not ready to give up without a fight. 'I'm better than that and you know it. Why did you ask me to create this costume if you only wanted a piece worker?'

'Because it amused me,' Frau Brodsky replied coolly. 'You had a nerve, marching in here and asking for a job, so why not put you through your paces? And I thought maybe you could teach that idiot Schwartz a thing or two. But money's tight around here and I doubt the owner's going to let either of us have an assistant.'

'You don't know that, though,' Freya insisted. 'There's no harm in asking him, is there? That's the least you owe me. And you'd better be quick. Imagine if I ended up working for Herr Schwartz rather than you. Think about it: if I were on your side, I could deal with him so you didn't have to. Wouldn't that be a weight off your shoulders?'

Frau Brodsky pursed her lips.

'Come on, Bubbe,' said a sepulchral voice, and they turned to find Perle had come to life – almost – and was squinting down her nose at them through half-closed lids. 'Give the girl a break,' she went on. 'We all have to start somewhere.'

'Thank you, Fräulein,' Frau Brodsky remarked. 'When I want the opinion of a drunken guttersnipe, you can be sure I'll ask for it.' All the same, she stood with her hands on her hips for a minute or so, then plucked the dress from Freya's arms and sailed out of the room with it.

'Thanks,' Freya said awkwardly.

'Don't mention it.' Perle swallowed a mouthful of egg and brandy, shuddered and wiped her mouth with the back of her hand. 'Wouldn't kill the old trout to help someone else up the ladder.' She closed her eyes again.

Taking the hint, Freya retreated to tidy up the workroom while she waited for Frau Brodsky to return.

The lady was back within an hour, with a determined set to her jaw. 'Schwartz got there first,' was all she'd say. 'But the battle's only just beginning.'

And now Freya knew she had a chance. It would have been foolish to throw in her lot with Herr Schwartz – he was far too flighty, and who knew how long his position at the club would last – but she could use him to make Frau Brodsky want to hire her instead. Piece work was no use; she had already decided to clear out the workroom at home and turn it into a bedroom, which they would rent out for a steady income. The Amsels' apartment was well-located at the front of the building, rather than in the *Hinterhaus* at the back where the factory workers, street sweepers and labourers lived, and where gypsy children sang for small change in the courtyard. It was a respectable address with a balcony and she could charge extra for breakfast and supper. If Ernst and Otto didn't like having a stranger in their home, they'd have to lump it. Grief and worry had hardened Freya from a dutiful daughter and sister into someone altogether more ruthless. If an opportunity came her way, she wasn't going to let it slip by.

The battle for Freya's services lasted a week, at the end of which she was summoned back to the Zaubergarten and informed she was to work for Herr Schwartz in the morning and Frau Brodsky in the afternoon. She would start at eleven and finish at seven, just before the evening's first performance began, and her wages would be low but better than nothing. That night, she took off her apron after cooking the supper and told her father and brother she'd secured a job in costume design. Without telling an outright lie, she managed to imply that it was at the much larger Scala theatre down the road, rather than what was essentially a cabaret club. She'd be working for a proper variety theatre, she told her father – a respectable, well-run place. Ernst wasn't overjoyed about the idea of his daughter in such a precarious profession, especially if it meant his supper would be late, but the news she'd be earning a regular salary was cheering. Similarly, he was persuaded to accept the need for a lodger when he heard that he or she would pay two hundred marks a month for bed and board; housing was scarce in Berlin and people lucky enough to have jobs were always looking for cheap rooms.

So Freya finished off the last few orders in her book, put a cover over the sewing machine and stowed it away under her bed. She sold the workbench and bought a second-hand bed frame and mattress (carefully checked for stains and any signs of infestation), moved her own chest of drawers into the room and added a jug and washbasin to stand on top. The place looked cosy when she'd finished, and she'd cleaned it from top to bottom. She put up a card on the front door of the apartment block, and within a few days her advertisement was answered by one Walther Grube, who'd been visiting a friend on the third floor. Herr Grube was interviewed by Ernst and pronounced satisfactory. He was a bank clerk and also, Freya was alarmed to learn, a member of the National Socialist party.

'Would you rather have a Commie or a Jew?' her father retorted – to which the answer was yes, though she knew better than to say so. To hear Ernst talk, anyone would think Jews were responsible for all that was wrong in the world. Painting the comfortable homes of Jewish families sent him into a state of sullen fury. Their businesses were flourishing while his had folded because they were corrupt swindlers, in league with the banks. Take the Wertheim department store on Leipziger Platz, for example, with its glass atrium, frescoes and the colonnaded entrance that so fascinated Otto: how could such a monument to extravagance have been built, if not for dirty money? The architect had been Jewish and so were the brothers who'd founded the Wertheim chain; they were all in cahoots with each other and no one outside the tribe of Israel stood a chance. And as for that quack, Rosenthal, letting his poor wife suffer . . .

'That's not fair!' Freya had protested, stung at last to defend the man who'd looked after her mother with such patience and compassion. 'Herr Doktor did everything he could for her, you know that. All those times he visited and never charged us, even late at night. Mutti loved him. It wasn't his fault she didn't get better.'

Ernst didn't pay her any attention. He was a bitter man these days; Adolf Hitler might have been speaking directly to him.

'It could be useful to know someone like this Grube fellow,' Otto told them. 'The Nazis are going from strength to strength.'

The Nazi party had increased its share of the vote sevenfold in the election that September, and now the brown-shirted stormtroopers seemed to be everywhere in the streets, strutting around and expecting people to salute them. All those scruffy, unemployed youths who used to hang about on street corners had been given a haircut and an identity: one that made Freya shiver.

Still, the Amsels needed money and no one else replied to the card, so Herr Grube moved into the apartment the same day Freya started at the Zaubergarten. In some ways, he was an ideal lodger: he was quiet and clean, and spent most weekends cycling or hiking in lederhosen through the countryside south of the city, no matter the weather. On weekday mornings he left promptly for work at eight o'clock, wearing a navy-blue suit that had become shiny at the knees and elbows and a grey shirt that was just a little too tight, its buttons straining across his chest.

Freya didn't trust him. He had an uncanny habit of materialising from nowhere, appearing suddenly before her when she was washing the dishes or on her way to the bathroom. He liked to walk around bare-chested, and his pale, smooth skin repelled her; she imagined it would be clammy to the touch, like that of some sea creature, and the thought made her shudder. His eyes were pale, the colour of slush, and always sliding away rather than meeting anyone's gaze. She couldn't bring herself to call him Walther, unlike her father and brother. Otto admired Herr Grube because he was fit and muscular, and possessed a set of weights that he occasionally allowed Otto to borrow. Ernst appreciated the fact their lodger kept himself to himself and didn't indulge in unnecessary small talk.

Freya was to inhabit two different worlds. At home, she

lived among taciturn men; at the club, she was surrounded by laughing, weeping, squabbling, struggling, loving, jealous women. For the first few weeks, she was so busy trying to find her way around and carry out the jobs Frau Brodsky assigned to her that she mainly knew the girls by sight – apart from Perle, for whom she would always feel a special affection. They accepted her straight away, and before long the dressing room echoed with cries of, 'Freya? Come here, right away!' Soon she could fit names to their faces too and, listening to their conversations as she fixed a broken shoulder strap or helped the dresser with a costume change, form an idea of their individual characters.

There was blonde Angelika with the lazy eye, who always arrived at the very last minute and smoked like a chimney even when in costume; the two Sophies, one who sang like a lark but couldn't dance and the other who cartwheeled across the stage as though she were made of India rubber; motherly Gisela, everyone's friend and confidante; angry Helga, in love with a banker who would never leave his wife; Karin, who was so thin and pale that she must surely be ill; Irmgard, who worked as a teacher in the daytime and was usually exhausted; and last but not least, the eccentric English girl, Violet.

The fashion at the time was for bobbed hair but Violet's was dramatically cropped, shorn at the nape of her long, graceful neck. Heads turned wherever she went, partly because of her strange clothes – she was as likely to appear in a jacket and tie as a satin evening gown, and might have been mistaken for a beautiful boy were it not for the voluptuousness of her figure – and partly because of her dazzling skin, large grey eyes fringed with dark lashes and wide, generous mouth that turned down so fascinatingly at the corners. She had an unpronounceable second name so everyone simply called her

Fräulein Violet. Nobody quite knew what she was doing in Berlin, let alone the Zaubergarten, but she was funny and the customers loved her, both men and women, so the other girls let her be. Violet and Helga were the tallest girls in the troupe and alternated in solo roles, but there could be no doubt that Violet was the star. There was a wildness about her, a lack of inhibition that made her performance magnetic. When Violet danced, Freya ached with indefinable longing: for freedom, for Leon, for a life full of drama and desire.

Inspired by Violet and the glamorous world in which she now moved, Freya began changing the way she dressed. She took scissors and needle and thread to her mother's wardrobe, slashing necklines and hems, remaking the old-fashioned sleeves of blouses and embellishing Ingrid's black work frocks with pintucks, sashes and ribbon – developing a style that, she liked to think, was both elegant and bohemian. And then one Saturday, she had her long brown hair cut into a bob that emphasised her cheekbones and determined jaw.

*'Mein Gott!'* Ernst exclaimed when he saw her. 'Your beautiful hair, ruined! That was the one thing you had going for you. What would your mother say?'

'She'd say I was being sensible,' Freya replied. 'She was always complaining about having to brush it every morning when I was small.'

'Very full of yourself since you started working at that theatre,' Ernst said, glowering.

Freya didn't pay much attention to his disapproval. She would never have dared speak so boldly to her father in the old days but now she had to stand up for herself if she was ever to break away. With Ingrid no longer around to act as the family peacemaker, there was no buffer between Freya and Ernst, and his blinkered views were increasingly hard to put up with. Although he'd been forced to accept her job and the necessity for a lodger because they needed the money, he would sooner have her at home all day, cooking and cleaning. He didn't care whether or not she was fulfilled; her growing independence only threatened him. Freya was sad this should be so and yet, selfishly, her father's shortcomings made it easier for her to think of leaving him. He was alone and grieving but she couldn't sacrifice her life for his. Ingrid had given her permission to escape and as soon as she'd saved enough money, she would.

It wasn't long before Freya felt as though she had been working at the Zaubergarten for years. Herr Schwartz didn't make too many demands on her time. Some days he only appeared in the middle of the afternoon, and when he summoned her to his office along the corridor (his *atelier*, as he liked to call it), he mainly wanted to talk about his troubles. Frau Brodsky had the artistic sensibility of a donkey, he complained, and the owner was beginning to take her side over his. Freya had been introduced to the owner, Herr Goldstein, a balding, jolly man in a brocade waistcoat that stretched across his stomach.

'He's too soft for his own good,' Frau Brodsky told Freya privately. 'If I wasn't here to keep an eye on things, the Zaubergarten wouldn't make any money at all.'

Frau Brodsky, on the other hand, certainly needed an assistant. Although the costumes were made up by piece workers and she had a girl to take care of the mending and laundry, there was still a lot of work involved in day-to-day wardrobe maintenance and supervision. The dancers often had to change in a hurry and were hard on their clothes, which could end up torn, stained or mislaid. Furious arguments often erupted as shoes went missing, lipsticks were pinched or laddered stockings were secretly swapped with pristine ones. Yet when the lights dimmed, the piano quartet began to play and the velvet curtain rose, the girls all wore radiant smiles as they high-kicked their way on to the stage, flashing their glorious legs in unison: the epitome of glamour and physical perfection.

There were several other acts: two middle-aged men who sang satirical songs at the piano, an escapologist, an acrobat who juggled, a redhead who played swirling Alpine folk music on a fiddle, and a handsome, drunken poet who prowled the stage like a caged tiger. They were all introduced by Willi, a young man in evening dress with a monocle and an air of barely suppressed menace. Freya stayed to watch a whole performance from the wings one night and discovered that she did, after all, love the spectacle as much as she'd claimed. The music was so exhilarating and the girls so graceful and lovely that she couldn't help but be entranced. The club wasn't one of those tawdry places where you could hire a room by the hour with the girl of your choice, and where the dancers came dressed as milkmaids, schoolgirls or cats with false tails. Herr Goldstein had created an atmosphere of elegance and refinement, appealing to a discriminating clientele. The pianist was a virtuoso and the girls were well-trained and athletic; a choreographer dreamed up new dances and supervised rehearsals with them in the afternoons. Frau Brodsky's costumes were truly beautiful creations, titillating but not tawdry, and although most of the dancers ended up naked, that was accomplished in the best possible taste.

All evening, a cigarette girl threaded her way among the round tables, dimly lit with rose-shaded lamps, while waiters were on hand to bring more bottles of champagne. The men in the audience craned forward, mesmerised by the long, lean legs of the Zaubergarten girls; the women smoked and drank, indifferent, or pretending indifference. Prostitutes – both male and female – were sitting with many of the men, that was clear, but they were a different class from those who hung about on street corners. Customers could buy champagne for the dancers to drink at their table and talk to them, but that was the extent of their contact. Herr Goldstein was in attendance most evenings and the barman, a bare-knuckle street fighter, was on hand in case of trouble.

The Zaubergarten was a well-run place, by and large, and Freya felt safe there from the beginning. The girls liked her because she was quiet and helpful, and a good listener. Soon they were telling her their secrets: Violet's escape from life as a debutante, Karin's recent stay in a sanatorium, Perle's struggles with cocaine, Helga's plan to tell her lover she was pregnant so he'd divorce his childless wife, and then pretend to have had a miscarriage. So many stories of love, desire and loss.

Freya began writing in the early morning and deep into the night, taking some detail one of the girls had told her as a starting point and letting her imagination embroider the rest. She hardly knew why, but for some reason she wanted to think more deeply about these young women and capture their fragile, precarious lives on paper, as though she were pinning gorgeous butterflies to a board. No one would have recognised them as she'd taken a feature from one and a habit from another, adding a background that was pure invention. Anyway, the pages were for her eyes only. Writing liberated her mind and crystallised her thoughts; it helped her see the world more clearly, and consider the type of person she might become. She wasn't going to be a seamstress for ever. One day she would find her voice, as her mother had urged, and the world would hear what she had to say.

# Chapter Four

*Portland, Oregon, April 2024*

Maddie took out a book, stowed her jacket and backpack in the overhead rack and sat down. She'd left it too late to reserve an overnight cabin but the business-class seats were roomy and reclined all the way back, so she figured she'd be able to sleep for at least some of the time. She wasn't sleeping much these days, anyway. She'd reserved a spot in the quiet car so she wouldn't be tempted to use her phone and wouldn't be inflicted with other people's conversations either. All she wanted was to stare blankly out of the window, listen to music and read. Of course, she could have flown the same distance in a couple of hours, but she'd been promising herself this journey for years and now seemed the right time to take it; she'd have some precious time by herself to think and take stock. With a bit of luck, the seat next to her would stay empty, or be occupied by a private person with the same attitude; she couldn't bear the idea of spending thirty-three hours next to someone who wanted to chat or, even worse, knew who she was. She looked quite different now from her profile picture: her blonde highlights had grown out and her hair was longer, tied back in a ponytail. That afternoon, she was also wearing sunglasses and a baseball hat for extra camouflage. Glancing warily around the carriage, she was relieved to find no one watching her.

Ten minutes before the train was due to depart, a woman with silver hair in a pixie cut and a tanned, smooth face sat down beside Maddie. She looked edgy and cool in a black skirt, black chinoiserie jacket splashed with red and orange flowers, chunky black boots and a turquoise necklace to match her earrings. Maddie felt suddenly boring in her sweatshirt and jeans. They exchanged brief noncommittal smiles before she returned to her book and her companion settled down with an iPad and a tote bag, which turned out to contain – Maddie snuck a sideways look – a pair of knitting needles, from which hung a woollen scarf flecked with a rainbow of colours. Perfect. Maddie's shoulders relaxed a fraction and she went back to her book, although she realised she'd been reading the same page over and over again. Only when the Coast Starlight pulled out of Union Station did her tension truly start to ebb away. The train rolled past a group of tents under the freeway where homeless people lived and crossed the Steel Bridge, picking up speed. Maddie leaned back, suddenly exhausted. Her hand closed over her phone but she wouldn't look at it; she just needed to know it was there.

'You're running on empty,' Vanessa, the features editor, had said. 'When's the last time you had a vacation? Go away somewhere for a couple of weeks and take a complete break. By the time you come back, the fuss will have died down and these people will have found something else to obsess over.'

Maddie wasn't so sure. She worried that disappearing for a while would look like an admission of defeat, a sign the trolls had won. Maybe her reputation was trashed for good and no one would ever take her seriously again. On the other hand, Vanessa was right. Maddie had come to the end of her rope, and the thought of spending a couple of weeks chilling out in her childhood home with the people she loved most in the world was irresistible. She wanted to hug her grandpa, taste her mom's cooking, hear her brother's infectious laugh. Ben would set her back on the right path; he had an unerring sense of right and wrong, and couldn't care less about the opinions of strangers. He was joyful, too, and she needed a dose of uncomplicated joy right now.

'Of course we'd love to see you,' her mom had said. 'And actually, you could be so helpful right now. Gramps is going through an odd phase. He's become obsessed with something called Swedish death cleaning. Have you heard of it? Apparently you're meant to throw out most of your belongings so the house is tidy after you've passed. He says he's doing us all a favour, but it's been driving me nuts.'

Now an image of Maddie's eccentric grandfather flashed into her head: the bow ties he wore, a little looser around the neck these days; his leather shoes, slip-ons now, but always well-polished; the kindness in his rheumy eyes. She felt the usual stab of guilt for neglecting him in favour of her career – for all the good that had done. Her hand strayed to her phone again but she resisted the urge to switch it on. Beyond the window, miles of forest flashed past while her neighbour's knitting needles clicked a comforting rhythm. Maddie closed her eyes and sank into sleep.

When she woke up a few hours later, they were passing through farmland: fields of rippling grain or pasture where animals grazed, a tractor in the distance crawling over the earth like a giant bug, the sails of wind turbines turning slowly on the horizon. Houses clustered together in occasional isolated settlements, and a woman sitting on her porch waved as the train roared by; Maddie waved back. The sun was sinking behind the hills, and shadows were pooling in woods and valleys as the countryside prepared for night. She gazed at the scene, refreshing as a cool glass of water on a hot day. She had always loved travelling by train. Snatching glimpses of different worlds and other people's lives was endlessly fascinating, and the act of moving forward helped her think.

Hungry and keen to stretch her legs, she walked along to check out the dining car. The seat beside her had been empty when she woke, apart from the knitting bag, so she guessed her silver-haired neighbour might have had the same idea. And there she was, alone at a table for four. Dining on the Coast Starlight was part of the adventure: passengers were directed by the steward to any table where there was space. For a moment, Maddie wished she'd brought sandwiches; she hadn't the energy or desire to make conversation.

Inevitably, the steward showed her to the seat opposite her neighbour. 'Hello again,' Maddie said, resigning herself to the inevitable. 'You can't get away from me anywhere.'

The woman smiled, her eyes crinkling at the corners. 'We must be on the same schedule.'

Yet it was just one meal, and Maddie was used to asking people about themselves. It didn't take long before she'd found out that her neighbour's name was Kate and she was a retired nurse, travelling back to Sacramento after visiting her son in Portland. He'd been living in the city for a year and had just opened a vegan restaurant there.

'Is that why you're eating steak?' Maddie asked.

Kate laughed. 'I must admit, it tastes pretty damn good.'

Maddie ordered salmon and a glass of wine, feeling herself relax a little more. They talked about whether it ever stopped raining in Portland, although at least that kept the grass green, how vibrant the arts scene was and how friendly folks were, by and large – the usual kind of chitchat, though it was enough to tell Maddie she liked this woman, they had a similar sense of humour, and that Kate had no idea who she was. So when Kate asked, 'And what about you?' Maddie was able to say quite calmly that she was a staff reporter, going home to visit her family.

'That must have been a tough profession to break into,' Kate commented. 'How did you get started?'

'I wrote an article when I was fifteen,' Maddie replied. 'About choosing a prom dress with my mom, would you believe. I sent it to the local paper and they published it.' She shrugged. 'That was that, really. I knew what I wanted to do with my life from then on.'

The thrill of seeing her words in print, and being paid for them, was unlike anything she'd experienced before. She had a neat turn of phrase and had always done well in English and Literature, so it was natural she should choose a degree in communications and pursue a master's in journalism. Natural, too, that one of the many regional papers to which she'd applied should offer her a job – at the bottom of the pile, but she would work her way up. Everything seemed to fall into place, as she'd assumed it would. She had been so sure of herself back then. Where had all that certainty gone?

'It's getting harder all the time, though,' she added. 'It's more about an online presence than print editions nowadays, and hundreds of regional papers are closing down. There's just so much content available for free.'

Kate groaned. 'Tell me about it. We're constantly bombarded with other people's opinions. Life before the internet seems like another age and it was a simpler one, that's for sure.'

Maddie winced, feeling automatically for her phone.

Kate glanced at her. 'Are you OK?'

'Sure. I'm just in the middle of a . . . situation, that's all.' Ben's favourite euphemism for whenever things went wrong.

'Do you want to talk about it?'

And suddenly, Maddie did. She was never going to see this woman again, this stranger who seemed good-hearted and sensible, and mature enough to have weathered a few storms of her own. Maddie hadn't been honest with any of her friends about what she'd been going through; she'd shrugged and said she was fine when they asked if she was having a tough time. She hadn't confided in her mother, either, because Mom was a worrier with enough on her plate.

She took a deep breath. 'Look, you'll probably think this whole thing is a tempest in a teapot,' she began – and then stopped, uncertain how to carry on.

'Try me,' Kate said. 'Start at the beginning, and take your time.'

It had all begun with a trip to the zoo. What could have been more innocent? Maddie had thought, bewildered, at the start of it all. She'd heard about the zoo's involvement in the California condor recovery programme, whereby the endangered birds were bred in captivity and released into the wild: a great initiative which deserved to be more widely known. She'd visited the zoo and learned about the main threat to the condors' survival: poisoning from eating the carcasses of animals shot with lead bullets or killed with DDT, or from scavenging trash and ingesting microplastics. The zoo was also home to several condors that couldn't be released into the wild, and Maddie had watched in awe from a covered viewing area as the magnificent creatures wheeled through the sky. They were huge, the largest birds in North America, with a wingspan ten feet across. From a population of twenty-two birds in the 1980s, there were now 400 condors, half of them flying free. This was a good news story, surely?

Vanessa the editor had frowned when Maddie pitched the idea for her article. 'I don't know,' she'd said. 'Zoos are controversial. Some people think keeping animals in captivity is wrong.'

Maddie remembered a desolate tiger she'd once seen, pacing up and down behind bars in a small concrete pen. This zoo was completely different, though. The grounds were beautifully landscaped and maintained, and the animals seemed content and in great condition, with freedom to roam. Of course, she had no idea whether they'd have preferred to be in the wild, and maybe they would, but did that mean she couldn't write about the condors?

'OK,' Vanessa had said in the end. 'But just concentrate on the birds. Don't mention anything else or people may get upset.'

Yet people had got upset anyway. From a few expressions of disapproval online after Maddie's article appeared, suddenly a maelstrom of indignation engulfed her. Those opposed to zoos were loudly appalled by what she'd written, ignoring the conservation angle, and Maddie had been taken aback by their tone. There were so many awful things to agonise about: climate change, the opioid crisis, homelessness, school shootings – not to mention what was happening in Israel and Ukraine. Should zoos be added to the list? And was she a terrible person for not having realised that already? The general reaction had been so hysterical that it had seemed ridiculous at first. Maddie was used to a certain level of abuse online and usually managed to rise above it, but the comments she was getting on her social media accounts and in direct messages were becoming increasingly vicious.

Shortly after that, Maddie had found herself featured on a gossipy website dedicated to 'exposing the dirty truth about Portland people and places'. She was accused of having slept her way up the career ladder, of not checking her facts and inventing sources, of being paid by companies and individuals to say positive things about them. Anything she'd ever written was used as an excuse to attack her.

Someone calling themselves 'Nightshade' was usually the first to tear her apart in the comments, encouraging the others to wade in. 'I know where this girl lives,' he or she had posted recently, before the comment was deleted. 'Different guy every night, the ugly slut.'

This would have been laughable, were it not so unpleasant. Maddie's last relationship had fizzled out by mutual agreement months before and she still hadn't found the enthusiasm to start dating again. No wonder she needed to get away for a while. This Nightshade person was probably bluffing but the thought they might actually know her address made her afraid – along with all the messages saying she deserved to be run over by a truck, or raped, or tortured like the poor beagles in a science lab.

'I love animals,' she told Kate. 'We always had pets when I was growing up. How can people be so full of hatred towards someone they've never met?'

Kate sighed. 'I don't understand. We're living in the land

of the free, and look how beautiful it is.' She gestured out at the view: rolling fields and a couple of horses grazing in a paddock, their pale coats gleaming through the dusk. 'When I was growing up, kids were still getting killed in Vietnam. We have so much to be thankful for these days. Why do folks have to turn on each other?'

Maddie shrugged. 'Beats me. In the old days, people were thrown to the lions for sport – now we just tear them apart on social media.'

'Can't you ignore the abuse?' Kate asked. 'I mean, you don't have to read it, do you? Stay off your phone for a while and don't let these idiots upset you.'

'That's easy to say,' Maddie muttered. 'I need to have a profile for work, though. And even if I don't see the comments, I know they're there.'

It was hard to explain how much her confidence had been dented, how diffident she felt about expressing any kind of opinion now. She was finding it almost impossible to write anything for fear of the inevitable backlash, and viewing stats showed her articles weren't as popular as they used to be.

'Well, I'm from another generation so it's all a mystery to me.' Kate stood up. 'Think I'll head back. Are you coming?'

'Thanks,' Maddie said, 'but I'm going to check out the observation car.'

Kate was kind and meant well, but she didn't understand the issues and her advice to just ignore the trolls grated. Maddie knew she needed to be on her own for a while.

She spent the next couple of hours gazing out of the floor-to-ceiling windows as darkness fell, trying to soothe herself with the wonders of nature as the train thundered through the mountainous wilderness of southern Oregon. It didn't work.

# Chapter Five

*Los Angeles, April 2024*

It took Maddie a while to fall asleep once she was back in her seat and she was only dimly aware of Kate leaving the train early the next morning, too drowsy to fully rouse herself. When she woke properly a little later, the seat beside her was empty but the rainbow-coloured scarf had been tucked into her chair pocket, with a note that read, 'Finished in the nick of time and wanted you to have this. Stay strong, Maddie – the world is still a good place, and it needs people like you.'

She wound the scarf around her neck, inhaling the faint smell of sandalwood and feeling its soft warmth seep into her skin. What a horrible person she was: grumpy and unappreciative to a kind woman who'd only been trying to help her. Rubbing her eyes, she glanced out of the window. By now the train had reached the Californian coast, and she reached for her sunglasses to look at the expanse of sparkling water, ruffled by the wind into a glittering silver mosaic. In places, the rail tracks ran so close to the shore that they might have been travelling over the sea. The ocean rose and fell in constant motion, swelling into waves that broke into foam before being sucked back to rejoin the surf. The rhythm was soothing. Maddie picked up her phone to take a picture, then laid it down again and simply watched.

The hours passed slowly and uneventfully. She took a shower, read her book, dozed, finished a crossword puzzle, took a sandwich from the café to the observation car, dozed and read some more, until finally she was stepping out into the warm night at Los Angeles station. From there it was only a short bus ride to Silver Lake, where Maddie's mother and brother lived. Her parents had gotten divorced when Maddie was ten and Ben five, their father remarrying soon after and moving to the east coast. Maddie hadn't heard from him in years and hardly thought about him; he hadn't been a great dad even when he was around. Her mother had brought up the kids with the help of her own parents, and Maddie's grandpa meant a hundred times more to her than her father ever had. She was suddenly eager to see him, suppressing the usual stab of guilt over not having kept more regularly in touch.

She'd only got halfway down the path before the front door opened and Ben was walking down the path to meet her, beaming.

'He's been waiting for you for a day and a half,' said her mom, Sharon, as her children came into the house together. 'Lord knows why you couldn't have flown and spared us this torture.'

'Great to see you, too.' Maddie hugged her mother close with the arm that wasn't thrown around Ben. She was home, with a pot roast in the oven and everything exactly as it should be: the grandfather clock ticking in the hall, the coiled rag rug in front of the stove and a jug of tulips from the garden standing on the battered kitchen table. She slid into her usual seat, her fingers feeling for the notch she'd naughtily carved into its edge when she was eleven – for reasons she still couldn't fathom – and let herself relax.

Over supper, she caught up on the news they hadn't been able to share in rushed phone calls.

'I've been trying to help Gramps with the death cleaning,' Sharon began, 'but I haven't really got time and we're driving each other crazy. He doesn't seem to realise that I might find talking about his death just a tad upsetting.'

'I'll go over tomorrow and see what I can do,' Maddie said.

Sharon squeezed her hand. 'Thanks. By the way, don't be alarmed if he acts a little strange.'

'How do you mean?' Maddie asked, but before her mother could elaborate, Ben stood up.

'I'm going to my room,' he announced. 'Good night.'

'Ben!' Sharon protested. 'Maddie hasn't finished eating. Sit down till we're all done.'

Ben ignored her, carrying his plate to the dishwasher and taking an age to slot it carefully into place. He left the room without looking at them.

Maddie raised her eyebrows. 'Is he OK?'

Sharon frowned. 'He's been a little unsettled recently. Don't worry, it'll soon blow over.'

Now Maddie thought about it, Ben had been uncharacteristically quiet over dinner. He usually loved to repeat the same stories over and over again, with as much enthusiasm as if he were telling them for the first time, but there had been no familiar anecdotes today. He'd also refused to answer when Sharon had asked him a question, which wasn't like him at all.

'I'll check in on him later, once he's finished his chores, and see if he'll open up,' Maddie said. Ben had an evening routine that never varied: tidying his room, putting out clothes for the next day and watching reruns of *Friends* on his iPad.

Sharon fetched them both another beer. 'That's enough about us. How are things with you, honey? Sorted things out with Steve?'

'We broke up a few months ago, but it's no big deal,' Maddie replied. 'A relief for both of us.'

'I'm sorry,' Sharon said, patting her hand. 'Why didn't you tell me?'

Maddie shrugged. 'Like I said, it wasn't a big deal. And I didn't want you to worry.'

'I do worry, though,' Sharon said. 'None of these boyfriends of yours' – she made them sound like they were figments of Maddie's imagination – 'seem to last very long. That dreadful business with Aaron is bound to have affected you. Maybe you should have counselling.'

'Mom, please!' Maddie exclaimed. 'When will you get it through your head that I don't want to talk about that?'

'I'm sorry,' Sharon said again. 'What a terrible mother I am.'

'Yeah, you are,' Maddie replied through gritted teeth. 'If I'd bought you, I'd take you back to the store for a refund.'

'Seriously, though,' Sharon said, scooping back her grey-blonde hair, 'I've been thinking a lot about your childhood recently, wondering whether I got the balance right between you and Ben. Do you feel like you missed out? There must have been so many times when I wasn't there for you.'

'Relax, it's fine,' Maddie told her. 'In some ways, Ben took the heat off me – I could get up to all kinds of stuff while you were focused on him. And Grandma and Gramps were always around.'

Ben had had open-heart surgery when he was three months old, and he'd been in and out of hospital for another year after that. He didn't develop at the same rate as other babies or toddlers his age, and needed physical therapy sessions several times a week to help him progress. Throughout Maddie's childhood, Sharon was constantly ferrying him to some appointment or attending yet another meeting to discuss the next steps in his care. Maddie couldn't remember when she first heard the words 'Down syndrome', let alone 'Trisomy 21', the more formal name for Ben's condition. He was just her precious brother, uniquely himself. She'd loved him from the moment her parents had brought him home from hospital, and had received unquestioning devotion in return. They fell out sometimes, like all siblings, but never for long.

All the hours she'd spent helping Ben with the exercises needed to develop muscle tone and help with his balance had strengthened the bond between them. As soon as he could walk, Ben had insisted on meeting her off the school bus, no matter how bad the weather, and he could never settle to sleep until she'd kissed him goodnight. Ben brought out the best in their family – except for his dad, sadly – teaching them to be patient and kind, open to embracing people who marched to the beat of a different drum. He had bucketloads of charm and a wicked laugh, and she wouldn't have changed a hair on his head.

She helped her mother clear the dishes and sat with her on the couch for a while, trying not to fall asleep, before climbing upstairs. When Ben answered her knock, she opened the door to see him sitting up in bed in his pyjamas and perched nearby, choosing her spot with care. He hated the duvet being rumpled.

'So, anything new to show me?' she asked, looking at the trestle table on which Ben's art materials were meticulously arranged. He'd shown an early passion and talent for drawing, and with Sharon's help, the year before had started a business producing greeting cards and T-shirts featuring his designs.

He shook his head. 'Still sunflowers and birds.' Birds were Ben's speciality: a line of them on a wire, all identical, with one doing something crazy like hanging upside down, wearing a top hat or a tutu, flying a plane or catching butterflies in a net. Sometimes he'd add a slogan: 'Follow your own path', or 'See the world in a new way'; sometimes he'd let the picture speak for itself.

'Can I have a look?' Maddie asked, wandering over to the table. Ben's sketchbook lay open, showing a drawing of one of his characteristic stick men with a round head and blobby nose, sitting with his legs drawn up in a bird cage. She studied it, looking for meaning, but was unable to find any, beyond a general air of sadness.

'Here, I brought you something,' she said, spotting the rainbow scarf at the top of her backpack. Surely Kate wouldn't mind her handing on the love.

Ben examined the scarf solemnly, holding it against his cheek and looking suddenly so vulnerable that her heart ached for him. Everyone had their struggles but his were harder than most.

She draped the scarf around his neck. 'When you wear it, you can think of me and it'll feel like we're closer together.'

'Thank you.' Ben grabbed her arm and pulled her close, burying his face into her shoulder.

'Ben, is everything OK?' she asked, when eventually he released her. 'You're not worried about anything?' She was on risky ground here: her brother often couldn't find the words to express his feelings and the effort left him frustrated.

'Gramps has his own home and so do you.' Ben tied the scarf in a careful knot. 'I want one too.'

'You mean, move out and live on your own?' Maddie asked. He nodded. 'Have you talked to Mom about this?'

'She won't let me. It's not fair.'

'Let me have a word with her,' Maddie said. 'This is a big step, Ben. We need to think about it carefully.' She hugged him again. 'But I'm so proud of you. My little brother, growing up.'

Sharon had always been careful to tread a fine line between encouraging Ben to develop new skills but not pushing him so far that he failed and became frustrated. Maddie could see her mother might have reservations, but surely Ben wanting some independence was a positive move? She was too tired to think straight now; they could all discuss the matter together tomorrow. Shouldering her backpack, she walked along the landing to the bedroom where she'd agonised, studied and dreamed her way through adolescence. Torn patches in the wallpaper showed where posters of boy bands had once looked down on her, and some of her old clothes still hung in the wardrobe. Lying back on the bed, she took out her phone to check for any messages – and then, because she couldn't resist, to flick through her various social media accounts.

Some anonymous person had kindly alerted her to a new line of attack. On the discussion board devoted to annihilating her reputation, she saw a photograph of Ben that had been used a while back to promote his artwork. Underneath, Nightshade had commented, 'Her brother's retarded. Guess her mom had him when she was old,' and someone else had added, 'Prolly a smoker and drinker too.'

Maddie sat bolt upright. It was one thing to attack her, but to go for her family was crossing the line. And that word! How dare anyone reduce talented, funny, caring Ben to some ignorant label that was merely designed to hurt? How could they be so cruel? She was filled with a blind, irrational fury that had nowhere to go. If Nightshade had been in front of her, she would have let rip.

# Chapter Six

*Los Angeles, April 2024*

'Madeleine, honey! At last!' Gramps threw his arms wide and Maddie bent down for a hug. He'd never been a tall man but he seemed to have shrunk further every time she saw him. Stepping back, she searched his face for signs of the strange effect that her mother had mentioned, and was relieved to find he looked as good-natured and unruffled as ever. In fact, she noticed a new light in his eyes and a sense of purpose about his movements. It was a warm day but he was colourfully dressed in a blue plaid shirt under his tweed vest with a red bow tie. When she was a teenager, Maddie had been embarrassed by the eccentric outfits her grandfather wore. He was a little more restrained these days, and she'd matured enough to appreciate his style.

'Come on through,' he said, ushering her down the hall of his duplex at top speed. 'Would you like a coffee? You look exhausted. Did you get in late last night?'

'I didn't sleep too well,' Maddie replied. 'But no more coffee, thanks – I've just had one. Tell me about this death cleaning, Gramps. Sounds morbid to me.'

'You couldn't be more wrong,' he said. 'It's the most life-enhancing thing you could imagine – clearing the decks, you might say, for the next phase. Of course I got rid of a pile of things after Betty died and we sold the house, but I seem to have accumulated just as much junk since then. Once it's gone, I can look ahead with a clearer mind to focus on the things that really matter. You'll thank me when I'm dead.'

'Gramps! I don't like to think about that,' Maddie protested.

'Well, I need you to,' he said. 'Madeleine, I want you to be my ally. That's what they call it nowadays, isn't it? Your mom doesn't understand and I don't want to worry sweet Ben, so I need you to speak up for me. Don't worry, I'll explain.'

He opened the door to his study and stood back to let her pass. Maddie's heart sank when she saw the state of the room: piles of books and papers all over the floor, and teetering stacks of cardboard boxes.

'Most of this can be taken to the recycling centre,' her grandfather said. 'You've brought the car, haven't you? But I want to go through a few things with you first.' He moved a file from his chair to the desk and sat, motioning Maddie to do the same. 'Now listen. I'm preparing for the end, Madeleine, and I want you to help me.'

Maddie stared at him, lost for words. 'Not too soon, I hope,' was all she could manage to say.

'You never know.' Gramps glanced at the photograph of his late wife in a silver frame on the desk. 'You probably don't remember your grandma's death but it was very sudden – here one minute, gone the next. A blessing for her, of course, not having to suffer, but so much unfinished business for those of us left behind. All the conversations we never had, the decisions that should have been made together . . .' He shook his head. 'It won't be like that when I die.'

Maddie shifted uncomfortably. 'This is a bit downbeat, Gramps. Maybe you need a holiday? Or perhaps a new hobby? If you're not playing so much golf, you could always try bowls.'

He tutted with irritation. 'You're as bad as your mother. What's the matter with everyone nowadays? Death is a part of life. It's coming for all of us sooner or later and we might as well acknowledge the fact. Madeleine, you disappoint me. I thought at least I could talk to you.'

'But I hate to think of you passing away.' Her eyes filled with tears.

'Dying, you mean,' he said.

'All right then, if you insist – dying,' she went on. 'It would be awful if you weren't around. We'd miss you so much.'

He took both her hands in his and squeezed them. 'But it's going to happen one day, honey. Why don't we get used to the idea together?'

'I guess,' Maddie said doubtfully.

'Good job.' He smiled at her. 'It's going to be fine. My mother showed me the way, you see. When she got sick, she sat me down and we went through the options together. She was German, if you recall, and they're a much more logical race. She'd lost her own mom when she was young with no preparations made, so she was determined to do things differently.' He gazed into the middle distance, his eyes far away. 'She was a force of nature. You'd have loved her.'

'Tell me about her, Gramps,' Maddie said, but he shook his head.

'Another time. That's a long story and we need to press on.' He passed her a ring binder labelled 'Robert Cole's Last Act'. 'So these are my plans for the funeral: favourite music and hymns, a couple of poems and a prayer, where to hold the service and the wake. Also, a copy of my will and a signed form saying I don't want to be resuscitated or kept alive on a machine. Got that? I tried to explain all this to your mom but she wouldn't listen, so I'm telling you. I'm eighty, I've had a good life and I'm ready to go when my time comes.'

Maddie opened the folder reluctantly. It was going to be a long day.

They worked all morning, Gramps directing Maddie from his chair as she held up items for his verdict. He'd been a history teacher and was a voracious reader so there were dozens of books that she put aside on his instruction to take to a dealer. Most of them were in English but there were also a few in German, including a volume bound in burned leather that left dark streaks on her hands. Sections of pages were welded together, charred at the edges, and a faint aroma of smoke still clung to the paper. From the layout of the text, she guessed it was a collection of poetry.

'Do you really want to keep this?' Maddie asked, wiping her palms on her jeans. 'It looks a little the worse for wear.'

'Of course!' he exclaimed. 'My mother brought it all the way from Germany; it must have meant something to her. I wonder . . .' He turned the book over in his hands.

'Wonder what?' Maddie asked.

'Well, you remember the Nazis banned a whole heap of authors because they were Jewish, or gay, or held views that weren't acceptable – and then burned their works, to show they meant business?'

'Oh yes.' Maddie sat back on her heels. 'I've seen a photo somewhere.' She shivered. 'Awful.'

'What if this was one of those very books?' Gramps asked. 'At any rate, I wouldn't dream of throwing it away.'

So there were evidently limits to death cleaning. Two photograph albums also escaped the cull; Maddie was particularly interested in the first, which showed various pictures of her grandfather as a child and then a young man. There didn't seem to be any baby photos but he was a cute little boy, with round cheeks, curly hair and the same gentle, wondering expression on his face she knew so well.

Maddie paused at a snapshot of a young woman, probably in her mid-thirties, smiling at the child she held in her arms as though they were sharing a private joke. She had thick wavy hair and a mischievous expression.

'That's my mom,' Gramps said. 'Your great-grandmother, Freya.'

'She was lovely.' Maddie felt instantly they would have been friends.

'She sure was.' Gramps sighed. 'I've always thought she deserved an easier life than the one she got, but I guess that's the luck of the draw. My father was killed in the Second World War before I could even meet him, so Ma brought me up on her own.'

Maddie sat back on her heels. 'How did she end up in California?'

Gramps shrugged. 'Hitler, I guess. She wasn't Jewish but she could probably see the way things were going. She didn't like anyone telling her what to do, or what she could and couldn't say. I think she had a rough time in Germany before she came to the States in 1938, before the war. She wouldn't talk to me about what happened but she never wanted to go back.'

'I can't believe we've never had this conversation before,' Maddie murmured.

'Well, I didn't like to say too much about my mother in front of Betty,' Gramps replied. 'They never got on, you see. It had been the two of us on our own for so long when I was growing up that I guess Mom found it hard to share me with another woman.' He clapped his hands. 'Now, on we go! No time for chit-chatting.'

Maddie took a last look at Freya's picture before closing the album. Here was a young woman who'd escaped true evil, travelling thousands of miles on her own to make a new life in a strange country. She wasn't the type to let some anonymous cowards dictate her life, and there was a lesson for Maddie in that.

They broke for lunch an hour or so later, feasting on a strange assortment of food from the fridge and store cabinet: instant noodles, cheese on graham crackers, potato chips with cocktail sauce, canned peaches and peanut-butter cups.

'Is anything on your mind, dear?' Gramps asked, after they'd finished eating. 'You seem a little out of sorts.'

'Oh, it's nothing, really,' Maddie replied. 'Just a stressful time at work.' It seemed so feeble to talk about her worries, compared to the hardships of previous generations. 'Tell me some more about your mom, Gramps,' she went on. 'Did she have a job?'

'Sure,' he replied. 'She was a wardrobe mistress for some of the big movie studios. Sounds glamorous but it was hard work. Just about covered the bills but we lived pretty much hand to mouth. I never realised we were poor at the time, though – my childhood seems idyllic, looking back. Mom and I were happy with the little we had.'

'So she wasn't bitter about what she went through?'

'Well, if she was, she hid it from me.' Gramps searched in the cabinet. 'Sorry, honey, I'm out of coffee. Will tea do instead? Oh no – I'm out of that, too.'

'No problem.' Maddie replaced the mugs. 'I'll run by the grocery store on the way back from the recycling centre this afternoon and pick up a few things.'

'Set your face towards the light, that's what Mom used to tell me,' he went on. 'Look outward rather than inward and don't be afraid to stick up for yourself. That advice has served me well my whole life. Maybe it'll help you, too.'

Look outward rather than inward: those words ran through Maddie's mind as she worked. She'd been obsessing about her own problems rather than sparing any time for her family; it had been weeks since she'd had a proper conversation on the phone with either Ben or her mother. Well, at least she was here now, and maybe she could put things right.

After another couple of hours, the study was more or less clear and the car loaded with boxes of books and bags of paper for recycling. Maddie had emptied the shelves of the tall, glass-fronted cabinet, but when she opened the double doors beneath, she was dismayed to find a couple of cardboard boxes pushed to the back.

'What's all this?' she said. 'I thought we were done.'

'No idea,' Gramps replied. 'Let's investigate and find out.'

One of the boxes was surprisingly heavy. Maddie reached inside to find a wooden case with a sloping front and a metal carrying handle, fastened by two brass hooks. Opening them, she lifted the lid to reveal a gleaming black typewriter, its ivory keys ringed with silver.

'Would you believe it!' Gramps said, delighted. 'I thought that old thing was lost.'

'Is it yours?' Maddie asked, releasing a couple of clips and carefully lifting out the machine.

'No, it was Mom's.' He shook his head. 'The number of nights I used to fall asleep listening to the sound of her clickety-clacking away.'

'But I thought you said she was a dressmaker?'

'Well, I guess she had correspondence,' he replied vaguely. 'You know, bills and so forth.'

Maddie looked at him. 'Really?'

'We must keep it in the family, at any rate,' he said. 'You're the writer, Madeleine – it should be yours.'

'Thanks. I'd love that.' She ran her fingers over the keys her great-grandmother had touched, watching the cascade of metal levers rise and fall, before turning to investigate the other carton. It was full of film magazines from the thirties and forties: *Daily Variety*, *The Film Daily* and several other titles. There was also a sheaf of signed photographs of movie actors: women in furs and soft focus, men in evening dress.

'We can't throw these out,' Maddie said. 'I could sell them for you online, or maybe we should give them to a library somewhere.'

'Sure, whatever you think.' Gramps yawned. 'Listen, honey, I'm done. I might take a quick nap, if you don't mind. Thanks for everything.' He squeezed her hand. 'Now, there's one last favour I have to ask: somewhere special I want to visit . . .'

'So how did it go?' Maddie's mother asked warily, wiping her hands on a dish towel.

'Fine, I think,' she replied. 'But I see what you mean about Gramps.'

'Did he show you the funeral file?' Sharon asked.

Maddie nodded. 'And he's asked me to take him to the Death Café. Apparently they all sit around talking about the end over tea and cake.'

Sharon sighed, shaking her head. 'He's obsessed. It's so gloomy.'

'But he doesn't seem depressed. He says he's making it easier for us when the time comes.' It was certainly the case that Gramps had seemed energised by his plans for the future. And yet, could he really contemplate death with such equanimity? Maybe he was just whistling to keep his spirits up.

'Is Gramps going to die?' Ben asked, materialising behind his mother.

'No, of course not,' Sharon said briskly, turning around.

'He's old, though,' Maddie added, 'so it'll happen sooner or later. He wants to be prepared.'

Sharon frowned at her, but Ben merely nodded and went back into the kitchen.

'He can cope,' Maddie told her mother. 'I mean, Gramps is taking things too far, but we can't pretend he's immortal.'

'You know Ben hates uncertainty, though,' Sharon said. 'Just tread carefully.'

Maddie followed her brother into the kitchen. 'Have a look at what we found in Gramps' study,' she said, laying the typewriter case on the table. 'This is what everyone used before computers came along.'

Ben was mystified by the lack of a screen, though he enjoyed hearing the bell ring when the end of a line was reached. The typewriter would need a new ribbon and several of the keys stuck together when Maddie pressed them, but it was generally in good condition.

'Will you help me unload the car?' she asked Ben. 'There's some more cool stuff you might like to see.'

She and Ben carried the box up to her bedroom and unpacked the contents. This was exactly the kind of task her brother enjoyed: sorting and arranging a collection of items according to his own particular system. He lived in the moment, focusing only on what lay before him.

'I don't want this one,' he said, handing the last magazine back to her. 'It's different.'

Maddie looked again and realised it was not a magazine at all, but a faded brown envelope. Inside was a notebook bound in embossed leather, fastened by a rusty brass clasp. Its pages were covered in handwritten German and a complete mystery; Gramps had tried to teach her a few words of the language when she was a child but she'd forgotten most of them. The book looked like a diary, as some of the entries were dated, although there were several pages of continuous text with underlined titles that might have been articles or stories.

'What's that?' Ben asked.

'I'm not sure,' she replied. 'We'll have to ask Gramps to tell us what it's about.'

She tried to slip the notebook back in its envelope but it wouldn't fit smoothly; investigating, Maddie found that a black-and-white photograph of two young women was caught at the bottom. The girl on the right had a cool, androgynous look, her hair cropped short at the nape of her long, graceful neck and falling over one smoky eye. A silk blouse slipped off her naked shoulders and strings of beads hung around her neck and the waist of her low-slung harem pants. Her arm was draped around the neck of a girl Maddie immediately recognised as Freya, although she was a few years younger and slimmer than in the previous photographs. She wore a tight-fitting black dress with a tasselled sash and stood with her hand on her hip, head tilted. Her eyes were also outlined in kohl and her skin was dazzlingly pale. She looked in need of a good meal and a decent night's sleep. Both girls were gazing directly at the camera but with very different expressions: Freya's was wary, while her companion stared brazenly at the unseen photographer, chin lifted.

Maddie turned the picture over. '*Violet und ich, der Zaubergarten*' was written on the reverse, in the same hand as the words on the envelope. 'Violet and me, the Magic Garden', according to Maddie's translation app.

Her great-grandmother was becoming more intriguing by the minute.

# Chapter Seven

*Berlin, December 1930*

The first Christmas without Ingrid was hard for the Amsel family, although they did their best to carry on with the usual traditions. Freya rolled dough for the cinnamon-spiced *Lebkuchen*, stamping them out with her mother's star-shaped cutter and loading tray after tray into the oven. Her father said when he smelt them baking, as he did every year, 'Surely it can't be Christmas already? Somebody should have told me.' Yet the biscuits weren't as light and crisp as her mother's, and none of them had the heart to eat more than one or two. Freya gave the rest away to their neighbours.

Ernst went to the market on Christmas Eve and came back with a small fir tree under his arm, filling the room with a painfully familiar scent of pine forests and excitement. Freya remembered the year she and Otto had got up in the dead of Christmas night, having convinced themselves it was morning, to discover a box of tin soldiers and a skipping rope under the tree in the living room. How golden the days seemed then, looking back! She and Otto had had their squabbles as children, but they'd played together for hours, building forts in their bedroom and racing each other on scooters around the park. They had been so close once; surely that bond couldn't simply disappear? Otto never talked to her about his plans or hopes for the future these days, and she couldn't think how to start the conversation in a way that seemed natural. As they decorated the Christmas tree with the usual candles and strands of tinsel that evening, Freya could sense her mother looking down on them. Ernst and Otto must have felt the same, but none of them could bear to mention the person on all their minds, the one whose absence had changed everything.

The only consolation, as far as Freya was concerned, was that Herr Grube was spending the holiday with his family in Bavaria. She disliked him more than ever, although he'd ingratiated himself with Ernst and Otto, and he'd certainly improved the household finances: he paid his rent promptly every month and he'd recommended her father as a decorator to several of his colleagues in the Nazi party. In fact Ernst already had jobs lined up for the first three months of the new year – and he'd be working for decent German folk, he declared with satisfaction, not flashy Jew trash. 'He's a solid fellow, that Walther,' Ernst pronounced. 'Let's hope he stays for a while.'

Otto had taken to cycling or hiking with Herr Grube at weekends. When the pair returned from their expeditions on a Sunday evening, windblown and ruddy-cheeked, the apartment seemed too small to contain their sweaty, masculine energy. Their studded shoes clattered up the stairs as they chatted together in harsh voices, Walther apparently liberated from his shell by Otto's company in the great outdoors. Freya resented the fact her brother preferred to spend time with their reptilian lodger rather than her, and she missed seeing Leon at her brother's side; he was never invited along on the trips.

'He doesn't have a bicycle,' Otto replied curtly when she asked why not. 'And anyway, he couldn't keep up. Walther sets a fast pace.'

Grube had smirked, turning away, but not before Freya noticed and disliked him more than ever.

If Herr Grube had been with them, he and Otto would probably have gone hiking or skiing on the afternoon of Christmas Day; in his absence, Freya told her brother she was planning to visit their mother's grave and invited him along. The headstone wasn't yet in place but she wanted to decorate the mound with ribbons and branches from the Christmas tree, so that Ingrid would be included in the festivities. Somewhat to her surprise, Otto agreed to come with her.

It was bitterly cold and fresh snow squeaked under their boots as they tramped through streets ringing with the cries of children sledging or pelting each other with snowballs. A few other people were gathered at the cemetery, tending graves or standing about, stamping their feet or rubbing their arms for warmth. Freya knelt to arrange the pine boughs around the wooden cross that marked Ingrid's grave, feeling a little self-conscious. Otto stooped to join her, lighting a small candle in a jam jar that he'd produced from his pocket, and they exchanged rueful smiles.

'Drink?' he asked, passing her a hip flask, and she raised it in a toast to the mother who had brought her up with such fierce love and ambition.

'Do you think she'd be proud of us?' she asked, returning the flask.

Otto shrugged. 'Well, I guess we're managing. She'd say Vati was drinking too much but that's always been the case. I don't think she'd blame you for not making a success of the business.'

'That's good to know,' Freya retorted, stung.

'All the same, this job of yours . . .' He hesitated.

'What about it?'

'Well, I'm not sure Mutti would have approved. There are a lot of sleazy types hanging around those places and you don't want to get a bad reputation. Walther thinks a respectable girl shouldn't be working there.'

'Walther?' She stared at her brother in disbelief. 'What business is it of his?'

'He has the right to an opinion, and you should pay attention,' Otto said. 'He has your best interests at heart.'

Freya swallowed her indignation and it was a few seconds before she could speak calmly. 'I'm sorry, I know you spend a lot of time with Herr Grube, but I don't care for him, and I don't like to think of the two of you discussing me behind my back.'

'That's why I'm talking to you now, face to face,' Otto said. 'Freya, listen to me. Germany's on the brink of change and it's going to be huge. We're in a mess at the moment, but Adolf Hitler can see the way out and guide us through it. Once we've got rid of all the Jews, Commies and degenerates, our country will become healthy and strong again.'

Freya scrambled to her feet. 'You can't really believe that man and his thugs are the answer!'

Otto stood too, his eyes bright and hard. 'All right, some of the brownshirts take things too far, but who else has a vision for the future? That's why people are cheering for Hitler: he's given them something to believe in. You should hear the plans he has for building new houses, creating jobs and helping families like ours get back on their feet. He's passionate about architecture, for one thing, which will mean plenty of work for me.' He might as well have been reading from a propaganda leaflet.

'Has Herr Grube been telling you all this?' she asked.

'I've been doing my own research,' Otto replied. 'Joined the Nazi party and gone to a few meetings.'

Freya's heart sank further. 'I wouldn't trust Hitler as far as I could throw him,' she said. 'Have you forgotten how he tried to take over the government by force and ended up in jail?'

Eight years before, Herr Hitler had marched into a beer hall in Munich where the governor of Bavaria was making a speech and announced the 'Berlin Jew government' was finished and the Nazis were taking over. The putsch hadn't succeeded but the following trial and then imprisonment of Adolf Hitler had brought his name to everyone's attention.

'These jobs he promises are all about preparing for another war,' Freya went on, 'and that's the last thing we need.'

'He's impatient for change, and who can blame him? Sometimes you have to burn the old wood to make room for new growth.' Otto took another swig from his hip flask. 'Just think about what I've said, Freya, and open your eyes. Loafing about the Schöneberg district won't do much for your prospects. And don't dismiss Walther out of hand. He likes you, despite his reservations, and you could do a lot worse. He has excellent prospects and he gets on with Vati, which is important. The three of you could live together quite amicably once I've left home.'

The thought of being confined to their apartment with

Walther Grube and her father was so appalling that Freya was momentarily lost for words. 'I'm not sure I want a husband,' she said eventually. 'Not for years, anyway. I might prefer to study, or travel, or have a career of some sort – like Leon's mother.'

Otto snorted. 'A career? There aren't enough jobs for men these days, let alone women. And what more important role could you ask for than motherhood? Mutti always said having children was the greatest joy of her life.'

Freya looked at the mound of earth shrouded in dark-green branches, the tiny candle flame at its head guttering in the wind. 'Mutti never liked Hitler.'

Otto smiled. 'Mutti wasn't interested in politics.'

He was so certain, so cocksure. Freya knew their mother would have found his revolutionary zeal as troubling as she did. Herr Grube might have accelerated the process, but her brother had turned into someone she no longer recognised and didn't particularly like. Shivering, she wrapped her coat more closely around her.

'By the way,' Otto added, as they turned to leave, 'I'd keep your opinion of Herr Hitler to yourself in front of Walther. At the very least, he'd never propose if he heard you talking like that, and at worst, he might even report you to the Nazis. They could make life extremely difficult for all of us.'

A harsh wind blew through the corridors of the Zaubergarten over the course of the following year. Patrons bought fewer bottles of champagne and their tips were smaller. The stage manager was discovered to have been selling half-price tickets on the street and keeping the proceeds; Herr Schwartz reluctantly took his place, abandoning hopes of artistic direction, and the number of dancers was reduced to six. Helga's plan to ensnare her lover had misfired: she'd become pregnant in reality, rather than myth, only to discover he had four children already and still had no intention of leaving his wife. Yet his offspring were all daughters and he wanted a son, so he was prepared to fund Helga until she'd had the baby, and even longer if it turned out to be a boy.

'So I've got a fifty-fifty chance,' she said cheerfully, eating grapes in the dressing room with her feet up on a chair, 'and maybe I'll keep the baby anyway, even if it is a girl. I should like to have something of my own.'

'Look at the size of you already!' Frau Brodsky exclaimed. 'If you ask me, it's twins.'

Helga only laughed and said that made the odds even better. She left soon afterwards, to be followed by Irmgard, who married a fellow teacher, and Karin, who went back to the sanatorium for a longer stay. They weren't replaced, and in due course the piece workers who made up new costumes were dispensed with, followed soon after by the girl who took care of mending. Freya agreed to work longer hours for a raise in salary and told her father she'd no longer be able to cook the evening meal. Since he was working regularly and Herr Grube was now in residence, they could surely afford a maid – either that, or live off bread and cheese. Ernst blustered and Otto sulked, but Freya didn't give in. The Zaubergarten had become everything to her; the less time she spent in the apartment, the better. Grube had installed a large framed photograph of Herr Hitler above the mantelpiece, and the glorious leader's cold eyes seemed to follow her around the living room. In due course, Hedwig arrived to help with the shopping and cooking: a sullen girl with skin as pasty as uncooked dough and small, suspicious eyes. Freya was nominally her mistress, but she felt uncomfortable giving orders and they had the same uneasy relationship she'd suffered with Elisabeth.

One Friday in the spring, Otto brought Leon around for supper. He hadn't called by for weeks, and her warm glow of happiness now made Freya realise how much she'd missed him. She usually ate her meal in the kitchen after the men had finished – Hedwig leaving after she'd prepared the meal – but that evening Leon persuaded her to sit at the dining table with them for the venison stew with red cabbage. She saw him glance at Hitler's portrait and then at Otto, but he made no comment. He asked her what she'd been up to and she told him about life at the Zaubergarten, ignoring Herr Grube's obvious disapproval.

'My brother doesn't think it's a suitable place to work,' she said, 'although he's never been there.' She pulled a face at Otto. 'But beggars can't be choosers and anyway, I enjoy the work.'

'Sounds like fun,' Leon said. 'We should visit one evening, Otto, to see for ourselves whether Freya is safe. And maybe you'd like to come too, Herr Grube?'

Freya could tell Leon didn't think much of their lodger from the way he looked at him, and knew that the offer was only being made out of politeness.

'No, thank you,' Grube replied, with an expression of distaste. 'I'm not in the habit of frequenting cabaret clubs.'

'And yet you might come across people you know,' Freya told him. 'From the party, I mean.' There was usually a scattering of men with swastika armbands among the audience, and lately their numbers had been increasing. Frau Brodsky regarded the Nazis with loathing but the owner,

Herr Goldstein, treated them with deference, not wanting to have his windows smashed in the middle of the night.

'That surprises me,' Herr Grube said stiffly. He turned to Freya's father. 'Were you aware the place is run by Jews?'

Ernst raised his hands in a gesture of defeat. 'What can one do? They have business interests everywhere, and where there is dung, you will find flies buzzing around. I've had to work for Jews myself in the past and didn't like it one bit, let me tell you, but needs must.'

'Herr Goldstein is a good employer,' Freya said, getting up to clear the plates. 'He pays me fairly and treats me well. And Frau Brodsky is like a mother to the dancers.'

Despite her gruff exterior, all the girls knew they could come to Rosa Brodsky if they were in trouble and she would do her best to help. When Perle had gone missing for several days without warning, Rosa had searched the streets and bars for hours until she'd found her and brought her back to the Zaubergarten. Freya had even heard a rumour Frau Brodsky had taken Karin to a sympathetic doctor, following complications after a back-street abortion. She went through to the kitchen, avoiding Herr Grube's gaze.

Shortly afterwards, Leon joined her there. Closing the door behind him, he said softly, 'So this is the famous Grube fellow Otto's been talking about for months. What do you think of him?'

'He makes my flesh crawl,' Freya whispered, 'and he's turning our apartment into some sort of Nazi headquarters. He salutes that picture of Adolf Hitler every morning and he wants to hang a swastika flag from the balcony.'

They laughed, though it wasn't really funny, and Leon took a cloth to dry the dishes Freya had washed. 'Perhaps you should move out,' he said. 'Can you afford a room somewhere?'

Freya paused with her hands in the water. Living on her own was a dream for the future, and it was strange to hear Leon suggesting the idea so matter-of-factly. 'It would be a struggle,' she said. 'I need to save some more money first. And I worry about my father. He seems so lonely and helpless, somehow.'

Yet she wasn't much company for Ernst, in reality, hurrying away to Schöneberg at the first opportunity and returning home as late as she could. Maybe she was simply frightened of having to manage by herself.

'Always thinking of other people.' Leon smiled at her. 'What do you want for yourself?'

I want you, Freya thought, looking at his dark eyes and the curve of his mouth. I want you to put down that cloth, take me in your arms and kiss me until our lips are raw. Can't you tell?

'I should like to become a writer,' she said, surprising herself. 'The Zaubergarten is fine for the moment but I'm not staying there for ever.'

Leon nodded, as though this was a perfectly sensible proposition. 'And are you writing now?'

She told him about her portfolio of short stories and he asked whether he might read any, making her both nervous and exhilarated. She would have to consider carefully which to choose and give them a final polish before exposing a part of herself that had always been so precious and private. Showing her work to anyone else was unimaginable but she knew Leon would give it his full attention – and perhaps he would think differently about her afterwards. His view of her might already have changed, merely for harbouring such an unexpected ambition.

'It will be a hard life,' Leon said. 'And if Herr Hitler ever comes to power, harder still. There will be no place for—'

Freya shook her head briefly in warning, widening her eyes. The door had opened silently and now Walther Grube was standing behind Leon, his arms folded.

'I'm sorry to interrupt, Herr Kohl,' he said, his voice flat, 'but Otto and I are going for a drink and wondered whether you'd like to join us. I'm sure Fräulein Amsel can manage the dishes by herself.' He glanced briefly at Freya before looking away.

'Of course.' She took the cloth from Leon's hands, forcing a smile. 'You go, I'll be fine. Enjoy yourself!'

The look on Grube's face made her deeply uneasy, especially remembering her brother's words in the cemetery. She might loathe their lodger but she didn't want to provoke him into making life difficult for Leon, of all people.

Summer came, and Freya decorated her mother's grave with linden blossom. Times were hard, despite the sunshine. People hung around street corners throughout the city, looking for work; one day she saw a young woman with a placard around her neck, announcing she would take any job going. And then in June, the government announced there was no longer enough money to pay reparations for Germany's part in the war.

'I told you the country's been bled dry!' Ernst cried, and he and Herr Grube had a long and heated conversation about the iniquities of the Treaty of Versailles.

In July, the banks suddenly closed. It seemed that anarchy might break out at any moment as desperate people beat on the doors of those imposing, uncaring buildings – for all the good that would do – demanding their money, and trading insults and blows with each other as none of the bankers was available. The Nazis strode about more importantly than ever in their swastika armbands, as though their moment had come.

'Out of chaos will come order,' Herr Grube told Freya with satisfaction as he prepared for a long bicycle ride, taking advantage of the indefinite bank holiday. 'It would be as well to prepare yourself for the new regime, Fräulein.'

'I beg your pardon?' Freya was taken aback: he hardly ever spoke to her directly and now he was looking her straight in the face, with an intent expression.

'Allow me to give you some friendly advice,' he went on, packing a haversack with hardboiled eggs and slices of ham wrapped in greaseproof paper. 'You dress modestly and without make-up, which is commendable, but I happened to see you smoking the other day, and that's no good for your reputation.'

'My reputation?' She found herself echoing his words, playing for time.

'Yes. These things are noticed and I'd be neglecting my duty if I didn't warn you. A woman with a cigarette is a most unwholesome sight.' He smiled, but it didn't reach his eyes. 'Forgive my frankness. I should like to help your family through these tumultuous times in whatever way I can. There may still be a place for you in this music hall once it is Aryanised, but it would be as well to act appropriately now.'

For a second, Freya considered ignoring Otto's advice and telling Grube exactly what she thought of the Nazi party. And yet he frightened her, with his bulging muscles and stealthy ways; she would have to come up with a strategy for opposing him subtly, rather than risking head-on confrontation.

'Thank you, Herr Grube,' she replied. 'I'll certainly think about what you've said.'

He nodded, apparently satisfied, swung the haversack over his shoulder and strode out of the room.

Freya sat at the table, smoking a cigarette to calm her mind. 'Aryanised'. It was the first time she had heard the word and she wasn't sure exactly what it meant.

All she knew for certain was that she and her family would be on different sides in the battle yet to come. She had no idea then how far that battle would divide them, or how it would end.

# Chapter Eight

*Berlin, August 1931*

Freya came to know the English girl, Violet, a little better over the course of that summer. Violet had been changing into her own clothes one evening after the show was over and torn a ruffle off the hem of her gown; she'd waited, lounging in her underwear, while Freya stitched it up for her. She was completely at ease with her body, like the other girls; naked or clothed made little difference to them. Swinging her legs over the arm of the chair, she drank champagne and chatted while Freya stitched.

'You must have a drink, too,' she insisted, pouring a glass. 'Poor little Freya, always missing out on the fun.'

Violet was usually on a high when she came off stage: sparkling and effervescent, looking around for an audience she could carry on captivating. That night, she had been in a gentler, more thoughtful mood, as keen to listen as she was to speak. In response to her questions, Freya found herself talking about life with her father and brother, and the loathsome Herr Grube. Violet let her ramble on, her chin propped on one hand and her lovely eyes fixed on Freya's face. Everyone else had gone home, the dressing room felt cosy and intimate, and Freya went into more detail than she'd intended. When she confided her ambition to earn a living from writing rather than sewing, Violet told her she had a friend who was a novelist and teacher, and Freya must definitely meet him: she would arrange an introduction at the first opportunity.

'And how about you?' Freya asked, a little shyly, aware of having held the floor for too long. 'What brought you to Berlin?'

'Goodness, I can hardly remember.' Violet topped up her glass and lit a cigarette, sending a casual smoke ring drifting into the air. 'Actually, I can. You've told me your secret; now I'll tell you mine. I want to be a movie actress so this is the obvious place to come – apart from Hollywood, that is. The film industry's positively booming in Germany. The cleverest directors in Europe are here, if only one could get at them, and brilliant screenwriters and cinematographers, too. You must have heard of the Babelsberg film studio, surely?'

'And you speak German like a native,' Freya said, wanting to sound encouraging. 'Where did you learn the language?'

'I spent a lot of time here as a child,' Violet said. 'My father's sister married a German and lives here with her family. I see them occasionally, though they're too busy sucking up to Hitler in Munich to have much time for me.'

'And have you had any auditions?'

'Not yet, but things may be changing. I've met a very interesting man with an address book full of contacts who thinks he might be able to help. I'm having dinner with him tonight, actually.' Violet stubbed out her cigarette. 'How's the dress coming along?'

'Almost there. Give me another five minutes.'

'Thank you, Freya. What a darling you are.' Violet kicked

a bare leg up to the ceiling and linked hands behind her thigh, pulling it towards her body. 'I think we're going to be terrific friends, don't you? The actress and the writer. One day we'll make a movie together and become famous, and we won't tell anyone where we met.'

Freya had sailed home on a cloud of happiness that wasn't merely down to the wine. The next day, Violet had hugged her and said again how grateful she was, and that the dinner had been a success. She had been distracted, though, and hurried away at the end of the performance without saying goodbye to anyone. The invitation to meet Violet's writer friend never came, and there were no further late-night chats over champagne in the dressing room. Freya couldn't help feeling disappointed, because she was lonely and the thought of a friend, however unlikely, was appealing. The English girl, she decided, was simply in the habit of charming everyone she came across; it was a reflex action, like flicking a switch, and shouldn't have been taken seriously. She probably hadn't even been listening when Freya was pouring out her heart. She'd have been thinking about dinner with her influential acquaintance, a much more interesting prospect.

Freya soon met this man, as he began bringing Violet to the Zaubergarten or occasionally taking her home at the end of the night. His name was Maxim Fischer: a short, dark-haired man in his forties with heavy-lidded eyes and an undershot jaw that gave him a pugnacious air, like a bad-tempered English bulldog. It was clear from the proprietorial way he treated Violet that they had a personal relationship, and rumours were soon swirling around the dressing room that he was paying for her apartment near the swanky Kurfürstendamm boulevard, not far from the Zaubergarten but a million miles away in terms of prestige. Freya was inclined to believe it as she couldn't see any reason beyond ambition for Violet to have been with Maxim, who was neither handsome, funny nor charming. Still, Freya couldn't blame her for that. She had ambitions of her own, and who was to say how far she might have to go to achieve them.

Freya had thought her brother would never set foot in the Zaubergarten, but Leon must have persuaded him. One sultry evening in September, she saw the two of them take a table near the front of the stage, settling down with a bottle of champagne. Violet happened to be starring as a particularly risqué Queen of Sheba, so perhaps it wasn't the best time to convince Otto of the club's respectability. Freya watched him from her viewpoint at the side of the stage, his gaze fixed on Violet's slender yet voluptuous body, and wondered whether any of the club's magic had entered his soul. Leon was clearly entranced, his eyes shining in the glow of candlelight and a smile on his slightly parted lips. His expression sent a hot pang of jealousy tinged with alarm shooting through Freya's heart. Violet would eat him for breakfast.

Otto and Leon came to find Freya after the show – although she quickly realised she wasn't the one they really wanted to see.

'Can you let us in?' Otto asked, craning over his sister's head when she opened the dressing-room door in answer to his knock. 'We want to pay homage to the Queen.' He was smiling, much to Freya's relief.

'We'll behave ourselves, we promise,' Leon added, leaning against the door frame.

'Go away,' she hissed. 'You're not meant to be here.' Luckily it was a Friday night so Frau Brodsky wasn't there:

she always celebrated Shabat at home, leaving Freya in charge of the dressing room.

'Oh, let them in,' Angelika said, opening the door wider on her way out, wearing a feather boa and a cloud of perfume. 'They look like nice boys. And when the cat's away . . .'

The two Sophies were arguing over a broken heel on a pair of shoes one had loaned the other, Gisela was buttoning up the back of Perle's dress while Perle held her hair scooped out of the way, and Violet was rolling on her stockings, her skirt bunched around her waist, one leg propped up on a chair and a cigarette clenched between her teeth.

'Your Majesty,' Otto declared, threading his way towards her and bowing so low that he almost toppled over, 'we've come to swear our allegiance.'

Freya hurried to introduce him, cringing a little inside. Her brother was flushed, his bow tie askew and his blond hair dark with sweat, slurring his speech. He looked like a boor, the type of man girls would avoid and bouncers would keep an eye on.

Violet let him kiss her hand, glancing at Freya with wry amusement. 'Freya's told me all about her dashing brother,' she told him. 'What a pleasure to meet you at last.'

'And this is our friend, Leon Kohl,' Freya added, as Leon joined them.

Violet reached out to shake his hand with her usual laconic smile, but her expression changed as she looked at him, her hand resting in his. The two of them stood there, gazing at each other as though they'd already met and were trying to work out when and where.

'Will you join us for a drink, my lady?' Otto interrupted, with a clumsy attempt at gallantry.

Violet turned to him, dropping Leon's hand. 'I'm sorry?'

And then, collecting herself, 'I would have loved to, but I'm meeting a friend tonight. Perhaps another time?'

She didn't look at Leon again as she slipped on her shoes and wished them all good night, but she was clearly intensely aware of him, as he was of her. Something had passed between them and Freya felt with a sinking heart that it could only lead to trouble. Surely Leon had more sense than to fall for a girl like Violet? Before Maxim, there had been a succession of different men calling for her at the club and none of them had lasted more than a couple of weeks. Leon was clever and sensitive, and she would break his heart.

Otto looked pale at breakfast the next morning and his eyes were bloodshot. 'You may carry on working at the Zaubergarten,' he said to Freya, clearing his throat, 'but that part of Schöneberg is a rough area. I shall meet you after work whenever I can and walk you home at night.'

'Thank you,' Freya said. If they had been alone, she might have retorted that she didn't need his permission, and that clearly her safety wasn't the first thing on his mind. Herr Grube glanced at them both but made no comment.

'It was lovely to meet your brother,' Violet told Freya later that day. 'And his friend. Have they known each other long?'

'Since school,' Freya replied, as briefly as she could. 'Frau Kohl was a great friend of our mother's.'

Violet looked as though she were about to ask another question, but Freya was already turning away. She had no intention of acting as a go-between.

The evening's performance was about halfway through when Freya became aware of a disturbance among the audience: a ripple of consternation, muttered conversation growing louder and chairs being scraped back in hurried departure. The two gentlemen at the piano were finishing their last number and the Zaubergarten girls were waiting to go on when Herr Schwartz lowered the velvet curtain, to catcalls from those still unaware anything was amiss. The owner, Herr Goldstein, stepped in front of it, rubbing his hands awkwardly.

'Ladies and gentlemen,' he began, 'I'm afraid trouble's brewing. There are reports of rioting on Kurfürstendamm. We shall be closing early as a precaution and suggest you make your way home avoiding the area.'

In the wings, Freya tugged at Herr Schwartz's arm. 'What's going on?'

'It's those Nazi brutes,' he told her, 'hundreds of them. Apparently they're beating up anyone on Ku'damm who looks Jewish.'

The dancers crowded around him, demanding more details. He shrugged. 'That's all I know. Go and see for yourselves if you want to find out more. Except for the two Sophies, unless you have a death wish.' Dark-haired, dark-eyed and olive-skinned, those girls would be obvious targets. Perle was Jewish too, but no one would have guessed that from her colouring.

Freya was seized by sudden dread and it took her a few seconds to work out exactly why. Frau Brodsky! That day was Jewish New Year and she had the evening off to celebrate; she might easily have been at one of the synagogues in the area. 'Please God, Rosa isn't caught up in it,' she said. 'Should we go and check?'

Schwartz snorted with derision. 'Sounds like it's chaos out there – you'll have no chance of finding her. It's every man for himself.' And with that, he walked off as quickly as possible without actually running.

Herr Goldstein appeared to calm everyone down. 'As long as we stick together, we'll be fine,' he told them. 'Once the club is cleared, I shall escort everyone to safety.'

'Thanks, but we'll be better off without you,' Perle muttered.

The other dancers evidently thought the same: one by one, they were slipping away to change and make their own way home. The bar staff and doorman were already boarding up the club's windows as Freya left. In the teeming street, people were rushing in every direction and cars roared past with their engines straining, while an armoured police car lumbered through the dark like a vast scarab beetle. The racket grew louder as she skirted around the Kurfürstendamm boulevard, a few streets away: breaking glass, the blast of car horns, the clanging bell of an ambulance or police car. A woman with blood streaming down her face hammered on a nearby door, which opened briefly to receive her before slamming shut, bolts grating back into place.

Ahead of Freya, someone crossing the street turned to glance behind and Freya recognised Violet, her hair whipping across her face. Instead of avoiding the trouble, though, she seemed to be making straight for it – turning left towards Ku'damm rather than right to head away from it. Maybe she was concerned for Frau Brodsky, too? Freya watched the resolute figure hurrying forward and, on an impulse, followed. She could be just as brave; they would rescue Frau Brodsky together. Violet walked quickly and Freya was soon out of breath, attempting to keep up. Only now did she remember that Violet lived near the boulevard.

Catching up at last, Freya laid a hand on Violet's arm. The English girl whirled around, her eyes wide. 'Are you trying to get home?' Freya shouted above the hubbub. 'You'll never make it!'

The scene before them was chaotic: people were running in all directions, trying to escape the men in brown uniforms armed with truncheons, knives and clubs. Tables and chairs were overturned in front of the fashionable cafés on each side of the street while, above the shouts of abuse and terrified screams, a deafening voice yelled encouragement. An open-topped Jeep was driving slowly up and down Kurfürstendamm, carrying a man who urged the attackers on through a megaphone. 'Death to the filthy Jews!' he cried. 'Purge our beloved country of their stain.' Men and women in their weekend finery were being dragged from the crowd, hands over their heads in a futile attempt to protect themselves. Freya turned away, sickened, as a middle-aged matron in a flower-trimmed hat was beaten at the knees and fell to the ground, curling into a ball while three Nazis kicked her with all their strength, faces contorted in fury.

'This is hopeless.' Freya pulled Violet away. 'You'd better come with me.'

Violet nodded and the girls broke into a run, retracing their steps. When they were a safe distance away, near the entrance to Tiergarten, Freya paused to catch her breath, bent double with her hands on her knees.

'Was that Hitler in the Jeep?' she asked, when she could speak. 'I couldn't see his face.'

Violet shook her head. 'He'll only come to Berlin on sufferance – thinks the place is decadent. From a quick look, I'd say it was von Helldorff. He's head of the Berlin SA.' She was surprisingly well-informed.

'You'd better stay with me tonight,' Freya said. 'Is there anyone waiting for you at home?'

'Luckily not,' Violet replied, brushing down her coat. 'Thank you, darling. What a kind offer.'

Freya glanced back towards Ku'damm. 'I'm so afraid for Frau Brodsky. Do you know which synagogue she attends?'

'Haven't a clue,' Violet replied, putting her arm through Freya's. 'But don't you worry about our Rosa, she has a nose for trouble. The best thing we can do is look after ourselves.'

By the time they'd reached the straight, wide avenue that ran through the centre of the park, the only sign of trouble was the number of police cars and trucks crammed with stormtroopers hurtling past. All the same, they walked quickly with their heads down. When at last the apartment building came into view, Freya broke into a run, dragging Violet with her.

'Thank God you're here,' Otto said, as she and Violet burst through the door. 'We were about to come looking for you.'

Leon was there too, holding a cloth to the side of his face.

'You remember Fräulein Violet?' Freya told them. 'She's going to be staying here tonight.'

Otto straightened his back. 'It will be an honour. Fräulein, you can have my bed and I'll take the sofa.'

'I wouldn't dream of it,' Violet said. 'I'll sleep on the floor in Freya's room, if she'll have me. But are you hurt, Herr Kohl?' And there it was again, that flash of connection between them as she met Leon's gaze and held it.

Turning to Leon, Freya realised there was blood on the cloth pressed against his cheek, and his knuckles were bruised and dirty.

'My pride as much as anything,' he replied, taking away the towel to show them an eye swollen almost shut. 'A couple of the brownshirts convinced themselves I was a Jew, but luckily Otto managed to talk our way out of trouble.'

Otto looked complacent. 'I told you joining the party would come in handy one day.'

The two of them had been drinking in a bar near Ku'damm when the commotion had begun, they explained, so they'd headed in the direction of the noise to find out what was happening.

'A mistake, in retrospect,' Leon said drily.

'And where were the police?' Violet asked.

'We saw a few but they were outnumbered about twenty to one, so in the end they gave up and retreated.' Leon shook his head. 'The Nazis have never gone this far before. They must believe they're untouchable, and tonight will have proved it.'

Freya glanced at Otto, but he said nothing. 'Where's Herr Grube?' she asked.

'Out,' Otto replied briefly. 'Vati's off somewhere, too, but I doubt he'll have got involved.'

Freya jumped up suddenly, seized the tablecloth and draped it over the portrait of Hitler that gazed so ominously down on them.

Otto stood up too. 'You can't do that. Take it off.'

'Grube should never have put up that picture without asking us first,' Freya snapped. 'Herr Hitler's a brute. I bet he's behind what happened tonight, even if he wasn't actually there.'

Otto tore down the tablecloth and stuffed it under his arm, glaring at her. 'Don't ever let me hear you talk like that again. Can't you see the risk you're running?'

'This is my home,' Freya said. 'I'll say what I like!'

'Then you're a damn fool,' Otto growled.

Leon raised his hands in a gesture of peace. 'Come, we're all shocked and tired. Let's calm down, have a drink and talk things over in the morning.'

'Good idea,' Violet said, producing a packet of cigarettes from her bag.

Otto took four glasses from the dresser without speaking, his jaw set, and Leon uncorked a bottle of schnapps. The four of them chinked glasses but nobody could think of an appropriate toast so they merely drank 'to Germany', whatever that meant, the air fraught with tension and resentment on Otto and Freya's side, and a fascination so obvious one could taste it on Violet and Leon's.

Freya's rage subsided a little, though she was still too angry to make polite conversation. How could her brother boast about being a member of the Nazi party tonight of all nights? And why should they all be expected to kowtow to Walther Grube? She should have objected as soon as that portrait appeared, but their lodger's worship of the odd little man who ranted and raved in a thick Austrian accent had seemed almost comical at first.

'There are tough times ahead,' Violet said later, as she and Freya settled down for the night. 'Not just for the Jews but for people like us: anyone who wants to think for themselves and live as they please.'

Freya was flattered to be included in that group, although now she couldn't help wishing Violet were spending the night somewhere else. She wouldn't have issued the invitation so readily if she'd known Leon would be at the apartment. Ashamed of such an unworthy thought, she dismissed it from her mind and asked quickly, 'Will you go back to England?'

'God, no.' Violet flexed her calloused dancer's feet, disconcertingly close to Freya's face as they lay top to toe in the narrow bed. 'There's nothing for me at home but marriage to some dreary creature and years of boredom, pushing out a suitable number of babies. I am most definitely not the maternal type. None of the Framley-Chambers women are.'

'Don't you miss your family, though?'

'Not really. My darling mama spends most of the year in South Africa and Papa has no use for girls.'

They were silent for a while.

'How can you bear to live like this?' Violet asked suddenly.

Freya didn't know how to reply. She assumed Violet was referring to the Hitler portrait and Otto's rebuke, yet maybe she had something else in mind. 'It's been manageable so far,' she said eventually. 'Anyway, nothing's perfect. I could ask you the same question.'

'*Touché.*' Violet laughed, apparently not at all offended. 'I suppose we all have to make compromises of one kind or another. But seriously, you don't have to spend your whole life skivvying for men. You can decide what you want and go after it.'

It took Freya a while to get to sleep – some time after Violet, to judge from the slow, steady breathing at the other end of the mattress. She was still tortured by an image of Rosa Brodsky under a hail of blows from a stormtrooper's baton, and this particular worry expanded into a general concern about the future. Violet's question had shaken her. She could just about afford a cheap room in some down-at-heel area and her father and brother would have to manage with the help of their maid, so what was holding her back? She had lived her entire life in this apartment and her mother's presence was still strong in every room; if she moved out, she'd be losing Ingrid all over again. Yet sooner or later, she'd have to accept that her mother had gone, and she would always carry memories of Ingrid in her heart. Maybe the time had finally come to make a break for freedom.

# Chapter Nine

*Berlin, September 1931*

Violet slept late the next morning, Freya was relieved to see. Since Hedwig the maid didn't work on Sundays, she got up to put on a pot of coffee, lay the dining table and prepare for breakfast. Herr Grube was the first to emerge, materialising silently as usual and sliding into a chair with a nod in her direction. Freya had switched on the wireless and reports of the previous night's violence on Ku'damm spilled into the quiet room.

'Did you hear about this?' Freya asked. 'Otto and Leon were caught up in the trouble and Leon has a black eye.'

'I did,' Herr Grube replied, with an air of quiet satisfaction. 'The rout is beginning.'

'So you're happy to live in a city where ordinary people going about their business are attacked while the police stand by?'

'I shall be happy to live in a city free of Jews,' Grube replied, pouring himself a cup of coffee. 'The end justifies the means.'

Ernst joined him shortly afterwards, and Freya went off to the kitchen to cut bread, cook eggs and arrange slices of ham. Sunday breakfasts were as elaborate as funds allowed. She couldn't bear to hear her father and Herr Grube glorying in the Jews having got their comeuppance, and could only pray they'd have exhausted the topic before Violet appeared. By the time she returned with laden plates, Otto and Leon were also sitting at the table, and the atmosphere had become distinctly chilly. The skin around Leon's left eye was purple and shiny, like a ripe plum, and he still couldn't open it.

'Herr Amsel,' he was saying, 'I've always felt welcome in your home. You and your wife were unfailingly kind to me, and Otto has been my friend since our schooldays. There's something you don't know that I should share now: my grandfather was Jewish, though I haven't been raised as a Jew. Does that change your opinion of me?'

A look of distaste spread over Ernst's face. 'Yes,' he replied simply. 'Of course.'

'So you are a Jew after all,' Otto said, staring at Leon. 'I shouldn't have defended you last night. Why have you never mentioned that before?'

He shrugged. 'Because it hasn't come up. Look, I'm still the same person you've known for years. Why would you turn against me just because the Nazis tell you to?'

'I don't need the Nazis to warn me not to trust a Jew,' Ernst growled.

'Herr Kohl,' Grube said, leaning back in his chair, 'if I were you, I would keep this information to yourself. I shall try to forget what you've said but others may not be so charitable. I'm afraid you are hopelessly naïve.'

Freya slammed a plate of fried eggs on the table with such force that one of them slid greasily to the floor, and turned on her heel.

She found Violet sitting up in bed, reading the portfolio of stories she'd left on her bedside table.

'Hey! That's private,' she said, making a lunge to grab the folder from Violet's hands.

'Why?' Violet asked. 'You write pretty well, actually. I really must introduce you to my friend Wolfgang, the novelist I mentioned. He'd be happy to give you some advice.' She closed the folder, though, and laid it back on the table.

How was it possible to look ravishing first thing in the morning? Freya wondered sulkily. Violet's creamy skin was flawless and her eyes were clear and bright, despite the previous night's alcohol and cigarettes.

'Well, well.' Violet smiled at her. '*Kleine* Freya, you are a dark horse.'

'There's coffee next door,' Freya said, seething. 'With eggs and ham. I'm afraid Herr Grube's in evidence but you'll have to put up with that.'

'I'll be interested to meet him,' Violet said, getting out of bed and stripping off the nightshirt Freya had lent her. 'He might know more about what happened last night. Do you have a hairbrush I could borrow, darling?'

Ernst had left the breakfast table but the other three were still there, finishing their breakfast in awkward silence. Herr Grube looked predictably disapproving when Freya introduced Violet. He and Otto had made plans to go hiking but when Violet announced she had it in mind to visit Lake Wannsee as it was such a beautiful day, Otto said that sounded a splendid idea.

'With Freya, of course,' Violet said, taking her arm. 'She can be my chaperone. And Herr Kohl too, if he would like.' She glanced at Leon almost shyly.

'I shall not come to Lake Wannsee,' Grube announced. 'It will be horribly crowded.'

'What a shame,' Violet murmured. 'Another time, perhaps.' And despite her irritation, Freya had to bite her lip not to laugh.

After she had cleared the breakfast plates, Freya put together a picnic of some leftover potato salad and sausage, Otto and Leon packed beer, towels and a rug, and the four of them caught the small suburban train to the lake, an hour's journey south-west of the city. Leon wore a pair of dark glasses to hide his eye and, apart from his bruised hand, there was little to remind them of the previous night's violence. There were fewer people about than usual and those they passed looked more sombre than usual, although Freya might have been imagining that. She felt guilty setting off on a jaunt, but she had no idea where Frau Brodsky lived and so they could only wait until Monday for news.

In other circumstances, the outing should have been glorious. The sun shone out of a bright blue sky and she was spending the day with Leon – who hardly seemed to notice she was there. It was strange, being with Violet in the fresh air rather than the dark, smoky confines of the Zaubergarten, and Freya felt self-conscious – even though she knew she'd only been invited along to make up numbers, and nobody was paying her much attention. Violet kept up a stream of chatter about nothing in particular, deffusing a growing tension between the two boys. Leon was quiet and when he did speak, Otto took issue with whatever he said. There was no chance they'd be able to discuss the previous night's attack without arguing so, by tacit agreement, the subject wasn't raised. To increase Otto's jealousy, Leon spoke English with

Violet and did it well. He had an ear for languages and his mother was a great Anglophile.

Herr Grube was right: the wide beach along the lakeshore was packed with bathers, lying on towels or lounging in deckchairs. Fathers had taken off their ties, rolled up their shirt sleeves and trouser legs and dug their bare feet into the sand as they read newspapers. Mothers dozed under sun umbrellas, supervised picnics or tucked up their skirts and paddled in the water, keeping an anxious eye on their children. Rowdy gangs of teenage boys played football, despite the lack of space, showing off for the benefit of any girls who might be watching.

'Dear Lord, they're everywhere,' Violet groaned, shading her eyes with her hand as she scanned the view.

Freya followed her gaze to see an encampment not far away, marked out by a swastika flag fluttering at each corner and packed with tanned, bare-chested young men drinking beer, wrestling, throwing quoits, shouting and singing. There were swastika badges on their swimming trunks, too. Instinctively, she turned to look at Otto.

'So?' he asked, glaring back at her.

They headed in the other direction to find a spot large enough to unroll the rug. As soon as they were settled, Violet peeled off her red polka-dot dress with professional ease, revealing the knitted bathing costume of Ingrid's she'd borrowed – although their mother had never made it look so alluring – and called over her shoulder that she was going for a dip. Stripping off his clothes and shoes, Otto hurried to catch up.

'Don't feel you have to stay,' Freya told Leon. 'I'm happy by myself.'

'But I should like to,' Leon said, smiling as he passed her a beer.

They sat companionably together, gazing at the sparkling water thronged with swimmers. Violet had waded out to mid-thigh and was standing there, occasionally scooping up handfuls of glittering droplets, while Otto swam in showy circles around her. Now and then she glanced back at the shore; to see whether Leon was watching, Freya guessed.

'What's on your mind?' Leon asked her. 'You look very serious.'

'You don't really think people are going to vote for Hitler, do you?' she replied. 'Can't they see what he's like?'

'They're poor and unhappy,' Leon replied, 'and Hitler gives them someone to blame. "It's all the fault of the Jews and the Communists," he says, and they're only too willing to believe him. Look at those Nazis, having the time of their lives. They can indulge their most savage instincts and feel justified because they're fighting for the sake of a greater Germany. But how can a country hope to be great when it's founded on hatred and fear?'

Freya gnawed her lip. 'Don't tell anyone else your grandfather was Jewish.'

'I probably won't.' Leon sighed. 'And so the secrecy begins. Maybe Grube's right and trying to reason with your father was hopelessly naïve.'

'Grube said something about the Zaubergarten being Aryanised,' Freya told him. 'Do you really think the Nazis could take Herr Goldstein's business away from him?'

'I can't believe that would happen,' Leon replied. 'We still have the rule of law in this country, thank God.' Freya couldn't see his expression behind the dark glasses, but his voice was firm and reassuring.

They lapsed into silence again. Eventually she said, 'I have a couple of stories ready to show you, but I'd like to type them up first. I've seen a second-hand typewriter for sale and . . .'

She could tell Leon wasn't listening and her voice petered out. His eyes were fixed on Violet, walking towards them with her hair lifting off her forehead in the breeze and the wet costume clinging to her extraordinary body. Tossing away his cigarette, he picked up a towel and hurried to meet her. She let him put the towel around her shoulders, gazed up into his face and said something that made him laugh. Freya felt as though a skewer had pierced her heart. She looked quickly away, resting her head on her knees so that her hair fell over them in a warm, soft curtain. What a fool she'd been! How could she ever have thought Leon would be interested in her when girls like Violet existed in the world? She was angry and ashamed of herself. At least, thank God, she'd never told him how she felt.

Otto had joined them, shaking water from his ears like an overenthusiastic, clumsy dog. Yet his swagger lacked conviction and Freya felt a pang of sympathy at the sight of his crestfallen face as she passed him a towel. Had she been so obvious, mooning over Leon? The sting of humiliation smarted all over again.

'Don't you want a swim?' Violet asked, but Freya shook her head. The sun had gone behind a cloud and a chilly wind ruffled the lake's surface. They ate and drank, smoked and talked – or mainly, listened as Violet told them stories about her family: her older brother who was due to inherit their huge country house but would rather have led a carefree bachelor life in London; her two sisters, one of whom was already married with two children she didn't seem to like, the other of whom was an artist living in Paris; her younger brother, who was a wanderer and currently walking through Spain.

‘And here are you in Berlin,’ Leon observed. ‘Why did you come to this country?’

‘It seemed like a good idea at the time,’ Violet said airily, brushing sand off her dress and getting to her feet. ‘Now, I fancy an ice. Anyone else?’ A boat selling ice cream was moored in the shallows, a little way further down the beach.

‘I’ll come with you.’ Leon jumped up too and they walked off, so fast that Otto had no chance of following. He watched them go, tossing a pebble from one hand to the other with a face like thunder. Freya pretended to concentrate on reading her book but she was constantly aware of his glowering presence, the tension building until she felt the sky might crack. Out of the corner of her eye, she saw her brother practise press-ups and squats till his face turned red and his chest gleamed with sweat. Then, knotting a towel around his waist, he lit a cigarette and paced up and down while he smoked it, peering towards the ice-cream boat.

‘What can be taking them so long?’ he muttered finally, throwing away the stub and setting off in the same direction.

‘Wait for me,’ Freya cried, closing her book and struggling to her feet in the vain hope she might be able to smooth things over. She had to break into a run to catch up with Otto, who paid her no attention whatsoever, striding ahead with his eyes fixed on the shoreline.

There was no sign of Leon or Violet in the queue for ices standing knee-deep in the shallows. Gazing around, Freya suddenly caught sight of a scrap of red spotted material fluttering in the breeze by the trunk of a willow tree close to the water’s edge. Otto had noticed it too. Clenching his fists, he stormed up the slope to investigate while Freya ran behind, dreading the sight that might greet them. Leon was standing with his back against the tree trunk and Violet in his arms, and they were kissing passionately, hungrily, in just the way Freya had dreamed Leon might one day kiss her. Oh, but they made a handsome couple.

With a roar, Otto launched himself forward and tore them apart, seizing Leon by his shirt and punching him furiously in a volley of blows. 'You swine!' he roared. 'Taking advantage of our guest!' This was such a ridiculous accusation that Freya was almost tempted to laugh, although the expression on Otto's face and the ferocity of his attack were shocking.

Leon put up his fists in an attempt to shield himself but didn't fight back. 'Come on, you coward!' Otto spat, dancing around him. 'Too much of a pansy to stick up for yourself?'

Violet grabbed Otto's arm and held on to it. 'Stop that,' she commanded. 'No one's taking advantage – this was my idea as much as his.'

Otto broke free of her grip, glaring at her contemptuously and wiping his hand on the towel as though it were contaminated.

Freya scrambled to join them. 'Please, Otto,' she implored, taking his other arm. 'Leon is our friend.'

Breathing heavily, Otto's eyes focused and he gradually came back to himself. 'Not anymore,' he said. 'He's a filthy Jew and blood will out.'

He aimed one last kick at Leon, then spat on the ground and walked away – with as much dignity as someone wearing only a knotted beach towel could muster. Leon gave a shaky, awkward laugh. He was ashen, a trickle of blood running from his nose.

Violet took a handkerchief from her handbag and passed it to him. 'Twice in one weekend? You're not having much luck.'

'Sorry you had to witness that,' he replied, feeling his jaw and wincing. 'And Freya too, of course.' He couldn't bring himself to look at either of them.

Without a word, Freya turned to follow her brother back along the beach.

It was only a kiss, Freya told herself. Violet probably kissed people all the time and thought nothing of it. When she bumped into her at the Zaubergarten a few days later, Violet merely thanked her airily for coming to the rescue on Saturday and said she'd had a lovely time. Maybe that would be that, Freya thought, and could only hope she was right. Yet a couple of weeks later, she was returning from a lunchtime trip to the fabric warehouse at Spittelmarkt when she saw a familiar figure in a café near the Zaubergarten, cropped hair curling into the nape of her neck and her back to the window. Leon sat opposite, gazing at his companion with a rapt expression. Freya shrank back before she could be spotted, lowering her head, but the pair had been too engrossed in each other to notice anyone else. She took shelter in a nearby doorway and risked another look – in time to watch Violet reach out and cup Leon's cheek with her palm, and see him take her hand and press it against his mouth. Anyone could have walked by and seen them, as she had done. What if Maxim Fischer had been passing?

As Freya watched, horrified, she saw Leon stand up and hand Violet her wrap before the pair of them left the restaurant. They walked quickly along the pavement without speaking, their bodies almost touching, while Freya followed at a safe distance behind. They traversed the length of one street, turned left into another and then took a right turn into an alley that led to a parade of shops. Stopping at a blue door on the corner, Leon took a key out of his pocket and unlocked it, standing back to allow Violet to pass while glancing beyond her to check they were unobserved.

Luckily, Freya was far enough away to escape detection. She immediately dropped to one knee to tie a shoelace, and by the time she straightened up, the blue door was closing. Numbly, she turned and retraced her steps.

Freya found it hard to concentrate for the rest of the day. The dancers were having their rehearsal for the Rhinemaiden number that afternoon, in front of the owner and Herr Schwartz as well as Frau Brodsky and Freya. Violet arrived late, tearing off her clothes and slipping into her costume so hurriedly that Frau Brodsky growled at her to take more care. Freya helped adjust the gauzy panels of blue and green silk that so alluringly failed to cover Violet's flawless skin. She was breathing quickly, her bosom heaving; it was a warm day and her body was covered in a faint sheen of perspiration. She smelt of cigarette smoke, and wine, and sex. Freya retied a ribbon on her alabaster shoulder with clumsy fingers and let a wave of sadness wash over her – yearning, as she so often did, for her mother. She had loved Leon for so long and never given up hope that one day, when she was a little older, perhaps, he might come to love her in return. Now that door had closed. Even if he and Violet only had a brief affair, Violet's ghost would constantly be hovering in the background. Freya would always be second best, a consolation prize, if the idea of her as a girlfriend ever crossed his mind at all.

She told herself to be sensible. What was the point in wishing Leon felt differently? Maybe he would bring out the best in Violet, and maybe their initial attraction would deepen into something lasting and worthwhile. Remembering the expression on his face as he gazed at Violet in the café, Freya tried to be glad he was happy. Yet she could not shake off the strongest sense of foreboding. She felt in her bones that this relationship was bound to end badly.

# Chapter Ten

*Los Angeles, April 2024*

This had to be the strangest social event she'd ever attended, Maddie thought, following her grandfather into the community centre. They stood in the foyer – a bright, airy space, with posters on the wall advertising bake sales and baby yoga classes – wondering where to go next.

'Are you heading for the Death Café?' asked an elderly lady, walking through behind them. 'It's right this way.'

'Thanks. We'll tag along with you,' Maddie said. She caught the eye of the guy whose arm the old lady was holding – most likely her grandson, to judge from his age – and they exchanged looks that said, 'You, too? What on earth are we doing here?'

'We've not been to one of these events before,' Gramps said. 'Can't wait to hear what it's all about, though my granddaughter isn't quite so keen.' He had dressed for the occasion in purple slacks, a red shirt and a red-and-yellow striped blazer, accessorised with a Panama hat.

'Oh, these kids are too soft for their own good,' the lady said. 'Just wait till it's their turn. Old age is no place for sissies.'

'My thoughts exactly.' Gramps hurried to hold the door open for her to pass through. They were much the same height and she was also stylishly dressed in orange leggings with flatform sneakers and a pink tunic dress that matched the pink streaks in her white hair. From behind, she and Gramps could have been a couple of kids going to a festival. Maddie hid a smile.

'What you have to bear in mind,' the old lady was saying, 'is that this isn't a counselling session, and it's not some kind of death cult, either. It's just a forum for people to discuss what seems to be a taboo subject these days.'

'With refreshments,' added the probable grandson. 'Though sadly not of the alcoholic kind.'

They found themselves in another light-filled room with around twenty or so other people, standing alone with glazed expressions or making stilted conversation in groups. Tables and chairs were dotted about, and a coffee urn stood to one side, along with plates of sandwiches, cookies and cakes. A woman with cornrow braids and a clipboard came to meet them, introducing herself as Gabrielle and asking for their names, which she ticked off on a list.

'Eva! Great to see you again,' she greeted the pink-haired lady.

'And you remember my grandson, Daniel.' Eva pushed him forward and he gave an awkward wave.

Gramps and Eva began chatting immediately, leaving Maddie and Daniel looking at each other. Maddie wished intensely that she hadn't come; she couldn't think of a thing to say and she still wasn't comfortable around groups of strangers. It might have been her imagination, but this guy seemed to be staring at her intently. Did he know who she was? His brooding, suspicious gaze made her nervous.

Maddie turned away and pretended to be fascinated by a leaflet about woodland burials. Part of her had been thinking that a visit to the Death Café would make great copy, but she could guess the shower of abuse that would rain down on her head if she dared write about it.

After another few minutes, Gabrielle clapped her hands and announced the meeting could start. There was no agenda: they would chat in groups about whatever was on their minds, taking care to be respectful and making sure everyone had a turn to speak. A page of conversation starters was provided on every table, for use if required. Maddie took a quick look. 'Would you prefer to be buried, cremated, or some other kind of ritual?' she read. 'How would you like to be remembered? Would you prefer to die suddenly or over a period of months?' She flipped the paper face down.

Luckily there was no need for any prompts with Gramps around. He talked about clearing out his home and the comfort he'd gained from looking back over his life that enabled him to think calmly about its end. Soon the others were joining in: Brad, who was caring for his father with terminal cancer; Devika, heavily into Tarot and spiritualism; Charmaine, recently diagnosed with a life-limiting condition she didn't want to specify; Alison, whose husband had passed away a couple of years before after a long illness, and who was thinking of training as a death doula. A death doula, she explained, was someone who could help a person out of life in the same way as a midwife brought a baby into it.

'Now that sounds fascinating!' Gramps said. 'Tell me more.'

Maddie had seen her grandfather's charm at work so

many times: people warmed to him because he was open-minded and curious. And why shouldn't he be interested in what lay ahead of him, maybe sooner rather than later? Maddie didn't contribute much to the conversation, feeling she was there under false pretences, but it was fascinating to eavesdrop on these discussions between like-minded strangers who had no axe to grind, no skin in the game. She regretted her previous squeamishness. Gramps was trying to make things easier for all the family, and there might come a time when they'd thank him for that.

Now they were deciding what would be the ideal way to die. Alison's sister-in-law had suffered a stroke in the passenger seat of her carer's car while out shopping. 'What a mercy,' Charmaine commented enviously. 'She didn't even have to fall down.' The winner, though, was Brad's boss, who'd had a heart attack on the eighteenth hole, having just declared that was the best round of golf he'd ever played. They were laughing when Maddie glanced across the room to find Daniel looking at her again with that odd, calculating expression. What was wrong with him?

Shortly afterwards, Gabrielle announced it was time for coffee. Before she could lose her nerve, Maddie walked over to Daniel and asked, 'Do I have spinach in my teeth or something?'

He gave an embarrassed laugh. 'God, no. Sorry. I feel like I know you from somewhere, that's all. Just trying to work out where.'

'I don't think so,' Maddie said coldly. 'You don't look at all familiar to me.'

She turned on her heel, torn between anger and fear. How dare some creep make her feel uncomfortable? She'd been doing so much better after a week at home, settling back into the usual family rhythms: taking Ben to the art supplies store, yoga classes with her mom, cooking a special dinner for Gramps. Now all her insecurities came rushing back. Daniel must have seen her picture online; he'd realise where he recognised her from eventually and another storm cloud would break. She'd probably be accused of wanting her grandfather to die. Could she not escape judgement anywhere? For a second, she wondered about making some excuse to leave, but her grandfather was enjoying himself and she had been too, up until then.

To make matters worse, after the coffee break they ended up on the same table as Daniel and his grandmother. Gramps was delighted to take the chair beside Eva but Maddie could only sit there, trying to pretend Daniel didn't exist. She didn't want to enter the general discussion, since anything she said might be used against her in some way or another. The woman beside her was quiet, too, though she smiled when Maddie said hello and introduced herself as Lauren.

'What brings you here?' Maddie asked.

'Well, that's a long story,' Lauren replied, her fingers twisting together. She looked plump and comfortable but her eyes were sad.

'Oh, sure. I probably shouldn't have asked,' Maddie said quickly. 'Have a cookie? The chocolate ones are delicious.'

'No, it's fine.' Lauren hesitated, glancing around the table, where a debate about assisted dying was in full flow. 'Where to begin? It's my mom, you see.'

Little by little, the story came out. Lauren's mother had originally been diagnosed with cancer four years ago and the disease had recently returned. She'd gone through various sessions of chemotherapy but her latest scans and test results had not been encouraging.

'We've been trying to stay positive for so long,' Lauren said, 'but now I'm wondering whether that's helping. I mean, maybe it's another burden for Mom, putting on a brave face when she doesn't feel that way underneath. On the other hand, I'm frightened of saying the wrong thing and scaring her to death.' She laughed awkwardly. 'Sorry, wrong phrase.'

'Sure,' Maddie said. 'You don't want to bring her down but it might be a relief for her to talk honestly.'

Lauren's face cleared. 'That's exactly it. I hope you don't think I'm an awful person.'

'Of course not!' Maddie exclaimed. 'Look, I haven't been in your situation but maybe you should let your mom take the lead. When the time's right, and you'll know when that is, you could just ask her how she's feeling and see what she says. She must be so worried about how you're coping. If she sees you can face the truth, no matter how hard it is, she might be reassured.'

'You're right. Thanks. Guess it's obvious, really.' Lauren gave a watery smile. 'Can I give you a hug?'

Human contact was so vital, Maddie thought as they embraced. Talking to someone when you could see the impact your words were having was a completely different matter from shouting into the void on social media.

'Well, I've had a great time,' Gramps said, fastening his seat belt. 'That Eva is some woman. Would you believe it, her parents came here from Germany in the 1930s too. Talk about a coincidence! They were Jewish so it was more urgent for them. She's an artist, as you can probably tell from her clothes. And you were at college with her grandson? He seems like a nice boy.'

'Hmm,' Maddie replied. The jury was still out on that one. Daniel had asked her where she'd gone to college and when she'd said UCLA, had replied that's where he'd studied, too, which must be why he recognised her. She didn't believe him for one minute.

'You know, it feels like I've been given a new lease of life,' Gramps said, looking out of the car window as they drew up at a traffic light. 'I've been mouldering away for so long in that apartment, worried about bills and grocery shopping and all the useless possessions I've accumulated over the years, and now I'm liberated. Look at Eva – she must be around my age but she's doing all kinds of things. She swims in the ocean all year round, and plays pickleball, and goes to German conversation classes. Makes me feel guilty I haven't kept up with the language.'

'She made quite the impression on you,' Maddie said, giving him a sidelong glance.

'Yes, I don't mind admitting she did.' Gramps inspected his fingernails with an air of concentration. 'She's invited me over to see some of her work.'

'Woo hoo, a date!' Maddie crowed, pulling out into the traffic.

'Don't be silly. At my time of life?' But he was smiling. 'Anyway, I thought Ben would like to come too and she says you'd both be welcome.'

'If Eva speaks German fluently, she might be able to help you translate your mother's journal,' Maddie said, careful not to look at her grandfather. He'd been curiously reluctant even to read the diary in front of her, and she was itching to know what it contained.

He sighed. 'I don't know. Feels wrong to be prying into someone's private life. I always had the sense there were things Mom didn't want to tell me about her family, things she wanted to keep secret.'

'Like what?' Maddie asked.

He shrugged. 'Why did she up sticks and sail halfway across the world to start over in America? It was the right thing to do, as it turned out, but she was so young. And why didn't she keep in touch with her family? She told me once that she had an older brother but we never heard from him. I couldn't even find an address to contact him when she got sick. And her father must have died at some point, though I don't remember her saying so.'

'Was she political?'

Gramps considered the question. 'Not exactly. I mean, she didn't belong to a political party but she had very strong beliefs. She was passionate about freedom of speech, for example. When I was growing up, Senator McCarthy was conducting a witch hunt against Communists, and my mother wasn't having any of that, no sir.' He laughed. 'I remember some woman in Indiana tried to ban books about Robin Hood because she said he stole from the rich to give to the poor, and that was Communist ideology.'

'And now books are being banned from school libraries all over again,' Maddie said.

Gramps shook his head. 'Mom would be turning in her grave. She said anyone who tried to restrict what people read and thought was not to be trusted. Even Hitler's memoir, *Mein Kampf*, should be freely available because it showed what he was like. Read as widely as you can and then make up your own mind, that was her philosophy.'

'Wish I could have met her,' Maddie said. 'She sounds great.'

'She was wonderful,' Gramps said. 'In some ways, you

remind me of her: both so thoughtful and creative. She made all her own clothes and mine, too, when I was little. I like to think I've inherited her sense of style.'

Maddie smiled. 'My goodness, what a gift to leave the world.'

Gramps ignored her. 'She hated war, that was another thing, which I guess was inevitable given her background. I remember going on marches with her to protest against Vietnam. I was born towards the end of 1943 so I just escaped the draft lottery, but kids I taught were killed or wounded out there.' He shook his head. 'All those young men whose lives were ruined. If I'd been born a couple of months later, in 1944, I might have been one of them.'

He was quiet for a while. When they were almost home, he turned to Maddie and said, 'Maybe you're right, and I should let Eva take a look at that journal. My mother lived through extraordinary times – she would probably want me to know about them.'

By the time Maddie had dropped Gramps off at his apartment and driven home, Ben had gone to his room for the night and her mother was alone in the living room, dozing in front of the TV.

She woke up when Maddie came in and gave her a bleary smile. 'So how was the Death Zone?'

'I enjoyed it, actually,' Maddie replied. 'It was interesting, meeting a load of random people and exchanging ideas. We should talk about the important things more often.'

'If you say so.' Her mother didn't look convinced.

'Look, this probably goes without saying,' Maddie went on, 'but you know I'd step up and take care of Ben if anything happened to you?'

'Thanks, honey,' her mother said, patting her hand. 'That's good to hear.'

Maddie hesitated, choosing her next words with care. 'Ben doesn't seem his usual happy self. The other day, he told me he wanted to live independently.'

Sharon groaned. 'I thought I'd talked him out of that crazy idea.'

'Is it so crazy, though?' Maddie asked. 'Shouldn't we at least consider the options? Maybe we could find a shared apartment, or a group home where he can be with other people but still have some freedom. It must be a strain for you, looking after him twenty-four-seven.'

'Are you saying I can't manage?' Sharon asked, flaring up.

'No, of course not. You take wonderful care of him. What if you got sick, though? Or had an accident? And let's face it, things aren't going to get any easier. You have Gramps to worry about and—'

'Ben couldn't cope on his own,' Sharon interrupted. 'He doesn't have the skills to look after himself, to shop and cook healthy food or do the laundry, let alone carry on with the art business. Remember that time he went away to camp and we had to fetch him back after three days?'

'But that was years ago,' Maddie protested. 'Mom, Ben's twenty-three now. If he wants to leave home, surely we ought to help him try? He should be able to live the way he wants.'

'That's easy to say,' her mother replied. 'I just don't think he has the capacity.'

'Well, perhaps we could arrange a meeting to talk about the idea with his support worker,' Maddie suggested. 'What was her name? Lisa something.'

'It would be setting him up to fail, encouraging wild dreams that can't ever come true,' Sharon declared. 'I'm not putting him through that.'

'You might be surprised,' Maddie persisted. 'He's started to do his own laundry now, hasn't he? I saw him loading clothes into the machine this morning. And I'm sure he could learn to cook. It would be a shame to assume he's going to fail without giving him a chance.'

'He can't manage without me,' her mother replied baldly. 'I'm sorry, but that's the long and short of it.'

'Some day he might have to,' Maddie said. 'Face facts, Mom – you're not going to live for ever.'

'Well, thank you for that cheerful reminder.' Sharon got heavily to her feet. 'On that note, I'm going to bed.'

It took Maddie a long time to drift into sleep that night, tossing and turning as her mind ran around in circles. She was perplexed by Ben's tentative steps towards a different life and her mother's refusal to contemplate them. Maybe Sharon depended as much on Ben as he did on her. Her mom had just turned sixty-five; what would happen to Ben if – or more accurately, when – she couldn't look after him anymore? Did she, Maddie, have the patience to become her brother's primary care giver, and how would that even work? Ben wouldn't want to move to Portland and she couldn't put her career on hold to come back to LA and take care of him. Perhaps that was selfish, but if she wasn't Maddie the journalist, who was she?

# Chapter Eleven

*Los Angeles, April 2024*

'Wow,' Maddie said, gazing around. 'Feels like we've entered a whole other world.'

'Is it magic?' Ben asked.

Eva laughed. 'I like to think so.'

Her garden was a jungle in miniature, alive with flickering shadows and dappled sunlight. Broad-leaved palm trees swayed above their heads; below their feet, a brick path bordered by mosaics wound through beds of grasses, ferns and fleshy succulents. The hum of traffic was muted here, overlaid by the sound of water trickling over rocks to fall in a pool and the crystal notes of wind chimes hanging from branches. And everywhere they looked, there were extraordinary statues standing among the plants: mythical creatures with claws, scales and horns, fashioned from an array of discarded garbage. Tiny plastic animals, dolls' heads, toy cars, flattened tin cans, ring pulls, tyre rims, bottle caps and a thousand other pieces of flotsam and jetsam had been arranged by colour and wired together to create large, friendly monsters.

Maddie was trying to think what the sculptures reminded her of when Ben said, 'This is where the wild things are!' and she realised, of course: his favourite picture book as a child. Sharon had even made him a wolf suit, which he wore until it fell apart.

'That's right,' Eva said, delighted. 'I love Maurice Sendak's work. We share the same heritage: his parents were Jewish, too.' Turning to Maddie, she added quietly, 'He lost most of his family during the Holocaust when he was young, and I believe it affected him deeply. You can sense a dark undercurrent in so many of his drawings.'

Gramps gazed around. 'Wonderful! Art from the contents of trash cans. But how did you collect all this? It must have taken years.'

'Oh, I was quite the beachcomber in my younger days,' Eva replied. 'I work on a smaller scale now. There are some of my more recent pieces inside the house but I thought you might like to see the garden. Feel free to wander wherever you like.'

Maddie followed Ben down the path, stopping to admire a troll with fishing-net hair and beer-can pointed teeth hiding behind a bottle palm.

'I love this place,' Ben said, running his hand over its traffic-cone nose. 'Can we come again?'

'Well, we don't want to bother Eva,' Maddie replied. 'I'd guess she's pretty busy.'

They found a bench set against a wall studded with seashells at the end of the garden and sat for a while, sunshine warm on their skin, listening to a pair of doves cooing to each other. That was perhaps the best thing about being with family: you could enjoy each other's company without the need to make conversation. 'Ben, maybe some time you could visit me in Portland,' Maddie said, as the idea occurred to her. 'Would you like that?'

'Yes,' he replied immediately, though he looked anxious. 'On a plane?'

'Not necessarily,' she replied. 'You can go by train, though it takes a long time.'

Perhaps he could come back with her when she returned to Portland, and then her mom could fly out to pick him up at the end of the trip. Although would it be safe for him to spend time with her there, given the attention she was getting?

'I'd like to show you where I live,' she told Ben, pushing away the unwelcome thought. They could go for walks along the riverbank, see the sculptures in the Art Museum, take a picnic to the Japanese Gardens, and just hang out together. Spending time with Ben now made her realise how much she'd missed him: his openness and affection, the joy he took in small things. Every day since she'd been in LA, he'd made her a card with a picture on the front and some funny little message inside: 'Wake up and smell the pineapple!' or, 'It's a lovely day for a trip to the grocery store!' Yet he hadn't tried to make her laugh, as he usually loved to do: singing numbers from *The Sound of Music* in a falsetto voice or putting on Sharon's coat and imitating her looking with increasing desperation for her car keys. He seemed to be running at half power.

Looking back, Maddie remembered the sense of liberation she had felt on leaving home to go to college. Sharon was a wonderful mother – almost too wonderful at times. Her whole being was wrapped up in her children: being the best advocate for Ben and making sure Maddie stayed on the right track. It would have been a relief if their mother could have eased off once in a while, though Maddie had never dared say so. Maybe Ben was beginning to feel stifled, too, trapped in a cage that was becoming too small for him.

'Let's go and see what Gramps and Eva are up to,' she said, stretching out a hand to pull Ben up.

'Do you think they're kissing?' he asked, screwing up his face.

Maddie laughed. 'Well, you never know.'

Their grandfather was a huge hit among the elderly ladies in his neighbourhood but he didn't seem to have any particular favourites; Maddie had certainly never seen him as animated as he was now with Eva. They fitted together perfectly, like two halves of a walnut in its shell.

Gramps and Eva were sitting at a table on the patio – not kissing but drinking tea, eating cake and talking ten to the dozen. 'Come and have some *Bienenstich*,' Eva said. 'Bee-sting cake. It's a German speciality I made for you, to celebrate our heritage.' Two circles of rich, buttery dough were sandwiched together with cream under a honey-glazed almond topping.

'It's weird but I've never really thought of myself as having German blood,' Maddie said, accepting a slice and attacking it with her pastry fork. 'Maybe we should take a trip to Berlin some time, Gramps.' Instead of obsessing about death, she might have added. She said instead, 'This cake tastes amazing, by the way.'

'It's so strange to think your parents and mine could have moved in the same circles,' Gramps said to Eva. 'There can't have been many German émigrés heading to California in the 1930s. Our house was always full of artistic types – my mother seemed to collect them.'

'My parents worked in the film industry too,' Eva

explained to Maddie and Ben. 'Mom was a set designer and Dad a violinist who specialised in playing film scores. But you're wrong, Robert: a flood of German writers and directors came to try their luck in Hollywood after Hitler came to power. Actors, too – Marlene Dietrich among them. My mother was in the audience at the opening of her film *The Blue Angel*. Marlene took a bow at the end for her standing ovation, then caught a taxi to the airport to leave Berlin for Hollywood. Five years later, my parents followed her.'

'May I have another piece of cake?' Ben interrupted, holding out his plate.

Maddie nudged him. 'Say please.'

Eva laughed. 'Of course, Ben. I'm glad you like it. Sorry to be boring. Who needs a history lesson?'

'No, this is fascinating,' Maddie assured her.

'But the person who can tell you the most about those times is my grandson.' Eva looked at her watch and tutted. 'He should be here by now. Serves him right if we've eaten all the cake.'

Maddie tensed immediately. Even the thought of Daniel made her feel uncomfortable.

'I love your wild things,' Ben said. 'Will you show me how you make them?'

'Sure,' Eva replied. 'When we've finished tea, we can take a look around my studio. I hear you're an artist yourself. Are you wearing one of your own designs?'

Ben beamed with pride, holding out his T-shirt and looking down at the picture as though he'd never seen it before: a sunflower with the caption, 'I am your sunshine'. He was telling Eva about his paintings when Daniel walked through the patio doors at the back of the house, apologising profusely for being late. Maddie felt her hackles rise. Why did he have to come and spoil the afternoon? The very sight of him in chinos and shirt sleeves was annoying; he was so pleased with himself. He was good-looking in a dark, rugged kind of way, and he sure knew it.

'One of my students kept me talking,' he said with a shrug. 'Not much of an excuse, I know.'

Maddie pasted a smile on her face for appearances' sake. Daniel shook hands with Gramps, smiled at her in return and clapped Ben on the back as they were introduced.

'Well, you nearly missed the *Bienenstich*,' Eva said, cutting him a generous slice.

'My favourite. You must be honoured guests,' he said, taking a bite and sending a dollop of cream squirting on to the table.

'Careful!' Maddie snatched up the envelope lying there that had narrowly escaped a splattering.

'Oh, sorry,' he said with his mouth full, not overly concerned. 'What's that?'

'It's my mother's journal,' Gramps said. 'I'm decluttering my house, you see. Have you heard of Swedish death cleaning?'

Daniel swallowed quickly and threw up his hands. 'No more death! Mr Cole, say that word again and you'll have to put a dollar in the swear jar.'

Ben laughed with delight. 'Pay up, Gramps!'

So arrogant, Maddie thought, choosing to ignore the fact she had felt exactly the same until ten seconds ago. Gramps only chuckled and told Daniel to call him Bob. 'So, we found this notebook among my mother's things,' he went on, 'and my German's too rusty to make much sense of it. Eva's going to see what she can do.'

'May I take a look?' Daniel asked.

'Only if you use this,' Maddie said, passing him a napkin.

'Yes, ma'am,' he said. 'Actually, on second thought, I should probably wash my hands. Won't be a minute.

'Daniel's in the movie business, too,' Eva told them, after he'd left. 'Well, he reviews films and teaches at USC. He wrote a thesis about the influence of German directors on the Hollywood movie business in the 1940s, so he knows more about the subject than I do.'

'We should have brought those movie magazines,' Gramps told Maddie, turning to Eva to add, 'My mother had a collection of issues from the thirties and forties that we found when we were clearing out my apartment. I'm sure Daniel would have liked to see them. Oh well, another time.'

He and Eva were talking proudly about their grandchildren when Daniel returned and, with a glance at Maddie, picked up the envelope and drew out the leather-bound journal.

He laid it carefully on his lap. 'Wow, this is precious. Kind of obvious, really, but have you made a photocopy?'

'We haven't, actually,' Maddie confessed reluctantly. 'That might be a good idea.'

'I can copy it for you at work,' he said, not lifting his eyes from the pages. 'Looks like a diary but there seem to be stories here as well.'

'My mother would never talk about her upbringing in Germany,' Gramps said. 'The writing might not be autobiographical, but any little clue about her early life would be so interesting.'

'Sure,' Daniel said politely.

Maddie had to fight an impulse to snatch the book out

of his hands. OK, she was being ridiculous, but this was her great-grandmother – her Freya, with the impish smile and cloud of wavy hair – and she didn't want a virtual stranger knowing anything about her.

'And what about your father?' Eva asked.

'I never met him,' Gramps replied. 'He was killed in France, during the war, shortly before I was born. It happened the year before the Allied invasions in 1944, and I gather he was there on some sort of reconnaissance mission. My mother always said he was the love of her life, but she didn't like to talk about him. I suppose it was too painful. He was German, too. I think he had friends in America who put him up when he first arrived, and then once he was settled, he sent for my mother. That's about all I know.'

'Did you miss him, growing up?' Maddie asked, thinking about her own childhood.

Gramps shook his head. 'Sometimes, maybe, when other boys' dads came to the football game or took them camping, but not often. My mom made sure I felt secure and loved.'

'And you don't have any of his belongings?' Eva asked. 'No medals, or books, or letters?'

'I have a photograph on the mantelpiece,' Gramps said. 'And I seem to remember a suitcase full of old clothes in the attic when I was clearing the house after my wife died, ready to move into the apartment. There might be something of his in there. Madeleine, maybe your mother has it?'

'Gramps!' Maddie exclaimed. 'How could you be so careless? You, a history teacher!'

Eva clicked her tongue. 'Robert, this decluttering is all very well, but you must be careful not to throw too much away. I have several treasures that my parents brought with them from Germany and they mean more to me than anything else in the house. Come and see.'

They walked through the long, low bungalow, crammed with as many interesting things to see as the garden: flowering vines drawn around doorways and climbing up walls; a glass table top resting on a massive section of tree trunk, its branches twisted and writhing; a seagull made out of discarded plastic – spoons and forks, coat hangers, a hairbrush – hanging in front of a porthole window; a painted sky-blue ceiling, dotted with fluffy white clouds. Eva's latest pieces were displayed in a light-filled studio at the side of the house: children's faces, composed of a collage of old photographs, film negatives, strips of contact sheets, even pieces of X-rays. Maddie couldn't stop looking at them, fascinated by the way so many tiny, ghostly images in black and white formed recognisable features when seen from a distance.

Ben was entranced, too. Daniel showed him how to make the seagull's wings flap by pulling a cord beneath it, and pointed out any delights he might have missed: a *trompe l'œuil* mousehole in the baseboard with a pair of beady eyes peering out; a real-life ginger cat asleep in a laundry basket. To be fair to the guy, Maddie had to admit, he was great with her brother – which simply meant treating him like a normal human being, rather than ignoring him completely or talking to him in a bright, false voice with the volume turned up. Any of her friends who'd failed the Ben test had been crossed off the list immediately.

Eva led them to a glass-fronted cabinet in a corner of the living room, its shelves crammed with objects. 'Pick up anything that interests you,' she said, opening the door. 'These belongings come alive when they're touched. When

I hold them, it feels as though my parents are speaking to me – and their parents, too.'

Maddie was content merely to look at first, taking in every detail of the display. Embroidered linen tablecloths and place mats were draped behind photograph albums, a stained recipe book, a gleaming silver cup engraved with lettering from the Hebrew alphabet, while a doll with a vacant china face, a stuffed calico dog and a teddy bear with a red bow tie sat around a miniature table laid with teacups the size of thimbles. Ben chose a misshapen leather football and tossed it high in the air.

'You'd better take that outside,' Maddie warned, but Eva told them not to worry.

'This is one of the most precious things,' she said, selecting a small book and flicking open its pages, which were crammed with dense handwriting. 'These are the addresses of my parents' friends and neighbours in the Jewish quarter of Berlin.' She sighed. 'The saddest book in the world, my father used to say. Just a handful of these people survived the war and nearly all their houses were bombed to smithereens. A whole community, destroyed in the blink of an eye. You can visit Berlin, Maddie, but I doubt you'll find your great-grandmother there. The world she grew up in has gone; it only exists in the stories handed down through generations.' She smoothed her thumb over the worn leather cover before putting the book back in place. 'My parents used to talk about the old days constantly. They might have escaped the Nazis but they were haunted by memories of those left behind.'

'And my mother never mentioned Germany,' Gramps told her. 'Strange, isn't it? I can't recall her seeking out any German friends and she had no desire to go back there after the war was over. Of course, she wasn't Jewish, and she was on her own throughout my childhood, but all the same . . .'

'Sounds like a mystery for you to investigate,' Daniel said to Maddie.

'How do you mean?' she asked, instantly defensive.

'Well, you're a journalist, aren't you?' he replied. 'Look, I'm not stalking you, but I've done some digging and I was right: we were at college together. There's proof!' He took out his phone and scrolled through some photos before selecting one. 'You were in the film society too. Remember this screening?'

'Vaguely,' Maddie said, squinting at the picture. There she was, in the middle of a group of five people standing in front of a movie poster, wearing her favourite red plaid shirt (she'd scarcely taken that thing off the whole of her freshman year – where was it now?) with her arms folded and her hair in a high ponytail, looking very sure of herself. She hadn't worried about voicing her opinions then; she was always sounding off about something or other. The other members of the film-society committee had been equally opinionated, as far as she could recall. It was a wonder they'd ever agreed on a single film worth watching. She had a dim memory of one person always turning up halfway through their meetings; perhaps that was Daniel.

'But where are you?' she asked him.

He came so close to peer over her shoulder that she could smell his cologne; she had to steel herself not to flinch. 'At the back. The one with the beard.'

'Oh, yes,' she said, 'of course. Guess I have an excuse for not recognising you. I left the film society after a couple of terms, anyway.'

'So once I had your name, I looked you up online,' Daniel went on. 'It's interesting to see what became of us all.'

Maddie passed him back the phone. 'And now you're teaching at USC.'

He smiled. 'Yeah, I haven't gone far. I write film reviews, too.'

'Good for you,' she said, more coldly than she'd intended. He'd found her on the internet so he'd know the things people were saying about her, and she hated that.

'And you've never tried to find your father's family?' Eva was asking Gramps. 'You can trace virtually anybody these days, you know. All you need is a name and a date of birth. I subscribe to a family history website so I could help you track them down.'

'I couldn't see the point,' he replied. 'They might turn out to be awful and then I'd be stuck with them.'

She laughed. 'Not necessarily. Anyway, look on the bright side: these people might be lovely. And even if they're not, they can probably tell you something about your father. Aren't you curious?'

Gramps considered the matter. 'Yes,' he said slowly. 'Now you come to mention it, I am.'

# Chapter Twelve

*Los Angeles, April 2024*

Maddie and Ben had a lot to tell Sharon that evening over supper. 'Eva's an artist too,' Ben said. 'She says I can come and draw in her studio whenever I want, and she's going to show me how to make collages.'

'That's cool,' Sharon said, with a glance at Maddie. 'And what's she like, this Eva?'

'She's great,' Maddie replied. 'I think Gramps really likes her – they have a lot in common, apart from death. She's going to help him research his family history.'

Sharon passed Ben a plate piled high with roasted peppers and pasta. 'I'd be interested to meet her. Why don't I give her a call and we can arrange a time to visit? Then I could give you a ride over there.'

'I'm going on the bus,' he said. 'There's a stop around the corner from her house. I'm not a kid, Mom.'

Sharon paused, her spoon in mid-air. 'But you hardly know this person. I really would like to talk to her before you start spending time together.'

'Why?' Ben asked. 'She's my friend, not yours.'

‘Don’t be so rude,’ Sharon snapped, the colour rising in her cheeks.

An uneasy silence descended. ‘Have some salad,’ Maddie said, passing her mother the bowl. ‘It looks great.’

They concentrated on their food for the next few minutes, Ben scowling and pushing pasta tubes around his plate, Sharon shooting him angry glances. ‘By the way,’ Maddie said at last, ‘Gramps mentioned something about a suitcase of old clothes that he thought you might have taken when he was clearing out the house on East Street. Does that ring any bells?’

‘What?’ Her mother’s gaze slowly focused on Maddie’s face. ‘A suitcase? Oh, I can’t remember. I took most of Grandma’s clothes to Goodwill, that I do know. You could have a look in the basement – if I didn’t throw the case out, that’s where it will be. I wouldn’t get your hopes up, though.’

‘Mom!’ Maddie had been pinning her hopes on this case. With so little to go on, the very thought of it was unbearably tantalising.

‘I’ve had enough,’ Ben said abruptly, pushing back his chair. ‘Going to my room.’

‘But you’ve hardly eaten anything!’ Sharon exclaimed.

‘I’m not hungry.’ He left the table, scraped the remains of his food into the trash and walked out of the room without looking at either of them.

Sharon laid her knife and fork together and wiped her mouth deliberately with a napkin.

‘We ate a lot of cake at Eva’s house,’ Maddie said, squeezing her hand. ‘But this was delicious, Mom.’

Sharon took a breath, looking down at the table. ‘I took longer to bond with Ben than I did with you. He spent so much time in the NICU and sometimes I had to force myself to leave you and go to see him. It was only when we took him home that love began to grow and I could be a proper mother to both of you. I swore that I'd make it up to him for my failings in those early days, that I'd do whatever it took to give him the best life he could possibly imagine. That's been my mission for twenty-three years. How can I stop now?'

'And you've succeeded brilliantly,' Maddie told her. 'Don't you see? It's because you've been such an amazing mother that he has the confidence to strike out on his own.'

'But he's so vulnerable.' Sharon raised her anxious eyes to meet Maddie's. 'I can't bear to think of people taking advantage of him. This Eva person, for example; you've only met her once.'

'Twice actually,' Maddie said. 'She was at the Death Café, too.'

Sharon shuddered. 'Well, that's hardly reassuring. And as for stuffing him with cake so he has no appetite for supper . . .'

'Mom, stop.' Maddie took her mother's hand. 'Ben eats healthily most of the time – a slice of cake now and then won't kill him. Eva's an elderly lady who wouldn't hurt a fly and anyone can see she's a kind, interesting person. Ben loved looking round her garden and the studio. He was so happy there.'

'Happier than he is here, you mean?' Sharon asked, bristling.

'Yes, actually,' Maddie replied. 'At the moment, anyway. Look, he's a young man; he's bound to want what he can see other people having. I think he might like to start dating again.'

Sharon groaned. 'Well, look how that turned out.'

The year before, Ben had started seeing Ruby, a lovely girl who had Down syndrome whom he'd met at summer camp. They'd gone to the movies together, and bowling, and out for meals – until Ben had discovered lovely Ruby was also dating several of the other boys from camp, and decided he didn't want to share her.

Maddie laughed. 'Come on! Just because it didn't work out that time doesn't mean he has to give up girls for ever. Look how many mistakes I've made in my brilliant dating career.'

Sharon smiled reluctantly. 'I guess you're right. And Ben took it on the chin, didn't he? He wasn't too upset when he and Ruby broke up.'

'Not at all. He believes in himself, Mom, and that's because of you. Now we just have to believe in him, too.'

Sharon looked her full in the face. 'Do you honestly think he could manage, living on his own?'

'I don't know,' Maddie replied. 'But I do know he'll be miserable unless we let him try.'

After she'd raced through clearing the plates and loading the dishwasher, Maddie hurried down to the basement storage room to look for a mythical suitcase that might only have existed in her grandfather's imagination. Locating anything in there was a nightmare, but the thought of finding even the tiniest clue to the mystery of her German great-grandparents spurred her on. Containers filled shelves around the sides of the room and the floor was stacked up to the ceiling with more boxes and paraphernalia; she had to drag most of it out into the passage to clear a space to stand. Here was the fabric of their life together, arranged and labelled by her mother: the Christmas and Hallowe'en decorations Sharon dragged out, put up and then packed away again, year after year; the crate that a succession of dogs had occupied as puppies; the picnic baskets, fishing nets, surfboards, tennis rackets, jump ropes and sagging footballs of their childhood;

the tricycle Ben had ridden until well into his teens. What a lot of work it took to raise a family, to create all the special occasions they had taken so much for granted, and their mother had done most of that single-handed. No wonder she was finding it hard to let go.

Once there was room to move, Maddie stood in the centre of the room with her hands on her hips, reading the labels in her mother's handwriting on the columns of plastic storage crates. Surely there had to be a few suitcases somewhere? And yet when was the last time Sharon had travelled anywhere and needed one? Maddie couldn't remember.

'How are you getting on?' Her mother's voice came floating down the stairs, to be followed shortly afterwards by Sharon herself, threading her way through the junk in the passage.

'Not well,' Maddie replied. 'I can't see any luggage at all.'

'You need to raise your eyes,' Sharon said. 'Wait, I'll fetch you a ladder.'

'How ever did you manage to get up there?' Maddie asked, peering at the bottom of a wire rack bolted to the ceiling that loomed over her head like a spaceship landing on earth.

'With difficulty.' Sharon unhooked a step ladder from the wall and pulled it open for Maddie to climb. 'Jeez, Maddie, you've turned the place upside down. I hope this won't be all for nothing.'

'Come on, Mom – go big or go home,' Maddie said, pushing aside a duffle bag and sending up a cloud of dust that made her cough. She pulled out a large wheeled suitcase that was obscuring her view and handed it down to Sharon. 'Could you take this for a second?'

Now she had room to move, she could sort through the pile of sports bags, backpacks and cases piled in the rack. And there it was, at last, pushed to one side: a small, chestnut-leather suitcase with reinforced corners, metal clasps and a worn handle.

'Yes!' Maddie's heart leapt as she reached for it. This had to be the one; the other bags might have been old, but they all had zips or wheels or modern plastic inserts.

'Promise I'll put everything back as it was,' she said, scrambling down the ladder. 'Let's take this case upstairs and go through it together.'

'No, you make a start,' Sharon replied, standing back to let her pass. 'If you tidy up in here, I'll never find anything ever again.'

Maddie could tell from its weight that the suitcase wasn't empty. She laid it on the living-room rug and set about the rusty metal clasps with a kitchen knife and a can of spray lubricant. At last she managed to prise them open and lifted the lid, releasing a faint scent of mothballs and mildew. Inside she found a swathe of tissue paper, yellow and brittle with age, which she drew apart with clumsy fingers to reveal several items of women's clothing: a couple of crêpe-de-chine dresses with dropped waists and ruffles around the neck and hem, an evening cloak with a Pierrot collar in striped silk, three pintucked blouses fastened by a row of tiny pearl buttons, and finally a gold brocade robe with a tasselled cord at the waist. Maddie shook out each garment reverently, admiring the tiny, exquisite stitching, and laid it aside for later inspection. The clothes were faded and deeply creased, but still intact.

Tucked between the layers of fabric she made discoveries that were even more intriguing. A framed picture was wrapped in another layer of tissue paper that fell apart in her hands: a watercolour painting of a large house built of honey-coloured stone, set in parkland with a dark forest behind. 'Beechwood Grange', read the caption beneath the painting. Maddie studied it for some time. A quick search by phone informed her that Beechwood Grange was a country house in Oxfordshire, England, home to the Framley-Chambers family since the eighteenth century. What could such a place have meant to Freya? This was definitely her great-grandmother's suitcase: an inscription inside the lid read, 'Freya Amsel, Holsteiner Ufer 40, Berlin'. Had she spent some time in England, then, as well as America?

Aside from the picture, Maddie found a silver-backed hairbrush and hand mirror, both badly tarnished, a pair of flat leather slippers and, most fascinating of all, a rectangular jewellery box made of shiny black lacquer, inlaid with mother-of-pearl birds and butterflies. The inside was lined with red velvet and contained something far more valuable than jewellery, as far as Maddie was concerned: a sheaf of letters, several of them still in their original envelopes, addressed to Mrs L Cole in Sherman Oaks, California. Her heart in her mouth, she carefully extracted the first sheet of flimsy paper and began to read.

'So, found any treasures?' Sharon asked, coming upstairs half an hour later. 'I hope it's been worth turning the basement upside down.' She looked around. 'And now the living room looks like it's been hit by a bomb.'

'Sorry,' Maddie murmured. 'I'll tidy up in a second.'

'These clothes are beautiful.' Sharon held up a dress against herself. 'Wonder if this would fit me? Far too precious to wear, though. Imagine if you spilled barbecue sauce on it.'

'Did you ever meet Gramps' mom?' Maddie asked.

'Once or twice, apparently,' Sharon replied, 'though I don't remember. She died when I was small.'

Maddie nodded, looking back at the letter she was holding.

'What's that?' her mother asked, kneeling on the rug to look over her shoulder.

'A letter from Gramps' father during the war. Except . . .'

'Except what?' Sharon smiled. 'You're being very mysterious. Spit it out.'

Maddie hesitated, wondering how to continue – and even whether she should. She wanted to confide in someone, though. 'Well, the other day Gramps told me he was born towards the end of 1943,' she began, 'which meant he escaped the Vietnam draft lottery that applied to men born from 1944 onwards.'

'That's right,' Sharon said. 'His birth date is 15 November, 1943. I happen to know it's his computer password.'

'Well, these letters are dated from June 1942 till August 1943, shortly before his father was killed,' Maddie said, feeling troubled. 'Once men had been posted overseas, they couldn't go back to the States until the war was over, could they? When they were given leave, I always assumed they took it locally rather than going home.'

'That's right.' Sharon's expression changed. 'Oh Lord, I see what you're getting at.'

'And there's no mention of a baby in any of these letters.' Maddie nodded at the envelopes scattered around her. The letters were written in English, presumably so the censor would let them through. 'Not even in the summer of 1943. He can't have known that his wife was expecting.'

Sharon sat back on her heels. 'Maybe she wanted to tell him face to face, once he was home. Or maybe she was going to wait until she was further along in the pregnancy.'

'But she would have been around six months pregnant by

then. Face facts, Mom: she didn't want to tell her husband at all because he wasn't the father. I can't see any other explanation.'

They sat in silence for a moment. 'Gramps mustn't know about this,' Sharon said at last. 'He adored his mother. Just put those letters back in their envelopes and forget about them.'

'You think?' Maddie frowned. 'I'm not sure what to do. Eva's helping him research his family history. What if he hears the truth from somebody else, and then discovers we knew all along?'

'You'll just have to put them off,' Sharon told her. 'Tell this Eva to mind her own business and distract Gramps somehow. Perhaps we could take him back to the Death Café, or for a tour around a cemetery – something suitably morbid.'

'But on the other hand,' Maddie said, 'we might be able to find out who his real father is. He might have half brothers or sisters, nephews and nieces. Wouldn't that be amazing? And come on, these are your relatives too. You must want to trace them.'

'No, I do not,' Sharon said grimly. 'I'm not having my father upset, not at his time of life – the shock could kill him. I'm telling you, Maddie, you need to keep this information to yourself. I wish you'd never uncovered it in the first place.'

Maddie watched her mother fold up the clothes with quick, angry movements. Yet again, they were at odds. She hated the idea of knowing something so fundamental about her grandfather's identity and keeping it from him. Didn't Gramps deserve to hear the truth, no matter how painful that might be? And what if his mother's journal revealed it anyway?

# Chapter Thirteen

*Berlin, March 1932*

Another strained Christmas without Ingrid had come and gone, and another interminable winter given way at last to an achingly beautiful spring. Germany teetered on the brink of change, though nobody could tell which way the political wind was blowing. In a March presidential election, Adolf Hitler and Ernst Thalmann, the Communist candidate, challenged the incumbent von Hindenburg. Hitler embarked on an ambitious propaganda campaign, using a private aeroplane to speak at rallies across the country, but von Hindenburg still managed to scrape a narrow victory. He lost support soon afterwards, however, and was forced to dissolve the Reichstag and call another election for July. Hitler had won a third of the vote and now had to be taken seriously as a politician.

The country seethed with discontent. Brawls broke out for the most trivial of reasons, or for no reason at all. People on the street hurried by with lowered eyes: looking at someone the wrong way could earn you a curse, a blow or a knife in the ribs. The violence reached such a pitch that in April, the Chancellor banned both the SA and SS from operating across Germany – much to the Nazis' outrage. Herr Grube and Otto became even more obsessed with fighting and fitness, cheering themselves hoarse at boxing matches. Grube intensified his early-morning exercise regime, repelling Freya more thoroughly than ever with his grunts of exertion and sweat-soaked vest. He'd been promoted to assistant treasurer of the Nazi party in Berlin, and was always hurrying off to evening meetings and rallies at the weekend. He'd also started taking part in regular security patrols with the SA, wearing the brown uniform and carrying a baton and a pair of handcuffs, so that he could enjoy a taste of the power they wielded. And Joseph Goebbels, the district leader and Hitler's propaganda chief, now greeted him by name – or so he claimed.

Freya avoided Grube as much as possible. She occasionally caught him staring at her but so far, her reserve (and stubborn refusal to stop smoking) had been enough to stop any advances he might make. Otto's company was also a trial, with the memory of that awful day at the lake still fresh in her mind. She wondered whether she'd ever see Leon again; naturally, he hadn't come to the apartment since then and his name was never mentioned. It was all Violet's fault, Freya thought, and wished for the hundredth time the girl had stayed in England and not come here to turn their lives upside down.

The only thing to be said for Violet was that, true to her word, she had finally introduced Freya to the writer she'd mentioned: Wolfgang Berger. His novel, *One Night in Berlin*, the story of an encounter between a young actress and a wealthy businessman, had caused a stir on the literary scene when it appeared twelve years before. Freya found the book's cynicism and lack of hope depressing, but Berger's prose was certainly powerful. Yet he'd had nothing published since then and had earned a living lecturing at Friedrich Wilhelm University until he'd lost his job the year before. Freya suspected that might have been on account of the amount he drank, although the fact he was Jewish couldn't have helped either. She never saw him completely sober: his morning coffee was always accompanied by a shot of schnapps and he became less coherent as the day wore on. He was an inspiring teacher in his more lucid moments, though, and paid her the compliment of taking her writing seriously.

She had been so nervous at their first meeting, in a café midway between the Zaubergarten and Berger's apartment on the edge of the Schöneberg district. He was an imposing figure, tall and thin in a threadbare jacket with a hooked nose, a sweep of black hair greying at the temples and pockmarked skin. He was in his late forties, Freya estimated, and would have been utterly terrifying were it not for the occasional flash of humour in his dark, intense eyes, and the warmth of his smile. She had bought her typewriter by then and clutched a manuscript to her chest: her most accomplished story, polished several times over before being laboriously typed with two fingers.

Berger glanced at the first page. 'Violet says you can write. We shall see about that. Now, tell me what you're reading.'

Hesitantly, she mentioned *Berlin Alexanderplatz* by Alfred Döblin, which Leon had recommended to her when it first appeared three years before: the sprawling, meandering tale of a small-time thief trying to stay on the straight and narrow.

'A good start, certainly,' Berger had replied, 'but hardly original. Anyone who claims to be an intellectual has a copy.'

Freya had no such pretensions but she'd been excited by the way Döblin immortalised her city in the language of the streets, with drinking songs, newspaper articles and biblical stories thrown in for good measure. He'd shown her that rules could be broken and prose didn't have to be convoluted, and that the feelings of ordinary people (even what some might call the underclass) were just as worthy of attention as those of the elite.

Wolfgang Berger told her about another ground-breaking book that had just been published – *Blood Brothers*, by Ernst Haffner, about a gang of boys eking out a precarious living on the streets of Berlin – and about the novels of Irmgard Keun: *Gilgi: One of Us* and, newly released that month, *The Artificial Silk Girl*. 'You absolutely must read Keun,' he said. 'She writes about female sexuality in a way no one has ever done before.'

After an hour of this, Freya's head was spinning and her body fizzing, driven by a new sense of purpose. Writing was a craft like any other, Berger told her, and had to be practised rigorously. When she could take her eyes off his face, she scribbled notes surreptitiously in a small book held under the table because he wanted her to listen and think, rather than copy his words by rote. She'd been tentative about her work until now, hesitant to assume her stories would ever be read by anyone else, but she had always loved the process: that sense of shutting a door on the outside world and being alone with her thoughts. Hours would pass without her noticing as characters and places sprang to life under her pen, so vividly they seemed more real than the people around her. With these imaginary characters in her head, it hardly seemed to matter that she had so few friends; in solitude she felt her true self unfurl. Now Wolfgang Berger was telling her she was on the right path and giving her permission – even encouraging her – to follow it. For the first time since Ingrid had died,

Freya felt a guiding hand on her shoulder. Only the thought she couldn't share this marvellous news with her mother cast a fleeting shadow over her joy; Ingrid would have been so delighted by Berger's interest in her daughter.

'Can we meet again?' she asked him, when her lunch hour was over and she'd surely bothered him long enough. 'And may I pay you for your time?'

He didn't want money, only for his glass to be regularly refilled and for her to listen attentively to what he said. They would meet next week at the same time and place to discuss her work, he told her, and Freya had rarely felt so happy.

'How did you come to know Violet?' she asked, gathering her things to leave. Wolfgang seemed an unlikely friend for the dancer.

'I met her through a friend at the British Embassy,' he replied, catching the waiter's eye to order another drink. 'Violet collects people like trophies. I'm never quite sure what she intends to do with them.' He drained his glass. 'Someone should write the story of her life – now *that* would make interesting reading.'

But Freya wanted to keep Violet at a distance. She hadn't seen her and Leon together since coming across them in the café the previous September, and wasn't sure whether they were still seeing each other. And then a couple of weeks before, Herr Goldstein had rushed down to the dressing room in the middle of the afternoon to say that Violet's gentleman friend, Herr Fischer, had appeared at the club unexpectedly and was demanding to see her.

'Apparently she told him she had a dress fitting this afternoon,' he said. 'I've made it clear she isn't here but he won't leave. Can you go upstairs and talk to him?'

Freya and Frau Brodsky exchanged glances. 'I have an idea

where Violet might be,' Freya said, and Frau Brodsky replied that in that case, she had better fetch her, and be quick about it.

'I'll tell Fischer I sent her to the cobbler's,' she said. 'He might swallow it.'

There was no telling whether Violet would be with Leon, but it was worth a try. Freya slipped out of the back of the club and ran through the streets until she saw a blue door on the corner of the parade of shops. A lad who was sweeping the street paused to lean on his broom and watch her. Freya beckoned him over, taking a handful of pfennigs from her pocket.

'See that door over there?' she asked, pointing it out. 'I want you to bang on it until somebody answers. Say you have an urgent message for Fräulein Violet that you have to deliver in person, privately. If you're alone, and only then, tell her that Herr Fischer is asking for her at the club. Got that?'

She made him repeat the message twice before she let him go. The boy rapped on the blue door several times before a window on the second floor was thrown up and Leon's head emerged. Shortly after that, the blue door opened and the lad propped his broom against the wall before being ushered inside. Freya shrank back, waiting, until he left the building a few minutes later – followed shortly afterwards by Violet, pulling on a jacket with her cropped hair sticking up in tufts.

Wordlessly, Freya fell into step beside her, making Violet gasp and put a hand to her chest. 'You! I wondered who was my guardian angel. How did you know where to find me?' She was smiling, and didn't seem at all embarrassed or guilty about having been discovered with her lover.

'I saw you and Leon going in there once,' Freya replied, setting off down the street. 'You should be more careful. Just so you know, Frau Brodsky is going to say you've been to the shoe mender's. And your shirt's done up wrong, by the way.'

'Well, thank you,' Violet said, adjusting her clothing. 'For being discreet, and for coming to get me today.'

'I did it for Leon, not you,' Freya replied, not caring how rude she sounded. 'He deserves better than this.'

'And can I trust you to keep quiet?' Violet asked. 'For his sake, if not mine?'

'Of course,' Freya replied.

They made their way quickly back to the club without another word, and she stood aside to watch Violet saunter through the front door as though she hadn't a care in the world, preparing to be surprised at the sight of Maxim. She was overwhelmed by the urge to let Leon know how Violet was deceiving him, but her mother's words rang in her ear: never betray a confidence or stoop to gossip. You have no idea what's happening in somebody else's life, so don't meddle in their affairs. For all Freya knew, Violet might have already told Leon about her involvement with Fischer. And what exactly was that involvement, anyway? Freya assumed Maxim Fischer and Violet were lovers but she didn't know for sure. It would look as though she were motivated by jealousy – and maybe she was. For the moment, she would hold her tongue.

And so for now, Freya and Violet were quits: Freya had repaid Violet for bringing Wolfgang Berger into her life and transforming it out of all recognition. Apart from educating her, Berger welcomed her into the circle of writers and artists who gathered in Schöneberg's various bars, drinking, gossiping and arguing until the early hours. She was wary at first, wondering what ulterior motive he might have, but it turned out he wanted nothing from her but a willingness to learn and dedication to her craft. He was intensely sociable and liked nothing better than being in the centre of a crowd, holding forth with a drink in his hand, or sitting back to watch connections firing between people who would never have met if not for him. Especially the young, he told her once: they had an energy that inspired him.

He was a hard taskmaster, nonetheless. Freya's heart sank the next week when he handed back her pages, covered in scribbled notes with whole sections crossed out.

'Don't look so downcast,' he said, laughing at her expression. 'I wouldn't waste my time if you didn't have talent.'

Reading through his comments, Freya saw he'd pinpointed the dramatic focus of her story and suggested ways she could increase its impact, while paring back inessential details that only diluted the tension.

'See here?' he said, pointing to a paragraph she'd struggled over for hours. 'You're over-explaining everything, telling the reader what to think. Leave some space for people to make up their own minds. Ambiguity can be interesting, you know. Paint a picture as vividly as you can but don't analyse it to death.'

Freya had started reading Irmgard Keun by then and saw immediately what Berger meant. She stayed up till the early hours that night, rewriting her story, and finally fell asleep with a pen in her hand and an ink blot soaking into the blanket. Even though she was still living at home, sleeping in her childhood bedroom, it felt as though a new, exciting life was within reach. She might not have found love, but she had art. She borrowed the books Berger recommended from the library or bought them, if funds allowed and the waiting list was too long, from a Jewish bookseller in Charlottenburg. She had to discipline herself, or all her money would be spent on books and – far less essential – bar and café bills. Her escape fund was growing, but slowly. It would be another year at least before she could afford to strike out on her own.

That Saturday, Wolfgang – as he told her to call him – invited her to meet some of his artistic friends in a nearby bar after she'd finished work. She was the youngest by several years but that didn't seem to matter, especially after a few drinks. Wolfgang introduced her as an exciting new literary voice and she almost believed him, though she was too shy to say much and spent most of the time glancing around, listening to conversations that became increasingly raucous. The bar was full of bohemian types – women wearing slouchy trousers, like she was, or satin slip dresses and long fringed scarves; men with long hair in waistcoats and shirtsleeves, gesticulating with cigarettes or playing chess – and she was in the thick of it, at the most interesting table of all. She sat between a tiny, exquisite photographer known as Maus – whose tilted nose and round, bright eyes were indeed a little mouse-like – and Rupert, an English writer with brown hair slicked back off his forehead, horn-rimmed spectacles and a world-weary expression. Maus was putting together pictures for an exhibition in the autumn and wanted Rupert's help with titles, and perhaps a short verse to accompany each section.

'But this is your artistic vision, darling, not mine,' he drawled. 'Your eye is too soft and feminine. If you'd photographed a few handsome boys, I might feel more inspired.' He nodded towards Freya and added, 'Why not ask Wolfi's latest protégée to come up with something?'

'I should love to see your work,' Freya said. 'It sounds fascinating.'

Maus was experimenting with solarisation, a technique whereby negatives were exposed to light before they were fully developed, so that some features were burned out while others leapt into stark relief, outlined in black. Next to her sat Elke, a graceful dancer with a loose chignon of dark hair and the serene expression of a Madonna, and beside her a journalist, Gunther, who was telling Wolfgang about the stormtrooper parade at Hitler's mountain retreat, Berchtesgaden, which he'd just covered for his newspaper.

'It was hypnotic: a river of uniforms like a great brown snake, with the jackboots pounding out a beat and the crowd half mad with cheering. Even a glimpse of their leader sends them into a frenzy – you'd think he were the Messiah. God knows what will happen if the Nazis win more seats in July.'

The ban on the SA and the SS had recently been lifted, thanks to a deal between Hitler and an ambitious army general, von Schleicher, who wanted power for himself – just in time for the Nazis to stand as a legitimate party at the upcoming election.

Freya leaned forward to catch Gunther's attention. 'Our lodger's a keen Nazi. He's assistant treasurer for the Berlin branch and knows Goebbels well – or so he says.'

'Does he indeed?' Gunther immediately bombarded her with quick-fire questions before adding, unnecessarily, 'I'd like to get the inside story on Herr Goebbels. He's a writer, too, don't you know? And a journalist.'

'I do.' Freya shuddered. Walther Grube subscribed to *The Attack*, the Berlin newspaper founded and edited by Goebbels, and left copies lying around the sitting room. She had once made the mistake of flicking through its pages, finding it full of Nazi propaganda and anti-Semitic hatred.

'Do you think your lodger would be willing to talk to me?' Gunther asked.

'Maybe.' But Freya wouldn't like to ask Grube; she couldn't bear the man knowing that she had told someone about him, that his existence had made any impression on her at all. Too late, she regretted ever having mentioned him. Luckily she was spared from going into more detail by the sight of Violet walking into the bar, dressed in crimson silk pyjamas with a white orchid in her buttonhole.

'Well, hello again,' she said to Freya, as it was only an hour since they'd been together at the Zaubergarten. 'Fancy running into you here. Just a quick visit, I can't stay long.' They'd been keeping each other at arm's length since Herr Fischer's surprise visit, and Violet would have been no keener to see Freya than the other way around.

She went around the table, kissing everyone on both cheeks and squeezing in beside Rupert. 'So, what do you think of our little wardrobe mistress?' she asked Wolfgang, fitting a cigarette into an ivory holder. 'Was I right to send her your way?' She gave Freya a tight smile.

'I'm not a parcel,' Freya replied sulkily, aware she should have been thanking Violet for the introduction but finding the words stuck in her throat.

'Quite right. You are a true original,' Wolfgang said, raising his glass to her.

Violet turned away and began an animated conversation with Rupert in English while finishing off his gin. She stayed for another twenty minutes or so, flirting with Wolfgang, teasing Maus and quizzing Gunther about Berchtesgaden before leaving in another flurry of kisses.

'Off to break a few more hearts,' Rupert said, while Maus and Elke exchanged significant looks.

'Violet's on a mission and I can't work out what it is,' Gunther commented, staring after her. 'There's more going on in her lovely head than one might imagine.'

'She likes to make people adore her and they generally oblige,' Maus said. 'Perhaps that's why she wants to be an actress.'

'Yet I gather Herr Fischer heard of an opening in America and she wasn't interested,' Gunther told them. 'She chose to stay in Berlin.'

'Do you think she's in love with him?' Elke asked, widening her large brown eyes, whereupon everyone burst out laughing.

'Violet, in love? Hardly,' Rupert said. 'If you ask me, she's waiting to see whether Hitler will get into power and smooth her path. I know her family in England and they're all terrific Fascists – they're bound to have connections.'

Freya's jealousy of Violet – for she had to admit that's how she felt – was turning to something nearer dislike. Admittedly, she'd never heard Violet railing against Jews or praising Hitler, but no doubt she'd be happy to make use of the Nazi leader if she got the chance.

Maus dug Freya in the ribs. 'I bet Violet's a nightmare to work with. Come on, spill the beans.'

But Freya merely laughed and shook her head. Her emotions where Violet was concerned were too complicated and intense to share with people she didn't know well; or in fact, almost anyone at all. Gunther lit a cigarette and looked at her through a cloud of smoke, narrowing his eyes as he waited for her to speak. She met his gaze, keeping her mouth shut.

# Chapter Fourteen

*Berlin, April 1932*

Adolf Hitler was back in the aeroplane on another whistle-stop tour of the country so that he could speak at bierkellers, town halls and stadiums in as many as four or five towns a day. Goebbels had organised the whole tour. A planeload of journalists flew in advance of these visits, filling newspapers the next day with photographs and reports of the adoring masses who had turned out to greet their glorious leader. He would start off quietly, telling them almost sadly how unfairly they'd been treated by the rest of the world since the war, how mercilessly exploited by their current government as well as the Jews, before whipping himself into a frenzy as he announced those days would be over once he gained power. If they gave him the chance, he would speak up for the working man and return the Fatherland to its former glory. He used short, catchy phrases that were chanted back to him by his audience, soon equally transported. He was on their side: passionate, fearless and honest, a contrast to the corrupt elite who'd been living high on the hog for years at their expense. No wonder they loved him.

Thousands came to hear Hitler talk at Berlin's Sportpalast arena in Schöneberg, and Freya had to fight her way through the streets to get home after work. Everywhere she looked, posters on lampposts and hoardings exhorted her to vote for him, and squads of passing stormtroopers waved the swastika flag she was expected to salute – the flag that now flew proudly from their balcony at home. Freya felt sick at the sight of it, and knew her mother would have been horrified, too. Walther Grube strutted about the apartment with renewed confidence, waiting for his hero to achieve due recognition, and was to be seen more often as a brownshirt, tapping his baton and with handcuffs dangling from his belt. He'd latched on to the family's maid and was often to be found in the kitchen, filling her head with visions of the promised land that would be theirs once the Nazis were in power. Hedwig proved to be a willing audience, to Freya's relief, as it meant Grube was paying less attention to her. Ernst was jubilant too. Why, hadn't Herr Hitler worked as a house painter himself before the war? He was a man of the people.

Meanwhile, brown-shirted stormtroopers and the fearsome SS paramilitaries roamed the streets, terrorising Jews, Communists and anyone else who displeased them merely by existing. There were running gun battles throughout the country on a scale that had never been seen before. In the middle of July, a gang of Nazis under police escort marched into a Communist area of Hamburg and opened fire; nineteen people were killed and over 300 injured. As the election neared, an Urgent Call for Unity was published in a national newspaper. Signed by over thirty scientists, authors and artists, it appealed to the Communist and Socialist parties to join forces and keep the Nazis out of government. Posters with the same message appeared throughout Berlin, jostling for space on the crowded hoardings.

'Ha!' crowed Herr Grube at breakfast one morning. 'See how worried those fools are? They know their days are numbered.'

And Freya was worried, too. She woke each morning to a sense of dread that the door to a brighter future, so tantalisingly within reach, was about to be slammed in her face. She felt the loss of her mother more acutely than ever, isolated as she was in an apartment full of Nazi sympathisers, and longed to talk things over with Leon – the Leon of before. He felt like a stranger to her now, the memory of their last, awkward encounter seared into her memory. Yet she couldn't bear to think they would lose touch for ever; she had to believe that someday she would find him again.

In Leon and Ingrid's absence, she confided in Wolfgang Berger. He'd become a friend by now, and she was as likely to talk to him about politics as writing.

'Do you think Hitler will actually gain power?' she asked.

Berger sighed. 'He might, but who knows whether he can keep it. Once people see his true agenda, they'll vote against him.'

'And what is that agenda, beyond persecuting Jews and Communists?'

'Another war, I believe,' Berger replied, his face grave. 'That's the point of all this marching, of the uniforms and brainwashing at youth camps. He's training young men to fight, and young women to bear children who will grow up to serve the Reich. I'm glad not to be teaching anymore. Today's students have been indoctrinated with Nazi propaganda at school and their minds are closed. There are professors they won't engage with and books they won't open because they don't want to be challenged.' He shook his head. 'Just when they should be reading anything and everything, and deciding for themselves what to think!'

'Can't people see how dangerous Hitler is?' Freya exclaimed. 'There must be something we can do to stop him!'

The walls were closing in around her and she alternated between anger and despair. When election day came around at last, one sunny Sunday at the end of July, she got up early to walk to the polling station alone. She'd only recently turned twenty so this was the first election in which she'd been able to vote, and she didn't want the gloating company of Herr Grube and her father and brother to spoil such a momentous occasion. She'd always been so proud of her country, not for its military might but for producing such giants as Beethoven, Wagner, Albert Einstein, Berthold Brecht and Thomas Mann. Her beloved Berlin had seemed the most exciting city of all, despite the wretched poverty and unemployment, because of the hotchpotch of people who lived there – making music, art, poetry, literature, films, inspiring architecture and so much more. Only recently, she had gone with Wolfgang, Maus and Elke to see *The Blue Light*, an extraordinary film starring Leni Riefenstahl as Junta, a girl who lived half-wild in the mountains. Fräulein Riefenstahl had directed the film as well as starring in it, using innovative camera techniques that left the audience breathless.

'You see? Women can do anything,' Maus had said afterwards, squeezing Freya's arm. 'We just need the chance.'

And Freya had a glimpse of the life she might lead, were she free to follow her dreams.

Election day itself passed peacefully, despite dire predictions of violence, with Berliners patiently queueing in long lines outside the polling places. After she'd cast her vote – for the Social Democrats, who seemed the least bad option – Freya found a quiet corner of the Tiergarten park to lie on the grass and doze in the sun for a while. On the way home, she passed a café where on past weekends, Leon would often meet Otto and other friends, but there was no sign of him. She spent the afternoon writing, locked away in her room, before leaving to join Elke and Maus at Haus Vaterland: a huge pleasure palace on the south side of Potsdamer Platz.

'One last hurrah before the curtain falls,' Maus had said, and suddenly all Freya wanted was to lose herself in the crowd, to drink and dance without having to think what the next day might bring. She wanted to grab life with both hands and wring it dry while she still had the chance. Darkness was falling as she approached Haus Vaterland, the lights on its vast dome winking at her in sequence as though they were moving. Thousands of people could be swallowed up in the restaurants, bars and dance halls on each of those six floors, so Maus had given her strict instructions as to exactly where in the Wild West saloon she and Elke were to be found. They were more than just friends, Freya had discovered, and lived together in a small apartment above a bookshop in the Jewish area of the city. Rupert, an inveterate gossip, had told her that Maus had once been in love with Violet but her feelings weren't reciprocated. It was all deliciously complicated and interesting.

Once inside Haus Vaterland, she ran up the spectacular staircases, one after another, until she reached the fourth floor and pushed open the swing doors to the American bar, where a Negro band played jazz and the bartenders wore cowboy hats. Maus had suggested the venue. They could have been drinking wine under grapevines in the Rhine

Terrace, where thunder growled and lightning flashed in a pretend storm every hour, but Maus declared she was sick of Europe and preferred the New World to the Old. She and Elke were sitting at a table beside a large fake cactus, bourbon glasses in hand. Maus wore a long gown in gold lamé and Elke crêpe-de-chine trousers and a velvet smoking jacket with nothing underneath, her hair tumbling in waves down her back.

'Freya! At last,' Maus shouted above the screeching music. 'We thought you might have stood us up.'

Like the rest of Wolfgang's friends, she and Elke seemed to have adopted Freya as their mascot. They regularly included her in their outings, asked her opinion about their work, their lives and their problems, and listened to what she had to say – even Gunther, who was terrifyingly well-informed about everything, and sophisticated Rupert, who introduced her to Virginia Woolf and Lytton Strachey, and quizzed her about Heinrich Heine.

'Why wouldn't we love you?' Maus told her once. 'You're young and sweet, and you think we're all marvellous. It's a winning combination.'

Yet sometimes Freya felt a hundred years old; tonight, especially. She slid on to the banquette and took a gulp of the whisky that Elke had pushed across the table, feeling its warmth spread through her veins. She was wearing Franz Schwartz's opera cloak, which he'd once let her borrow and luckily forgotten about, over an ivory silk nightdress of her mother's that she'd turned into a backless evening gown. What would Ingrid say if she could see her now? Freya lit a cigarette, tossed back her hair and glanced away from her reflection in one of the many mirrors dotted around the room.

'Done the deed?' Elke asked, squeezing her shoulder.

Freya nodded. 'For all the difference it'll make.' Elke was a Communist, despite her gentle demeanour, and Maus was Jewish, so there was no need to ask where their allegiance lay.

'And that's enough politics for now,' Maus said. 'Tomorrow will come soon enough.'

Besides, they couldn't hear themselves think. Freya sat back, surrendering to the jaunty music as she watched couples gyrating on the crowded dance floor: kicking out their feet, slapping their hips and throwing up their arms in versions of the Charleston and the Black Bottom – dances that had long since gone out of fashion but which seemed strangely appropriate now. If she narrowed her eyes, they looked like mechanical toys in the harsh light, their faces contorted in gaiety and their limbs jerking as though exorcising some inner demon. Maus caught Freya's eye and smiled, shaking her head, but when the next number began, she and Elke got up to take their turn on the floor.

Freya ordered another round of drinks and threw hers back in double time, relaxing in a haze of alcohol. The band had taken a break and only a single saxophonist stood under the spotlight, playing such a haunting melody that tears came to Freya's eyes as she watched Elke glide across the room with Maus in her arms. Her new friends had become inexpressibly dear. What lay in store for them all? But now a young man in a dazzling white shirt was approaching the table with his hand outstretched, asking her to dance. She pulled herself together and let him lead her into the throng, laying her cheek against his crisp cotton chest and closing her eyes so she could pretend he was Leon.

The night passed in a blur. At some stage Rupert joined

them, and then Gunther and Wolfgang. Freya could only remember isolated scenes, frozen in time: Rupert sending the cork of a champagne bottle ricocheting off a chandelier, Maus standing on the table to strike a pose like a shimmering column of gold, Wolfgang watching them all before turning to tell her solemnly, 'We are dancing on the edge of a volcano,' and then sliding to the ground.

He was right. Freya's hangover the next day was made worse by hearing on the wireless that the Nazis had won 230 seats – not sufficient to give them an overall majority, but enough to make them the largest party in the Reichstag.

Life went on, as it must. A few weeks later, Maus's photographic exhibition opened in a small gallery near her apartment: fleeting glimpses of everyday life, captured for posterity. A toothless old woman danced in a courtyard before a wind-up gramophone, hat on the ground for spare change; children fished for coins through the grate of a drain; teenage girls lounged among the chimneys in a roof garden, listening to the radio; a *hausfrau* with her hands in the sink and her eyes closed to feel the sun on her face; a horse-drawn cart delivering milk laboured up a cobbled street. There were several solarised portraits, too, and three superimposed images of a nude Elke forming one stunning picture: the centrepiece of the exhibition.

Freya had worked with Maus to suggest titles and a brief narrative for many of the pictures: a line or two evoking emotion or locating a setting, sometimes using the subject's own words if those were especially resonant. She was touched by Maus's trust in her, loved the collaborative process and felt proud of having played a small part in the display. Seeing her text in print on the wall was a wonderful thrill.

'You see? Freya was the perfect girl for the job,' Rupert told Maus. 'She has a feel for the domestic.'

The usual friends had turned up at the opening to toast Maus's success and then carry on the party back at her and Elke's apartment. They put on a brave front, but an undercurrent of melancholy ran beneath the celebration.

Wolfgang grew more sombre with every drink. 'How long before the brownshirts smash your windows and close you down?' he asked. 'We should run a sweepstake. I say a fortnight.'

'Don't be so pessimistic,' Gunther said. 'Hitler's not running the show yet.'

Maus reached for Elke's hand, the smile dropping from her face. 'Wolfi's right,' she said. 'Elke and I are thinking of moving to Paris. It's all right for you, Gunther. You're blond and blue-eyed and you have a girlfriend. Everyone knows how much Hitler hates queers.'

'No!' Freya burst out, unable to restrain herself. 'You can't go! Not when we've only just met.'

Elke smiled. 'Come with us. Why not? You can make costumes for the Folies Bergère.'

'The most wonderful city in the world, ruined by those louts,' Rupert said bitterly. 'I shan't go back to dreary old England; it would be the death of me. Maybe I'll try America next. Or Morocco? Tangier has a certain appeal.'

Freya wondered briefly whether Violet would leave too. What if Leon went with her? He wouldn't consider it, though, not with his mother alone in Berlin and his studies to finish. And she couldn't abandon her country either.

'There have to be people to stay and speak up for what's right,' she said. 'We can't let the Nazis drive everyone out.'

'That's the spirit,' Wolfgang declared, draining his glass. 'We must stand together and resist!'

'Good luck with that,' Gunther said. 'Half the country's mad for Hitler – they're not going to pay any attention to a few intellectuals worried about their artistic freedom.'

Wolfgang sprang to his feet. 'Then we have to make them listen! This isn't just a question of censorship, though that's bad enough. The man is evil. Have you read *Mein Kampf*? He wants to crush anyone who doesn't share his warped views. God knows what will happen if he gets a chance to put those ideas into practice.'

'Oh, don't be so dramatic,' Gunther replied, crossing his legs on the coffee table. 'Von Schleicher and the old elite might allow him the illusion of power but they'll be holding his puppet strings, you can be sure of that. Once he's helped them get rid of the Communists, they'll soon boot him out. Trust me, I know how these things work.'

'No, you don't!' Wolfgang's eyes were blazing. 'You shan't have the last word on everything. This is different. Hitler's . . . well, he's a . . . a maniac.'

But it was too late in the evening and he'd drunk too much to articulate more clearly than that; he slumped back in the chair, glowering.

To fill the awkward silence, Freya asked Gunther, 'Have you heard Herr Hitler's going to inspect the new Nazi members of the Reichstag tomorrow? There's to be a gathering of the party faithful at the Kaiserhof. Goebbels is going to be there too.'

The Kaiserhof was a smart hotel in the government district, opposite the Reich Chancellery, where Hitler stayed on his infrequent visits to Berlin. It was said that he took a corner suite with windows looking directly into the Chancellor's office: the very place he wanted to be.

'How did you find that out?' Maus asked. 'Are you on the guest list?'

Freya laughed. 'Our lodger, Herr Grube, told me. He's going along to pay homage. Apparently anyone can turn up – I was thinking of attending myself. Might be my only chance to see Hitler in the flesh.'

Elke shuddered. 'Who'd want to?'

It was a legitimate question. Yet Freya was curious: she wanted to watch Adolf Hitler in action, see his spell working on those around her and find out whether she was susceptible.

Wolfgang roused himself. 'I'll come with you. Let's see the whites of the devil's eyes.'

'I'd heard something to that effect,' Gunther said. 'I'll be there. But don't tell anyone else – we don't want this turning into a free-for-all.'

Luckily, there could be no question of Walther Grube taking Freya to the Kaiserhof, as he was attending a meeting near the hotel immediately beforehand. She told him she would be there, though, hoping to catch a glimpse of Herr Hitler.

'I'm glad to hear it,' he said with evident surprise. 'And does this mean you'll be supporting the party, Fräulein?'

'Who knows?' she replied, to keep him guessing. Gunther had asked her to pass on any useful pieces of information Grube might let slip and while she couldn't bring herself to be friendly to the man, she was less actively hostile. Herr Grube didn't affect her so much now that she had a circle of friends and a life outside work and home.

'We never see you,' Otto was prone to grumble. 'God

knows what you're up to. Playing fast and loose around town, no doubt.'

Yet he was out more often in the evening himself, courting the daughter of a builder working on the Horseshoe Estate. Liesl was the opposite of Freya in every respect: long blonde hair in braids, demure floral dresses – apart from the blue skirt, white blouse and heavy walking shoes of the Nazi League of German Girls that she wore as she set off to attend summer camp. She was eighteen and about to graduate from secretarial college. Hanging on his every word, Liesl's dreamy blue eyes focused on Otto's face as though she couldn't quite believe he was real. If he'd told her to lie down in the street in front of a tram, she would have obliged without question.

The famous housing estate was nearing completion; no doubt Otto had his eye on a choice apartment into which Liesl could be slotted, along with the mini Ottos and Liesls who would soon appear. Freya tried to get along with her brother for Ingrid's sake, but that was becoming increasingly difficult. She couldn't forget the expression on his face when he'd attacked Leon, and she hated the way he and Walther Grube held forth about the state of the country, shouting down any opposing view. Otto would have dismissed her friends as degenerates; he and Grube loved to make fun of 'warm brothers', or homosexuals, although Freya felt that Grube himself, like Rupert, admired the male body more than the female. She'd never been convinced by his supposed romantic interest in her, and had often caught him glancing lasciviously at Otto when he thought no one was watching.

Herr Grube certainly wouldn't have approved of Wolfgang's appearance that afternoon in the lobby of the Kaiserhof hotel. Unshaven, his eyes bloodshot and his hair unkempt, he'd thrown an unseasonally heavy coat over his clothes from the night before, which looked as though he'd slept in them. Freya was surprised he'd been allowed through the door.

'Are you feeling all right, Wolfi?' she asked cautiously. 'Maybe you should spruce yourself up in the men's room.'

'What?' He looked at her blearily. 'Oh yes, perhaps. Will you order me a brandy?'

Freya found an unobtrusive table for two beside a pillar in the grand, high-ceilinged room, ordered drinks from a waiter and looked around. Several Nazi officials in dark suits with swastika armbands sat drinking beer, and a group of foreign correspondents and photographers stood gossiping with each other, keeping an eye on the side doors for any glimpse of the Herr Hitler. She saw Gunther, who gave her a brief nod; he didn't like to mix business with pleasure. And there was Joseph Goebbels, immediately recognisable thanks to his cadaverous face and pronounced limp, entering the lobby with his statuesque wife. They struck up a conversation with a tall man in brown SA uniform, festooned with gold braid, insignia and medals, who'd been pacing around the room.

'Who's that talking to Goebbels?' Freya asked Wolfgang on his return.

'Count von Helldorff,' he replied briefly. 'Head of the Berlin stormtroopers. He was behind that trouble on Kurfürstendamm last year.'

So Violet had been right. Freya remembered the figure in the Jeep, screaming abuse as he was driven up and down the boulevard. She watched him now, so charming and urbane as he bent to catch some remark of Goebbels' which made him chuckle.

'Perhaps this wasn't such a good idea,' she said uneasily. 'Shall we go? Who knows when Hitler's going to turn up. He might not come at all.'

'You can leave but I'm staying,' Wolfgang replied. 'You're right: this might be our only chance to see the enemy up close.'

At least he looked more presentable now, but he was in a strange mood: distracted, jittery, tapping his fingers against his thigh as he stared about. Beads of sweat stood out on his forehead but he refused to take off the coat, merely mopping his brow occasionally. Time dragged by and the journalists gradually left in twos and threes, tired of waiting. Meanwhile, the lobby filled with Nazis and a few curious tourists. Walther Grube appeared in a group of identical crop-headed young men, casting disdainful glances at the hoi polloi around them.

Freya shrank behind the pillar so she wouldn't have to acknowledge Grube and he wouldn't see she was with Wolfgang, peeking out a few minutes later to witness several extraordinary things happen in quick succession. Firstly, the last couple in the world she expected to see walked into the Kaiserhof. The woman wore a halter-neck gown in green silk that showed off her beautiful back to its best advantage; the man was less remarkable, short and dark, also in evening dress. The crowd parted to let them pass and Freya watched, hardly believing her eyes, as Maxim Fischer walked up to the Goebbels, greeted them and introduced Violet. He kissed Frau Goebbels' hand and engaged her in conversation while Herr Goebbels talked to Violet, drawing her a little way apart; he was a notorious womaniser, despite his club foot and short stature. Violet listened with her head on one side and a radiant smile on her face.

Shocked, Freya nudged Wolfgang. 'Have you seen who's over there?' Violet should have been on stage at the Zaubergarten, rather than cosying up to Hitler's propaganda chief. What on earth was she up to?

Wolfgang didn't reply, because now the side doors were opening and a flood of senior Nazis poured into the room, their uniforms decorated with gold braid and colourful insignia. They strutted about like peacocks, ridiculous (to Freya's eyes) in their widely cut brown jodhpurs, before lining up in ranks. Black-uniformed members of the dreaded SS, Hitler's bodyguards, surveyed the action from the side of the room. Freya lost sight of Violet and was relieved she and Wolfgang were also hidden by the throng. And then, as a murmur of anticipation spread through the lobby, suddenly their leader was walking among them. She craned forward to catch a brief glimpse of that sallow, belligerent face with its toothbrush moustache, so familiar from posters and the portrait that dominated their living room at home. A forest of arms flew up and cries of *'Heil!'* filled the air.

Freya couldn't bring herself to do the same, and was relieved no one seemed to be looking at her. She turned to speak to Wolfgang, but the words died on her lips when she saw him. His hand was raised, though not in salute. He was holding a pistol, which he managed to cock with shaking fingers and aim at Adolf Hitler.

# Chapter Fifteen

*Berlin, August 1932*

Freya acted on instinct. She stepped forward without thinking, standing directly in front of Wolfgang to block his view and, just as importantly, hide the pistol in his hand. Miraculously, all eyes were on Hitler and nobody seemed to have noticed the strange man in the heavy coat with his arm extended, like so many others. She and Wolfgang locked eyes, his already defeated, before he lowered the gun. Trying to assassinate the leader of the Nazi party, in a room packed with SS guards! It was suicide. Besides, there was only the slimmest of chances he'd have found his mark. Hitler was in the middle of a crowd and Wolfi was even more drunk than usual; he'd have ended up killing innocent bystanders – even if they were Nazis – before being shot himself. And she would almost certainly have been killed along with him.

All these thoughts must have raced unconsciously through her head, together with the overriding conviction that taking any human life, even Hitler's, was wrong. Years later, though, when she was leading another life altogether, she would look back on that day and wonder whether Wolfgang had had the right idea all along. If by some miraculous chance his plan had succeeded, the world would have been spared unimaginable horror. At the time, all she could think about was getting him away from the Kaiserhof alive and unseen. She shielded him with her body until he'd replaced the pistol in his coat pocket and steered him through the hotel lobby and out of the double doors with her head down, avoiding anyone's gaze. He stumbled beside her in an apparent daze, unresisting.

When they were outside in the fresh air and a safe distance away, she took him by the shoulders. 'What were you thinking? Promise me you'll never try anything like that again.'

Wolfgang put his hand in his pocket and she flinched, but all he drew out was a handkerchief to mop his forehead. His face had a yellowish tinge. 'You were right. We have to do something.'

'But not that,' she said. 'Not murder.'

He shrugged, pulling away from her and weaving across the square. A squad of Hitler Youth came marching towards him, singing as they went, but he didn't alter his course to avoid them. Freya watched, her heart in her mouth, but the boys merely parted and flowed around him without breaking their stride or missing a note. It appeared that Wolfgang wasn't worth the trouble of beating up – this brilliant, damaged man who'd taught her to believe in herself. He seemed set on course to self-destruct and she couldn't bear it.

She also feared for Leon, certain he would have had no idea what Violet was up to. Instead of going home, she took a tram to the Schöneberg district and walked to the parade of shops with the blue door at the corner. She didn't know whether he lived there now or only used the place occasionally, but she couldn't think where else to try. There was no reply when she knocked on the door and the building was shrouded in darkness. She leaned against the wall, trying to remember the Kohls' home address. They lived in a second-floor apartment not far from the technical university, to the west of Tiergarten; she knew the name of the street but couldn't recall the number of the building. A sense of urgency sent her hurrying back to the tram stop, though she hadn't eaten since breakfast and her stomach was growling.

An hour later, she had rung at least five doorbells in Gutenberg Strasse without success before the last person she'd disturbed happened to know Frau Kohl and directed her to the right apartment, a little further down the street. Unexpectedly, Leon himself came down to the main door of the building to let her in.

'Hello, stranger! Come in,' he said, standing back to let her pass although obviously surprised to see her. The last time they'd spoken to each other was the disastrous outing to Lake Wannsee, almost a year ago.

'Thank you.' Yet now Freya's courage was failing her; she had no idea how he'd react to what she was about to say. Rather than have him throw her out of the apartment, she decided to broach the subject down in the courtyard.

'I'm sorry to call round out of the blue,' she began, 'but I need to tell you what's just happened.'

He paused under the archway. 'That sounds serious.'

'It concerns Fräulein Violet,' she said, her hands clenched by her sides, prickling with sweat.

'Is she in trouble?' he asked quickly. 'Has she sent you here?'

Freya shook her head. 'Nothing like that. She's fine, as far as I'm aware. But there's something about her you should know.'

Leon frowned. 'Very mysterious. Well, we can't talk here. Let's go upstairs.'

They climbed two flights without speaking, Freya's heart pounding in her chest and her nerves increasing.

'My mother's working late,' Leon said, opening the apartment door. 'I'm cooking supper – you'll have to excuse the mess.'

The kitchen was hot and steamy, the sink piled high with pans. He pulled out a chair for her at the table and sat opposite, his eyes wary. Without mentioning the part Wolfgang had played, she explained briefly what she'd witnessed at the hotel that evening.

'I don't believe you,' Leon said when she'd finished. 'Violet? With Joseph Goebbels at the Kaiserhof? It must have been someone who looked like her.'

'Nobody looks like Violet,' Freya replied. 'I saw her clearly – and her . . . agent, Herr Fischer.' A shadow crossed Leon's face but she ploughed on. 'He introduced her to Goebbels and they talked together until Hitler appeared. I lost sight of them after that. Maybe she spoke to him, too.'

A saucepan bubbled over on the stove and Leon got up to turn off the gas ring. 'Why are you telling me this?' he asked. 'What has Fräulein Violet got to do with me?'

'Leon, I know you're having an . . .' She hesitated, before continuing. 'I know you're more than friends. I saw you together once.'

He flushed and looked away.

'You don't have to pretend,' she went on. 'Of course I've kept your secret, and I always will, but I wanted to warn you. You can't trust Violet, Leon; an English friend told me her family are well-known Fascists. Don't share anything with her that could land you in trouble. Any mention of your Jewish grandfather, for example.'

Leon frowned, folding his arms. 'That's enough, Freya. I don't doubt you have the best motives and I thank you for your concern, but you have no need to involve yourself in my affairs. You don't really know Violet, do you?'

'Maybe not,' Freya replied. 'And maybe you don't, either.' An awkward silence descended, so after a moment she got to her feet. 'Well, I've said my piece. Goodbye, Leon. Take care of yourself.'

The smell of cooking meat was making her mouth water, and she was half-hoping he'd press her to stay for supper with his mother, who had been Ingrid Amsel's closest friend and whom Freya loved too. Instead, he said, 'Look after yourself, too, *kleine* Freya. These are dangerous times and we must each navigate them as best we may. Can you see yourself out?'

And now, too late, she bitterly regretted having come. She had damaged her relationship with Leon, probably permanently, to no great effect, and this glimpse of cosy domesticity in the Kohls' apartment had left her feeling more alone than ever. She leaned against the wall in the stairwell for a moment, imagining her mother's comforting arms around her and her voice whispering, 'Don't despair, little one. This too shall pass.'

Ingrid had known how Freya felt about Leon: she had once caught her daughter gazing after him as he and Otto left the apartment and cupped Freya's cheek for a moment, murmuring, 'There will be other boys, you know.'

How angrily Freya had batted her mother's hand away,

convinced she didn't understand, and what wouldn't she give for Ingrid's loving touch now!

Freya managed to avoid Violet at the Zaubergarten until Friday evening, when she was supervising costume changes in Frau Brodsky's absence. They were surrounded by the other girls so there was no chance to talk privately, but she was aware of Violet's hostile stare. When the performance was over, Violet drew her into the workroom and closed the door.

'So, I gather we have a spy in the ranks,' she said. 'And what were you doing at the Kaiserhof, Fräulein Amsel?'

'I was curious,' Freya replied, matching Violet's cool tone. 'I went there with Wolfgang. We simply wanted to see what Hitler was like – we weren't hoping for a private audience.'

'And you think I was?' Violet asked.

'Who knows?' Freya said. 'I can't imagine why else you'd be sucking up to Goebbels.'

Violet snorted. 'And who else have you gone running to with your scoop of the century?'

'No one. Wolfgang didn't see you and I let Frau Brodsky carry on thinking you had a migraine that evening.'

'And why should I believe that?'

'I don't care whether you believe it or not,' Freya retorted, her anger growing. Why was she the one to be questioned? 'I've kept your dirty little secrets long enough. Leon deserved to know the truth. I feel responsible: you only met him because of me.'

'And I bet you wish you'd never introduced us,' Violet said. 'But Leon's a grown man with a mind of his own – you can't keep him all to yourself for ever.'

'He's my friend and nothing more,' Freya said, her cheeks hot.

'You'd like there to be, though,' Violet said with a smile. 'Forget about him, Freya. Find someone who'll love you and be happy.'

'Shut up!' Freya cried, beside herself. 'Do you think I need advice from a, a . . .' She paused, not quite brave enough to continue.

'A what?' Violet asked icily.

'An Englishwoman,' Freya said at last, and Violet laughed.

Now they were truly enemies.

The weeks rolled by and summer turned to autumn. Adolf Hitler still hadn't been appointed Chancellor, despite leading the largest party in the Reichstag, but surely it was only a matter of time. Gunther reported that President Hindenburg had started negotiations with Herr Hitler. And Wolfgang was proven right: the windows of the art gallery housing Maus's exhibition were smashed and anti-Jewish slogans daubed over the photographs inside. Rumours spread around the Zaubergarten that the place could only stay open because Herr Goldstein was paying the Nazis protection money.

Life at the club became increasingly precarious: there seemed to be more Nazis in the audience every evening, identifiable by their swastika armbands and swagger, while the regular clientele were choosing to drink elsewhere. Willi, the emcee, was beaten up so badly after one too many jokes about Goebbels that he'd spent a fortnight in hospital and gone back to working in the Adlon hotel when he was discharged. Herr Schwartz took over the role but was too nervous and depressed to perform with any flair. The two men who sang satirical songs at the piano now made them so obscure no one could understand the joke, while the red-headed violinist had acquired a stormtrooper lover who didn't like her appearing on stage and so left the company. The Zaubergarten girls were down to four: Angelika's father had died, leaving her enough money to live on, and Sophie with the beautiful voice had found a job entertaining passengers on a liner sailing to America, and was hoping to stay there.

Frau Brodsky arrived for work later each day, the routes she took to avoid stormtroopers marching down the street becoming ever more circuitous. By now, she and Freya had developed a comfortable working relationship that suited them both. They talked about costumes, the club and the girls but left politics alone and kept their home lives private. Freya often thought how horrified Rosa Brodsky would be if she could see the picture of Herr Hitler in their living room, a copy of *The Attack* on the coffee table and a swastika flag hanging from the balcony.

Yet as they were stitching companionably together in the workroom one afternoon, Frau Brodsky stuck her needle in a pincushion, took off her spectacles and smoothed her face with both hands.

'You know, this month I will have lived in Berlin for forty-five years,' she said. 'Not all my life, but almost.'

Freya was taken aback by this confidence. 'Where were you before?' she ventured.

'I came here from Russia with my parents when I was a little girl,' Frau Brodsky replied. 'In Russia we lived in a place called the Settlement of Pale. Have you heard of it?'

Freya shook her head.

'There's no reason why you would,' Frau Brodsky went on. 'It was an area specifically for Jews. Anyone who wanted to travel elsewhere had to get permission and that was expensive. I was an only child but part of a big family, with many uncles, aunts and cousins who lived nearby. Times were hard but we were happy. At some point I must have realised the rest of Russia hated all of us in the Settlement, though I can't remember when, or how. The Czar had been assassinated and people naturally blamed the Jews, although we'd had nothing to do with it. Anyway, then the Czar's son had become Emperor Alexander III, and we were forced to put up his portrait in our houses and fly the Russian flag – the police would tear up your sheets to use if you couldn't afford one – even though life was worse under this Alexander than his father.' She shook her head, clicking her tongue.

'And that's why you came to Germany?' Freya asked.

'We were heading for America, but by the time we arrived in this country, we'd had to pay so many bribes along the way that there was no money left. So here we stayed.' Frau Brodsky gave Freya a weary smile. 'And now we have to worship at the shrine of Adolf Hitler, and hang a swastika banner from our windows. Man plans and God laughs, as they say.'

Freya hesitated, anxious not to cause offence. 'Do you think it might be time to think about making for America again?'

Frau Brodsky gazed into the distance. 'I can't leave. My husband is elderly and in poor health – he'd never last the journey. My son and his family have talked about trying to go, though. There's no future for my granddaughters here.' She shrugged. 'Yet who knows whether they'll be safe even there?'

Freya picked up her work with a heavy heart, wondering why some people's lives had to be so hard. To relieve her feelings, she bought a leather-bound notebook that fastened with a brass clasp and started writing in earnest. She wrote about the tramp of Nazi jackboots in the night, about a young man lying in hospital with a broken jaw, about the savage thrill of violence and destruction, about a love affair between a stormtrooper and a musician, about a young girl arriving in a strange country with a dream of safety. She even put herself in Walther Grube's shoes and wrote about a fanatic's love for Adolf Hitler, and imagined Liesl preparing to become a dutiful wife and mother in her camp for Nazi maidens. Writing became her way of making sense of an increasingly nonsensical world, a record of the extraordinary things that were happening around her so that one day she could look back and think, yes, that's exactly how it was. If something particularly noteworthy happened in real life, she would write a diary entry, too.

Several of the pieces developed into longer stories, which she typed and put into a yellow folder in the top drawer of her chest, hidden beneath underwear. One in particular had promise, she felt: the imaginary account of Gerda, a cabaret dancer trapped in an affair with a wealthy man who turns out to be a Fascist. He introduces her to high society, taking her to receptions and dinner parties where she meets important Nazis, whom she soon comes to loathe. Gerda is red-haired and blue-eyed, and no one realises she's Jewish. Rather than ending her relationship with this man, she decides to take advantage of the inside knowledge he allows her by devising a plan to assassinate the most important Nazi of all, Adolf Hitler, when he visits a prestigious hotel in Berlin. This story soon took fire and was a joy to write. Freya made Gerda an amalgam of Violet, both Sophies and Perle, with a touch of herself thrown in for good measure, and added background details from her other tales. She would ask Wolfgang to read it when it was finished – although it was considerably longer than anything she'd written before – and hoped he wouldn't be offended.

Then as she was getting dressed one morning, Freya opened her drawer and realised immediately that the folder was missing. Frantically, she rifled through all her underclothes and then the contents of the entire chest. Her notebook, thank God, was still between her mattress and the bed frame; some instinct had told her to keep this precious record separately and hide it even more securely. Now she remembered her underwear drawer had been slightly ajar the night before, though she'd thought nothing of it at the time. Yet who would want to steal a folder of stories? A terrible thought occurring to her, she pulled on a dressing gown, ran into the kitchen and pulled out the ash tray of the ancient stove. It was full to the brim. And when she unhooked the lid of the fuel compartment with clumsy, panicky fingers and peered inside, she saw a tiny scrap of yellow card at the edge of the smouldering coals.

Slowly, she replaced the lid and turned around. Otto was leaning against the door frame, watching her.

'You,' she said, too shocked to feel angry. 'But why?'

'Why do you think?' he retorted. 'To keep you safe – and the rest of us. Imagine if Walther had found those pages. An assassination attempt on Herr Hitler! How could you even imagine such a thing? Not to mention what you wrote about Walther himself. So disrespectful! He'd have reported you, for sure.'

'Walther would have had no business searching through my private things,' Freya said, 'and neither have you. I wasn't making fun of him; I wanted to understand how he felt.'

'You could never understand,' Otto said loftily, 'because your mind is focused on the gutter and the pathetic creatures who scrabble for a living there. If you must waste your time writing, focus on the strong, pure Germany that will come back again once Adolf Hitler's in charge.'

'You mean the strong, pure Germany whose people aren't free to say what they think?' Freya replied. 'Where ideas and words on a page are so dangerous they must be burned? Tell me exactly what it is about my work that threatens you.'

'Your work,' Otto scoffed. 'The ramblings of a depraved mind, more like. Father's always been too soft on you and this is the result. As long as you live under this roof, you'll conduct yourself decently.'

There was no point trying to reason with him. Without another word, Freya pushed past, went to her bedroom and packed a suitcase. She wrote a note for her father, propped it on the mantelpiece and left the apartment, suitcase in one hand and typewriter in the other.

# Chapter Sixteen

*Los Angeles, April 2024*

Maddie didn't like sharing her phone number, especially not these days, but Gramps had set up a WhatsApp group with the title 'German Journal' for the four of them (himself, Maddie, Daniel and Eva) and there it was. She sent Eva a message of thanks for the wonderful tea and Daniel waved hello. A few days later, she received a text from him, saying he'd copied the manuscript and would like to give her back the original; could they meet for coffee at the weekend, as there was something he wanted to talk to her about. She waited a couple of hours before replying, trying to understand how she felt about the invitation. He'd annoyed her at the Death Café and she didn't like the way he'd looked her up online, but, to be fair, wasn't that what everybody did? She'd checked him out, too, finding a paper he'd written about Nazi propaganda and the German film industry. It was pretty dry, though, and she'd fallen asleep after the first few pages. He must be clever to land a teaching job at USC, and he'd been great with Ben; perhaps she should give him the benefit of the doubt. And come on, it was only a coffee, and she had nothing else planned. She replied, saying she was busy all Saturday (a big fat lie) but Sunday morning would be great.

As soon as she saw Daniel, she would know what she thought about him, Maddie told herself, but that theory turned out not to be true. There was a flutter in her stomach when he stood to greet her in the coffee shop, but a corresponding flicker of irritation at the way he seemed so pleased – or rather, maybe so at ease – with himself, taking time to unfold his long limbs. She had to force a smile in return, already calculating how quickly she could make her escape.

'So here's your journal back,' he said, handing over the envelope once she'd ordered her coffee. 'Eva's working on a copy and I've had a quick flick through, though my German isn't as good as hers.'

'Better than mine, which is non-existent,' Maddie replied.

'There are diary entries but also what seem to be short stories. And several references to a cabaret club called the Magic Garden, *der Zaubergarten*.'

'*Der Zaubergarten?*' Maddie repeated. 'I found a photograph of my great-grandmother and her friend with that name written on the back.'

'I thought the name sounded familiar so I did some research,' Daniel said. 'Turns out I *had* heard it before: a movie called *The Magic Garden* was released in 1942, set in Germany but filmed in Hollywood. It was based on a novel of the same name, published a few years before. It's about a cabaret dancer who has an affair with a high-ranking Nazi and tries to assassinate Hitler at some luxury hotel in 1933, just after he was made Chancellor. It's great – brilliant dialogue, and the dancing and costumes are amazing.'

'You've seen it?' Maddie asked.

'Yeah, I found a copy in the UCLA film archive. I could arrange for you to watch it too.'

'I guess my great-grandma made the costumes,' Maddie said. 'Maybe she was writing production notes in her journal?'

Daniel pulled a doubtful face. 'But she was writing these entries in the 1930s, we can tell that from the dates. And some of the things she describes seem spookily similar to scenes from the film, though I'll have to wait for the translation to be sure. What if your great-grandmother had a more significant role in the movie? Come on, you're a journalist. Don't you want to do some digging?'

'I'm not sure,' Maddie replied. 'Seems to me like you're putting two and two together and making five.'

Daniel took a sip of coffee, looking at her over the cup as he waited for her to elaborate. She took a deep breath. 'Look, I found some old letters that tell a different story about my great-grandmother. I can't go into detail because it's private, but let's just say I promised my mom that I'd leave the past alone.'

'Very intriguing,' Daniel said. 'I'm surprised, though. Imagine if Woodward and Bernstein had promised their mothers not to bother nice President Nixon.'

Maddie felt herself flush. 'That's not the same at all!'

Daniel smiled. 'I'm only teasing.'

'I know,' Maddie snapped, 'and it's really annoying.' She picked up the envelope. 'Thanks for the coffee, and for copying the journal. I have to go now.'

Daniel stood too, holding up his hands. 'I'm sorry, I'm sorry. I was just trying to lighten the mood, that's all. Stay for another coffee, or a slice of pie or something. Please, I feel terrible.'

He looked so genuinely upset that Maddie relented, already embarrassed and ashamed of her outburst. What kind of person was she turning into? Daniel had touched a nerve but that was no excuse for being so rude.

'I'm sorry, too,' she said, laying the folder back on the table and sitting down. 'I'm a little touchy these days.'

'Seems like I've been annoying you since we first met,' Daniel said. 'Can we try to start over? Or at least, maybe you could tell me where I'm going wrong.'

Maddie buried her head in her hands. 'You're fine. I'm not in a good place right now, but that's my problem.'

'Don't move a muscle,' Daniel said. 'This place has the most amazing fried chicken sandwiches. I'm going to order two and you're going to tell me everything.'

'I just don't understand how anyone could be so horrible about Ben,' Maddie finished, swallowing the last mouthful of her sandwich.

'Because they don't see him as a real person,' Daniel replied. 'That's the trouble with the internet: you can disappear into this sad little vortex of hatred and spill your poison without thinking of the consequences. The trolls wouldn't dream of saying those things to his face – or yours, either.'

'I know I shouldn't give them the time of day,' Maddie said, 'but it feels like I'm constantly under attack. As soon as I try to write anything, I imagine what the reaction's going to be and wonder if it's worth the effort. Of course, I block the haters and delete their messages, but they keep on coming.'

'You can't let them win, though,' he told her. 'I've read some of your articles and they're great. You write so fluently.'

'Thanks.' Maddie crumpled her napkin into a ball. 'I don't know why you're being nice to me when I'm such a misery.'

It was beginning to dawn on her that she might have got Daniel completely wrong. He was a good listener, letting her talk without jumping in too soon to offer his opinion. Why had she been so quick to judge him and find him wanting? Couldn't she entertain the possibility he was simply a nice guy? There were still a few of those left in the world, surely, and he just might be one of them.

He smiled. 'Somehow I like you, misery and all. And I really like your grandpa.'

'He's great, isn't he?' Maddie replied, smiling too. 'We're so lucky to have him. And your grandmother's pretty amazing too.' She hesitated. 'Look, I shouldn't ask this, but if there's any chance you can persuade her not to help Gramps look into his family history, I'd be so grateful.'

Daniel raised his eyebrows. 'And presumably you won't tell me why? Well, I can try, though I wouldn't hold out much hope. There's no stopping Eva once she sets her mind on something.'

'I can imagine.' Maddie sighed, reaching for the folder and her purse. 'This has been great, Daniel. Thanks for listening.'

'My pleasure,' he said. 'But I was going to add, there might be something you can do about all this hate on the internet. It might be possible to find out who the worst offenders are. They're probably just bots, anyway, not real people at all. You mentioned someone calling themselves Nightshade? If you look into their internet profile, you could get some clues about their identity, even trace the IP address. I have a techie friend who's an expert in that stuff.'

'And then what?' Maddie asked.

Daniel shrugged. 'That's up to you. Knowledge is power, though. And if Nightshade turns out to be a program, you might not take the abuse so personally.'

Maddie was about to reply when her phone rang. 'Hi, Mom,' she said. 'Just heading home.'

Sharon's voice was high-pitched and breathy. 'Ben's not with you, is he?'

'No. I haven't seen him since last night,' she said. 'What's wrong?'

'He's gone. Packed some clothes and art materials and left me a note. Can you come back straight away? I don't know what to do.'

Maddie hung up. 'Everything OK?' Daniel asked.

'Not really,' she said. 'I need to get home right now. You couldn't give me a lift, could you? I came here on the bus.'

'Sure,' Daniel said. 'I'm parked right outside.'

She explained what had happened on the short ride home – as far as she knew, which wasn't much – and they arrived to find Sharon pacing up and down in the kitchen, her face pale.

'I came back from yoga to find the house empty and this note on the table,' she said, holding it out.

*Gone away for a while,* the note read, in Ben's characteristic scrawl. *Don't worry! Love, Ben.*

'Do you think I should call the police?' her mom asked. 'What if he's gone to the train station, or even the airport?'

'I don't think that's very likely,' Maddie said. 'He hates flying, and where would he go by train? Let's try to find him first – I shouldn't think he's gone far. He's set off on outings before, remember.'

'Have you tried calling his friends to see if they've heard

from him?' Daniel asked. 'I could do that for you, to keep your phone free.'

'Mom, this is Daniel,' Maddie said hastily. 'Eva's grandson. You remember, Gramps' friend?'

'Oh, yes. Thank you, Daniel,' Sharon replied. 'That's kind of you. Give me your number and I'll text you some details.' Her hands were shaking as she scrolled through her contacts.

'Try not to panic, Mom,' Maddie said. 'Everyone knows Ben in the neighbourhood. People will look out for him.'

Sharon didn't reply. When Daniel had gone to another room with his phone and a few names to call, she told Maddie, 'This is my fault. You were right – I should have let him go before now.'

'Well, it's a hard call to make,' Maddie said.

Sharon frowned, knitting her fingers together. 'Perhaps I'm just frightened of being left on my own. Gramps is always busy these days and of course Ben wants a life of his own. How selfish can you get?'

Maddie put an arm around her shoulder. 'Not selfish at all. You might have forgotten how to carve out any time for yourself, though. You'll need some practice.'

'Let's get this drama over with first,' Sharon said, squeezing her hand. 'But thanks, honey. I'm glad you're here.'

None of Ben's friends had heard from him, so Daniel suggested they drive around to see if they could spot him. Maddie directed him to some of Ben's favourite places – the skate park, the mall, the ice-cream parlour – but there was no sign of him anywhere. Despite Maddie's optimism when talking to her mom, the prickle of anxiety in the pit of her stomach was growing stronger by the minute. Ben leaving a note made this more than a casual outing. Where could he have gone?

It was Daniel's turn to reassure her. 'We don't need to panic yet. Like you said, this is Ben's home turf and people will want to help him.'

'Do you think so?' Maddie asked. 'It's a tough old world out there.'

'Sure,' he replied. 'I still believe in the kindness of strangers. Don't you?'

'Maybe.' Maddie wondered for a second whether Ben was wearing the rainbow-coloured scarf. 'Anyway, you're not a stranger but you're certainly being kind. A quick coffee seems to be turning into a day trip.'

Daniel smiled. 'Don't worry, I have nothing else on today – my girlfriend's away at a bachelorette party. There seems to be one every weekend. Either that or a baby shower.'

Maddie felt the blood rush to her cheeks. She didn't know why she was blushing – she'd never thought of him in that way, had she? – but for some reason she was, and could only pray he hadn't noticed. 'Tell me about it,' she said. 'Feels like everyone's coupling up these days.'

'How about you?' he asked.

'Things haven't exactly worked out for me so far. Never say never, though. Wait a minute!' Her eye was caught by a figure walking past in a grey sweatshirt with a backpack, who turned out to be a girl when she looked back. 'No, that's not him.'

They were driving out to the reservoir. 'So, your grandpa and my grandma seem to be getting along pretty well,' Daniel said, parking the car. 'They might hook up together – we could end up as family.'

'Whoa, now you're really getting ahead of yourself,' Maddie said. 'Still, my mom would like to meet Eva; I think she wants to check her out. Do your parents live around here?'

Daniel shook his head. 'My dad's in New York and my mom passed away when I was little. Basically, Eva and my grandpa brought me up. I don't know where I'd be if not for them. That's why I can't stand all this death stuff – I'm not ready to do without her yet.'

'My feelings exactly about Gramps. Do you think we ever will be?'

'Probably not.' Daniel smiled, his eyes crinkling at the corners. He wasn't so irritating after all, and actually, maybe the fact he had a girlfriend would make things more relaxed between them. They could get to know each other without any pressure – as long as he was prepared to overlook the way she'd treated him at first. They got out of the car and walked towards the Meadows at the edge of the lake, scanning the families, groups of friends and couples dotted about the grass.

'This is hopeless,' Maddie said. 'He could be anywhere.' She couldn't bear to think of Ben alone with his backpack and a head full of dreams. What if they hadn't found him before night fell?

'You don't think he might have gone to Eva's house, do you?' Daniel asked suddenly. 'He was very interested in the room I had as a kid, and I told him my grandma sometimes had students staying in it now.'

'But she'd have let us know, wouldn't she?'

'I might call her,' Daniel said, taking out his phone. 'Just on the off chance.'

Eva's phone went to voicemail so they decided to swing

by her house, as that seemed as good a place as any to look. 'Then I'll head home,' Maddie said. 'Honestly, I've taken up enough of your time.'

Daniel's suggestion made sense but she didn't dare allow herself to hope. Yet as they pulled into Eva's driveway, there was Ben, sitting on the porch with his backpack beside him. Maddie flew out of the car as soon as it came to a halt and threw her arms around him.

'What are you doing?' he grumbled, fighting to get free. 'I can't breathe!'

'We've been so worried,' she exclaimed.

'Why?' he asked.

'Because we didn't know where you were.' Maddie paused, not wanting to overwhelm her brother when he would be feeling vulnerable.

'But we've found you now,' Daniel said reassuringly, 'so all's well that ends well.'

'Nobody's home,' Ben told them, blinking anxiously behind his glasses.

'That's OK,' Daniel said. 'I'll show you where Grandma hides her spare key.'

Ben picked up his backpack expectantly.

'Why have you brought that?' Maddie asked.

'Because I want to stay for a few days,' Ben replied. 'Eva said I could.'

Maddie sighed, shaking her head.

Daniel unlocked the front door and let them in. 'We can talk about that later, once she's back,' he said. 'Now who's for coffee? I think that's enough drama for one day.'

An hour later, everyone had assembled: Maddie, Daniel, Ben and Sharon – and Eva and Gramps, who'd been out to lunch together. They were a little surprised to find the whole crew sitting in Eva's kitchen, but happy to share the coffee Daniel had brewed.

'And it's a pleasure to meet you, Sharon,' Eva said.

'Likewise,' Sharon replied, looking as though she meant it. 'Thank you for giving Ben such a great time the other day. He wouldn't stop talking about your artwork, and I can see why.' She gave her son's hand a squeeze and his face lit up. 'He's already shown me around your incredible garden.'

Daniel had persuaded Sharon to stay for a coffee when she arrived to pick Ben up, and she, Ben and Maddie had had a heart-to-heart about the future as they wandered among the wild things: the kind of conversation that somehow flowed more easily on neutral territory. Sharon had gradually calmed down as she listened to Ben explain how happy he felt at Eva's house, and how careful he'd been on the journey over there.

'I'm going to call your support worker tomorrow,' Sharon had promised Ben. 'Nothing's going to happen straight away but at least we can start talking about the options.'

'You can trust me, Mom,' he'd said. 'I won't let you down.'

'And I'm sure you can stay with Eva for a couple of days, but you have to ask her first,' Maddie added. 'You can't just turn up on the doorstep.'

'All right,' Ben had replied. And the three of them had had a family hug, which left everyone a little teary.

'Eva's so talented,' Gramps said now. 'And what's more, she's also a brilliant sleuth. We've been looking into my father's military service and we've actually found out where he's buried in France. I'm wondering about taking a trip to Europe in the fall to go visit the cemetery. Want to be my chaperone, Madeleine?'

'Why not?' she said, trying to summon a smile but only managing to bare her teeth.

'It would be so moving,' Gramps said. 'Some tangible evidence that he existed, that he mattered, beyond a photograph.'

'Well, time for us to get going,' Sharon said briskly, standing up. 'Daniel, I can't thank you enough for all your help. And Eva, you must come for supper at my house soon. Dad, do you need a lift home?'

'No, I'm staying here for a while,' Gramps replied, looking at her curiously. 'Eva and I are having another session on the computer.'

He followed them out to the car, though, and when Eva and Daniel had waved goodbye and returned to the house, he said, 'So what's going on?'

'How do you mean?' Sharon asked, pausing with the car key in her hand.

'I saw that look between the two of you just now, when I mentioned my father's grave.' He folded his arms. 'Is there anything I should know?'

Maddie glanced at Sharon again, waiting for her response. 'I have no idea what you mean,' her mother said after a couple of seconds, unlocking the car so she didn't have to meet his gaze.

'Madeleine?' Gramps asked, fixing her with his steady, trusting eyes.

'Yes,' she said slowly, unable to lie to his face. 'Gramps, I think you need to come home with us. We have something to show you.'

# Chapter Seventeen

*Los Angeles, April 2024*

'Of course you were right to show me those letters,' Gramps said, passing Maddie a cup of tea. He'd been quiet on the ride back to his apartment, but not as upset as she'd feared. 'It doesn't change the way I feel about my mother,' he went on. 'She was the best mom I could have wished for. It wasn't easy for her, bringing up a kid on her own, but she never let me see how hard things were, never made me feel a burden. Ours was a happy home, full of love. And she adored my father – or at least, the man she called my father – I know she did. She was always talking about him, telling me stories about how kind he was and how talented, the funny things he used to do.'

He glanced at the photograph on the mantelpiece: a handsome man gazing straight at the camera with a serious expression, dark hair cut short under an army cap, high cheekbones and a full mouth. He could have been a movie star.

'Mom said we had the same eyes,' Gramps went on. 'And apparently he used to chew his food the exact same way I do. I guess she was just trying to make me feel some kind of connection with him. Goodness knows how she'd have explained me away when he came home at the end of the war, but that question never arose.'

'Do you want to try and find out who your real father is?' Maddie asked.

Gramps sighed. 'I can't see how that's possible. It's too late now; all my mother's generation has died.'

'You could always send off for a DNA test.'

'I'm not doing that,' Gramps replied bluntly. 'It would seem like I'm spying on Mom, judging her, and I feel bad enough about reading her diary. Say we come up with some random name, anyway: we're never going to know the whole story. She must have been lonely during the war, with my dad away.'

'Did she have any friends that you particularly remember?' Maddie asked.

Gramps blew out his cheeks. 'Well, there was a guy I used to call Uncle Frank who would come visit. He was a work friend, I think, and they were obviously close, but I never got the feeling they were romantically involved. This man didn't seem the marrying kind, if you catch my drift. Anyway, whoever my dad was, he never played a part in my life, for whatever reason: he only fathered me in the biological sense.'

'Sounds familiar,' Maddie said wryly.

'Sorry, dear.' Gramps patted her hand. 'Have you heard from yours recently?'

'Nope. Not that I care.'

Although sometimes, when she was feeling low or had had one glass of wine too many, Maddie was tempted to call her dad and ask him whether he ever thought about her and wondered how she was doing, whether he still remembered her birthday even though he no longer acknowledged it. She didn't know if the phone number she had for him was still current. How could you bring a child into the world and just forget they existed? If she didn't have Gramps and a couple of good male friends in her life, Maddie might have decided men were assholes.

'His loss,' Gramps said. 'And you have a good mother, like I did.'

'That's true.' All the same, Maddie was glad to be going back to Portland soon; three weeks with Sharon was quite enough.

'Tell you what is intriguing, though,' Gramps went on, swerving abruptly into another subject. 'That painting you found in Mom's case: I have the strangest feeling I know the house from somewhere. I even dreamed I was there the other night. How crazy is that? I've never been to England in my life.'

'Can I have another look?' Maddie asked, and Gramps fetched the picture from his bedroom. There it was: Beechwood Grange. She'd discovered the name of the family who lived there, although she couldn't remember it now. Something double-barrelled and classy.

'Well, I can do some digging for you online,' she said, but Gramps only laughed and told her not to bother.

'I've probably been watching too many period dramas on Masterpiece, and you need to get on with your own life. I gather Ben's coming to stay with you in Portland?'

Maddie nodded. 'Just for a few days, then Mom will drive up to bring him back via San Francisco. They're going on a road trip together.'

'That's a lovely idea,' Gramps said. 'It'll do her good to have some time by herself.'

And this was just the start. Ben's support worker, Lisa, had told them about an organisation that provided support for adults who had Down syndrome and wanted to live independently. Ben could rent a room in a shared house with staff who'd help with tasks like shopping, laundry and cooking, and sort out any problems along the way. When he came back from Portland, he was going to look around one of the properties to see what he thought about the idea.

'I won't know what to do with myself,' Sharon had said, biting her lip. Lisa had told her that if she had any time to spare, the Down Syndrome Society was always looking for volunteers. With a little training, perhaps she could talk to parents whose newborns had been diagnosed with the condition.

'Mom, you'd be brilliant at that,' Maddie had said. 'Think of all the experience you have to share!'

They all were moving forward. Gramps' apartment was positively spartan and he seemed to like it that way. 'At last I have room to breathe,' he said, gazing around the near-empty room. 'Everything's in order and I'm free to enjoy myself. Thanks for all your help, Madeleine – it's been lovely spending this time with you.'

'I've enjoyed it too,' Maddie replied. 'Despite the D word.'

'You have to admit, I'd never have met Eva if it wasn't for the Death Café,' Gramps said. 'And you wouldn't have met Daniel, either. We could have a double wedding.'

'Gramps, stop it!' Maddie protested, laughing. 'You know he has a girlfriend.'

'Eva has reservations about her,' he said. 'I think you'd suit him much better.'

'Well luckily it's not up to you.' Maddie wasn't blushing now. She really had come to think of Daniel as a friend even though every now and then a flicker of attraction passed between them like a tiny electric charge and she let herself imagine a different relationship. No, she'd blown her chances there. The fact he was happy to spend time with her had to be enough. They'd met in the past week for a drink, and watched *The Magic Garden* together on a computer in the Film Archive's study centre. She'd been transfixed by the contrast between the sensual, seductive world of the cabaret and the dead hand of the Nazi party, throttling joy and creative freedom. Marching feet and martial music stamped over the gaiety of a chorus line, drowned the languid notes of a singer in the spotlight. This had been Freya's world, as remote to Maddie as the moon. She'd sat for a moment in silence when the film had ended, unable to express her emotions.

'Powerful, isn't it?' Daniel had said. 'I'm going to try and see if I can locate an original script. It seems such a coincidence that your great-grandmother wrote those words on the back of that photograph and describes some similar scenes. When the translation's ready, you'll see what I mean.'

'I guess,' Maddie said. 'Let me know if you turn up anything interesting.'

Her curiosity was piqued but she could see herself disappearing down an internet rabbit hole if she started researching some obscure movie from the 1940s, and she had to get back to earning a living. Daniel was the expert: she would leave this to him. He'd texted her the day before to say he had some news for her and could they meet but he'd cancelled first thing that morning because of some work emergency, and she was leaving for Portland the next day. He'd promised to call her instead, although there was no telling when.

'I'll come again soon,' Maddie told Gramps now, gathering her jacket and purse. 'And I won't leave it so long next time.'

'No, don't,' he said, hugging her goodbye. 'You look a hundred times better than when you arrived. You work too hard, dear. Have fun with Ben and remember to get out into the fresh air now and then.'

Maddie felt a hundred times better for her time out, too: more relaxed and able to cope. Restricting the hours she spent on her phone and reading instead had made her feel calmer. In some ways, she was ready to go back to work, although writing about garden makeovers and trends in kitchenware seemed a little unimportant after what she'd discovered. She no longer cared about the internet trolls, though. It had been so easy to lose a sense of proportion over some mean-spirited people who weren't worth the energy she'd wasted on them, and she felt a sudden pang of sympathy for anyone with nowhere to run when things got tough, no one to turn to when they needed looking after. The world could be a harsh place.

'You're not really thinking about getting married again, are you?' she asked her grandfather. 'Do I need to start choosing a hat?'

'I was only joking,' Gramps replied. 'Eva's a lovely woman, though, and it's nice to have someone to do things with. Let's hope I've a few years left in me yet.'

Which seemed a much more positive attitude than planning his imminent funeral, Maddie thought, and could only thank Eva for that. It was a relief to be leaving her grandfather in such a happy state of mind.

The idea of a journey with Ben was daunting because he didn't like crowds, and Maddie wasn't sure how he'd react to so many new experiences. To make life easier, she'd booked a cabin with bunk beds on the train – but what if he found that too claustrophobic? Luckily there were several videos showing every step of the Coast Starlight journey in detail, which they watched together so Ben would be prepared. They'd even taken an advance trip to the train station, checking out the waiting area and finding the right platform. Ben had spent days before the trip filling and emptying his backpack and she had to persuade him not to bring his entire collection of paints, brushes, pens and sketchbooks. Sharon hovered in the background, twittering and wringing her hands.

'Mom, everything's going to be fine,' Maddie told her, praying that would turn out to be true.

As soon as Sharon had hugged them goodbye at the train station the next morning, Maddie felt more relaxed. Ben was wearing the rainbow-coloured scarf that Kate had given her on the journey down, and the sight of it was reassuring. She couldn't wait to see the sights through his eyes. He was quiet as they waited for the train to arrive, sticking close to her side, but he loved the compact cabin with its own bathroom and later, a fold-down bunk bed that the attendant prepared for the night. The dining car was where Ben really came into his own. He was so friendly that even the grumpiest passengers couldn't help being charmed when he introduced himself, and Maddie, too.

'Ben, they don't need to know our life story,' she hissed, as he was telling the morose couple across the aisle about all the things he was going to see and do in Portland. But the woman actually cracked a smile and said it sounded like he would have a fun few days, and soon she was showing Ben photographs of the Victorian mansion where her son was getting married that weekend.

'There's a gazebo, and a fountain with courtyards all around it,' she said, 'and you should see inside the house! Stained-glass windows and sympathetically restored woodwork everywhere.'

She was about to run through the menu for the wedding

reception when luckily the woman sitting opposite leaned forward to say her daughter had just got engaged and was trying to find caterers who would respect food allergies – and they were off. Ben blinked a few times and retired from the conversation.

After lunch, he and Maddie went to the observation car to look at the Pacific shoreline past Santa Barbara and the Vandenburg Space Force base. This time, a couple of National Park volunteers were acting as guides, pointing out the rocket-launching pads and talking about what made the area so suitable for missile testing. Ben was fascinated, though Maddie's eyes soon glazed over and she sneaked a look at her phone. Reception had been patchy but a text had just arrived from Daniel that made her sit up and pay attention.

'My techie friend has traced an IP address for Nightshade, registered to a computer in Oregon City. Ring any bells?'

'Not that I can think of,' she texted back. 'Will rack my brain tho. Thanks! Sorry not to say goodbye but back soon.' She added a kiss and then deleted it.

Oregon City: less than half an hour's drive from Portland, and well within her paper's circulation area. The news that Nightshade was a real person rather than a bot disturbed her briefly but she soon managed to regain a sense of proportion; she was going to ignore him or her and write what she damn well pleased. With that in mind, she took a picture of Ben looking out of the huge observation window and began to make notes about their journey on her phone.

It wasn't until she and Ben were preparing to settle down for the night that another text arrived from Daniel: 'PS, seems Nightshade is a foodie. There's an Instagram account called @goodthingstobake linked to the same computer.'

Frustratingly, reception dropped out again after a few

minutes and she couldn't search Instagram. She tossed and turned on the thin mattress, hearing Ben shift on the bottom bunk as the train hurtled along the twisting track. Suddenly a thought flashed into her mind that sent her sitting bolt upright, cracking her head on the cabin ceiling and yelping with pain.

'Maddie? What are you doing?' Ben called from below.

'Nothing! Don't worry,' she replied, rubbing her head. She *did* know someone in Oregon City! Last year, the paper's regular restaurant critic had been off sick for a few months, so she'd taken a turn filling in for him. She'd gone with Steve, her boyfriend at the time, to review a seafood place that had just opened in Oregon, and they'd had a fairly disastrous evening. OK, she and Steve had not been getting on well anyway, but their food had taken ages to arrive and was lukewarm and congealed, and their server had been rude. On top of that, Steve had been violently ill during the night and reported the restaurant to the county health department. Although Maddie had tried to be constructive in her review – or at least, not unremittingly negative – she had to be honest. The restaurant had closed down shortly before Christmas and the owner had written a furious letter to the paper, blaming negative publicity for its failure. The woman had to be Nightshade: it all made sense. What was her real name? Maddie couldn't remember, but she would find out.

She woke early the next morning after only a couple of hours' sleep, dressed in the dark without waking Ben and made her way to the observation car. She'd managed to look up @goodthingstobake on Instagram during the night. The setup of her pinned post was perfect: sunlight streaming through an open window, soft music in the background, pretty enamel cake tins and a smiling blonde woman in a striped apron. 'My name is Lily-Anne and I love baking sweet treats in my country kitchen!' announced the bio. 'Come join my cookie crew!' And now Maddie remembered the signature on Lily-Anne's letter to the paper. Jaunty captions under various posts read, 'Swiss meringue buttercream is the best frosting!' 'My mom showed me how to bake the perfect brownie!' 'Did you know you can use beetroot to sweeten a red velvet cake? Crazy, huh?'

Yet comments under most of the posts told a different story. 'Way too much sugar for me,' someone had written, while another person added, 'The state of your oven! I'd be ashamed,' and somebody else asked, 'Why are you wearing plastic gloves? Worst germ spreaders ever.' Lily-Anne defended herself vigorously against each of these accusations with responses that became increasingly heated: the bitter back-and-forths contrasting with her idyllic pictures. For a second, Maddie had been tempted to weigh in herself, criticising Lily-Anne for using canned blueberries in her muffins or some other heinous crime. Her fingers had hovered over the keypad of her phone, but thankfully she caught herself just in time. What had she been thinking?

Putting her phone down, she gazed out of the window as the sky gradually lightened and the sun rose over soaring Mount Shasta, marking the start of a new day. The smell of fresh coffee drifted through from the restaurant car and she yawned, stretching her arms above her head, before making her way back to their tiny bedroom to see if Ben was awake and ready for breakfast.

Ben's trip to Portland could be counted a success. Maddie was back at work and hadn't been able to spend much time with him during the days, but that was fine: what he really enjoyed was exploring the streets around her apartment, finding his favourite park and coffee shop and sitting there to watch the world go by. One lunchtime, Maddie showed him around her newspaper office. He was fascinated by the cubicles crammed side by side, the constant hum of activity, and the overhead television screens broadcasting news throughout the day. She introduced him to her editor before they left for a sandwich in the café next door, and when she returned to the office on her own, Vanessa asked whether she'd ever considered writing about her brother.

'It's lovely to see the two of you so close,' she said, 'and he's such a charmer. This would be a feel-good story.'

'Let me think about it,' Maddie replied, wanting to consider all the implications. Yet she was already imagining a piece about Ben leaving home for the first time, navigating the challenge of living alone and finding his place in the world. Parents of kids who had Down syndrome would find it fascinating, surely, and even those with no direct experience of the condition might want to learn more. She would have to see what Sharon thought about the idea and make sure Ben was shielded from any negativity. He never paid any attention to social media, luckily, or she'd never have contemplated the idea.

They'd been planning to visit the Rose Garden that Saturday (Portland was the City of Roses, after all) but the night before, Maddie spotted a new post on Lily-Anne's @goodthingstobake account. 'Exciting news!' she chirruped. 'For one day only, I shall be running a pop-up café at the Hillside Mall tomorrow from 10 am to 3 pm. Everyone welcome!'

'Ben, do you fancy going shopping tomorrow?' she asked. 'You could look for a souvenir to take home.'

Although she'd been trying to put Lily-Anne out of her mind, checking in with her on Instagram was hard to resist, and so was the thought of confronting her in the flesh. Why should she get away with pretending to be this warm, homely person while spreading hatred on the internet? Let's see how brave she was when Maddie was standing in front of her. What was that speech from *The Merchant of Venice*? 'If you prick us, do we not bleed?' Maddie had a vision of declaiming the lines while Lily-Anne grovelled in shamefaced apology.

The sense of righteous indignation woke her up early the next morning, and she had to go for a run to let off steam. Showering afterwards felt like washing Lily-Anne's poison out of her hair; now she was strong, refreshed, and ready to take control of the narrative. After the short drive to Oregon City, they found a bookshop in the mall that also sold paints and art supplies, so Ben was happy, and then spent half an hour trying to find the café; Lily-Anne's signage was not great. Eventually they tracked the place down. A few strings of bunting had been draped across what looked like a recently vacated storefront and several tables and mismatched chairs were clustered inside at the back of the room. The floor was dusty and several empty display cases stood against the rear wall, while an attempt had been made to brighten up the place with a gingham tablecloth over a trestle table and some jam jars full of wild flowers. Brownies, chocolate-chip cookies and squares of carrot cake sat under glass domes beside an urn, a coffee machine and a stack of mugs. The café was completely empty apart from Lily-Anne herself, standing behind the table in her signature striped apron. She looked unhealthily thin in real life and her face was lined and tense, her jaw clenched. From the alarm in her eyes and the flush creeping up her neck, it was clear she'd recognised Maddie straight away.

All the biting remarks Maddie had planned flew straight out of her head and they stood there, staring at each other, until Ben asked, 'May I have a hot chocolate, please?'

Lily-Anne came back to herself with a start. 'Sure, honey,' she said, looking anywhere but at him. 'Coming right up. And for you, ma'am?'

'I'll have a coffee,' Maddie replied.

'Take a seat wherever you like and I'll bring them right over,' Lily-Anne said. 'There's plenty of room.'

'And a chocolate brownie, please,' Ben added.

Maddie found a table as far away from Lily-Anne as possible and they sat down. A pall of sadness hung over the pop-up, thick as frosting. The bunting sagged and the flowers drooped in their jam jars, scattering pollen across the tablecloth. Lily-Anne had tried so hard with her pop-up and nobody was here. What if Ben and Maddie were her only customers all day?

'Here you go,' she said, approaching their table with a tray. 'Extra marshmallows for you, young man!'

It was excruciating. The coffee burned Maddie's tongue but she wanted to get it down as quickly as possible, although Ben was taking his time with the hot chocolate and brownie, oblivious to the awkward atmosphere. He soon had a chocolate moustache but there were no napkins.

'Use your sleeve,' Maddie whispered. 'It won't matter, just this once.'

Back behind the table, Lily-Anne scrolled through her phone, flicked away a few non-existent crumbs and stared at people walking past the door as though she could magnetically attract them inside.

As soon as Ben had finished eating, Maddie got up to pay the bill. She tapped her card against the reader and put a generous tip in the jar, avoiding Lily-Anne's eye. What was the point in engaging with her? She would only be defensive and Maddie had the upper hand already. Lily-Anne could never bring herself to apologise but now at least she would know Maddie was on to her.

Ben came to join them, bringing his plate. 'Thank you,' he said. 'That brownie was so good.'

'Why, thank you, darling,' Lily-Anne cried. 'Glad you enjoyed it. And don't you have lovely manners?'

'He does,' Maddie said, linking arms with her brother. 'Ben makes the world a better place. I'm so proud of him.'

'I'll bet,' Lily-Anne replied, her mouth stretching into a rictus grin. 'Well, you guys have a great day!'

'You too,' Maddie said. 'Good luck with the pop-up.'

And just for a second, she caught the anger and suspicion on Lily-Anne's face before the mask of civility reimposed itself. How had Maddie let this unhappy, disappointed person take up so much space in her head? Vanessa had been right: the circus would move on and miserable Lily-Anne would be left behind, searching for someone else to attack so she could feel better about herself. She wasn't worth another minute of their time.

Later that day, she texted Daniel: 'Found Nightshade! An interesting encounter. Tell you more when I see you next.' The last sentence sounded a little presumptuous, so she changed it to, 'Must tell you about it some time.'

Daniel didn't reply that day, or the next, or the day after that. He was usually so quick to respond to her messages but now it seemed like he was ghosting her, which was disappointing. She'd ended up really enjoying his company and he'd seemed to feel the same. It shouldn't have mattered so much – he was only a friend, after all – but they had a lot in common and she'd been looking forward to seeing him on her trips back to LA. 'Are you surprised?' a voice whispered in her head. 'After the way you treated him? He's seen the real you, and who could blame him for running a mile.'

By the time her mom arrived to take Ben back to LA, Maddie had resolved to put Daniel out of her mind. Sharon was on great form, fizzing with energy but also more relaxed than Maddie had seen her for years.

'Honestly, I feel like a different person,' she said after lunch, while Ben was packing his belongings and she and Maddie were enjoying a quiet coffee alone. 'You were right, honey – I needed some time to get to know myself again. Thank you for setting me on the right track. And Ben's obviously had a wonderful time.'

'It's gone pretty well,' Maddie said. 'I'm going to miss him.' She felt suddenly bereft at the thought of being alone.

'Heard from Daniel recently?' Sharon asked casually, a few moments later.

Maddie stiffened. 'Why would I?'

Sharon shrugged. 'No particular reason. Just that you seemed to get on and he's such a lovely boy.'

'Stop trying to pair me up with every random male who comes into my life,' Maddie snapped. 'Daniel's fine but he has a girlfriend and he's not interested in me.'

'OK, OK.' Sharon held up her hands. 'I'm sorry. I'm your mother, though, and I can't bear to see you hurting. Of course things are still difficult. After what you've been through, no one could blame you for avoiding men for a while, I get that, or chasing guys who won't make you happy because you feel that's all you deserve.' She put a tentative hand around Maddie's shoulder. 'But you have to learn to trust again – other people, and yourself.'

Maddie found herself alarmingly close to tears. 'Do you really think that's what I'm doing?' she asked, her voice wobbly.

'Yes,' Sharon replied simply. 'You were betrayed in the cruellest way and that awful Aaron made you believe you're worthless. Listen to me: you're smart, and kind, and funny, and sure, I might be biased, but you also happen to be beautiful. You need to stop feeling sorry for yourself and get back in the saddle. I want my daughter back, the one who isn't afraid to set her sights high, the one who'll pick herself up and try again if things don't work out the first time. I know she's in there somewhere.'

'Then you have more faith than I do.' Maddie laid her head against her mother's neck and let Sharon rub her back.

'And as a matter of fact,' her mom added, 'a little bird told me Daniel might not have a girlfriend anymore.'

'Mom!' Maddie looked up. 'Enough!'

'Just saying,' Sharon murmured.

Once Sharon and Ben had left on their epic road trip back to LA, Maddie took a hike through Forest Park. As she tramped along the wooded trail with the sun warm on her back, her mother's words ran through her head. She'd been trying so hard not to think about the traumatic time in her life, a couple of years ago, that had nearly derailed her completely. Now she let herself remember what had happened and wonder whether she had been using the experience as an excuse to let herself slide, to settle for second or even third best because it was the easiest option. If she was honest, she'd have to admit her journalism had become formulaic, despite the compliment Daniel had paid her, and possibly even lazy. Her mom was right: these days, she didn't push herself, thinking it was enough to churn out the requisite number of words and hang on to her job. What kind of legacy would she leave behind with that approach?

She paused for a moment, staring up into the canopy of leaves above. An image of Freya's typewriter, refurbished now, came into her mind. It wasn't much practical use in a digital world but she felt like a real, authentic writer when she loaded up the paper feed and pounded the keys, channelling the spirit of her great-grandmother. The keyboard had more or less the same layout she was used to, although the Z and Y letters were swapped, and there were additional keys for the vowels with umlauts, which she just ignored. Still, she loved the smoothness of the keys under her fingers and the vintage feel of the type, even if the letter 'e' always jumped, which was irritating.

When Maddie was at college, she'd wanted her words to have a real impact: to make people think, as well as entertaining them. She'd even started writing a novel, and although her plot had fizzled out after a couple of chapters, the process had been exhilarating. It looked as though her great-grandmother, Freya, had been a story-teller, and Maddie might have inherited that talent. Shouldn't she make the most of it? She could string a sentence together and knew something about structure and narrative tension; perhaps now she was ready to write something that wouldn't be forgotten in five minutes. The idea of creating a world and filling it with characters born from her imagination burst in her head like a firework. Turning for home, she broke into a run, letting the shadows of the past evaporate in the sunshine.

# Chapter Eighteen

*Berlin, December 1932*

Winter had come, and the city streets glittered with frost. Another Christmas was approaching but nobody felt like celebrating, the country gripped by fear as insidious and penetrating as the bitter cold. None of the parties in the Reichstag could agree and President von Hindenburg, old and frail, constantly resorted to invoking Article 48 of the Weimar constitution, which allowed him to rule by decree. He'd appointed von Schleicher as Chancellor, but the general couldn't rally enough support and the government lurched from one crisis to the next.

'Von Schleicher wants to get back into bed with Hitler,' Gunther said. 'Offered to form a government with our Adolf as Chancellor, as long as he could keep control of the military. Hitler said no, of course. He'll never let anyone else get their hands on his beloved brownshirts and he's managing just fine on his own, thank you very much.'

He stood back to let a girl in a silk kimono edge past him to the sink, where she seized one of the dirty glasses waiting to be washed and filled it with wine. They were crammed into the tiny kitchen of Maus and Elke's apartment, along with half the artistic population of Berlin.

'And do you still maintain Hitler's nothing more than a puppet of the ruling class?' Violet asked, her eyes sharp.

'Hard to tell,' Gunther admitted, lighting a cigarette and holding it aloft to avoid setting anyone on fire. 'But they won't smash the Communists without him, that's for sure. Look, he might become Chancellor but if you ask me, he'll be no more able to hang on to power than the rest of them.'

'And then what will happen?' Freya asked.

Gunther shrugged. 'That's anyone's guess.'

'Elke, darling,' Violet cried, catching sight of her in the doorway. 'Come and cheer us up. Gunther's talking politics.'

'But I'm too sad to be leaving for any sort of cheerfulness,' Elke said, drawing Freya and Violet into a drunken embrace. 'How will we survive without you, my darlings?'

She'd been given a last-minute place at the Paris Opéra Ballet School as someone had dropped out; she and Maus were moving there for Christmas. Maus had an introduction to the French photographer Henri Cartier-Bresson and was hoping to pick up work in a studio to keep her going.

'You're going to be such a success that you won't have time to miss us,' Freya replied, disentangling herself. She and Violet had reached an uneasy truce as time had gone by, but being in such close proximity was still awkward. A few weeks before, Maus had been commissioned to take some publicity shots at the Zaubergarten and had asked the two of them to pose together; Freya had flinched at Violet's careless arm slung around her shoulder.

'And we'll be sure to visit,' Violet added. 'You know my sister lives there? You'll be sick of the sight of us eventually.'

'You must follow us to Paris,' Maus said, joining them.

'Seriously. Violet, you could live anywhere, and Freya, you're independent now. What's stopping you?'

Freya had spent a couple of nights sleeping on the floor in Maus and Elke's apartment after she'd left home, plucking up the courage to ask Frau Brodsky whether she might be able to stay at the Zaubergarten, as long as Herr Goldstein agreed. Now that only four dancers were left, there was enough space to move the work table out into the girls' dressing room and turn the workroom into a bedroom by adding a mattress on the floor and a camping stove. She would offer to pay a reasonable rent and keep an eye on the place overnight.

'You can always ask,' Frau Brodsky had replied. 'I don't mind one way or the other.'

Freya had been surprised she should be so amenable, but Frau Brodsky had become increasingly detached from her work at the club. Her husband was poorly and she seemed preoccupied by worries she didn't want to share. She handed over a little more responsibility to Freya every day, keeping an eye on things in the background and offering advice when it was asked for.

Herr Goldstein was delighted with Freya's idea and accepted immediately, though he was a little concerned to think of her alone in the club overnight. Without wishing to cause alarm, he showed her a way of slipping outside via an exit she hadn't known existed; if any brownshirts caused trouble at the front of the building, she could leave via the rear. Adjoining the workroom was a smaller room – more of a large cupboard, really – where costumes and props were stored. A narrow door to one side, usually concealed by a stack of boxes, opened on to a staircase leading up to the ground floor. According to Herr Goldstein, this escape route had been constructed thirty years before by the premise's previous owner, who'd run an illegal distillery in this basement and was frequently raided by the police.

Strangely, Freya didn't feel frightened in the Zaubergarten once everyone had left. This was her domain, every inch of the territory familiar and private. Here she could breathe. It was blissful to walk around without any chance of bumping into Herr Grube or seeing Adolf Hitler glaring down at her from the wall. She began retyping her stories and discovered she knew all of them pretty much by heart – and now she was liberated to go into greater depth. When she'd finally finished the story about Gerda the dancer and her attempt on Hitler's life, she told Wolfgang a summary of the plot and asked whether he would read it. By tacit agreement, they no longer mentioned what had happened at the Kaiserhof; she'd given up trying to persuade him not to pull a stunt like that again. She wasn't sure how he'd react to her request but he only smiled and said, 'An interesting premise. Everything's grist to the mill, I suppose.'

She would have liked to join forces with him and talk about other ways they might resist the Fascists, but Wolfgang was a lone wolf and too unpredictable to be a useful ally. The Zaubergarten dancers were too absorbed in their rackety, precarious lives for politics and she couldn't risk confiding in any of her old friends – whom she hardly ever saw now, anyway – in case they turned out to be Nazi sympathisers. Unexpectedly, she found herself becoming increasingly friendly with Franz Schwartz, who had given up trying to be an emcee and was now running the bar. Herr Goldstein had appointed an assistant, Werner, to collect each night's takings and keep an eye on things, while he spent less and less time at the Zaubergarten. Rumour had it he was trying to sell the place.

'Franz, what would you do if you lost your job here?' Freya asked him one day as she was locking up. It was a question that had been keeping her awake at night.

'I'm considering the movie business,' he replied airily, buttoning his coat. 'I have a contact at the Babelsberg film studios and the other night I met an American screenwriter at the Eldorado. He's called Grant and looks like a cowboy. Can you imagine? And he says there's plenty of work in Hollywood.' He shivered as a blast of icy air swirled through the open front door. 'Sunshine and oranges – sounds good to me. I'm on the waiting list for a visa at the US embassy.'

'Well, just be careful,' she warned. 'Remember what happened last time.' Schwartz was always being seduced by men who promised him the earth and inevitably failed to deliver. He'd recently fallen for someone who claimed to own a restaurant in Paris and was looking for a maître d'. The restaurant couldn't have been very successful, because its alleged owner disappeared in the middle of the night with Franz's wallet and his best suit.

'So young but so crushingly sensible,' he said, winding a scarf around his neck and stepping out into the night. 'Can there really be no romance in your soul?'

Freya smiled to herself as she slid the heavy bolts into place behind him. There was something endearing about Franz's optimism, his refusal to lose hope no matter how many times he was disappointed. He made her laugh, although he took himself extremely seriously; she would miss him if by any strange chance the movie business snapped him up. Brick by brick, the foundations of her world were crumbling.

That Christmas Eve, Freya walked through the snow to the family apartment with a batch of *Lebkuchen* biscuits baked in the Zaubergarten kitchens, and the bottle of champagne Herr Goldstein had given her. Ernst had refused an invitation to tea at her room in the Zaubergarten and asked her to come there for supper instead. Herr Grube would be away, thankfully, but she would have to see Otto, and she wasn't looking forward to that.

It was strange, being treated as a guest in what had once been her home. She discovered Hedwig the maid had moved into her old room – presumably so she could be on hand to work from morning till night – which was now crammed with clothes and china nick-nacks. The whole apartment seemed cramped and more fusty: crocheted mats on every surface, heavier curtains at the window, a salmon-pink tablecloth with a lace frill drooping to the floor and a sentimental picture of two kittens in a basket on the wall. A Christmas tree stood in the corner, already decorated, and the portrait of Adolf Hitler had been festooned with tinsel so that he glared out beneath an incongruously festive fringe. Surely Ernst hadn't been behind these developments? He looked much the same in his best tweed trousers and waistcoat, his face giving nothing away as he greeted her casually; she might have been gone for a night, rather than weeks.

'So this is what you're drinking now?' he said, eyeing the bottle of champagne. 'Living the high life.'

She flushed. 'Of course not. I brought it as a present.'

Hedwig appeared from the kitchen with glasses, looking lumpen as ever. 'Ah, there you are,' Ernst cried, strangely animated at the sight of her. 'Will you join us for a drink?'

Freya stared at him, flabbergasted.

'Why not?' Hedwig replied, simpering. 'I took the liberty of bringing an extra glass.' She seized the champagne from Freya's hands and made a performance out of failing to pop the cork before passing the bottle to Ernst. 'We need a man for the job,' she said, turning to Freya with a knowing smile and folding her hefty arms.

Freya watched the scene in growing disbelief: her father preening as he eased out the champagne cork, Hedwig flirting as she poured glasses and handed them out with a proprietorial air. Clearly, a drama was being played out for her benefit. The three of them stood making awkward conversation until Otto arrived, his cheeks pink from the cold. He didn't seem at all taken aback to find Hedwig included in the family celebrations, and Freya got the impression he was enjoying his sister's discomfort.

'And how's life in Schöneberg?' he asked, drinking half his champagne in one gulp and not listening to Freya's answer. What he really wanted was to tell her how smoothly the apartment was running now Hedwig was in charge, and how prosperous their household would become once Herr Hitler was made Chancellor.

'Walther Grube is destined for great things,' he said. 'It wouldn't surprise me if he ends up in the Reichstag.'

The table had been laid for four, Freya noticed, but she was prepared for anything now. Hedwig brought through a dish of roast carp with boiled potatoes and carrots and sat at the head of the table – Ingrid's place – to portion it out and pass round the plates. Ernst took the seat opposite, ate with his head down and acted as though nothing were out of the ordinary. Hedwig demolished a mountain of food, then fixed her eyes on a point somewhere in the middle distance with her hands in her lap and an infuriating smile on her face while Otto held forth about what the coming year might mean for Germany. He was hoping for everything that Freya dreaded, and she felt too depressed even to argue with him.

Hedwig refused her offer of help with the plates when they had finished the main course, although she allowed Ernst to carry the rest of the dishes through to the kitchen.

'How long has this been going on?' Freya asked Otto quietly, once they were alone and the kitchen door was closed.

'Since you left, pretty much,' he replied. 'She saw her chance and took it. She doesn't spend many nights in your old room, needless to say.'

Freya winced.

'Well, what did you expect?' he said, helping himself to another glass of schnapps. 'I imagine they'll get married soon. This is all your fault, so don't come crying to me when our inheritance is gone.'

Freya laid down her napkin. 'I have to leave, I've a terrible headache. Will you say goodbye to Vati for me? And goodbye, Otto. I hope things fall into place for you.' She couldn't bring herself to embrace him and he made no move towards her.

It had been a dispiriting visit. On the way back, she made a detour via the cemetery to sit by her mother's grave for a while and talk to her, as she did on special occasions such as birthdays and holidays. She didn't mention Hedwig; instead she confided her feelings about Otto and asked Ingrid's forgiveness. Her brother might have grown into a different person if he'd stayed friends with Leon instead of letting Hitler and Walther Grube turn his head, but as things stood, she wouldn't care if she never saw him again. It was a terrible thing to admit, but such a relief to let herself stop trying to like him.

# Chapter Nineteen

*Berlin, December 1932*

In the drab, empty days between Christmas and New Year, Frau Brodsky arrived at the Zaubergarten, surprising Freya, who wasn't expecting to see her until the club was open after the holidays. Her hair was dishevelled and her eyes were strangely blank, as though she couldn't process what was in front of them.

'Are you all right?' Freya asked in alarm. 'Has something happened? Sit down and I'll make you a coffee.'

'No time for coffee, I'm afraid. I've come to say a quick goodbye,' Frau Brodsky replied, taking a seat in front of one of the dressing tables and looking at herself in the mirror. 'Lord, what a sight.' She picked up a comb and tidied her hair distractedly.

'Where are you going?' Freya asked, panic rising in her chest.

'To Palestine.' Frau Brodsky's voice was flat, devoid of emotion. 'We leave next week. The exit papers came through and I've sold everything we own, apart from some jewellery and a few clothes.'

'And what about your husband?'

'He died,' she said simply, laying down the comb. 'Just before Hanukkah. There was some trouble in the street. The brownshirts roughed him up – not badly, but enough to give him a fright. He came home, sat in his chair and had a heart attack. I thought he was sleeping until I tried to wake him for lunch.'

'Oh, Rosa, I'm so sorry.' Freya took Frau Brodsky's hands in hers. 'What an awful thing to happen.'

Frau Brodsky smiled. 'Thank you, my dear. But he's safe now; no one can hurt him anymore. And it was a peaceful death, despite what had gone before: his favourite armchair, a fire in the grate and his wife close at hand, cooking potato latkes just the way he liked them. We should all be so lucky.'

'How will I manage without you?' Freya asked, unable to hold back the question any longer.

'You'll be fine.' Frau Brodsky patted her hand. 'You're running this place already, more or less. I've told Herr Goldstein he won't find a better wardrobe mistress in Berlin and that he's to give you a raise. He'll do his best, I'm sure, though I wouldn't expect too much. The club's barely breaking even and who knows how long he'll be able to hang on to it. If I were you, I'd start looking around for other opportunities. Maybe you should see if there's any work going at the Scala?'

'This is my home, though!' Freya gazed around the dressing room, less crowded now with costumes and paraphernalia than it had been when she first saw it, just over two years before. The Zaubergarten had taken her in, given her life structure and purpose in the darkest of times, and she couldn't imagine starting again somewhere else.

'You must carry home in your heart wherever you go,'

Frau Brodsky said. 'That's what life has taught me, and it's the only advice I can give.'

She took Freya's face between her hands and kissed the top of her head. 'Good luck, my dear. You're clever, resourceful and stronger than you think. God willing, you'll survive.'

Frau Brodsky had left the country just in time. At the end of January, President von Hindenburg bowed to the inevitable and appointed Adolf Hitler as Chancellor. That night the streets of Berlin flamed with a river of torches as SS and SA paramilitaries marched in celebration through the government district, singing as they went. Herr Hitler waved to the jubilant crowds below from the chancellery window, while it was von Hindenburg's turn to appear at the Kaiserhof hotel. Freya kept well away, listening to an account of the procession on the radio she had bought herself for Christmas. The announcer – whom she hadn't heard before – was practically screaming with excitement and, alone in her room, she felt like the one sane person in a country of lunatics. She had no idea what the next few months would bring; the only thing to be done, she decided, was to take each day as it came.

When the Zaubergarten reopened later in the week, Freya had to break the news of Frau Brodsky's departure to the dancers.

'Well, she'll probably be happier in Palestine,' Gisela said. 'Amongst her own kind.'

Perle and Sophie said nothing, exchanging a glance that Freya didn't understand. There was a subdued atmosphere in the dressing room that evening, with none of the usual backchat and bickering.

'Cheer up,' Freya said, trying to lighten the mood. 'Hitler might be Chancellor but life goes on.' The girls didn't even smile.

'Freya, can you have a look at the lavatory?' Violet asked, heading for the door. 'I think it's blocked again.'

Sighing, Freya went to oblige; her first day in charge was not going well. When they were in the corridor, however, Violet grabbed her by the shoulder, pulled her into the bathroom and shut the door behind them.

'Do you have a death wish?' she hissed, her fingers digging into Freya's flesh. 'You need to watch your tongue.'

'What do you mean?' Freya said, shaking her off.

'Gisela's in cahoots with the Nazis. If you say anything against our Adolf, she'll report you to the Gestapo.'

'Gisela?' Freya repeated. Kind, friendly Gisela who was everyone's confidante? 'I can't believe it. How do you know?'

'Because I go about with my eyes and ears open,' Violet snapped. 'That's why the other Sophie had to leave for America in such a hurry: Gisela was on to her. Let's hope you've got away with it this time, but you'd better toe the party line from now on.'

'Like you do?' Freya asked sardonically.

'Yes,' Violet snapped. 'Exactly like I do.' And she strode off without another word.

Freya was shaken. The Zaubergarten had been her sanctuary but now she felt unsafe even here. The Nazis in the audience every evening had no interest in humour or satire; they wanted drinking songs with choruses they could sing along to, stamping their feet, and pretty girls to look at. Elegant costumes were wasted on them: they would no doubt have preferred milkmaids and cats with long tails. Still, at least they brought in some much-needed income. Herr Goldstein employed three more dancers; all of them blonde, blue-eyed and inexperienced. Gisela took the newcomers under her wing and Perle, Violet and Sophie became more withdrawn than ever. The dressing room was a tense, watchful place.

In the wider world, a sense of order had been restored. Hitler gave a speech on the radio, calling for national unity in the fight against Communism and promising an end to unemployment and poverty. He sounded measured, statesman-like. The streets were quieter, apart from the Nazis rattling their collecting tins or marching in squads, singing as they went. Red and black swastika flags clothed the city and the Communist hammer and sickle graffiti on walls was painted over with messages of hatred for Jews. A baker opening his shop one morning greeted Freya with '*Heil Hitler!*' and a salute that he clearly expected her to return. She hurried past with her head down and bought her bread elsewhere.

A month or so after Hitler had been elected, she switched on her radio early one morning to hear that the Reichstag building had been set on fire during the night and virtually destroyed. The alleged arsonist, a Dutch Communist, had been arrested at the scene. Seized with misgiving, she hurried to Wolfgang's apartment at midday to hear his view of the matter. He opened the door a crack, saw who it was and hustled her quickly inside.

'You shouldn't have stopped me, that day at the Kaiserhof,' he said, lighting another cigarette from the stub of the first. 'We're in serious trouble now. It's the beginning of the end.'

'What do you mean?' she asked, her stomach in knots.

'I went there this morning – to the Reichstag, I mean.' He spoke rapidly, his words falling over themselves as he paced up and down. 'Not that you could get near the building, but I wanted to find Gunther and that seemed the best place to try. He thinks there's something fishy about the whole story – not that he'll be allowed to say so. This Dutch fellow they've arrested is a pathetic creature, apparently. How could he have burned down the Reichstag on his own without anyone noticing until it was too late? Hitler's claiming it's the start of a Communist uprising. He's going to use this as an excuse to crack down, you mark my words.'

He was right. That very day, the Reichstag Fire Decree was passed, 'For the Protection of the People and State'. Freedom of the press and freedom of expression were suspended, the right to assembly was banned, and the Chancellor and the President could overrule the Reichstag however they chose. Von Hindenburg was in Hitler's pocket, so essentially this meant the Chancellor could do as he pleased; he was answerable to no one.

'This is ridiculous,' Freya protested to Wolfgang. 'Why do I need protecting from ideas? How can they hurt me?'

She couldn't eat, couldn't sleep, couldn't write a word – even though Wolfgang had told her he thought Gerda's story was brilliant, the best thing she'd ever come up with. Her notebook pulsed under her mattress as though it were an unexploded bomb. What was the point in trying to express herself if she'd never be able to share her stories, and when even daring to write them could land her in trouble? It seemed that every time she went out, she passed men in long trench coats and Homburg hats, hammering on a door or bundling someone into a car which then drove off at top speed. The secret police were everywhere. They had even wormed their way inside Freya's head, infecting her most private thoughts. 'We're watching,' they whispered. 'Defy us and you'll be next.'

'It's a rout,' Wolfgang said. 'All the writers are leaving while they can: Gunther told me Brecht has gone, and your favourite, Döblin. Joseph Roth, too. So many people have been rounded up that the Nazis are setting up prison camps everywhere.'

'Aren't you worried?' Freya asked.

'Oh, no one will bother about an old has-been like me,' he replied. 'They have fatter fish to fry.'

Sadly, he was wrong. Rupert arrived at the Zaubergarten one sunny spring afternoon to pass on the news that Wolfgang had been arrested.

'We were meant to meet for a drink this morning but he didn't turn up,' he said. 'The bartender hadn't seen Wolfi for a couple of days, apparently, so I knew something was wrong, and when I called at his apartment, a neighbour told me the Gestapo had taken him away yesterday. I don't want to make too many enquiries in case they throw me in a cell too. Perhaps you could find out where he is? A pretty girl might have more luck than a foreigner with dubious connections.'

'I'll try, of course,' Freya said, already looking for her coat. The dancers wouldn't arrive for another few hours and she was up to date with her chores.

'You don't need to go right away,' Rupert said, putting his hand over hers. 'How is the writing progressing, dear Freya? Wolfi thinks you're terrifically talented. I'd be happy to read this manuscript of yours he mentioned the other day. He said it was rather marvellous.'

'Thanks, Rupert,' Freya replied, distracted. 'That's kind of you. In fact, Wolfi has it at the moment. I suppose I'd better go round to his place and try to get it back.' It occurred to her now that she only had the one copy.

'Once you've located our mutual friend, of course,' Rupert said smoothly, now apparently anxious for her to leave. 'You know the Gestapo headquarters at Prinz-Albrecht-Strasse? It's a huge building; you can't miss it.'

At that moment, Franz Schwartz put his head around the dressing-room door. 'Thought I heard a familiar voice,' he cried. 'Rupert, you old rascal! What are you doing here?'

It turned out they were acquaintances, if not friends, and Freya left them talking as she hurried towards Prinz-Albrecht-Strasse, full of misgiving. What if Wolfi had tried to pull another stunt? What if someone had spotted him pull the gun at the Kaiserhof hotel and waited for some reason until now to tell the police?

She was out of breath by the time she arrived at the police office and stammered out her request to the bored sergeant on the reception desk. He directed her to the top floor of the building, warning her there was a long queue. 'But I only have an hour,' she said, despairing, and he shrugged.

The room in which Freya was told to wait reverberated with the din of conversation and typewriters pounding away in a mechanical chorus. The noise was deafening, and she had to raise her voice to have any chance of being heard as she repeated her enquiry about Wolfgang Berger. All the seats were occupied, so she leaned against the wall until an official could spare any time to reply, listening to a hundred personal tragedies play out. An elderly woman was looking for her son, taken from his bed in the middle of the night two weeks before; a girl who could have been no more than ten or eleven with a baby in her arms was trying to find her parents, seized within hours of each other that morning; a heavily pregnant woman sat in the corner, clutching her stomach and weeping. Outnumbering the searchers by at least two to one were the informers, keen to do their duty by reporting neighbours who'd failed to return a Heil Hitler salute, or made a joke about Goebbels, or defaced a swastika flag, or . . . On and on went the litany, while clerks solemnly typed up every petty accusation.

Freya stayed for as long as she could, but it was clear she wasn't going to find out where Wolfi had been taken and the racket was making her head ache. After a last hopeless appeal, she made her way back to the Zaubergarten in time to prepare for the evening's performance. There was no sign of Rupert or Herr Schwartz, who'd probably gone off to a bar together.

When Violet arrived, Freya drew her to one side, well out of Gisela's earshot, and whispered, 'Have you heard Wolfi's been arrested? I've been to the Gestapo HQ but no one seems to know where he's been taken.'

'They probably have a good idea but they won't tell you, that's for sure,' Violet replied, her face impassive. 'I'll see what I can find out.'

How irritating she was, with her assumption of superiority! Yet Freya was glad to have someone to confide in, someone who might be a closet Fascist but was still Wolfi's friend and would care about him – if Violet cared about anyone apart from herself, which was open to debate.

Soon the invisible net that had been thrown around Germany was pulled into a stranglehold: an announcement was made on the radio that works by undesirable authors were to be banned. Jewish, Communist or pacifist writers, hostile foreigners and those with degenerate tendencies would no longer be published, and their books would be removed from public libraries. Indeed, everyone was 'encouraged' (i.e. ordered) to purge their bookshelves at home; there would be consequences if any such titles were found during the raids that were sure to follow. Books could be dropped off at designated collection points and ceremonial book-burnings would be held in two weeks' time in cities throughout the country. A new German culture would emerge from the flames: racially pure, martial and high-minded.

Freya listened in mounting disbelief before running outside to buy a newspaper to read the reports in black and white. There had been no mistake. All her beloved contemporary authors were to be silenced – Irmgard Keun, Alfred Döblin, Bertolt Brecht and Thomas Mann among them – and Heinrich Heine, her mother's favourite radical poet from the nineteenth century, was included among the undesirables. It would also be a crime to read Ernest Hemingway, F Scott Fitzgerald, Helen Keller, H G Wells, D H Lawrence and scores of other literary greats from overseas. And this move was said to have been instigated by university students!

Wolfgang's words echoed in Freya's head as she leaned against the wall: 'There are books they won't open because they don't want to be challenged. Just when they should be reading anything and everything, and deciding for themselves what to think!'

Now Wolfgang had been arrested she had no one with whom to share her dread – or almost no one. Summoning all her determination, she hurried through the streets to Potsdamer Platz, where she took a tram towards the Kohls' apartment. It was months since her last awkward meeting with Leon and she had no idea how he'd greet her, but she yearned to see him. This time, it was Frau Kohl who answered the bell in Gutenberg Strasse and came down to let her in.

'So good to see you, my dear!' she said, with a warm embrace. Freya let herself be held for a moment before she drew back and began to stammer out an explanation.

Frau Kohl put a finger to her lips. 'Not here. We can talk in the kitchen.'

Over coffee upstairs, all Freya's fears for the future came spilling out. 'I don't know how we've ended up in this state,' she finished. 'My mother would have been heartbroken. Why should those illiterate thugs tell me what I can and can't read? I won't put up with it!'

'Where you burn books, you will in the end burn people,' Frau Kohl said. Freya must have looked puzzled because she added, 'That's a line from a play by your mother's favourite, Heinrich Heine. But you must be careful, Freya. I promised Ingrid I'd look out for you and I haven't made a very good job of it so far. I'm telling you now, though, to choose your friends wisely. It's fine to blow off steam with me or Leon but don't speak like this to anyone else or you'll end up in prison faster than you can spit. It will be safer to keep your head down while the Nazis are in power.'

'But that will be for ever!' Freya exclaimed. 'No one is allowed to oppose them. Am I to keep quiet for the rest of my life? It's intolerable.'

'I know,' Frau Kohl replied with a sigh. 'What are we to do? I've lost my job but that came as no surprise. I'm thinking about emigrating but Leon doesn't want to abandon Germany.'

'Is he at home?' Freya asked, glancing towards the door.

'He's busy studying,' Frau Kohl replied, looking evasive. 'Exams soon. But I'm sure he'll be pleased to catch up with you another time.'

After another cup of coffee, Freya asked to use the bathroom before she left. On her way out, she noticed the door opposite was ajar, the sound of voices drifting through into the hall. Intrigued, she crept forward to listen. There seemed to be at least three people talking in hushed, urgent voices, though she couldn't make out what they were saying. A floorboard creaked under her tread as she inched closer, however, and the conversation stopped abruptly. After a few seconds' silence, Leon appeared. His face cleared when he saw her and he stepped outside, closing the door behind him – though not quickly enough to hide the four or five faces looking back at her in alarm. She caught the eye of a boy with flaming ginger hair, sitting on the edge of the bed.

'I'm sorry, Leon,' she stammered. 'Your mother told me you were busy but I just wanted to say hello.'

Frau Kohl appeared in the corridor, too, and Freya apologised again. 'It's all right, Mutti,' Leon said. 'I'll show Freya downstairs.'

He took her elbow and guided her out of the apartment. 'My study group,' he said briefly on the stairs.

She raised her eyebrows. 'Really?'

Once outside, she stopped him in the shelter of an archway and said quietly, 'Whatever you're planning, I want to help. I could be so useful. So many Nazis are coming to the Zaubergarten – I can pass on any useful information they let slip. And I could try to find out from Walther Grube what Goebbels is up to.' There was more point helping Leon than her friend Gunther; he'd only wanted information about Goebbels so he could write it up for the newspaper and that was forbidden now.

'We're not planning anything,' Leon replied.

Freya snorted. 'I don't believe that for a second. Look, I'm going mad by myself. If I can't join in with you, I'll make a plan on my own and that'll be a hundred times more dangerous. Surely you need all the support you can get?'

'I can't let you get involved at this stage,' Leon said, speaking honestly at last. 'It's far too risky and my mother would kill me if she found out. But let's keep in touch, Freya. I've missed you. Can we be friends again? Times are too hard to hold a grudge and people who think like us should stick together.'

She smiled and hugged him. 'Of course. You know where to find me and I'll come here again, I promise.'

At last, a glimmer of hope for the future. With Leon on her side, she could take on the world.

'Keep a record,' he whispered, pulling back. 'Make a note of everything you see and hear. One day, God willing, the Nazis will be held accountable.'

# Chapter Twenty

*Berlin, May 1933*

On her way back to the Zaubergarten, Freya made a detour via Wolfgang's apartment. She should have been back at work but was desperate to find Gerda's story before the police did. Her name was on the title page and it wouldn't take long for the Gestapo to track her down. Running into the building and up the stairs, she discovered the apartment was locked, but the caretaker knew her from past visits and was prepared to let her in for a modest bribe.

'Herr Berger has an essay of mine, you see,' she gabbled. 'About the glorious Prussian wars against Denmark, which I have to submit for examination.' The man had always seemed friendly enough but you could never tell; he was perfectly placed to be an informer.

Once inside, it was easy enough to imagine what must have happened the day before: the overturned chairs, ransacked shelves and smashed crockery told their own sad story.

'Poor Wolfi,' Freya murmured, and the caretaker sighed sympathetically.

'Ach, it's a bad business,' he said, which could have been taken to mean anything.

Stepping carefully over the debris in Wolfgang's study, Freya made her way to the large desk by the window and looked quickly through the open drawers. There was no sign of the envelope containing her typescript and nor was it on the bookcase or among the papers scattered over the floor, or on Wolfi's bedside table or in any of his cupboards. Eventually she had to concede that unless she was going to take the place apart even more thoroughly than the Gestapo, she would have to give up the search. If they had found her story already, she was done for, and a curious fatalism came over her. She stood looking at the devastation: Wolfi's precious books, their spines split and pages torn, lying on the rug like so much discarded rubbish. She could see him now, turning around in his chair to pick a title from the shelf, turn to a well-thumbed page and read out a passage in his husky voice, his face alight with appreciation.

'My library is my greatest treasure,' he'd once told her. 'Through good times and bad, I turn to these books for consolation, inspiration and delight. They never fail me.'

She picked up a copy of *All Quiet on the Western Front*, that extraordinary novel about a young, naïve soldier living through the horrors of the Great War. Naturally, this book had been banned. It was a story of humiliation, practically an advertisement for pacifism, when Germany could only be seen as a strong, victorious nation.

Smoothing its pages, Freya turned to the caretaker and said, 'Herr Berger could get into trouble if the police come again and find this book. I'll hand it in for him. And some others, too.'

She fetched a suitcase from under the bed and hurriedly

filled it with more gems from Wolfgang's collection: all forbidden now, of course. The most powerful stories were subversive and nuanced, testing boundaries while asking uncomfortable questions, and the Nazis could never allow that.

She had no idea whether the caretaker believed her story but he didn't try to stop her.

'Someone else came this morning,' he said, as she was closing the latches of the case. 'An Englishman. He took a couple of books too.'

Rupert must have had the same idea, which seemed uncharacteristically considerate, or maybe he just wanted to add to his own library while Wolfgang was out of the way. Dismissing such an unworthy thought, Freya lugged the case down into the street and stumbled straight into a squad of brownshirts marching past. She flattened herself against the wall, dropped the case and saluted with a feeble *'Sieg Heil!'* which they ignored. Her stomach fluttering with nerves, she kept her head down all the way back to the Zaubergarten.

Of course she wasn't going to surrender these treasured books to be destroyed, but where could she hide them? Step by laborious step, she formulated a plan that took her breath away with its audacity and filled her with a savage joy. She was probably doomed anyway; might as well go out with a bang. Arriving at the club, she bumped the suitcase down to the dressing room and through to the large store cupboard adjoining what was now her bedroom. Pulling out a couple of boxes filled with ostrich-feather fans, Venetian masks and grass skirts, she stowed the suitcase behind them and stood back, breathing heavily as she rubbed her aching palm. She felt sure Wolfgang would have approved.

That evening's performance was lacklustre, as usual.

Violet danced half-heartedly nowadays, scarcely bothering to hide her contempt for the baying audience, Sophie had disappeared and Perle's drinking was out of control now that Frau Brodsky wasn't there to look after her. The Zaubergarten girls were no longer a polished troupe, perfectly in tune with one another. How much longer could they carry on? Herr Goldstein hadn't been near the club for days. Freya stayed awake for hours that night, listening to every creak of the floorboards above her head, every passing vehicle or loitering drunk outside in the street. Her mind was too busy for sleep.

She rose early the next morning, despite her fatigue, and walked through Tiergarten park towards the place she had once called home. It was a Friday; after breakfast, Hedwig would be going to the market on the other side of the bridge. Wearing a hat pulled low over her face, Freya lurked in the doorway of an antique shop a little further down the road that never opened before eleven. With a basket over her arm, she attracted little attention. At a quarter to eight, she saw her father set off for work in his paint-stained overalls, a haversack slung over one shoulder. It was strange, watching him from a distance and realising how little he meant to her; she had no desire to run up and greet him. Herr Grube left promptly at eight, marching along in his shiny suit with the swastika armband proudly displayed, and at eight-thirty, Hedwig appeared, proceeding down the street in her dirndl and shawl like a ship in full sail. As Ernst became scrawnier, so she seemed to be expanding, as though she were sucking the meat off his bones. Finally, Otto wheeled out his bicycle, swung a leg over the crossbar and pushed off. Freya waited until the sound of his jaunty whistle had faded into silence, then crossed the road and slipped into the building, reaching for the keys in her pocket which she had never bothered to return.

The apartment was dark and quiet, with only narrow shafts of sunlight piercing the heavy curtains that now shrouded every window. Hedwig kept the place clean but it seemed joyless, the air smelling of cabbage and boiled fish. Freya went straight to the sitting room, her heart in her mouth. What if she were too late? But there they were: the books her mother had cherished, untouched in the glass-fronted cabinet. Quickly, she ran her fingers along the row of spines, selecting Ingrid's favourites on the banned list and piling them in her basket. The poems of Heinrich Heine and Rudyard Kipling, of course, and the novels of Herman Hesse, Aldous Huxley, Stefan Zweig and Thomas Mann.

Soon there was only room in the basket for a couple more copies and she was deliberating between translations of Proust and Mark Twain when she heard a voice ask, 'Fräulein Amsel? Can it be you?' and whirled around to find Walther Grube standing alarmingly close behind her.

'Herr Grube!' she exclaimed, her hand to her throat. 'My goodness, you gave me a shock.' She had no idea how long he'd been there.

'And vice versa,' he replied, in his soft, sly voice.

With a flash of inspiration, Freya dropped the basket, raised her arm and cried, '*Heil Hitler!*'

He returned her salute, a little nonplussed. 'And what is this? A change of heart?'

'Absolutely,' she replied fervently. 'I've been such a fool, Herr Grube. Seeing the Chancellor that day at the Kaiserhof, I realised how right you were. He *is* the man we've been waiting for: strong, principled and honest. Hearing him speak was a revelation.'

'But he didn't say anything at the Kaiserhof.' Grube regarded her quizzically. 'He walked through the lobby and into a side room without a word.'

'Of course,' Freya said. 'Hearing him talk later on the radio, I mean. That speech he gave after he was elected! So wise and compassionate. He is truly a hero for our times.'

'Well, this is welcome news, Fräulein Amsel,' Grube replied. Was he convinced? She had no idea. 'I always hoped you might come around to the right way of thinking, a clever girl like you.'

'My eyes have been opened,' Freya went on. 'I don't know why it took me so long to see the truth of what he says. That's why I'm here: to remove these corrupt books from our collection. My father and brother aren't great readers and have probably forgotten they're here, but I know my mother would have wanted us to abide by the rules.'

'But why come now, when everyone is out?' Grube asked. 'Why not wait until the evening and join us for supper?'

Freya dropped her gaze. 'To be frank, I'm embarrassed by my father's relationship with our maid. I find it painful to see her in my mother's place.'

After a short pause, he said, 'I understand. That must be very hard.'

'Thank you,' she said, seizing the basket with her eyes still downcast. 'Well, I'm sorry to have alarmed you, Herr Grube. I'd better hand in these books and get back to work.'

'Wait a moment and I'll come with you,' he told her. 'Let me just collect the ledger I'd left in my room and I can carry that heavy basket. There's a collection point for banned books at the Technische Hochschule library, I believe. We might even run into your brother there.'

There was no use Freya protesting that she didn't want

to delay him and could manage perfectly well by herself; in the end, she had to give in. She walked beside Herr Grube for the next half hour, listening to him hold forth about their dear leader's glorious vision of Germany, freed at last from the corruption and decadence of the Weimar Republic and the evil influence of Jews. The forbidden authors contaminated their country's purity; burning these works would show the world that the old order had gone for good.

'And it's the students who've come up with this inspired idea,' he said, his eyes gleaming. 'Our young people! That gives me the greatest hope for our future. Herr Goebbels approves, of course. I believe he's agreed to deliver a speech when the bonfire is lit.' He shifted the basket from one arm to the other. 'But keep that to yourself. It might not be common knowledge.'

'Of course,' Freya said. 'I should very much like to hear him. Where is the book burning to take place? The one here in Berlin, I mean.'

'The Opernplatz,' Grube replied. 'It will be a tremendous occasion. Perhaps one day you will tell your children you were there.' He bared his teeth in the approximation of a smile.

Freya did her best to smile back, digesting the information. The Opernplatz was a public square off the wide Unter den Linden boulevard, bordered by several imposing buildings: the State Opera, the Old Library, which had been taken over by Friedrich Wilhelm University, and its law school, where Leon was enrolled. She wondered whether he knew about these plans.

At last they arrived at the library of the Technische Hochschule. No longer a place of studious silence, it now thrummed with purposeful activity. The barriers had been thrown open and students in brown shirts, their sleeves rolled up, tramped through with armfuls of books which they threw into waiting wheelbarrows. They looked a little doubtfully at Herr Grube advancing with his oddly feminine basket but warmed up after a few Heil Hitlers and were happy to accept its contents. Freya had to watch as the volumes her mother had cherished were tossed carelessly among the rest and then wheeled away to be stored elsewhere until the great day came. At least she didn't have to see them being burned, but it was heartbreaking nonetheless.

'A good job done,' Herr Grube said, handing back her empty basket. 'I'm glad to have bumped into you today, Fräulein Amsel. As a matter of fact, we may be seeing more of each other soon.'

'That sounds intriguing,' she said, trying to conceal her alarm. 'Tell me more.'

'I can't go into detail, but your place of work has been of interest to the party for some time,' he went on. 'Let's just say our plans should come to fruition in the near future.'

'Then I'll look forward to finding out about them,' she told him. 'Goodbye, and thank you for your help.'

Her legs were weak as she walked away. Grube was no fool: she suspected he knew exactly what she'd been up to, and his parting words were ominous. Only once she was safely back at the Zaubergarten did she retrieve the volume of Heinrich Heine's poetry that she'd tucked into the waistband of her skirt while Grube was fetching his forgotten ledger, and add it to the collection in Wolfgang's suitcase.

Violet was in a strange mood that evening, jumpy and distracted. Freya was looking for a chance to draw her to one side but Violet seemed to be avoiding everyone. She wouldn't wander among the tables or drink champagne with anyone in the audience, hurrying downstairs as soon as her number was over. After the performance had ended, however, Freya got her chance. Violet lingered in the dressing room and once the other girls had gone, she took Freya's arm and said quietly, 'Can you let me out the back way?'

'What back way?' Freya asked, instantly wary.

'Through the storeroom,' Violet replied. 'I tried the door but it's locked. Come on, don't pretend not to know what I mean. Frau Brodsky showed me those stairs the last time I needed to leave discreetly.'

'Of course,' Freya said. 'I'd forgotten about them for a moment.'

'So this basement is your personal kingdom now?' Violet asked wryly. 'You control the comings and goings?'

Freya snorted, reaching into her pocket for the keys. 'Hardly. Listen, have you heard any rumours about the Zaubergarten? I bumped into Walther Grube this morning and he told me the Nazis are interested in the place. Do you know what's going on?'

'Not exactly,' Violet said, 'but I have a hunch. Let me make some enquiries and see if I'm right.'

Freya unlocked the storeroom door and switched on the light, her eyes flickering immediately to the stack of boxes behind which Wolfgang's suitcase was hidden. Inadequately hidden, as it turned out. Violet followed her gaze and immediately spotted one leather corner. 'What's that?'

'Nothing,' Freya said. 'Just something I'm keeping for a friend. Clothes, that's all.'

She forced herself to look Violet in the face. 'They're Wolfi's, actually.'

Violet gave her an appraising stare. 'Be careful, *kleine* Freya. By the way, I've found out where he is. They've taken him to a concentration camp near Munich. Apparently one of his neighbours turned him in; he had a copy of *The Communist Manifesto* on his bookshelf.'

'And how long will they keep him?' Freya asked as they went upstairs. 'Can I visit, do you think?'

Violet laughed. 'Fat chance of that. They might let him out after a while, though. Wolfi's never been a member of the Communist party and there might be people who can vouch for him.'

'How do you know all this?' Freya asked.

Violet shrugged. 'Friends in high places.' She stood for a moment at the back door, looking out into the night and gathering her coat around her, although it wasn't cold. Abruptly, she turned to Freya and said, 'Do you fancy a nightcap?'

'Why not?' Freya replied after a moment. She still didn't trust Violet, or even particularly like her, but she wanted to keep on her right side and they were allies of a sort – or at least, she hoped they were.

'Just go ahead and make sure the coast is clear, would you?' Violet asked lightly. 'Whistle if you spot anyone lurking.'

With some misgivings, Freya crossed the small yard where dustbins were kept and entered the street that ran parallel to the Zaubergarten's front entrance. Nobody seemed to be about, apart from a stray dog and a boy walking past with his hands in his pockets. She waited until he'd turned the corner, then waved for Violet to join her. Violet led the way through a zigzag of streets to a small, unobtrusive bar, where she chose a table near the back and ordered cherry brandies.

'Is everything all right?' Freya asked. 'You seem a little nervous.'

Violet took a swig of brandy. 'Nothing I can't handle. It's wise for me to keep a low profile at the moment, that's all.' She had one eye trained on the door, Freya noticed. 'In fact, I might not be around for much longer.'

'I'm sorry to hear that,' Freya said.

Violet raised her eyebrows. 'Really? I'd have thought you'd be delighted.'

'Not at all,' Freya protested, as convincingly as she could manage. 'I'd never have met Wolfi if it wasn't for you and it feels like all his friends are disappearing, one by one.'

Violet nodded. 'And now Rupert's off to America.'

'Is he? Strange, he never mentioned that yesterday.' The doubt that had been niggling away at the back of Freya's mind pushed its way to the front. 'Do you happen to know where he lives?'

'I do, as a matter of fact,' Violet replied. 'He has rooms in a house near Savignyplatz. Why do you ask?'

'Only because there's a chance he might have borrowed something of mine,' Freya said. 'I'd like to ask him about it before he goes.'

Violet laughed. 'Rupert's a magpie: he steals shiny things. Well, I wouldn't hang about if I were you.'

'Actually, I might go there now,' Freya said. It was late but she knew Rupert stayed up half the night and slept until midday. 'What's the address?'

Violet drained her glass. 'Wait, I'll show you the way. Sounds like this could be entertaining.'

She set a brisk pace through the streets, seemingly invigorated. Savignyplatz lay about half an hour to the west, with Rupert's house five minutes' walk beyond.

Violet nodded towards a glowing upstairs window. 'Looks like he's still up.'

Freya had been prepared to wake him but she didn't want to disturb the whole house. 'Should we throw some pebbles against the window?' she asked.

Violet shook her head. Walking up to the front door, she took what looked like a nail file out of her pocket and spent a few minutes fiddling with the lock before quietly pushing the door open with impressive ease and turning to Freya, a finger on her lips. Together they crept up the stairs. Violet led the way along a wide landing, stopping by a door on the left through which faint strains of music drifted. She put her ear to the wood, then stood back, smiling with anticipation, and let Freya knock.

Freya pounded on the door. Rupert's plan seemed obvious to her now and she would have rumbled him at the time if she hadn't been so worried about Wolfi. The thought that he could be so deceitful made her blood boil. They heard footsteps approaching before the man himself appeared at the door in a paisley silk dressing-gown, looking understandably wary. He wore a hair net and his face gleamed with some sort of skin cream.

'Evening, Rupert,' she said, insinuating herself through the narrow gap. 'You should have told me you were leaving. I wanted to come around straight away to wish you luck.'

'I'm not off yet,' he said, standing back reluctantly to let her pass. 'But this isn't particularly convenient. I was about to go to bed. Hello, Violet.'

'Don't think you can slope away without a proper sendoff,' Violet said, following Freya into the room.

'I shall be in Berlin for at least another week,' he replied.

'I'll be throwing a party, no need to worry about that, and of course you're both invited.'

Freya looked around the sitting room, comfortably furnished with a sofa, two armchairs, several lamps and layers of soft drapery: rugs, fringed tablecloths, velvet cushions and curtains. Preparations for Rupert's departure had already begun; books were heaped in piles on the floor and a desk in the window was covered with files and folders. She approached for a closer look and quickly rifled through the papers, her back turned to the others, while Violet chatted to Rupert about America. And there it was: the brown envelope containing her typescript, hidden under a newspaper.

'What are you doing with this?' she asked, pulling out the envelope and showing it to Rupert.

'I saved it for you,' he replied, without a second's hesitation. 'There was no time to waste, so after you left for Prinz-Albrecht-Strasse yesterday, I went to Wolfi's apartment and found your manuscript before anyone else could. From what he'd told me, no doubt the Gestapo wouldn't have approved of your storyline. I just wanted to have a quick read before I gave it back.'

'That's kind of you,' Freya said. 'But I'll take it now, if you don't mind.'

'Suit yourself.' Rupert looked at her coldly, thrusting his hands into the pockets of his dressing-gown. 'You might be missing a trick, though. I can show your script to my agent if I think it has potential.'

'That's a risk I'll have to take,' Freya replied, not bothering to be polite. What a fool she'd been! Rupert had always been so kind to her, if a little patronising: asking after her progress, recommending authors she should read, telling her about English culture. She'd admired him and thought they were friends, yet he hadn't had the slightest scruples about pinching her work. He was probably planning to pass it off as his own.

'We'll let you get to your bed then, Rupert.' Violet took Freya's arm. 'Sweet dreams. And remember not to slip away like a thief in the night.'

'As if I would,' he said, guiding them to the door.

'Well, well,' Violet said, when she and Freya were out in the street again. 'Your story must be worth something if Rupert wants to steal it. He has taste, if not morals. Nor talent either, come to that.'

It might have been grudging praise but Freya accepted it happily nonetheless, hugging the envelope to her chest as though it were a precious child. She would look out for herself from now on; no one else was going to. That night, she levered up the loose floorboard beneath her bed and took out the locked cash box containing her savings. (Hardly anyone in Germany trusted the banks anymore.) She'd been working long hours since Frau Brodsky had left, and managed to put aside at least a quarter of her salary each month. Counting her money gave her a sense of security. If she lost her job tomorrow, she could manage for a few weeks, surely long enough to find work and a new home elsewhere. Rupert's appreciation of her manuscript and her courage in confronting him had made her feel she could take on the world. She was not going to give up without a fight, no matter how high the cost.

# Chapter Twenty-One

*Berlin, May 1933*

So the Gestapo had not, after all, got their hands on Freya's account of defiance in the face of Nazi brutality. She was free for the moment to carry on with her secret campaign of resistance: a campaign that gave her life meaning and purpose – despite, she had to admit, making very little difference in the great scheme of things. Early each morning, she would set off in a coat with voluminous pockets and a leather satchel over her shoulder, and rescue as many books as she could manage. Her favourite Jewish bookseller had long since closed, his windows daubed with anti-Semitic graffiti; rumour had it he'd moved to England, and she could only hope that was the case. In his absence, she searched out other bookshops, looking for any piles of forbidden books that might be waiting in some cupboard or back room for collection. Wherever possible, she left money in return for what she had taken, although once a woman ran after her and pressed the note back into her hand.

'I cannot be found to have sold these titles,' she hissed angrily. 'Come around here again and I'll call the police.'

Public libraries were fertile hunting grounds, too, though she had to be particularly careful since there were often officials hanging around and the staff were more suspicious.

'What are you up to?' an officious youth with glasses and pockmarked skin demanded one day, appearing out of nowhere as she crouched beside a crate.

'Just curious,' she said, dropping the copy of Sigmund Freud's *Interpretation of Dreams* she'd been about to slip into her satchel. 'Good riddance to bad rubbish, filthy Jew.' And she spat on the floor for good measure.

The youth nodded, apparently satisfied, but she sensed his eyes on her back as she left the library, walking as quickly as she dared without breaking into a run. Once safely back at the Zaubergarten, she hid her spoils in the storeroom. Wolfgang's suitcase had soon become full, so she'd transferred twenty pairs of tap shoes and top hats from a trunk into a burlap sack to make room for her growing collection. Sometimes she remembered Grube's remark about her place of work being of interest to the Nazis, but the threat was too vague and she couldn't think of another hiding place. These books were under her protection, safe for the time being. What if this copy of Irmgard Keun's latest novel at the bottom of the trunk turned out to be the very last one in existence? One day, she told herself, the Nazis would be gone, Wolfi and so many other prisoners could come home, and she would have made some gesture, no matter how small, to stand up for truth and civilisation. She would no longer turn a blind eye to the terrible things that were happening every day. When windows were smashed and people beaten up on the streets, she would watch and take note, as Leon had asked; she would not pretend she hadn't known, and hate herself for it afterwards.

Yet soon Freya became dissatisfied with these fishing expeditions. Collecting books surreptitiously wasn't enough; she wanted people to be aware of the stand she was taking so they might feel encouraged to protest in some small way themselves. And she wanted the Nazis to know that at least one person couldn't accept what they were doing and was prepared to say so. 'Find your voice and use it,' she heard her mother whisper.

One sleepless night, the line of Heinrich Heine's that Frau Kohl had quoted came back to her: 'Where you burn books, you will in the end burn people.' The next morning, Freya wrote the words in capital letters with a black pen on to a plain white postcard, the sort anyone could buy from a street kiosk, and took it with her when she slipped out of the club. She would leave the card somewhere it could be easily found, in an area far from Schöneberg where she had no connections. Always careful to make sure no one was following her when she went out on these trips, now she was doubly wary. This was an extraordinary risk and perhaps she was mad to consider taking it, but there were only a couple of days left before the book burnings and she had to make a final effort before it was too late.

As she was sitting on a tram heading eastwards through the city, the perfect spot flashed into her mind. She got off at the next stop and walked the rest of the way through the eastern side of Tiergarten and on to the Opernplatz. An ominous wooden pyre was being constructed in the centre of the square, like the gallows awaiting a public execution. Casually, she walked closer. Scaffolding boards and shorter planks of wood criss-crossed in an elaborate structure, about ten feet tall, that Otto would surely have been proud to have designed. A ladder leaned against one side and three or four labourers stood admiring their handiwork, hands on hips. Freya still found it hard to believe this ceremony was actually going to take place; it seemed inconceivable that people would stand around this bonfire to watch the work of so many brilliant minds going up in flames.

'Why do you need all that wood?' she asked one of the workmen.

'Because books are hard to burn,' he replied, taking the stub of a cigarette from behind his ear and lighting it. 'Get the blaze going first and then toss 'em on, that's the way to do it.'

Freya nodded, gazing around the square at the Old Library and the law school next to it. She wondered whether Leon had been watching the bonfire take shape, and whether he might be looking out of the window even now. She had met him at the library once – it must have been at least three years ago – bringing a message from Otto to cancel some outing they'd planned. Any excuse to see Leon had been welcome. He'd shown her around the library as if she had a right to be there, and the future had seemed so bright and full of promise. Anyone wanting to use the library had to show their green student pass but Leon had told her to tell the guard she'd forgotten hers and slip him a couple of marks to enter.

This time, the official by the turnstile at the library entrance didn't even need a bribe. When she approached with her most winning smile and trotted out her excuse, he nodded her through with a bored jerk of the head. Keeping her head down, she followed a group of students along the marble corridor as though she knew where she were going, although she could remember very little of the library's layout. Glimpses through doors to the right and left showed rooms lined with bookshelves from floor to ceiling, but none of these places seemed appropriate for what she had in mind as they were well-staffed and busy, and it would soon become obvious she had no reason to be there. She would walk about the library to get the lie of the land, she told herself, and if necessary, she could just walk right out again.

The students were mostly male, with a few women striding confidently among them. Freya watched them enviously, wondering whether they knew how fortunate they were. Several of the young men wore brown shirts with swastika emblems, aping those of the stormtroopers, and must have been members of the Nazi Students' Union. They had no business being in a library at all, she thought, her fingers closing over the card in her pocket.

A pair of double doors stood open at the end of the corridor, and beyond them was a large hall, filled with row upon row of gleaming mahogany desks, each with two chairs side by side and a shared lamp and inkwell stand in the centre. A plaque on the wall announced, 'Reading Room. Silence, please!' Freya followed an older woman through – a lecturer, perhaps – and stood on the threshold, looking about. Around half the desks were occupied with students, most reading or making notes from piles of books open in front of them. A couple, she noticed, were asleep with their heads on their elbows. Only a scratching of pens and the odd cough disturbed the quiet. Her heart thumped so loudly that she was sure someone would hear and her legs trembled. It wasn't too late: she could sit down and read for a while before heading back to the Zaubergarten. But then how would she feel? Summoning all her resolve, she picked up a book that was due to be reshelved from a nearby table and carried it to a seat at one of the empty desks in the middle of the room.

She had ended up with a weighty tome that described the Prussian criminal code of 1851 in more detail than anyone could ever have imagined necessary. Freya sat looking at it, turning the odd page every so often and thinking about the kind of life she would have had if she'd been born a boy, with the chance to study in a place like this. After half an hour or so, her heart had gone back to beating with its usual rhythm and her breathing had calmed. Glancing casually around, she retrieved the postcard with its stark inscription from her pocket, leaned across the desk to turn off the lamp and, in one swift movement, propped the card against the stand. Then she closed the book, her actions measured and deliberate, picked up her satchel and turned to leave.

A blond youth in a brown shirt was standing almost immediately behind her, ready to take the seat she was about to vacate. 'Excuse me,' he said politely as she took a step back, half paralysed with fear, the blood rushing into her cheeks.

He was looking at her curiously when – either by accident or design, she didn't know which – the book she was holding fell from her grip and tumbled noisily to the floor. The boy tutted in alarm and bent to retrieve it. Coming to life at last, Freya reached for the card on the lampstand and crammed it back in her pocket.

'You should be more careful,' the youth said sternly, straightening up and smoothing the book's pages before returning it to her. 'This is a valuable edition.'

She mumbled an apology and turned away, forcing herself to walk at a normal pace to the exit, where she replaced the book on the table for reshelving. No one was about; the doorway was empty and a quick look over her shoulder confirmed nobody had followed her or was watching her now. This could not be the end of it: she wouldn't go back to Schöneberg having failed in her mission. She dropped the postcard with its neat black capitals in the centre of the table and left the reading room, joining the stream of students going about their business. As she slipped out of the library into the square, she wondered how soon the card would be discovered, and whether the first person to see it would look away, pretending not to have noticed, because even to read such a subversive statement was inviting a whole host of trouble.

That afternoon, Franz Schwartz announced he was leaving the Zaubergarten. Two extraordinary things had happened: he had been granted a visa to emigrate to the United States, and his relationship with the American screenwriter was still going strong. They would be travelling to Hamburg in a few days' time, and catching a boat from there to New York, before travelling on to California.

'Your friend Rupert's coming with us,' he told Freya, 'but you probably knew that already.'

'I didn't, actually,' she replied. There had still been no word of Rupert's promised farewell party. 'Well, I'm pleased for you, Franz, but I shall miss you very much.'

'Dear Freya,' he said, hugging her. 'Why don't you come, too? Go to the embassy today and start the process. It'll take months but Grant will be happy to sponsor you.'

'I'm not leaving. Write and tell me how you get on, though – you know where I'll be.' Such misplaced confidence!

'Then you should think about looking for another job,' Franz told her. 'This place is on its last legs. I haven't even been able to get hold of Herr Goldstein to tell him I'm going so Kurt will have to run the bar tomorrow night. At least find somewhere else to sleep. It's not safe for you here alone.'

Freya's thoughts turned immediately to her collection of books in the storeroom. She'd been in a fever since returning from the Opernplatz that morning, giddy with terror and exhilaration, and now fear threatened to get the upper hand. But she took a breath, straightened her spine and said, 'Don't worry about me, Franz. I'll be fine.'

Violet was later than usual for the evening's performance and eventually it became clear she wasn't going to turn up at all. Gisela – who was now supervising the dancers, much to Perle's irritation – merely shrugged her shoulders and gave a solo spot to her favourite among the new girls. Apparently she had always thought Violet's performance undisciplined and overrated.

Freya had mixed feelings about Violet's departure. There was no denying life was more interesting with the English girl around, but it was just as well for Leon's sake that she was leaving – and for Freya's, too, since Violet might well decide to investigate that mysterious suitcase of Wolfgang's in the storeroom. Wolfi was a friend of hers, in theory, and she wouldn't want to incriminate him further, but she might have been glad of a chance to take revenge on Freya. Life was precarious enough without that added complication.

Time was running out: in a couple of days, book burnings were due to take place across the country, so Freya decided to distribute several postcards in one go. The next morning, she left the Zaubergarten through the back entrance just as Schöneberg was waking up, walked up to Nollendorfplatz and took a tram heading north through the city. A light rain was falling. If the cards became wet, she thought, no one would be able to decipher them, and even if they could, they might dismiss her message as the work of a crackpot. The Nazis would seize the cards as soon as they were found, and only one or two passers-by might have seen them before then. Was this whole mad escapade nothing but a pointless gesture? Absolutely not, her mother's voice replied; Freya was lighting a fuse and even if the spark only reached one other person, that was enough.

Half an hour later, she got off the tram, pulled her hat low and turned up her coat collar to walk another mile to the Technical University, where Otto studied. What if she ran into him there? The thought of how he'd react to what she was doing made her smile, even as her heart pounded. The architecture of this building was as impressive as those around the Opernplatz, with a sweeping circular drive in front of the main entrance. Freya had visited a couple of times, for a public lecture and then a prize-giving ceremony, and could roughly remember the layout. It was early still, and not many people were about. Opening a side door off the main corridor at random, she found an empty lecture hall with seats arranged in ascending tiers. Closing the door behind her, she walked to a lectern in the middle on which she propped one of her cards, then ran up the steps to the back of the room and out through the rear door into a smaller passage, which took her on a winding route down some stairs to a side exit and out into the damp, quiet day.

It had been so easy, the work of a moment! Her mind raced ahead as she walked towards the Tiergarten park. She would carry on distributing cards around the city, even after the book burnings had taken place. There were all kinds of messages she could write, and other people might be inspired to protest in the same way; so many must feel as she did but not know how to translate those feelings into action. Even if she were caught, the movement would continue. The thought of being discovered made her stop for a moment and cling to a nearby railing, breathless. She would be sent to one of the concentration camps that were springing up all over the place, and quite possibly tortured, if not killed. The Nazis wouldn't tolerate any opposition, no matter how mild. Yet she'd gone too far to turn back now. Her small postcard bombs were worth the risk.

Rain dripped mournfully from the trees in Tiergarten and her boots crunched along paths shining wet. She'd planned her route the night before: a straight line that would take her through the park, passing the Victory Column topped by a bronze winged statue overlooking the city, then out by the Brandenburg Gate and along Unter den Linden to the Opernplatz. The symmetry pleased her. She'd wondered about climbing to the viewing platform near the top of the Column and leaving a card there, but she'd have to queue for a ticket and the space would be confined and probably crowded. Instead she wandered around the base until she was alone, then knelt to place her message against one of the huge granite columns. Running steps nearby and a child's cry made her jump to her feet, but luckily the mother chasing an escaping toddler was too fraught to pay her any attention.

She carried on through the park, glancing behind every so often to make sure she wasn't being followed. Her breath came fast as she walked by the Brandenburg Gate, dodging the inevitable sightseers, then past the green-roofed Hotel Adlon with its uniformed doormen and line of idling limousines, like gleaming black sharks. She was in the heart of official Berlin, the burned-out Reichstag building only half a mile away. In the cold light of day, her plan to leave a postcard somewhere near the Gate seemed far too risky. She would, though, look for a spot at the site of the bonfire. This was where an act of desecration would take place the next day, where the values by which she lived and her hopes for the future would go up in flames.

The wooden pyre loomed uncompromisingly in the centre of the square. The workmen and their ladder had gone, replaced by a single guard who strolled at a leisurely pace around the structure's perimeter with a rifle over his shoulder. Freya stood under an arched entrance to the opera house, assessing the situation. The guard's circuit took about thirty seconds; it would be hard to place her card and get away without attracting his attention. She decided to cross to the law school and watch from a closer vantage point. There were only a few other people walking by and they kept to the outer edge of the square; she felt as vulnerable setting off into the centre as if she were naked. Rows of windows looked down from every side, and she had to remind herself that nobody would be taking any notice of her, and that even if anyone did happen to spot her solitary figure, they wouldn't be able to see her face under the hat she wore.

Just as she was passing the bonfire on her left, an opportunity suddenly presented itself. Another armed figure approached from the direction of the library, and the guard walked some distance away to meet him. As they exchanged salutes and cries of *'Heil, Hitler!'* Freya changed direction, swerving towards the structure, her hand already reaching for the postcard in her pocket. She was about to spear it over a splintered branch sticking out waist high when a voice from somewhere behind her cried, 'Hey, you! Stop right there!'

She caught a glimpse of a figure in a brown shirt and black trousers before she started to run, panic shooting through her body, with this person racing in hot pursuit and gaining ground every second, she could tell from the sound of his boots and his breath, until it seemed he would only have to reach out to grab her. She was tiring quickly, a stitch burning in her side. The law school wasn't far now but she had no chance of reaching it; would it be better to stop and fight? For a second she wondered whether there was enough time to chew and swallow the postcards in her pocket and she was about to stuff one in her mouth when she heard a scuffle close by, the footsteps now staggering and sliding rather than chasing, and thumps and groans of pain. Before she could turn to see what was happening, her arms were pinioned by her sides and she found herself virtually lifted off her feet and half-dragged, half-carried towards the building. A door was opened by an unseen hand and she was thrust inside, the door slamming shut behind her and bolts scraped into place.

# Chapter Twenty-Two

*Berlin, May 1933*

Freya clenched her fists, but the girl who stood before her didn't seem inclined to fight; she merely stared back coldly. She had shoulder-length dark hair and wore khaki trousers with the hems rolled up around her ankles and a grey checked shirt. Grasping Freya's arm, she pulled her down the corridor, muttering, 'Don't draw any more attention to yourself, if you can possibly manage that.'

They were followed by the person who'd bundled Freya into the law school: a young man who seemed somehow familiar. He was breathing hard, and revealed a head of ginger hair when he took off his cap to wipe the sweat from his forehead.

'But what about . . .?' Freya asked, glancing over her shoulder at the door into the square, where someone was presumably getting beaten up on her behalf.

The girl shook her head. 'Josef can look after himself. Let's hope so, anyway.'

Freya wasn't in a position to argue. The three of them walked briskly along the hall into a wider passage, where knots of people hurried to and fro. She kept her eyes down, listening out for any alarm that might be raised, her heart still beating frantically. She had no idea where she was being taken or why she should have been rescued – if that was indeed what was happening – but her only option now was to do as she was told. They hurried along the main corridor until they'd reached the end, then ran up several flights of stairs on the left, the girl peering anxiously down the stairwell as they went. She took them through a door on the right and along a circuitous route of passages and internal steps, sometimes doubling back on themselves, until they were near the top of the building and approaching a landing with a door in the centre. They had passed fewer and fewer people along the way, and now they were quite alone. Glancing around to make sure, the girl walked up to the door and unlocked it with a key from her pocket. The lintel was so low that Freya had to duck as she was pushed through.

She found herself in a long, narrow attic in the eaves, its massive beams interlocking just above her head. The place was cold and dusty, and her eyes took a while to adjust to the shadows. What light there was filtered through knee-high windows set in the outer walls and chinks in the roof tiles. The floor was mostly boarded, with the occasional joist to stumble over. Freya followed the girl as she threaded her way to the left through crates, filing cabinets and random pieces of furniture until they had reached the corner of the building. The next section of the attic was less crowded with junk, although the sloping ceiling was lower, so they had to watch their step. A couple of armchairs were placed by a window halfway along, and someone levered themselves out of one as they approached. It was Leon.

'You made it! Thank God,' he said, embracing her briefly.

'At some cost,' muttered the girl in khaki trousers. 'Do we know what's happened to Josef?'

Leon turned to her. 'They've given him a beating but they let him go. You know Josef, he'll have spun them some story about getting the wrong end of the stick and protecting a damsel in distress. The main thing is, nobody seems to have seen where you went, or followed you either.'

'What about the guards?' the ginger-haired boy asked, and Freya suddenly realised where she'd seen him before: sitting on the bed in Leon's room, that morning she'd rushed to the Kohls' apartment.

'They were too far away,' Leon replied, 'and focused on Josef. By the time they'd worked out what had happened, the pair of you were long gone.'

The girl raised her eyebrows. 'Well, that's a miracle we didn't deserve.' She turned to Freya. 'What were you doing there in the first place? And why the hell did you run?'

Three pairs of eyes were fixed on her, waiting. Slowly, she drew the postcards out of her pocket and held them out. The red-headed boy whistled, and the girl clicked her tongue in irritation.

'Come, Magda,' Leon said. 'We're on the same side.'

'Yes, but she's putting us all at risk.' The girl glared at Freya. 'And now the brownshirts will be doubling security around the fire, so thanks for nothing.'

Freya glanced around the confined space. The attic had been set up for a prolonged stay: she noticed a mattress with a sleeping bag and pillow further along, some plates and mugs, a camping stove and a jerry can of water next to a crate of food supplies. A pair of binoculars lay beside the armchairs. 'What are you planning?' she asked.

Leon hesitated. 'I can't tell you,' he replied, as she'd known he would. 'But you mustn't come here again. Do you understand? This is important.'

'Wait a minute,' Magda said, narrowing her black eyes at Freya. 'Egon spotted you yesterday, too. Did you leave one of these cards in the library? The Gestapo were crawling all over the place.'

'Yes, I did.' Freya lifted her chin. 'I'm sorry if I interfered with whatever you're trying to do, but since Leon wouldn't tell me what that was, I couldn't possibly have known.' She'd had enough of being interrogated by this hostile creature who got to spend hours a day closeted with Leon – her Leon, who was determined to keep her in the dark. Yet her postcards seemed naïve and foolish now, and dropping one by the bonfire, the idea of a lunatic.

'Of course you couldn't,' Leon said. 'You've been very brave, Freya. Now, if you can stay here until we're sure the coast is clear, I'll take you back downstairs.'

He was humouring her as though she were a child, which was worse than Magda's animosity. Freya bit her tongue and, studiously ignoring the other girl, knelt by the window to look down on the square. Two guards were now stationed at the wooden pyre, which the next day would be lighting up the night sky as thousands of books burned. The Nazis were setting her world on fire and there was nothing she could do about it.

There was still no sign of Violet as the girls prepared for the evening's performance, which left Freya feeling even more unsettled. She was afraid for Leon and bitterly regretted having made his life more dangerous. He had hugged her before they parted that morning, telling her to be careful, and she was left with an overwhelming dread that they might never see each other again. Before she went to bed, she unlocked the storeroom and spent some time sitting on the floor, browsing her books for comfort. The writers felt like friends and she would not abandon them. The American author Helen Keller had written an open letter to the Nazi students, published in *The New York Times* and reproduced in German newspapers that afternoon. 'History has taught you nothing if you think you can kill ideas,' it had begun, which would have made the perfect message to share on Freya's postcards, were she to carry on distributing them. The shock of so nearly being caught had made her think twice about that.

She hadn't been planning to attend the book burning in the first place, so Leon's request – more of an order, really – that she should keep away from Opernplatz was easy to obey. Werner, Herr Goldstein's assistant, had announced the night before that the Zaubergarten would be closed the following evening, in view of the celebrations. Celebrations? Freya was in no mood for a party. After a restless night, she spent a quiet morning mending and doing the laundry. She was distracting herself in the afternoon by hemming a new set of dirndls (the Nazis were keen on traditional dress) when she heard the front door open, followed by footsteps and voices on the floor above. This was alarming: the cleaner had left hours ago and, as far as she knew, she was alone in the club. Arming herself with a pair of scissors, she ran upstairs – to find Maxim Fischer and Walther Grube standing by the bar.

'Herr Fischer, may I present Fräulein Amsel?' Grube said, when they had exchanged salutes and Heil Hitlers. 'She is the young lady I mentioned who lives on the premises.'

'We know each other by sight,' Fischer said smoothly, 'though we've never been formally introduced.' Freya shook his cold hand, her stomach churning. 'You'll be pleased to know the Zaubergarten will reopen in a few days' time under new direction,' he went on. 'I shall be appointing a general manager shortly, but Herr Grube will be taking immediate control of the accounts and making an inventory, starting tomorrow. You must answer any questions he might have.'

'Of course,' Freya murmured, and Grube gave her one of his ghastly smiles, his eyes gleaming.

'Herr Grube has vouched for you,' Fischer went on, 'so I'm sure you'll work well together. You may continue in your current accommodation, at least for the time being. Goodbye for now, Fräulein Amsel. No doubt I shall see you again soon.'

Freya had been dismissed. She went back downstairs, her legs shaking, to sit over her work while straining to hear the murmur of conversation overhead. It had finally happened, then, the Aryanisation that Walther Grube had mentioned. She was glad Frau Brodsky wasn't there to see it and that Franz Schwartz would soon be leaving, but what could have happened to Herr Goldstein? For a moment, she wished Violet were there, to tell her what was going on – if even Violet knew. Was this takeover the reason why she had to lie low? Or had her relationship with Maxim Fischer ended badly? So many questions which would never be answered.

Then suddenly a phrase of Fischer's came back to her: 'Herr Grube will be making an inventory, starting tomorrow,' and her blood ran cold.

At that moment the front door slammed and she jumped up, weak with relief: they had gone. Before she could reach the storeroom, however, she heard the ominous sound of someone descending the stairs, and a few seconds later, Walther Grube appeared in the dressing room.

'Remember what I told you, Fräulein Amsel?' he said, walking towards her and pulling out a chair. 'The Zaubergarten has been badly managed for months, if not years, but now we have a chance to put things right.' He sat down, rubbing his hands as though about to start work there and then. 'I'm glad to have been able to tell Herr Fischer that you're a trustworthy employee.'

'Thank you, Herr Grube,' Freya said, twisting aside her knees under the table to avoid his. He was sitting uncomfortably close.

'Please, call me Walther.' He smiled. 'We have known each other for a while, and now we shall be working together. You must be my eyes and ears on the ground, keep me informed of morale among the troops, so to speak. Will you do that?'

'Of course – to the best of my ability.' She could think of nothing worse than being Grube's spy, but then the whole idea of working for Maxim Fischer and his new, no-doubt Nazi manager filled her with horror.

Grube looked around, smoothing his hands along his shiny-trousered legs. Half the dressing room was taken up with Freya's work table and sewing machine, and the walls were now entirely covered with layers of costumes hanging from hooks. 'So this is where the magic begins,' he said. 'It's a little untidy, if you don't mind me saying so.'

'I've been rather busy since Frau Brodsky left,' Freya told him, her resentment growing. 'The two of us used to manage the wardrobe together, and now there's just me.'

'Discipline and order, that's what you need.' Grube got to his feet and wandered about, arranging shoes in pairs, tidying hairpins into pots and replacing the lids on jars. What was he after?

'Forgive me, Herr Grube,' Freya began (she still couldn't call him Walther), 'but I need to finish these dresses today. May we have a proper discussion tomorrow? Unless you have any urgent questions, that is.'

She caught a flicker of anger in his eyes. 'I should like to see your room,' he said abruptly. 'I need to assess its value and suitability.'

Freya's stomach lurched. She stood, keeping hold of the scissors in her apron pocket. 'Of course. It's just through here.'

They walked through the dressing room to the door at the back, which Freya opened before standing aside. Grube entered and looked about, hands clasped behind his back. Her room was such a pathetically barren cell that Freya felt oddly ashamed. Her bed was neatly made, thank goodness, her clothes put away in the chest and her typewriter in its case. Her notebook, as always, was hidden between the mattress and the bed frame, and her typescript lay safely in her top drawer. A copy of *The Count of Monte Cristo* sat on the nightstand, which was innocuous enough. The books she loved most lay hidden in the trunk next door.

'And where does this lead?' Grube asked, approaching the storeroom door and trying the handle.

'To a store cupboard, for props and suchlike,' Freya replied.

'Well, we can investigate tomorrow,' Grube said. He stood there, making no move to leave, and then he sat on the bed and patted the mattress beside him. 'Come closer, Freya. You are always so reserved. Why don't we get to know each other better?'

Sickened, Freya shrank back, clutching the scissors more tightly. She'd sensed all along that this was what he'd been leading up to, and nothing on earth would make her enter that room. 'No,' she blurted. 'I'm sorry, I can't.'

'You can't?' Grube repeated, dropping the false smile. 'That's a shame. I'm quite offended, given all the trouble I've taken on your behalf.'

And suddenly he was looming in front of her, seizing her

wrist and twisting it back so the scissors she was holding clattered to the floor. She screamed as he threw her down on the bed, kicked out and tried to punch him with her free arm. It was hopeless: he was far too strong and determined.

'You think you're so much better than everyone else,' he snarled, his face inches from hers, 'when you're nothing but a common dressmaker. You aren't even pretty!'

Drops of his saliva landed on her cheek and his breath was stale. She jabbed her fingers in his eyes, and as he drew back, roaring, she made a desperate attempt to wriggle out from underneath his body. She'd managed to get both legs off the bed before he grabbed her hair, drew back her head and slapped her across the face with such force that her ears rang.

'Little tart,' he growled, wrenching at the belt of his jacket with one hand as he held her by the throat with the other. 'I'm going to teach you a lesson you won't forget, Miss High and Mighty.'

She wrenched at his fingers, screaming – and then suddenly, extraordinarily, their pressure eased, and Grube was rearing up to look through the open door. She couldn't see what had made him let go of her, but she heard footsteps running towards them, and a man shouting, 'Stop! I have a gun! I've called the police!'

Grube flung her down and got off the bed, breathing hard. Adjusting his clothing, he walked out of the room, pushing past whoever had come to save her.

It was Franz Schwartz. 'My God, Freya!' he cried, picking her up. 'Are you all right? Who was that man? Did he . . .?'

Freya couldn't speak for a moment. She shook her head, massaging her neck, and eventually croaked, 'No, but he was about to. Thank you, Franz.'

He held her tight, rubbing her back and murmuring

words of comfort. When she'd recovered a little, she asked, 'What are you doing here? I thought you'd already gone.'

'I came to say goodbye,' he replied. 'We leave tomorrow. Freya, do you know the man who attacked you? Is there any chance he could come back? You can't stay here a minute longer.'

'You're right,' she said – although where could she go? Well, she would have to think about that later.

'I didn't really call the police, although maybe I should have,' he said. 'Do you want me to telephone now?'

Freya shook her head. 'What good would that do? Grube's a Nazi, he can act as he pleases.'

Franz actually did have a gun, unlikely as that seemed. He passed it to her and said, 'Then you must have this. I can't take it out of the country so you'd be doing me a favour.'

Patiently, he showed her how to hold the pistol in both hands and aim, how the safety catch worked, and how to load and empty the bullets. 'I can't imagine ever using it,' she told Franz. 'But thank you anyway.'

'Look after yourself, dear girl,' he said, hugging her. 'And come to California as soon as you can. Stay with a friend tonight. Grant and I will be at Rupert's since we're all off first thing tomorrow, or I'd invite you over to ours.'

'I'll be fine,' Freya promised, with more assurance than she felt.

She and Franz went upstairs together to make sure Grube had gone. Franz poured them each a brandy from the bar which they drank standing up, and then he left, and she was alone. She closed her eyes for a moment, driving her fingernails into her palms. Later, there would be time to think about what Grube had done to her. For now, she had a more urgent problem to solve, and if she panicked, all was lost.

# Chapter Twenty-Three

*Berlin, May 1933*

'Please, Leon. It won't take long, just an hour or so. I can't think of anyone else to ask.'

He frowned. 'To move some luggage? Can't Werner help you?'

'The club is closed today and I need someone I can trust,' Freya told him. 'If anyone finds that trunk, I'm in serious trouble.'

'So where are you taking it?'

She bit her lip. 'That's the thing. I need to find another hiding place – or maybe we can just dump it somewhere.' Her nerve had gone. Walther Grube would be delighted to punish her for his humiliation, and hoarding banned books would see her locked away for years.

'I won't ask what's inside,' Leon said, 'as long as you promise it isn't a dead body?'

Freya smiled and shook her head. 'Nothing like that. I'm sorry, I can see you're keen to get going but I'm desperate.'

It had taken her a while to summon the courage to venture out from the club, with the gun Franz Schwartz had given her strapped in a holster around her waist. Even pulling the trigger seemed inconceivable, but its solid weight reassured her. She had come to the Kohls' apartment on the off-chance Leon might be there, or if not, that his mother might know where he was. She'd wondered about looking for him at the law faculty, but her chances of finding the attic room again were slim and Leon had ordered her specifically to stay away. Thankfully, she'd caught him at home, packing to leave the city. He didn't tell her where he was heading and she knew better than to ask. He was clearly preoccupied, and Frau Kohl was similarly anxious and tight-lipped. Freya felt guilty about bothering them at such a time, and if there had been any other alternative, she would never have done so. Leon was her last resort. How would she manage without him?

'I'll wait in the courtyard till you're ready,' she said. 'Thanks, Leon. I can't tell you how grateful I am.'

Fifteen minutes later, he appeared: grim-faced, with a haversack over his shoulder. They took a tram part of the way back to Schöneberg and walked the rest. Leon wore a cap and kept his head down, avoiding anyone's gaze, and she did the same. They didn't speak. Approaching the Zaubergarten by the rear entrance, Freya's heart began to pound and her throat became constricted. What if Walther Grube had come back? He had keys and could let himself in whenever he wanted. Franz was right: she couldn't spend another night in this place. She'd find a cheap hotel for tonight and start looking for a room the next day. Once they'd dealt with the books and her mind was clear, she'd make a plan.

'I'll go first,' she told Leon, unlocking the back door, and locking it again behind them once they were inside. She made a quick sweep of the ground floor, her hand on the gun barrel. It was empty, as far as she could see, waiting for the chandeliers to blaze and the still, dusty air to fill with music and laughter. Dear Lord, but she would miss this place. She opened the unobtrusive door and led the way down the back staircase, straight into the storeroom.

'Wait here,' she whispered to Leon, and tiptoed through to her bedroom. The rumpled blankets told their own story, and for a second she was back there, defenceless, with Grube grinding her body beneath his. She could feel his suffocating weight and the white heat of his rage, and for a second she thought she might faint. Taking a few deep breaths, she walked on into the dressing room. It was similarly deserted. Leon is here and you have a gun, she reminded herself; nothing bad is going to happen.

'All clear,' she said, returning to the storeroom.

Leon had taken the suitcase into the middle of the room and thrown open the lid. 'Oh, Freya,' he said, looking at its contents. 'You don't do things by halves, do you?'

'And there's this,' she said, moving aside a couple of boxes and dragging out the trunk. 'More of the same, as you can see. I can't get it up the stairs by myself, but if you help me, we could take it out through the back door and load it on to the porter's trolley. I can probably manage by myself from there, actually.'

'Why have you collected all these books?' Leon asked. 'What were you planning on doing with them?'

Freya shrugged. She didn't even know anymore. 'I wanted to save them. It seemed important to make a stand and this was all I could think of. I'm not sorry, Leon. You once said we'd each have to find our own way, and this is mine. Better than nothing, isn't it?'

He smiled, but so sadly she could hardly bear it. 'I know somewhere we could take them. I have the keys to an empty apartment not far from here. They'd be safe there for a while, at least – as long as nobody ambushes us along the way.'

Freya knew instantly the place he had in mind: an apartment with a blue door, on the corner of a parade of shops. 'Thank you,' she said. 'That sounds perfect. I'll get the trolley in place upstairs.'

She flung open the storeroom door – and gasped. On the other side stood a Nazi in brown uniform, a khaki cap pulled low over his forehead. She stood there, frozen with horror, and the man laughed. It was Walther Grube. He grabbed her around the waist, turned her around and pushed her back into the room, slamming the door behind them. Leon bunched his fists but it was an unequal struggle; in three strides, Grube had reached him, drawn a baton and winded him with a single blow to the stomach, followed by two vicious punches to the jaw that left Leon semi-conscious on the floor. Grube's fist gleamed with brass knuckle dusters and his eyes shone with bloodlust as he kicked Leon's prone body.

'Leave him alone!' Freya screamed, launching herself forward.

Grube slapped her twice in quick succession, once on each cheek, then wrenched her arm behind her back and held it there as he hissed in her ear, 'You and I have unfinished business, don't we, Fräulein?'

Taking a pair of handcuffs from his pocket, he snapped one half around Leon's wrist, dragged him across the floor, towing Freya behind him, and locked the other cuff to the pipes that ran from floor to ceiling. Leon groaned, writhing with his knees to his chest, and spat a bloody tooth from his mouth.

Walking over to the trunk, Grube flipped open the lid with his baton and looked inside. 'Ha, I knew it! You didn't fool me for a second. I'm assuming these books were never going to end up on the bonfire tonight. Well, I shall take them there myself later. But first, I'm going to have a little fun before I turn you in.'

Leisurely, he unbuckled his belt, unknotted his khaki tie and took off his jacket, which he draped over a stack of boxes. Underneath he wore a thin singlet, and the muscles bulged in his pale arms. He was standing between Freya and the door, and was quick and lithe as a cat; she had no chance of getting past him.

'You'll be glad to hear that there's no chance of us being disturbed,' he went on. 'I've bolted the doors from the inside and we're quite alone, the three of us. Shall we go into your bedroom, Fräulein, or do you think your friend Herr Kohl would like to watch us here?'

Leon let out a roar. He pulled himself upright, holding on to the pipes, and lunged impotently towards Grube, who laughed again. He still had a smile on his face when Freya raised the gun, holding it in both hands as Franz had taught her, and squeezed the trigger. With a flash of light and a crack that sounded ear-splitting in the confined space, the pistol jumped in her clenched fingers and a jolt travelled all the way up her arm. She couldn't even tell whether she'd hit Grube, although how could she have missed, at virtually point-blank range? He stared at her in disbelief, his smile fading. When he raised a hand to his shoulder, she saw blood oozing between his fingers. He looked at them in wonder, then came to life: snarling as he threw himself towards her.

She stepped back, aimed at his chest and fired again, and then once more to make sure. Grube staggered a couple of paces before dropping to the floor, his body dropping like a felled tree. His head rolled to one side, and he lay without moving.

The storeroom still rang with the echoes of those three deafening shots, like ripples spreading over the surface of a pond. Leon stared at Freya, his eyes wide. She replaced the safety catch on the gun, her fingers trembling, and put it back in the holster around her waist. I have killed a man, she told herself, but the fact was impossible to comprehend. What frightened her as much as anything was the momentary sense of power and excitement that had flooded her body when Grube had fallen. Was she no better than a Nazi? She walked to his body and crouched beside it. His face was blank, emptied of all expression, his eyes fixed and unseeing. She tried not to look at the scarlet mess of his torso as she felt gingerly in his trouser pockets for the handcuff key.

'Try the jacket,' Leon said, his voice low and indistinct.

Grube's outer jacket pockets contained another pair of knuckle dusters, a neatly folded white handkerchief, a letter in a handwritten envelope that she didn't want to open, and a set of door keys. She searched the inner breast pocket and found a couple of smaller keys on a ring, along with his Nazi party membership card and a photograph of a boy with white hair, aged around ten, sitting on a doorstep between his parents. Freya didn't like to look at that, either; she couldn't think of Grube as somebody's son. She took the keys over to Leon and attempted to fit one with shaking fingers into the minuscule lock on the handcuff. Eventually the cuff snapped open and he rubbed his wrist.

'Are you all right?' Freya asked. His lip was split and swollen, and blood was caking along the cut on his jaw.

He nodded, looking at her with an expression she couldn't make out. Before he could speak, they heard a crash of breaking glass on the floor above, followed by the sound of a bolt being drawn back. Freya reached for the gun at her waist but her hand hovered above the holster; she was afraid of what she might do. Footsteps advanced down the stairs. There was nowhere to hide the bloody corpse on the floor, no time even to throw a blanket over it, so she waited, as if in a dream, to see who would be revealed when the door swung open.

'Dear God!' Violet exclaimed, taking in the scene. She was holding a gun herself, Freya noticed, and wearing a raincoat over a tweed suit. 'What the hell happened here? And who is that?'

'Walther Grube,' Freya replied. 'He was going to turn us in, so I shot him.'

'In the circumstances, that might be just as well.' Violet put the gun back in her coat pocket and looked down at Grube's body. 'Not bad for a first attempt: thorough, if lacking in finesse.' She turned to Leon. 'I've come to tell you the game's up. The brownshirts found that little surprise you left in the bonfire and raided the attic. Egon picked up a tail last night. They took him in and he must have cracked because there's a warrant out for your arrest. Grube would have been the hero of the hour if he'd brought you back.'

Leon's face had turned deathly pale. 'What about Magda?' he asked hoarsely. 'And Josef?'

'I assume they're on the run,' Violet answered. 'And so should you be, though heaven knows how far you'll make it.'

'How did you know I was here?' he asked.

'Your mother told me,' Violet said. 'She took some persuading but eventually she realised I'm on your side.'

'Are you though?' Freya said. 'How do we know that?'

Violet laughed. 'You'll have to take my word for it – apart from the fact I'm not marching you down to the nearest police station.' She frowned. 'But we're wasting time. If we don't dispose of your friend here, and quickly, you'll be joining Leon on the Most Wanted list.'

Freya was to make several difficult and dangerous journeys throughout her life, but this had to be the most surreal. She walked arm in arm with Violet, while a Nazi brownshirt wheeling a porter's trolley piled high with luggage followed behind. None of them spoke. Rain was falling steadily and she wondered whether the bonfire would stay alight or even catch fire in this weather. The ceremony might have to be postponed and Goebbels would never get to make his speech about purifying German culture. She remembered Walther Grube proudly sharing his inside knowledge and her gut clenched. She hated the man, viscerally, but taking his life would change hers for ever.

Violet was in charge of the situation, which was fine with Freya; Leon, too, apparently. We're amateurs, Freya thought, watching the English girl decide what needed to be done. She was the professional, and it seemed ridiculous that Freya could ever have thought of her as nothing more than a cabaret dancer. After she had stripped Grube of his trousers, watch, cap and boots, she told the other two to help her empty the trunk of books.

'What shall we do with them?' Freya had asked, her arms full.

'That's the least of our worries,' Violet had replied, glancing up as she crouched by the trunk. 'You could dump them in Herr Goldstein's office, I suppose. He's in Switzerland so he won't care.'

And that's what Freya had done, adding Wolfi's books from the suitcase to the pile. Repeated trips upstairs made her nervous but she reminded herself the club's main entrance at the front was bolted from the inside, and Violet would deal with anyone who tried to enter through the back. When she returned from the last sortie, Leon was holding Grube under the arms, his head lolling grotesquely to one side, while Violet grasped his knees. Freya looked away as they wrestled his body into the trunk, breathing heavily over the various thuds and crunching of bone.

'He's stiffening up,' Violet had muttered. 'Press his head down, Leon. For God's sake, he's already dead – you're not going to hurt him.'

It had been a tight squeeze but they'd at last managed to force the lid shut and stood back.

'We'd better wait till it's dark,' Violet had said. 'That's only a couple of hours, and with a bit of luck, everyone will be so taken up with this ridiculous book burning, they won't pay so much attention to us. What are you going to do, Freya? Stay here or come with us?'

'I don't know,' she replied, dazed. 'Come with you, I suppose.'

'Then you'd better pack a few things,' Violet said. 'No one will be looking for you. Not yet, anyway. I can give you some money for a train ticket but that's it, I'm afraid. I shouldn't even be here.'

'I thought you were meant to be back in England already,' Leon said, rousing himself.

'I was,' Violet replied. 'But they owe me a few days' leave and I knew you'd need some help. I'll be going home with the ambassador's party tomorrow. There's a new chap arriving to take over so some of the staff are changing.'

They held each other's gaze for what seemed like a long time, and Freya excused herself to start packing in case they wanted privacy. Where could she go? It would have to be a big city, where no one would be curious about a young girl turning up out of the blue. She had a second cousin in Munich; perhaps he would take her in to start off with. Or maybe she would make her way to Hamburg and apply for a visa to America, as Franz Schwartz had suggested. Will I have to keep running all my life? she wondered, throwing some underwear into Wolfi's suitcase. And what about Leon? Where could he hide to escape the Gestapo? Suddenly she was desperate for them both to get as far away from Germany as possible. Her fingers trembling, she levered up the loose floorboard and took the wad of notes from her cash box, stuffing them into a canvas bag which she bound against her chest.

When she returned to the storeroom with her luggage, Violet was mopping blood from the floor with a bucket of soapy water and Leon was wearing Grube's uniform. The jacket was too big for him and the trouser legs had a few blood spots, which he was dabbing with a damp cloth, but the clothes would probably pass muster in the dark.

'Thank you,' Freya told Violet. 'And I'm sorry I thought you were a Fascist.'

'I suppose that's understandable,' Violet said, squeezing out a mopful of pink suds. 'I'm glad I convinced you, at least.'

After the floor and walls had been thoroughly washed,

Freya emptied the bucket in the bathroom and helped Violet and Leon heave the trunk containing Grube's body upstairs and load it on to the porter's trolley. And suddenly they were back in the outside world, walking through the night while the city heaved, taut with excitement. The streets were busy, despite the weather; lorries crammed with stormtroopers thundered through puddles in the road, while couples and families in their Sunday best hurried eastward, their faces alight with anticipation. Brownshirt brigades were out in force and the police patrolled in packs, looking for any excuse to arrest passers-by, or at least have fun beating them up. Shutters had been pulled down over shop windows but nobody seemed in the mood for looting. Somewhere in the distance, they could hear the tramp of feet and hundreds of male voices raised in unison – a beautiful, thrilling sound, Freya thought, until you heard the words of those Nazi songs: death to Jews and Hitler's banners flying in every street.

The three of them crossed the canal and pressed on towards Tiergarten. People might have wondered why a uniformed member of the SA should have been acting as a porter, but nobody cared enough to give Leon a second glance. He had to stop occasionally and wrestle the trolley from a pothole, and once he called out and Freya and Violet turned to see the trunk toppling slowly into the street. Freya gasped, her heart in her mouth. A motorcycle had to swerve to avoid it and a leather-booted policeman shouted at Leon to watch his step. They must have caught him in a good mood, though, because he helped Leon right the trolley and load the trunk back in place.

'Dear Lord, that's heavy,' he said, taking off his cap to mop his brow. 'What have you got in there?'

'My winter wardrobe,' Violet said. 'I have a large collection of shoes, which this oaf should treat with more care.' And the policeman had smiled, pocketing the five-mark piece she'd given him for his trouble.

They would make their way through Tiergarten, Violet had said, and then along the river until they found a secluded stretch or some kind of shelter. Freya and Violet would keep watch while Leon tipped the trunk into the water, pushing it as far out as possible. She made it sound so easy. As they walked beside the rushing Spree, swollen with rainfall, Freya realised they were heading in the direction of her old apartment. She remembered sitting by the river that night she'd gone to fetch her father while her mother lay dying, almost three years ago. It was a relief to know Ingrid didn't have to see how the country had changed since then and that she was at peace, her suffering over. Freya would never have considered leaving Germany had her mother been alive, but now there was nothing to keep her here. Nothing apart from Leon, and she'd lost him already.

Violet squeezed Freya's arm and nodded ahead. They were approaching a bridge, its base shrouded in darkness. Violet stood aside to let a couple walking towards them pass by, waiting for Leon to catch up. 'This is a good spot,' she told him quietly, once the strangers were a safe distance away. 'I'll guard the other side and Freya can stay here. We'll make a noise if anyone comes. Push the trunk as far out as possible – midstream, if you can.'

Freya stood in the centre of the path, looking back along the way they'd come. An idea had come to her for a possible escape route and the more she thought about it, the more brilliant it seemed. Her breath was shallow, her heart thumping. If only Leon could get rid of the trunk, this nightmare would be a step closer to ending. Seconds later she heard a grunt followed by a splash, and turned to see the brass corner of Grube's coffin gleam in the eddying current before sinking beneath the black water. Before she could think twice, she drew back her arm and hurled the gun after it.

The three of them regrouped under the bridge. 'Good job,' Violet said. 'Now I suggest we split up right away. Do either of you need any money?'

Leon shook his head. 'I have enough.'

'Wait!' Freya grabbed Violet's arm. 'I have a plan that might work. For Leon, that is.'

'Spit it out, then,' Violet said. 'There's no time to hang around.'

'We need to go to Rupert's apartment,' Freya said. 'You know they're setting off for California tomorrow? Rupert's travelling with Franz and his boyfriend Grant. Well, Leon could go in Rupert's place. I mean, he and Rupert look similar enough, especially if Leon wore spectacles. He could travel on Rupert's passport with the visa stamped in it, and then later, once he's left the country, Rupert can say his passport was stolen and reapply for exit papers. He's English – there won't be a problem.'

'And why on earth would this Rupert fellow agree to that?' Leon asked. 'He hasn't even met me.'

'Because I have something he wants,' Freya replied. 'And he'd do anything to get it.'

Violet stared at her, and then laughed. 'You might be on to something. It's worth a try, at any rate.'

'But what about Freya?' Leon asked Violet.

'What do you mean, "What about Freya?"' she repeated.

'Take her with you to England,' he replied. 'You know

it's not safe for her to stay here, not after what's happened. They're bound to link her with Grube's disappearance sooner or later.'

'I haven't got exit papers or a visa, though,' Freya stammered. They both ignored her.

'No,' Violet said flatly. 'I'm in enough trouble as it is. I can't go back with a stowaway.'

'Yes, you can,' Leon told her. 'Say she's an informer who's been working for you and her life's in danger. It's half true, anyway. Please, Violet – I've never asked you for anything. Will you do this for me?'

Violet looked at him for a long time, her face half hidden in shadow. 'Dear God,' she muttered at last, turning away. 'All right, then.'

# Chapter Twenty-Four

*Portland, Oregon, August 2024*

Maddie did her best not to think about Daniel and his relationship status over the coming weeks. His loss of a girlfriend might have been the reason he hadn't contacted her, or something completely different might have been keeping him away. Speculating was pointless, and what did it matter anyway? He was just a friend: one she hadn't known for very long, even if it didn't feel like that sometimes. Whenever her thoughts started to wander, she corralled them firmly back in place. And then, well into summer, the German Journal WhatsApp group sprang to life with the news that Eva had finished her translation, and a friend was currently typing it up.

Shortly afterwards, Daniel texted Maddie separately. 'Sorry for the radio silence. I've seen a handwritten copy of the translation and it gave me chills. We need to talk. Can you call me when you have a minute?'

Maddie sat on her hands for a couple of hours. The sight of his name coming up on her phone made her heart miss a beat, but she decided to wait until the next day before contacting him. That turned out to be impossible, though; she couldn't concentrate on anything until she'd spoken to him. He answered her call immediately. 'So go ahead, shoot,' she said. 'Tell me what's so startling about my great-grandmother's journal.'

'The fact that the entire *Magic Garden* movie seems to be based on her writing – and probably the book, too, though I can't get hold of a copy.' Daniel's voice was emphatic on the other end of the line. 'There are so many similarities: plot twists, lines of dialogue reproduced verbatim, characters' names, background details . . . It's all Freya Amsel, but her name doesn't appear anywhere in the credits. According to my research, the film was based on a novella written by a British guy called Rupert Harrington. It was published in the States in 1939 but went out of print in the fifties. Harrington wrote the movie screenplay, too – supposedly.'

'Rupert Harrington,' Maddie repeated. 'Why was his novel published in America if he was a Brit?'

'Because he moved to California in 1933 and made his home there,' Daniel told her. 'And where do you think he'd been living before?'

'Berlin?' Maddie guessed, and Daniel practically crowed with delight.

'Exactly! Bet you a hundred dollars he and Freya knew each other. We need to look into this more deeply, Maddie. I know your mom doesn't want you digging up the past but there might have been a terrible miscarriage of justice.'

'But how could we prove that?' she asked.

'I'm not sure we can. It has to be worth a try, though, right? I'd like to find out more about Rupert Harrington and his circle. I've come across his agent before: Frank Schwartz, a German who came to Hollywood around the same time as Harrington. *The Magic Garden* was a success for them both, especially once the movie came out. Schwartz went on to represent some big names on the Californian literary scene, though Rupert Harrington never wrote anything else. Or at least, never had anything else published.'

'Interesting,' Maddie said, although privately she was thinking the connections sounded a little tenuous. 'Thanks for taking so much time and trouble over all this.'

'You're welcome. Must admit, I'm hooked. Listen, are you coming down to LA to see your folks some time? It would be good to talk face to face.'

'I'm actually visiting in a couple of weeks' time,' Maddie said. 'Ben's moving out to live in a shared apartment and my mom could do with some moral support.' She paused for a beat before asking, 'How are things with you, anyway? I haven't heard from you in a while.'

'Yeah, sorry,' he replied – perhaps embarrassed, although she might have been imagining that. 'A little up and down. I'll tell you more when I see you.'

Maddie was even more unsettled after the call. She was intrigued by what Daniel had told her, but more than that, hearing his voice had lifted her spirits in a way she hadn't expected. Only now did she realise how much she'd missed him – which was ridiculous, really, given the fact they didn't even know each other that well. To distract herself, she concentrated on the substance of what he'd said, rather than the effect he had on her. She'd saved the picture of young Freya and her friend Violet at the Zaubergarten on her phone, and looked at it now, wondering what secrets lay behind that closed, wary face. Gramps could remember Freya typing in the evenings, long after she'd left Germany. So what had become of her later work? Had this Rupert Harrington stolen all of it? Or any at all? And then a disturbing thought occurred to her: what if Rupert and Freya had been lovers, and he was Gramps' father? She Googled him quickly but every biographical entry mentioned Harrington's homosexuality. He seemed to have a complicated love life – there were suggestions of a *ménage à trois* with Frank Schwartz and his boyfriend of the time, Grant Williams, a screenwriter – yet his relationships with women were all platonic. In fact, Rupert Harrington was widely considered misogynistic in real life, despite his sensitive portrayal of female characters in *The Magic Garden*.

Freya Amsel was an elusive quarry: Maddie would have to sneak up on her in a roundabout way. She ran through the clues they'd found so far, turning them over in her mind. This Violet person had to be significant, or Freya wouldn't have bothered to keep a photograph of them together. Violet wasn't a German name; it sounded more British than anything. And then Maddie remembered the painting of a country house – Beechwood Grange, home to the Framley-Chambers family – that she'd found in Freya's suitcase, which had made such an impression on Gramps. What if Violet were a Framley-Chambers? She'd be the black sheep of the family, obviously. Well, the possibility was worth investigating; Maddie opened her laptop and got to work, even though it was late.

Several hours were to pass before she shut her computer down, and sleep would be hard to come by that night.

'So tell me about your encounter with Nightshade,' Daniel said, passing Maddie a glass of beer and settling down himself. 'Did you actually confront him?'

'He was a she. And that's old news – I'll save it for later.' Maddie didn't care about Lily-Anne anymore. 'What's more important is the fact I've found Violet. You remember, Freya's friend from the Zaubergarten?'

They were sitting under the vine-covered terrace of her favourite bar in LA on a warm late-summer Friday evening, and it felt strange to be talking about such long-ago times in Europe.

'Go on, then – shoot,' Daniel said, tossing a peanut into his mouth.

'She was Violet Framley-Chambers,' Maddie began. 'Born in 1911 and died in 1946, the youngest daughter of Sir Anthony Framley-Chambers. He was a great friend of Oswald Mosley, the British Fascist, and had links with Germany: his sister married a German and went to live in Munich. Violet was brought up in Beechwood Grange, the family seat in Oxfordshire, and educated at home by French and German governesses. She spoke both languages fluently and – get this – spent two years in Berlin, where she worked as a part-time artist's model and cabaret dancer.'

'In the Magic Garden, I assume.' Daniel sat back, folding his arms.

'That's right. Remember the photograph of her and Freya that I showed you?' Maddie took a sip of beer. 'Anyway, she left Germany before the war and lived in France for several years before returning to England. After the war broke out and France was occupied by the Germans, she was parachuted back into the country as a member of SOE. You know, the Special Operations Executive that Churchill set up to secretly fight the Nazis?' Daniel nodded.

'Of course, nobody realised that at the time,' Maddie went on, 'not even her family. It was only when the documents were declassified about thirty years ago that she was revealed as an agent who transmitted radio messages back to London. Her code name was Pearl, apparently, and she was one of the bravest and most daring of them all. The Gestapo were desperate to find her but they never did.'

'And she died soon after the war ended?' Daniel said.

Maddie nodded. 'I'm not sure how. Sad, isn't it? She wasn't married and didn't have any children so she hasn't left much of a trace.'

'It is,' Daniel agreed. 'Though I can't see how identifying Violet is going to help us find out whether Rupert Harrington stole Freya's movie script.'

'It might not, but she's the one person I've come across who knew Freya and might be able to tell us more about her.'

'Except she died in 1946,' Daniel said, 'which is a bit of a disadvantage.'

'I know,' Maddie sighed. 'I just can't help feeling that Violet and the house she was brought up in play a major part in Freya's story. It must be significant that Gramps felt such a connection to Beechwood Grange when he saw the picture in Freya's case. Why would she have kept it?' She shook her head. 'I'm becoming obsessed with Freya and Violet – they seem to have led such mysterious, interesting lives.'

'Wait till you read Freya's journal,' Daniel said, running a hand through his hair. 'We need to talk about that. In the meantime, would you be interested in hearing what I've discovered about Rupert Harrington and Frank Schwartz?'

Maddie almost choked. 'Oh my God, yes. Tell me!'

'It's not much,' Daniel said, 'but it might be a start. Well, you may already know that Rupert Harrington died quite young, in the 1950s – drove his car into a tree while he was blind drunk. His agent, Frank Schwartz, became literary executor of his estate, handling all the copyright issues and so on. When Schwartz died, years later, he left the Harrington archive to his nephew, a guy called Waldo Brookes, from San Francisco. Schwartz's sister had followed him out to the States, you see: she was an interpreter who fell in love with an American GI stationed in Berlin after the war. They lived in Germany for a couple of years and then moved to San Francisco, where Waldo was born. The good news is, he still lives there and he'd be happy to meet me. Or us, actually. I thought you might like to come too.'

'I'd love to,' Maddie said, her head still spinning from too much information. 'I'm only here till Sunday, though.'

'Sure. He's busy for a couple of weeks, anyway.' Daniel drained his glass. 'Just give me a few dates that are good for you and I'll try to fix something up.'

'Let me get you another beer,' Maddie said, glancing at her watch. There was just about time. 'Thanks for going to all this trouble, Daniel. I really appreciate it.' He was looking tired and his voice was a little flat. She wanted to give him a hug, or at least let him know she understood how he felt.

When she came back from the bar, he was gazing morosely into the distance. 'So how are things with you?' she asked.

Daniel took a sip of beer and winced. 'Not great, to be honest. Christina and I have split up. You know, my girlfriend. Ex-girlfriend, I mean.'

'That's a shame,' Maddie replied, her heart beginning to thump. She was glad her mother had given her some warning and she didn't have to make a fool of herself by blushing or blurting out something inappropriate.

'Yeah.' Daniel sighed. 'Turns out there weren't so many bachelorette parties after all. She was having an affair with a guy from work, and I was the last to know.'

'I'm so sorry,' Maddie said. 'How did you find out?'

'One of her friends took pity on me in the end. It's just so humiliating! How come I didn't realise what was going on when it was staring me in the face?'

They were both quiet for a while, absorbed in their own thoughts. Maddie took a deep breath and said, 'If I tell you my own break-up story, you might feel better.'

'You don't have to,' Daniel said.

'No, I will.' She'd never willingly shared the excruciating details with anyone else, although her mother had wormed them out of her eventually, but now she was several years down the line and could honestly tell Daniel that life goes on, that you wake up each morning and force yourself to walk through the day with your head held high, even though you might feel like curling into a tiny ball of shame and pulling the covers over your head.

'We were going to get married,' she said. 'We'd been engaged for a year. And then one morning, I opened an envelope addressed to me that had been hand-delivered to the newspaper where I work.' She closed her eyes for a second, reliving the moment when her world had fallen apart. 'And inside were photographs of my fiancé, Aaron, with another girl. They were kissing, eating dinner and drinking wine, walking along holding hands, lying together on the grass.'

Daniel said nothing, just stared at her.

'There were copies of text messages, too,' she went on. 'He was arranging to meet her when I'd gone with my mother to choose a wedding dress. And they sometimes joked about what an idiot I was for believing him.'

'Oh my God,' Daniel said slowly. 'That is awful. And you got this package at work?'

Maddie nodded. 'In an open-plan office.'

'But who sent the pictures to you?' Daniel asked. 'Why would anyone be so cruel?'

'Turned out this other girl was married. Her husband suspected she was cheating on him, so he had her followed by a private detective. When he had proof, he sent it to me. He was trying to get back at Aaron, I suppose, and I was just collateral damage.'

'If I could find that guy . . .' Daniel shook his head. 'What a complete asshole.'

Maddie smiled. 'I don't know, maybe he did me a favour. Imagine if I'd ended up marrying a jerk like Aaron?' There were tears in her eyes, though, which she tried unsuccessfully to blink away.

And then Daniel surprised her. He leaned across the table, took her face in both hands and kissed her on the lips. Maddie felt the colour rush to her cheeks. She had no idea how to react once he'd let her go.

'I'm sorry,' he said, sitting back in a daze. 'I don't know what came over me. That was so stupid!'

'No, it wasn't. It was . . . lovely,' Maddie stammered. But she couldn't think what to say; she could hardly carry on talking as though nothing had happened. Or could she? Dammit, she wasn't a teenager. She should have gained a little more poise by now.

Flustered, her cheeks still burning, she glanced at her watch again. 'Sorry, Daniel, but I have to go. Ben's moving out tomorrow and we're having a family supper tonight. Listen, thank you so much for everything. I'll text you about dates for San Francisco.'

Should she kiss him now? No, that would be weird. And if she went to hug him, he might think she was moving in for a kiss. He was sitting and she was standing, which made things doubly awkward. She settled instead for a sort of half-hearted wave, as though she were drowning languidly at sea.

'Sure,' he said, raising a hand without looking at her. 'Let's keep in touch.'

Admit it: you're falling for him, Maddie said to herself in the back of the cab. Maybe he likes you too – or at least, doesn't hate you – otherwise why would he be spending so much time on your family history? Because he's interested in the Hollywood angle, of course. And now you've screwed everything up anyway, because you're such a klutz.

Although, there was still San Francisco . . .

'Where have you been?' Sharon asked as soon as Maddie walked through the door. 'Supper's almost ready.'

'I'm sorry,' she replied, holding up her hands. 'I was out for a drink and lost track of time.'

'With Daniel?' Gramps asked, smiling knowingly at her. 'Eva told me you were meeting up. How did that go?' He turned to Sharon and added, 'You remember he's broken up with his girlfriend? She was two-timing him. Eva always said she was a piece of work.'

'Gramps! It was just a friendly drink.' Maddie took off her jacket and slung it over the banister, aware she was blushing. 'Talk about making something out of nothing.'

'Well, now you can help Ben set the table,' Sharon said, 'and then can you make your famous salad dressing?'

Ben looked up as she came into the dining room. 'Are they nagging you?'

'Not really.' Maddie hugged him. 'So how are you feeling? Excited?'

Ben nodded. 'It's going to be so cool. I have my own bedroom and there's a lounge where we can all hang out together.' He told her about the guys he'd be sharing with: Josh, who loved video games and was going to show him how to play Minecraft; Ethan, who worked in a deli and loved to cook; Steve, who was older and didn't say much, but that was OK because he was like that with everyone and it didn't mean he was angry – it was just the way he was. There was also a tabby cat who lived in the house, Jellybean, and a lady called Maria who helped to run the place.

But then Ben put down a handful of cutlery and looked at her tentatively as he asked, 'Do you think I can manage by myself?'

'I don't see why not,' Maddie replied. 'It's bound to be a little strange at first, but the others sound nice, and Maria will be there.'

Ben smiled. 'It'll be nice to have people to talk to whenever I like.'

He'd probably been lonely for a while, Maddie realised. 'I can't wait to see your room tomorrow,' she said. 'We're going to make it look great.'

Now Ben was beaming, and hugged her again.

'Remember, you can always call Lisa if you have any problems,' Maddie said. 'And Mom won't be far away. I bet you'll be fine.'

'Well, isn't that lovely,' Sharon said, bringing through a bowl of salad. 'My two wonderful children. Couldn't be prouder of you both.'

She was doing well, and she kept up a positive front throughout supper: a succession of Ben's favourite dishes.

They ate meatloaf and corn muffins with tomato and avocado salad, followed by pumpkin roll with cream-cheese frosting, even though it was nowhere near Thanksgiving and Sharon had had to use canned pumpkin purée. Maddie looked at the smiling faces around the table and thought how much happier everyone seemed than the last time she'd been home. Ben was moving on, Sharon was about to embark on a two-day orientation course so she could volunteer at the local Down syndrome association, and Gramps went for weekly walks with Eva. He'd joined her book group, too. And he hadn't mentioned his funeral once, although Sharon told Maddie in the kitchen – raising her eyes to heaven – that he and Eva had each bought build-your-own caskets, which they were using as bookcases in the interim.

'But now what do you think of my mother's journal?' Gramps asked, as they were sitting over coffee after Ben had gone upstairs to bed. 'Isn't that the most fascinating thing?'

'I haven't read it yet,' Maddie confessed. 'Give me a chance! You only emailed it to me this afternoon.'

'And I've been too busy with Ben,' Sharon told him. 'I'll have a look tomorrow, I promise.'

'Eva thinks we should get the thing professionally translated,' he went on. 'She says she doesn't have the skill to do the writing justice, though it seems to me she's done a pretty good job.' He shook his head. 'What a life my mother must have led. Eva's going to see what she can find out about her years in Germany: where she lived in Berlin, that kind of thing. I sure wish Mom could have told me more about it.'

'You can't force people to talk if they don't want to,' Sharon said. 'You have to respect their privacy.'

'Yes, but this notebook . . .' Gramps sighed. 'Well, it raises more questions than it answers, and it's made me desperate to find out about my mother's early life. Read the translation, Maddie, and you'll feel that way too.'

Sharon turned to her daughter with a look that clearly said, 'See what you've started?'

There were dishes to be cleared and washing-up to be done. 'Well, my girl, I just hope you know what you're doing,' Sharon said, as she and Maddie carried a stack of plates into the kitchen. 'Who knows where this is going to lead.'

'To the truth, maybe?' Maddie replied. 'Isn't that worth something?' But Sharon merely raised her eyebrows.

Maddie stayed up late again that night, even though they'd have to be up early the next morning to pack the car and drive Ben to his new home. She couldn't resist a quick look at Eva's translation of Freya's journal, and she needed a distraction from endlessly turning over her encounter with Daniel. Was she making too much of it, or had something significant happened between them? Would it lead anywhere? She wondered for a moment whether Gramps had deliberated in the same way about Eva, and whether you ever reached an age when the answers to these questions came more easily, or if you simply stopped asking them.

The first page of Freya's diary had Maddie sitting bolt upright in bed, startled out of her reverie. The writing was as clean and bracing as a cold shower, plunging the reader straight into the violent, teeming heart of Berlin.

*Yesterday Frau Apfelbaum fell out of her fourth-floor window into the courtyard, narrowly missing the old man who plays his concertina there in the evening,* read her first entry.

*I say 'fell' but who knows whether she jumped or was pushed. She's been a sitting duck since her son was killed in the May Day demonstrations, the year before last, and today a major from the SS moved into her apartment with his wife and two children. Apparently they are a respectable family and having them here will be good for our security. Yet I miss Frau Apfelbaum, whose only crimes were to have been Jewish, and to have raised a Communist son.*

This was a world Maddie knew already from the movie she'd watched with Daniel. She could absolutely see what he meant: almost everything Freya described made its way into the movie, and was probably to be found in the book, too. Interspersed with the factual entries were vignettes, germs of stories that described a country on the brink of collective insanity as the Nazis gradually, inexorably took control. Freya's sense of despair was palpable.

Her very last entry was the saddest of all.

*Today at dawn, I walked through the city I love for the last time,* she wrote.

*I could sense my mother beside me and when I reached Opernplatz, she sent me a sign: a book to rescue. I can never come back here, never again decorate her grave with linden blossom. Forgive me, Mutti, for leaving you, and for the terrible thing I have done.*

And now Maddie realised what her grandfather had meant.

# Chapter Twenty-Five

*Berlin, May 1933*

'You can have my story,' Freya said, holding out the envelope. 'Show it to your agent, say you wrote it – I don't care. Obviously you'll have to translate it into English first, or have it translated, but that should be easy enough to arrange.'

Rupert took a long pull on his cigarette, squinting at her through the smoke. 'And in return, you want me to let this gentleman,' he gestured towards Leon, pale and tense in his Nazi uniform, 'travel on my passport with my boat and train tickets.'

Freya nodded. 'Once the ship has sailed, you can report the passport as stolen and apply for another one, and an entry visa for America.'

'Which will take weeks, if not months,' Rupert said.

'I can pull a few strings at the passport office,' Violet said. 'And we'll reimburse you for the tickets, obviously.'

'I'll pay you back,' Leon said quietly, and she shrugged.

'You'd be doing a good thing,' Freya told Rupert.

He laughed. 'Since when has that ever swayed me? I won't ask what this fellow has done to require such a speedy exit.'

But he stubbed out his cigarette and took the envelope from Freya's hands, pulled out her typescript and leafed through the first few pages.

'Obviously you'll be writing your own novels soon enough,' Freya told him. 'You could think of this as a calling card, so to speak, which might open a few doors at first.'

'Well, it will need work,' Rupert said. 'And how do I know you won't change your mind if by any chance I managed to make this manuscript a success?'

'I could write a letter, relinquishing all rights to you,' Freya replied. 'I'll do that straight away, if you like.'

'What are they saying?' whispered Franz Schwartz's American boyfriend, Grant somebody or other, in English. He had startlingly white teeth and extremely blue eyes, and looked altogether unreal.

'I'll tell you later,' Franz whispered back.

'I have, in fact, read your little story already and I might be able to do something with it,' Rupert said loftily. 'All right, Freya. Perhaps at last it's time for me to play the knight in shining armour. Write your letter and we have a deal.'

He pulled out the chair at his desk, took a pen out of the pocket of his blazer and a sheet of paper from the drawer. Freya sat and wrote something she hoped would satisfy him, though it probably wasn't legally binding and the sentences flew out of her head the moment she laid down the pen. Rupert took the note to Franz and Grant so that they could sign as witnesses, then tucked it into his jacket pocket. Freya's head swam as she stood and shook his hand, not wanting to meet his cunning, greedy eyes. She should be grateful to him for saving Leon, but she was giving away part of her soul and despised him for accepting it. Instead she glanced at Franz, and they exchanged small, sad smiles.

'We'll take good care of your friend.' Franz clapped Leon on the back. 'And we'll keep a chair warm for you, Rupert.'

'This is all very moving,' Violet said, looking towards the dining table, 'but is that food going to waste?' The platter of pork knuckles lying on a mound of sauerkraut looked hardly touched.

'Please, come and eat,' Rupert said, rubbing his hands together. 'We'd planned a nostalgic farewell meal but my landlady's *Eisbein* proved less than tempting in reality. And there are a couple of bottles of wine that need to be drunk before morning.'

They took their places at the table while Rupert fetched more crockery and glasses from the sideboard. Freya's hand shook as she raised the wine to her mouth.

'You should eat something,' Violet said impatiently from across the table. 'We have a long journey ahead of us and you need to keep up your strength.'

But Freya couldn't chew or swallow anything solid; her throat was too constricted. The sight of Walther Grube's mutilated body kept flashing into her mind. What if the trunk hadn't sunk after all but floated away downriver, to be washed ashore with the tide tomorrow? She glanced up to find Leon staring at her, his expression enigmatic. He wasn't eating much either. This whole situation was her fault: that's what he must have been thinking. If she hadn't gone near the pyre at Opernplatz, security wouldn't have been increased and Egon might not have been followed and arrested. But we are both alive, she told herself, and soon, please God, we shall be leaving Germany. She was desperate to go, even though Violet clearly resented being lumbered with her, and she had no idea where they were heading or what was waiting for her once they got there. She had become a child again, waiting to be told what to do.

When at last Violet had laid her knife and fork together, she wiped her mouth with a napkin, threw it down and said, 'I suppose the time has come for us to part ways. Franz, can you lend Leon some clothes for the journey? I think you're nearest his size. And Rupert, perhaps a spare pair of specs? And some Brylcreem? Once his hair is smoothed back, you won't look too dissimilar.'

'Yes, ma'am,' Rupert replied, raising his hand in an ironic salute.

Violet got to her feet with the air of someone preparing to shoulder a burden. 'Come on then, Freya. We'd better say our farewells.'

Freya obediently stood too, holding on to the back of her chair as her legs were suddenly weak.

'Goodbye then, Leon,' Violet said, holding out her hand. A tiny muscle twitched in her jaw and her eyes were fixed wide open. She was trying very hard not to cry, Freya realised with a shock, as Leon shook hands with her, then turned away and opened his arms to Freya.

'Thank you,' he whispered in her ear as they embraced.

'I'm so sorry,' she said quietly. 'For everything.' But he only shook his head.

Violet kissed Rupert and Franz on both cheeks and shook hands with Grant, who said, bewildered, that it had been a pleasure to meet her, and Freya did the same.

'Right then,' Violet said, with evident relief. 'Off we go. Good luck, everyone.'

And then they were out in the street again. Freya took Violet's arm, though she could tell Violet didn't want to be encumbered by her.

'I suppose you absolutely had to bring this?' Violet asked, holding up Freya's typewriter case, which she had offered to carry. 'I did tell you to only bring necessities.'

'That is a necessity,' Freya replied. 'I'd sooner ditch my suitcase.' Violet shook her head.

Freya was overwhelmed by the rush of people who swept them along, by the strange orange glow in the night sky, as though dawn were already breaking, and by a distant, pulsing roar.

'We'll have to take the tram,' Violet snapped, as though this were an added irritation. 'It's too far to walk all the way.'

'Where are we going?' Freya asked.

'To the British Embassy,' came the reply. 'In the same direction as everyone else, so at least we don't have to swim against the tide.'

The same direction: into the official heart of the city, towards the Brandenburg Gate and Opernplatz, where books were to be burned and Goebbels was to make the speech that his admirer Walther Grube would never hear. It was still drizzling. Freya lifted her face to the sky and felt raindrops, like tears, run down her cheek. She kept a tight hold on Violet's arm with one hand and held her suitcase in the other as they boarded the tram and stood in a crush of passengers by the rear window, jammed too tightly for there to be any danger of falling. A familiar landmark from her childhood vanished into the dark: the southern perimeter of Tiergarten and the Asian-style gate to the zoo, guarded on each side by the two vast stone elephants which she and Otto had once climbed upon. They had been shouted at by a policeman, she remembered, but Ernst had ruffled their hair and bought them doughnuts from the café. Otto might bring his own children here one day, and tell them that story.

'We'll get off here,' Violet said as the tram approached Potsdamer Platz.

Freya had never seen the square so crowded. Hordes of people lined the pavement outside the imposing Palast Hotel, swastikas flapped in the rain and the swelling sound became deafening: stamping feet, pounding drums and voices raised in song and cheers. Violet nudged Freya's side and jerked her head backwards, and Freya gasped as she caught sight of the advancing stormtroopers, each carrying a flaming torch which lit his stern, implacable face. The Nazis knew what she had done and they were coming to get her. Instinctively, she broke into a run.

'Stop!' Violet hissed, grabbing her elbow. 'We're nearly there.'

She kept a tight hold on Freya's arm as they walked briskly along Leipziger Strasse, turned down a side road and then hurried up the steps of an imposing colonnaded entrance and pulled open one of the double doors. She showed some form of identification to the official who stepped forward to meet them and Freya held out her passport, which seemed to do. The man glanced at both documents and ushered them inside.

Violet let out her breath. 'Right, now I'm going to talk to a few people while you stay put. Understand?' And she led the way towards a vast double staircase, soaring up to a panelled dome that wouldn't have looked out of place in a cathedral. They took the lefthand side of the staircase, hurrying now, and turned left along a corridor at the top. Violet opened a door at the end of the passage and hustled Freya into a smallish, bare room with an enormously high ceiling. A mahogany desk stood at one end, facing two rows of chairs, and two plump horsehair sofas faced each other on opposite walls. Violet sat Freya down on one of them, dropped the typewriter case at its foot and stood back to catch her breath.

'Give me your passport,' she said, holding out her hand. 'I'll be back as soon as I can, and you're not to worry. I'm going to lock the door but that's just for your own safety.'

Freya nodded, past caring, although she did wonder why she should need protection inside an embassy. The question was not reassuring. She closed her eyes and then, overcome by a bone-deep weariness, laid down her head, tucked up her legs on the fat, unyielding cushions and fell asleep.

Violet reappeared some hours later with a suitcase of her own and a couple of rugs, one of which she tossed to Freya. 'We'll be spending the night here and then in the morning, we'll leave for England,' she said, giving Freya back her passport. 'You'll have to work as a domestic servant – to start off with, at least. My parents have a house in the country and they're always looking for staff.'

'Thank you, Violet,' Freya said. 'This is very good of you.'

'Well, you'll be earning your keep,' she replied, unlacing her boots and kicking them off. 'But it'll be a roof over your head until you can find your feet. It'll give you a chance to learn the language, too.' And with that, she bundled her coat into a pillow and lay down on the sofa, closing her eyes.

Freya was wide awake now, open-eyed in the dark. In one day, her life had changed beyond all recognition; she would be leaving her beloved city in a few hours, never to return. As the square of sky beyond a window set high in the wall began imperceptibly to lighten, she sat up, reached for her coat and shoes, and tiptoed towards the door. The lobby below was quiet, with only a security guard asleep in a chair beside the main entrance. She crept downstairs and headed towards the rear of the building in search of a more discreet exit. Eventually she found a side door through the kitchens and let herself out into the street as dawn was breaking. Evidence of the previous night's revelry lay in gutters: broken glass, a swastika banner trampled in a muddy puddle, lengths of charred wood, a drunk sprawled by the side of the road. A few other people were about, picking their way through the debris, but no one paid Freya much attention.

She headed north towards the Brandenburg Gate and Unter den Linden, turning right into Opernplatz. This was what she had come to see: the great smoking ruin of everything she held dear. The ground beneath her feet was softened by a damp, sooty sludge that coated her shoes, and the air smelt of cinders. Nobody was guarding the site anymore and she was able to walk right up to it and poke at the blackened spars. Lifting her head, she gazed up at the attic windows of the law faculty, wondering whether haughty Magda were safe, and if Egon were still alive.

Turning to leave, her eye was caught by a flicker of movement and she saw pages fluttering in the half light, like the wings of a large white moth. She dropped to her knees and reached through a lattice of burned wood to retrieve the book that had somehow escaped the blaze, singed but intact, and smiled as she recognised a collection of Heinrich Heine's poetry. She kissed its blackened cover and slipped the book into her pocket. Ingrid was wishing her God speed and watching over her even now. Perhaps, after all, she would get through.

They left for the train station only a couple of hours later, in three identical black limousines. The outgoing ambassador, referred to by Violet as Sir Horace, travelled in the first with his wife, his private secretary, a valet and a bodyguard. Violet and Freya went in the second car, alongside two female secretaries who were returning to London, and the third was full of security staff, according to Violet. The party boarded a train bound for the Netherlands at Friedrichstrasse station, beside the River Spree, where they divided: Sir Horace's party heading for first class, the secretaries for second, and Violet and Freya taking seats in third. Freya had reimbursed Violet for her tickets, which had taken most of the money she had. Neither Sir Horace nor his wife had acknowledged her presence in any way, and the secretaries had ignored her, too. Now Freya leaned back in her seat and closed her eyes, terrified that if she were to look out of the window, she might see a trunk bobbing past in the water. Only when the train had pulled out of the station with a shriek and a tremendous blast of steam did her shoulders relax a little.

It took hours to cross the gently undulating countryside of North Germany, stopping at various stations along the way where there was sometimes a chance to buy black bread, sausage and milky coffee from women who held their trays up to the train windows. Around mid-afternoon, they reached the Dutch border, where their papers were checked again. The first time she'd presented her newly stamped passport at Friedrichstrasse station, Freya's heart had been in her mouth, but the guard had merely glanced at it before clipping her train ticket and passing the documents back to her.

'Don't look so frightened,' Violet muttered this time as two of the border police boarded the train, so she forced herself to smile as she handed her passport to them. It seemed to her that he took a particularly long time to check it, glancing back at her, but at last he closed the booklet and returned it to her with a curt nod. The guards disembarked and the train drew away, and then they were leaving Germany for the flat, marshy Dutch coast, heading towards the Hook of Holland and the night boat which would take them across the North Sea to England.

Violet had been quiet for most of the journey. She looked so different in her tweed suit and raincoat, a silk headscarf tied over her cropped hair. Was she glad to be leaving Germany for home, or wretched at parting from Leon? It was impossible to tell.

The two of them were sharing a cabin on the ship and Violet went to stretch her legs on deck and watch the boat leave harbour while Freya changed into her nightclothes. She had no desire to be out in the open; she wanted to lock the door and hide away in the dark. When the ship's vast engines roared into life and she sensed movement through the swell of water beneath, she felt nothing but relief.

Violet came down below deck an hour or so later. She sat on the edge of Freya's bed, stretched out her legs and stared at her sensible shoes.

'I took the bottom bunk,' Freya said. 'Is that all right?'

'We'll have this conversation only once,' Violet replied, 'but I wanted to tell you a few things before we reach England.'

Freya nodded.

'Well, the first and most important thing is that I'm trusting you not to mention any of my extra-curricular activities to anyone at home,' Violet went on. 'Or outside it, for that matter. A lot of people could get into trouble if you breathe a word. Is that clear?'

Freya nodded again.

'As far as anyone else is concerned, I've simply been sowing my wild oats in Berlin, but now I'm coming back to Blighty because I never stick at anything for longer than five minutes.' Violet untied her headscarf and shook out her hair, and for a moment, she looked like her old self again. She folded the scarf into a neat triangle and tucked it in her coat pocket.

'Now as for you, life will seem very strange for the next little while. I suggest you try to learn English as quickly as possible. There are plenty of people who fought in the Great War and won't look at you kindly. With your skills, the housekeeper will probably want you as a lady's maid, but you might be better off working in the kitchen. Most women of my mother's type are insufferable, especially where servants are concerned, and the less you have to do with them the better.'

'All right,' Freya said slowly, the realities of life in service beginning to hit her.

'You may have to swallow your pride but you'll be safe, and well looked after.' Violet patted her knee under the blanket. 'And don't keep brooding about what happened yesterday. I know it's shocking but you did the right thing.'

'I killed him,' Freya whispered.

'It was a fight for survival,' Violet said briskly. 'You against him, and you won, thank goodness. He was about to turn you in to the police, and Leon too, and that would have been it for both of you.' She drew a finger across her throat. 'So don't think about that anymore. If you get into a complete funk, you can come and talk to me, but don't for God's sake tell anyone else.'

'Can I ask you a question?' Freya said.

'Well, you can try,' Violet replied. 'Whether I'll answer is another matter.'

'What did Leon leave in the bonfire?'

She smiled. 'Some high explosives, primed to go off when the thing was lit. The Nazis aren't fools: they'd been watching him, and the others, too, waiting for them to show their hand. Let's hope he can make it to America. You've almost certainly saved his life, if that's any consolation.'

'It was all pointless,' Freya murmured. 'We had no chance, any of us.'

'But you tried,' Violet said sharply. 'You recognised Hitler for the madman he is, and that's not nothing. Sir Horace understands, too, but who knows whether the government will listen to him, or whether his replacement will see the danger. I'm very much afraid it's too late for Germany now. There are interesting times ahead.'

# Chapter Twenty-Six

*San Francisco, October 2024*

'I'm so sorry, Daniel,' Maddie texted. 'My flight's been delayed and now I won't arrive till 1.30. Shall I meet you outside the apartment?' They'd been going to have lunch before meeting Waldo Brookes in his Nob Hill apartment, but now there wouldn't be time.

'There's a deli across the street,' Daniel replied, and sent her a pin with the details. 'See you there whenever you can make it. DW if yr late, you can always join us later.'

Maddie leaned back in her seat, closing her eyes. She'd had hardly any sleep the night before and her head was spinning. Deep breaths, she told herself; take it one step at a time. She and Daniel had been texting regularly since her previous visit home and had managed to hit the right tone: businesslike when necessary, friendly but never, ever flirtatious. She couldn't stop thinking about him, though, and now she would arrive even more flustered and distracted. She would have to empty her mind and concentrate on the job in hand: seeing if there were any connections between Freya Amsel, the mysterious Rupert Harrington and his agent, Frank Schwartz. Daniel had told her that Waldo Brookes managed his late uncle's estate meticulously, and he had a large collection of manuscripts, photographs and correspondence which they might be able to consult.

'He seems a bit anal to me,' Daniel had texted. 'Like he doesn't want anyone else touching his uncle's things. If he hadn't read my latest review and approved, he prob wouldn't have agreed to see us.'

Maddie rushed through the arrivals hall and took a cab towards the Golden Gate Bridge, through the city and, at last, up one of San Francisco's vertiginous hills to the deli where Daniel was waiting. She'd booked an Airbnb nearby for the night and would explore the city tomorrow, maybe take some notes for an article. She wondered whether Daniel had made any plans to stay and whether maybe they might have dinner together – but no, she wasn't going there. Not when her mind was in enough turmoil already.

'You made it!' Daniel said, rising to greet her with a hug as she rushed through the door. 'I got you a cappuccino to go and some water. And a muffin, but you can save that for later.'

It was lovely to see him, it really was. 'Thank you,' she said, taking a bite of the muffin and a mouthful of coffee. 'You're a lifesaver.'

'Now we'd better go.' Daniel took her arm. 'I'm guessing Mr Brookes is a stickler for punctuality. Apparently he used to be an interior designer, so his place should be impressive.'

Waldo Brookes himself was certainly stylish. He wore a dark blazer with an open-neck shirt and a paisley-silk cravat, impeccably cut chinos and polished tasselled loafers. He was probably in his seventies, Maddie estimated, but well-preserved. She wanted to ask him about his skin-care regime.

'Do come in,' he said, eyeing Maddie's takeaway cup doubtfully.

'Shall I leave this in the kitchen?' she asked, stuffing the muffin and water hurriedly into her purse.

'Let me take it for you,' he said. 'The bathroom is just here' – he opened a door off the hall – 'if you'd like to freshen up.'

Maddie looked at herself in the mirror as she washed her hands and groaned inwardly: hair all over the place and poppy seeds caught in her teeth. The bathroom was immaculate. A white orchid in a pot on the black marble countertop was lit by a single spotlight, and every surface gleamed. The handwash smelt of old leather and libraries.

'You have a spectacular apartment,' she told Mr Brookes, rejoining him and Daniel in the open-plan living and dining room. 'My goodness, that view! How do you ever get anything done?' Beyond the huge windows and wraparound balcony, you could see right down to the bay, where at that moment a ferry was sailing majestically by.

'It is rather special,' he replied, adjusting his cravat. 'But let's go through to my office and get down to business. I don't want to take up too much of your valuable time.' Or give you too much of mine, was the implication.

The office was a spacious room, three walls entirely taken up by bookshelves from floor to ceiling and the third panelled in dark wood. Waldo Brookes sat behind a large desk in the centre, while Maddie and Daniel took the two chairs opposite. Maddie felt as though she was about to be interviewed for a job she had no chance of getting, though Daniel seemed as easy and relaxed as ever. He explained their interest in European émigrés to Hollywood in the thirties and forties, thanks to their family history, and in

*The Magic Garden* in particular, both the book and the movie which followed.

'As you told me in your email, Mr Lewin,' Brookes said, reaching for a pile of documents on top of a box file and passing a folder to Daniel. 'I have the original typescript here, if you'd like a look. The book was published in 1939, just before war broke out in Europe, and it did quite well. Nazis make very good baddies.' He smiled. 'Although sales really took off once the movie appeared, in 1943.'

Maddie looked over Daniel's shoulder. 'The Magic Garden, by Rupert Harrington,' she read on the first thin, yellowing page – typed in a font that was nothing like that of her great-grandmother's typewriter. The 'e's were all perfectly aligned and only the letter 'k' seemed to stick.

'Could you tell me a little about your uncle, Frank Schwartz?' she asked Mr Brookes. 'Did you know him well?'

Waldo Brookes' face lit up as he smiled. 'Oh yes, we were very close,' he said. 'He was a lovely man with a wonderful sense of humour. Of course, he could drive a hard bargain, but he was generous and kind-hearted, and all his authors adored him. Here he is.' He turned around a framed photograph to show her.

Maddie saw a man in his fifties with grey, wavy hair swept back off his forehead and smiling eyes. 'He looks so nice,' she said. An anodyne word she'd always been told not to use, but it seemed appropriate here.

'He certainly was,' Brookes agreed. 'I loved Uncle Frank. He was the perfect role model: a single man, without a family, but so warm and leading such an interesting, creative life. I still miss him.'

'Uncle Frank': that phrase rang a bell, but before Maddie could ask herself why, another thought occurred to her.

'I don't suppose there was ever a German version of the text, was there?' she asked. 'I mean, both he and Rupert Harrington came from Berlin, didn't they?'

'Now, how did you come to know that?' Mr Brookes asked, sitting back in the chair. 'As a matter of fact, there *is* a German version. I have it here.' He pulled out the box file and rifled through it. 'Here we are.' And he passed her a large envelope.

'The Magic Garden, by Rupert Harrington,' proclaimed the title page in the same type as before, and Maddie's heart sank again. When she looked at the manuscript itself, though, it felt as though an electric current had run through her.

'It's strange,' Brookes went on, 'because Rupert Harrington wasn't bilingual by any stretch of the imagination and he never wrote anything else in German. Or that much in English, come to that. Uncle Frank encouraged me to learn the language and I can still speak it, although I'm a little rusty, and read it. I'll tell you something else that's odd: the German *Magic Garden* is much more powerful. It has a poetry that the English translation lacks.'

'And I know why,' Maddie said, in a faint voice. 'It's because my great-grandmother wrote it.'

'I beg your pardon?' Brookes asked, and Maddie was aware of Daniel staring at her.

She cleared her throat. 'I have a typewriter at home that belonged to my great-grandmother, Freya Amsel – the same typewriter she used to type this script. Not the title page, which must have been added later, but the rest. It's unmistakeable: the "e" jumps and the top of the "m" is faint.' She showed Mr Brookes a page from the stack in front of her.

'So we were right!' Daniel exclaimed. 'Rupert Harrington must have stolen the story.'

'That's a serious allegation,' Brookes said. 'You'll need proof if you want to take it any further.'

'Mr Brookes—' Daniel began.

'Please, do call me Waldo,' Brookes interrupted. (Such an inappropriate name for him, somehow.)

'Waldo, is there any correspondence between your uncle and Freya Amsel?' Daniel went on.

'I don't think so,' he replied. 'It's not a name that sounds familiar. Let me check, though.' He swivelled around in his chair to press one of the wood panels behind him, which swung open to reveal vertical racks of filing cabinets. 'Now let me see. Amsel, Amsel . . .' Springing to his feet, he drew a fat folder out of the top drawer and began leafing through it.

And all of a sudden, Maddie heard her grandfather saying, 'There was a guy I used to call Uncle Frank who would come visit. He was a work friend, I think.'

'Waldo, may I take a picture of your uncle and send it to my grandfather?' she asked.

'Sure,' he said, without looking up.

'Random question: do you recognise this man?' Maddie typed, pinging the photo across to Gramps.

'Nothing, I'm afraid,' Brookes said, shaking his head as he reached the end of the folder.

'Try under her married name,' Daniel suggested. 'Freya Cole, wasn't it, Maddie?'

Brookes replaced the folder and ran his fingers along the next row, muttering, 'Cole, Cole, Cole.' Then he took out another folder, had a quick look and slapped it down on the desk. 'Now this might be more promising.'

Maddie was desperate to tear the papers Brookes was reading out of his hands, but he made her wait. At last he glanced up at her with a smile and said, 'Yes, it would seem they knew each other well. See for yourself.' And he passed her the open folder.

Freya Cole sprang immediately to life before Maddie's eyes. Business letters were typed in that characteristic font but the more personal correspondence was handwritten. Freya had a bold, looping hand and her notes were generously sprinkled with exclamation points and sometimes tiny drawings in the margins. She was warm and witty, thanking Frank for trips to the theatre, dinners and cocktail parties, or inviting him to birthday picnics for Bobby, barbecues on the beach and Thanksgiving dinners – always in English, as were Frank's replies.

There was only one note handwritten in German, which she passed back to Waldo Brookes. 'Can you understand this? Daniel speaks the language, if not.'

'I can,' Brookes replied. 'As I said, my uncle insisted I learned.' He read the page and said, 'Well, there's your proof. Freya Amsel is relinquishing all rights in *The Magic Garden* manuscript and assigning them to Rupert Harrington. So I'm afraid you won't have any legal redress, but you're right, she was clearly the original author.' He looked into the distance, adding, 'I got the impression from Uncle Frank that Harrington wasn't a particularly nice man.'

'And nothing else of hers was published,' Maddie murmured.

Freya's typed letters and the carbon copies of Frank's were less personal in tone. They referred to a collection of short stories, at least one of which Freya was working up into a full-length novel. Frank reassured her that the writing was exceptional but said he was having trouble finding an editor who would commit to publishing them. He listed all those he'd approached before eventually concluding,

*I'm afraid word seems to have gotten around that you are a Communist; I believe our mutual friend may have been spreading rumours. We both know how ridiculous that accusation is, but the book trade is wary and libraries are now under pressure to remove 'dubious' material from their shelves. Ironic, isn't it, when you think what we went through. Or perhaps heart-breaking would be a more accurate word. At any rate, we may have to accept that now is not the best time to bring your writing to the world's attention. Your day will come, though, I'm sure of that. Don't despair.*

'I understand,' Freya had replied to this letter. 'Perhaps it's just as well – I would have wanted the stories to be published anonymously, anyway. Maybe it would be safer to wait until after my death.'

'These stories they mention,' Daniel said to Waldo Brookes. 'Would your uncle have kept copies?'

'I'm trying to find them right now,' he replied, standing on a small stepladder to reach the upper bookshelves. 'He returned most unpublished typescripts, but this one might have had sentimental value. Let's see.'

Maddie's phone pinged just then with a reply from Gramps. 'That's Uncle Frank!!! I remember him clearly. Might even have a photograph of him in one of Mom's albums. Where did you find that picture, and how did you know?!!'

'Tell you later,' Maddie texted back, and turned off her phone.

Waldo took down a couple of box files and placed them on the desk. 'This is the Miscellaneous section,' he said briskly. 'If the script is anywhere, it'll be here.'

Maddie offered to look through one of the boxes and he let her, though she could tell that another person going through Frank's papers made him nervous. In any event, it was Waldo who drew out a folder, rifled through a few pages and cried, 'Aha! We've struck gold.'

'Let me see,' Maddie demanded, coming around to his side of the desk.

'It's from the same typewriter, I believe?' he said, looking up at her – and so it was.

The typescript was inches thick: story after story in Freya's distinctive, elegant voice, and all written in English. The title page read 'Underground Whispers', and the author was listed as 'Anonymous'. Overleaf, Maddie read an extract from a poem she had never heard of, *A Map of Verona*, by Henry Reed, written in 1942 about a city at war, the unreliability of memory and the 'underground whispers of music beneath the years'.

Maddie hugged the folder to her chest. She already knew so much. Could these stories be the final pieces of the jigsaw?

'Can we take a photocopy of this typescript?' Daniel asked Waldo.

'You may have the original,' he answered. 'It belongs with Maddie's family, and my uncle would have wanted me to return it to its rightful home.' Their time was evidently up, as he stood to usher them out. 'Well, from an unpromising beginning, this has turned into quite an exciting afternoon. Let's keep in touch.'

'Daniel, I can't thank you enough,' Maddie said when they were out in the street again. 'I'd never have found these stories without you. It feels like Freya's within touching distance. I've learned something extraordinary about her that I can't wait to share with you.'

'Sounds intriguing.' He smiled, then put an arm around her shoulder. 'But first, let's get some lunch – you must be starving.'

They went back to the deli and sat at a table in the window. 'I'm just so relieved you agreed to come,' Daniel said, looking at a chalked menu above the counter. 'After I jumped on you last time, I mean. I thought you might not want to see me again.'

A warm, happy glow filled Maddie's entire body. Maybe she hadn't screwed everything up, after all. She waved her hand. 'Oh, come on! You didn't jump on me. It was cute.'

'But I should have asked your permission,' Daniel said, still not meeting her eye. 'You know, boundaries and everything.'

'But where's the fun in that?' Maddie asked him. 'Can't anyone be spontaneous anymore?' And she leaned across the table, took his face in both hands and kissed him back – a little longer than was strictly necessary, because his lips were so soft and lovely, and the kissing melted her from the inside.

'There,' she said, letting him go. 'Now we're quits. See, it's just a kiss.'

'Well, that was fun,' he said, laughing. 'You'll be giving me ideas.'

'Oh, Daniel, I have so much to tell you,' Maddie went on. 'But can I talk to you in confidence? Could you keep a secret from Eva, at least for the time being? I don't want to put you in a difficult position, but I really need advice from someone I can trust.'

'Sure,' he replied. 'Let's order some food and then you can go ahead.'

Maddie shrugged. 'I'll have what you're having, whatever. My head is so full, I think it might explode. But first things first.' She took a large, slim book from her backpack and held it up.

'*Beechwood Grange: A House Through History*,' Daniel read.

'That's the book I mentioned – you know, the one I found online?' She rifled through the pages. 'And look! The photograph on the right, the one of all the household staff in 1933 – Freya's in the back row.' She passed the open book across the table.

'You think?' Daniel said, examining the page up close. 'It's hard to tell for sure.'

'No, it isn't!' Maddie exclaimed. She scrolled to the picture of Violet and Freya on her phone and gave it to him to compare. 'See? I was certain it was her – and in point of fact, I know I was right because I've been in touch with the Framley-Chambers family at Beechwood Grange.'

'Seriously?'

She nodded. 'I wrote to them initially, and we've been emailing ever since. Actually they're called Covington-Chambers now, and they have another name with a title that's even more confusing, but still . . . Anyway, I always thought Freya's friend Violet was the key to the whole mystery, and it turns out she is. I had a Zoom call with Felicity Covington-Chambers yesterday and she told me everything. You're not going to believe this.'

'Try me,' Daniel said, leaning back in his chair.

So Maddie began, right at the beginning. She talked until the waitress had cleared their table and clearly wanted them to leave, so they ordered takeaway coffees and found a bench further down the hill, and she was still talking when Daniel suggested they find a bar for an early-evening drink. Occasionally, he asked her a question but for most of the time he just listened, his eyes fixed on her face.

'My God,' he said, when at last Maddie was all talked out, 'that is some story.'

'I know.' Maddie sipped her wine. 'But how am I going to tell Gramps? What if he gets upset and has a heart attack or something?'

Daniel considered the question. 'I don't think that's very likely. This is too big, Maddie. Now you've found out, you can't keep it to yourself. Your mother's involved, too.'

She groaned. 'My mother. She wanted me to leave the past alone.'

'But I bet she'll be glad you didn't. Once she's got over the shock, that is.' Daniel put his hand over Maddie's for a moment. 'It's not fair that we know all this and your grandfather doesn't. You need to tell him right away. Don't go back to Portland – come to LA with me this evening instead. You can fly home from there tomorrow.' He took out his phone. 'Let me see if they have a last-minute ticket, or maybe you could try standby.'

'That'll cost a fortune,' Maddie said, though her heart was beginning to race.

'I'll split it with you,' Daniel said. 'We're in this together.'

And somehow, miraculously, it was all arranged. The Airbnb would have to go to waste but Maddie cancelled her flight back to Portland and bought a ticket to LA on the same flight as Daniel that evening instead. She couldn't let him pay for any part of it; he'd done enough for her already. They were sitting a couple of rows apart on the plane but he bought a tiny bottle of champagne and passed it forward to her, via a kind woman in the middle – whereupon Maddie's neighbour offered to swap seats with Daniel so they could sit together.

‘Look out,’ he said, chinking his bottle against hers. ‘I might forget myself and kiss you again.’

‘Don’t spoil the surprise,’ she replied, and then of course they were kissing, though who could say who’d started it, and the kiss was wonderful – but too public. Luckily it was a short flight.

‘Does your mom know you’re here?’ Daniel asked as they walked through the arrivals hall at LAX. He had taken her hand, which felt perfectly natural.

‘Not yet,’ Maddie answered. ‘I’ve told her I’ll see her in the morning.’

He smiled. ‘Good. Let’s take a cab to mine.’

They managed to keep apart in the Uber out of consideration for the driver, although it was difficult, and then at last Daniel was punching in a code outside a building somewhere in Glendale, and they were hurrying through the lobby and into an elevator and kissing properly now, hungrily, and Maddie felt she had never been so blissfully happy in her entire life.

‘My apartment’s not as tidy as Waldo’s,’ Daniel said, unlocking the door.

It had a bed, though, and at that moment, nothing else mattered.

# Chapter Twenty-Seven

*Los Angeles, October 2024*

Maddie asked Daniel to drop her off a block away from her house the next morning. She knew if her mother saw them together that questions would be asked. Inevitably, questions were asked anyway.

'So what is it?' Sharon demanded as soon as Maddie walked through the front door. 'Have you lost your job? Are you sick, or pregnant? You look even more tired than usual.'

'Nothing like that,' Maddie replied, taking off her coat and slinging it over a chair. 'I just want to talk to you both.'

'Let the poor girl sit down,' her grandfather said, patting the couch beside him, and Maddie gave him a grateful hug.

'How are you?' she asked. 'And Eva? Still having fun discussions about death?'

'I'll pour the coffee while you catch up,' Sharon said. 'Are you hungry? I have fresh bagels too.'

'Ravenous,' Maddie replied. 'Fill me in, Gramps.'

'Well, we've moved on from funeral arrangements,' he said. 'Eva's been tracing my mother's history.'

'OK,' Maddie said, though a pang of alarm had shot through her stomach. 'Tell me more.'

'So she's traced the Amsel family in Berlin,' he said. 'At the address you found on that old suitcase? There was a census in Germany in 1925, and they're all there: Freya's mother, who was called Ingrid, and her father, Ernst, and her older brother, Otto. She and Otto were schoolkids then, and her mother is listed as a dressmaker and her father a house painter. Solid working-class folk.'

'That's so interesting,' Maddie commented, keeping her voice neutral.

'Just wait,' Gramps went on. 'There was another census at the beginning of May 1933 and by then, the household had changed. Ingrid Amsel was no longer living at that address, and neither was Freya. Her father and brother were still there, though, with a maid called Hedwig Müller, and a lodger by the name of Walther Grube. Eva's trying to see if there's a death certificate for Ingrid Amsel. I remember Mom telling me her own mother had died relatively young. Isn't it amazing what you can find out on the internet these days?'

Sharon was back with a tray and fussed about for a while, handing out coffee, bagels with smoked salmon and cream cheese, plates and paper napkins.

'Well, that's kind of why I'm here,' Maddie said, when they were relatively settled. 'Sit down, Mom. Nobody needs black pepper and this is important.'

'Sorry, I'm sure,' Sharon said, perching on the edge of a chair. 'Go ahead, then.'

'This is a long story, so prepare yourselves. You might find it hard to take in – I did, at first.' Maddie took a deep breath, squaring her shoulders. 'This is your mother's story, Gramps. So we know Freya Amsel went to America in 1938, but she didn't go straight there from Germany. In 1933 she went to England with her friend, Violet Framley-Chambers, to work as a kitchen maid at the family home, Beechwood Grange, in Oxfordshire.' She heard a sharp intake of breath and looked up to see Gramps staring at her, coffee cup poised halfway to his mouth.

'Freya stayed there for five years,' Maddie went on, 'learning English and saving her wages. Then in 1938, Adolf Hitler annexed Austria. She realised war was coming and there was every chance the Germans would invade Britain, too, so she left for California, to join the love of her life, Leon Kohl – or Leonard Cole, as he was now known. He'd emigrated to the States back in 1933 and become a permanent resident by then.'

'Don't we know most of this already?' Sharon asked, picking crumbs off the rug.

'As I was saying, war broke out in Europe in 1939,' Maddie continued, 'and the United States came to help the Allies at the end of 1941, after the attack on Pearl Harbour.'

Sharon sighed. 'Thanks for the history lesson.'

Maddie ignored her. 'In 1942, Leonard Cole went to work for the US military against the Nazis in France. He was an invaluable asset, being a native German speaker, and managed to infiltrate the highest diplomatic circles. And while he was in France, he met up with Violet Framley-Chambers again, who was living there as a member of the Resistance. They'd been lovers in Berlin and they must have rekindled their affair, despite the fact he was now married to Freya.'

She gave Gramps a rueful smile, but he only shook his head and said, 'Passions run high in wartime, it's inevitable. People live for the moment when they don't know what the next day will bring.'

'How did you find all this out?' Sharon asked, curious at last.

'Because I've been in touch with the Framley-Chambers family,' Maddie replied. 'I had a Zoom chat with Felicity Chambers a couple of days ago. She's great, I love her. Anyway, Felicity's husband, Henry, is the son of Nigel, who was Violet's nephew.'

Sharon shook her head. 'You've lost me now.'

'It doesn't matter,' Gramps said impatiently. 'Go on, Madeleine.'

'Well, Leonard was tragically killed in France in the summer of 1943, as you're well aware. He'd been betrayed by an American double agent who was also working for the Nazis, and was lured to a remote spot and shot in the head. Not long after that, Violet was sent back to England.' Maddie hesitated for a moment, then forged ahead. 'Because she was pregnant.'

The room became utterly silent. Nobody moved. Maddie could hear the grandfather clock ticking away in the hall.

'Violet gave birth to a baby boy,' she continued eventually, balling a paper napkin tight in her fist, 'at home, Beechwood Grange, on the fifteenth of November 1943. She called him Robert.'

'Dear Lord in heaven!' her mother cried, jumping to her feet. 'Are you serious?'

'Sharon, sit down and shut up,' Gramps ordered, in a voice Maddie had never heard him use before.

'But the story doesn't end there,' she went on. 'Violet survived the war, returning to France as soon as she could while Robert stayed behind with a nanny at Beechwood Grange. They had hot and cold running servants in those days, I gather.' She didn't dare look at Gramps. 'But tragically, Violet fell seriously ill in 1946. When it became obvious she was going to pass away – sorry, Gramps – when it became obvious she was going to die, Violet wrote to Freya, asking her to come back to Beechwood Grange one last time. Transatlantic flights were just beginning and she wired her the money for a plane ticket. So Freya came back to England, met little Robert and understood immediately what had happened. Violet didn't need to explain. He looked so like his father, you see.'

Maddie took a sip of water, her mouth dry. 'And here's the most extraordinary thing: Violet asked Freya to adopt Leon's child and bring him up as her own. She knew her son would have a miserable life in England, with both his parents dead and his father a German into the bargain. Her family was cold and unloving, according to Felicity, and would probably have put Robert in an orphanage. Violet's two brothers had been killed in the war but her sister, Annabel Covington, already had a son, Nigel. As Robert was illegitimate, there was no question of him being in line to inherit the house or title, and the family would have seen no reason to keep him around. He'd have brought them nothing but shame.'

Maddie took Gramps' hand and squeezed it. 'So Freya went home to California,' she finished, 'and took Robert with her.'

There was nothing more to be said. Even Sharon, mercifully, stayed quiet.

After a minute, Gramps got to his feet. 'Would you excuse me? I'd like a moment to myself.' He left the room, not looking at either of them.

Maddie and her mother sat in silence for some time.

'Oh, my Lord,' Sharon murmured at last, shaking her head. 'Oh, my Lord! So Dad's real mother was this Violet something Chambers, who was brought up in an English stately home? She was my grandmother, then? Are you absolutely sure?'

Maddie nodded. 'Felicity emailed me copies of his birth and adoption certificates. It's all true, Mom. I can prove it.'

A smile crept slowly over Sharon's face. 'Wait till my book group hears about this.'

'Jeez, Mom,' Maddie exclaimed. 'You are such a snob!'

She went through to the back yard, to find her grandfather by himself on the bench, staring into space.

'OK, Gramps?' she asked, sitting beside him and squeezing his hand again.

He nodded, though there were tears in his eyes. Maddie pretended not to notice, looking away as he took a spotted handkerchief from his pocket and blew his nose.

'What a woman,' he sighed, shaking his head.

'I know,' Maddie said, though she wasn't sure to whom he was referring.

He turned to her, his eyes shining. 'Can you imagine the courage it must have taken to fly across the ocean to Europe in 1946, return with a child she didn't know and bring him up as her own? The child who must have been a constant reminder of her husband's infidelity? And for her to never make that little boy feel less than special, but to love him with her whole heart and give him the most wonderful life he could ever have imagined?'

'Don't, Gramps,' Maddie said, her voice breaking.

'What a woman,' he repeated. 'God, I was lucky to have her. When I think how things might have turned out . . . She might not have given birth to me, but I was blessed to call her my mother.'

He put his arm around Maddie and drew her close. 'Thank you, darling. You've done more for me than you could ever imagine.'

# Epilogue

*Los Angeles, November 2024*

It was the best Thanksgiving Maddie could remember. Daniel and Eva came to dinner and of course Ben was there, too, along with his housemates, Josh and Ethan. Steve had been invited but preferred to stay at home, which was fine. Ethan helped Sharon in the kitchen, mashing potatoes and making cranberry sauce, while Ben and Josh played video games in the family room. Sharon had pulled out all the stops in terms of decorations and the dining table groaned with so many pumpkins, china turkeys, candles and dried leaves, there was hardly room for the plates and cutlery. This year, she had added bright-green candles in the shape of asparagus stalks and silver-plated candlesticks and napkin rings; the discovery of an English grandmother seemed to have gone to her head. She was messaging Felicity Covington-Chambers almost every day, from what Maddie could make out, and plans were already being hatched for them all to visit Beechwood Grange in the spring – including Eva.

'Well, my father should see where he was born,' Sharon said. 'Do you think they still have servants at the Grange?'

'They'd be called staff now, Mom,' Maddie replied, 'and I wouldn't get your hopes up. Felicity's very down-to-earth – she's not like a character from *Downton Abbey*.'

Still, at least finding out about her British heritage distracted Sharon from interrogating Maddie about Daniel. Word had soon leaked that they were a couple, since Eva had guessed what was going on and told Gramps, so Maddie had to tell her mother before he did.

'I'm happy for you,' Sharon said, hugging her. 'He's such a lovely boy, not your usual type at all. Looks like you've finally picked a good one.'

Ben was pleased, too. He was in a good place: life in the shared house seemed to be working out as well as anyone could have dared to expect. He had been a little homesick at first, but Sharon visited several times a week and he became more settled as the days went by.

'We're getting on so much better,' Sharon told Maddie. 'We were suffocating each other before, and now it feels like we can breathe again.'

She was volunteering regularly with the local Down syndrome association, and loved it. 'I'm actually making a difference,' she said. 'If only I would have reached out for help all those years ago, when Ben was born and I was groping around in the dark. Honestly, Maddie, this is what I was born to do.'

So this year they had a lot to be thankful for, all things considered. The turkey hadn't dried out, the new bread stuffing recipe was a success and the pumpkin roll was as delicious as ever; Ben had three helpings. When they had finally finished eating, Gramps tapped a knife against his glass and got to his feet. He was wearing a new burgundy velvet smoking jacket with a yellow bow tie and looked blooming.

'Well, here we are once again,' he began, almost shyly. 'I want to thank you all just for being yourselves, my dear family and friends. This has been one of the most remarkable years of my life, and who knows how many more I'll be granted. As you know, I've spent some time putting things in place for my departure—' And here he broke off to say, 'Sorry, Daniel. I'm not going to dwell on the D word,' before clearing his throat and adding, 'But now I'm going to focus on the future, and making the most of every precious day.'

He turned to Eva, who'd been sitting beside him, and his eyes softened. Maddie's heart contracted, and Daniel took her hand underneath the table and squeezed it. They could sense what was coming.

'This morning, I asked this wonderful woman to marry me,' Gramps went on, 'and I'm delighted to say she agreed. It may seem a sudden proposal but at our age, it doesn't pay to hang around.'

Eva got up too, and they kissed, and then everyone around the table clapped, whistled and cheered, and Daniel went to open two bottles of champagne that had magically appeared from nowhere.

'Did you know this was happening?' Maddie asked him.

'Grandma told me this morning,' he answered, grinning. 'She was so excited, but she made me promise not to spoil the surprise. Apparently your grandad wanted to take her to Europe as his wife, rather than his mistress. He thinks that wouldn't have been respectable. They're going to visit his father's grave in France after they've been to Beechwood Grange.'

Everyone sat around the table for hours, talking about weddings and honeymoons and English stately homes.

Maddie went to the kitchen to brew some coffee and Gramps followed her.

'Will you come outside for a moment, Madeleine?' he asked mysteriously. 'There's something I'd like to show you.'

They walked into the yard and she sat beside him on the bench.

'Such wonderful news, Gramps,' she said. 'I'm so happy for you both. Eva's just lovely.'

'What about a double wedding, then?' he asked.

She laughed and shook her head. 'Daniel and I are taking things slowly. And to be honest, I'm not sure I ever want to get married. Not after what happened before.'

'Maybe if we decide to have children,' Daniel had said the other day. So actually, not that slowly. She was crazy about him and the feeling seemed to be mutual.

Gramps took an envelope from his pocket. 'This is what I wanted to show you. Felicity sent it to me, unopened. It's a letter my mother wrote for me – my English mother, not my German one – shortly before she died. If it wasn't for you, I probably would never have read it. I showed it to Sharon earlier today but you should see it too. Is there enough light?' It was growing dark.

Maddie switched on her phone's flashlight and unfolded the paper, soft with age.

*My dear Bobby,* the letter began . . .

*I should have written this note months ago and given it to Freya to keep until you are old enough, but I didn't think of that so here we are. I could send this letter to her in America, I suppose, although to be perfectly honest, I'm not sure whether she would pass it on. In spite of everything we've been through, I'm not sure we entirely trust each other, even now. Isn't that odd? So instead, I've told my family to give you this letter if you ever come looking for me.*

*Anyway, I just wanted to let you know that giving you up has been the hardest thing I have ever done. I could only go through with it because there isn't a better person in the world to take care of you than Freya Amsel – sorry, Freya Cole. She is capable of great love and will tell you all about your father, Leon, whom we both adored. I couldn't marry him for various reasons, mainly to do with the war, so I was glad he married her, rather than a complete stranger. I think they made a go of things and I'm sorry for her sake that he and I fell in love all over again in France. Although, am I? The most wonderful thing to come out of our affair was you, darling Bobby: my hope for the future. I believe you will make Freya happy too.*

*I don't like talking about my feelings but needs must, so here goes. I love you with my whole heart, dear little Robert: the most passionate and selfless love that I never imagined was in me. I haven't let Nanny bath you once – much to her fury – and for the first six months I took you out of your cot in the nursery at night and smuggled you into bed with me, which was heavenly. I don't particularly mind about dying but I do mind not seeing you grow up, find a nice girl (or boy, if you're that way inclined – it's all the same to me) and perhaps have children of your own. That's bloody awful, if you'll excuse the language. But the doctors have told me that my time's running out and sadly they seem to be right.*

*I've left Freya some money in my will to put towards your education and I'm sure she'll make good use of it. She's very conscientious, as you probably know by now. By the way, if she ever starts droning on about something that made her leave Berlin in a hurry, don't pay any attention and tell her to buck up. That's all in the past and she needs to look ahead.*

*Now I'm getting tired and there's nothing more to say. I hope you do read this letter one day, Bobby, and that you'll come back to Beechwood and see the place where you were born and lived for a couple of years. Don't be sad about Nigel inheriting the house – there's dry rot in the attic and it needs a new roof. Much better to grow up without that millstone around your neck!*

*Good luck, dear boy, and try to be happy,*
*Your loving mother*
*Violet Framley-Chambers*

Maddie didn't know whether to laugh or cry. 'I'd say both your mothers are pretty awesome,' she told Gramps, putting the letter back in its envelope and passing it to him. 'No wonder you turned out well.'

'You're right there,' he said. 'About the awesome mothers, that is. Violet sounds quite the character – wish I could have known her.'

'But you did know her,' Maddie said. 'And she knew you, like no one else.'

They sat for a while in silence, and then Gramps said, 'What do you think she meant about Freya having to leave

Berlin in a hurry? Mom never mentioned anything about that to me.'

'I guess we'll never know,' Maddie replied.

In fact, though, she had a good idea. She had read Freya's collection, *Underground Whispers*, so many times that she practically knew the stories by heart. One of the most powerful concerned a young girl who had killed the man who was about to rape her, a Nazi stormtrooper; she stabbed him with a kitchen knife and loaded his body into a packing crate, bound for the hold of a cargo ship. Coincidentally, Eva had mentioned that she'd been researching what had happened to the members of the Amsel household. The maid, Hedwig Müller, had married Ernst Amsel in 1934, but the lodger, Walther Grube, had met a grisly end. A short newspaper report revealed that his body had been discovered one day in 1936, packed inside a trunk washed up on the bank of the River Spree. He had been identified by his dental records.

'It doesn't matter now, anyway.' Maddie reached out a hand to help her grandfather up. 'We need to look ahead, like Violet said, and there are plenty of exciting things on the horizon. Daniel's going to ask how you'd feel about submitting Freya's stories for publication. A friend of his is an editor at one of the top publishing houses and she wants to look at them, if you agree.'

'Sure,' Gramps said. 'The more people who get to read them, the better. Are you disappointed not to be related to Freya by blood? From the writing perspective, I mean.'

Maddie shook her head. 'We've all inherited so much from her. Look at what she taught you: to be loving and steadfast, not to turn away from difficult things but to embrace life's challenges and make the best of them. You passed those lessons on to Mom, and she's handed them down to Ben and me. I lost my way for a while but now I'm back on track.'

'And how's the book going?' Gramps asked.

'I've started a new idea,' Maddie replied, 'one that's closer to home. I'll tell you more about it when I'm a little further along.'

She'd been writing a novel about a woman taking revenge on an internet troll but progress had been slow and she didn't actually like any of the characters she'd invented. 'It all seems so trivial,' she'd said to Daniel. 'I mean, compared to what Violet and Freya went through.'

'Then why don't you write about them?' he'd suggested.

'Do you think I should?' she'd said. 'Maybe their stories aren't mine to tell.'

'Well, no one else is going to, and I can't think of anyone better qualified.' He'd kissed her forehead. 'Do your research and trust your imagination and your great-grandmothers will be delighted.'

And so Maddie had started writing about a young woman who adopts a child in a country that is still new to her, and through loving and caring for him, begins to recover from the trauma of her past. It was hard work, dreaming up something out of nothing, and sometimes she doubted whether she could – or should – continue. Reading her story back, though, it seemed the most authentic, interesting work she had ever produced. She pictured Freya leaning over her shoulder and urging her on.

Now she and Gramps walked back to the house to find Sharon waiting for them in the open doorway.

'Have you read the letter?' she asked, and Maddie nodded.

'You know, it is kind of exciting, discovering I have

English relatives who live in a huge country house,' her mother went on, 'but actually, Dad, I'm so happy Freya brought you back to America. I wouldn't change a thing about my life. Everything that's happened has brought me to where I am now, and that's a pretty good place.'

'Same here,' Maddie said, smiling. 'We're lucky, aren't we?'

Gramps put an arm around each of them. 'We sure are. In fact, I'd say we've won the lottery.'

Acknowledgements

I should like to thank my agent, Sallyanne Sweeney, and my editor at Avon Books, Amy Baxter, for her enthusiasm and encouragement as well as her editorial skills, together with the rest of the friendly, professional Avon team. Thanks are also due to my American friend Linda Oliver and her sister, Joann Smith, for saving me from too many Britishisms; any remaining mistakes are all mine. I'm so lucky to have a niece, Zoe Spurgeon, conveniently living in Berlin, and also thank her friend, Lewis Shields, for his wonderfully informative walking tour of the city. Stuart Mills, from the UK Down's Syndrome Association, was kind enough to read the relevant text and steer me tactfully in the right direction; for those in the UK, I would recommend the Down's Syndrome Helpline as a great source of information and advice. In the US, Heather Rodriguez from the National Down Syndrome Society and Charlotte Woodward, who read my text, were also extremely helpful. While writing this book, I was lucky enough to stumble across Nikki Geib's Instagram account @makingmilliestones, featuring her three gorgeous girls, one of whom – Millie – has Down syndrome. Part of this book features the darker side of social media, but Millie and her family are a daily dose of joy!

**The world is at war.**
**And time is running out . . .**

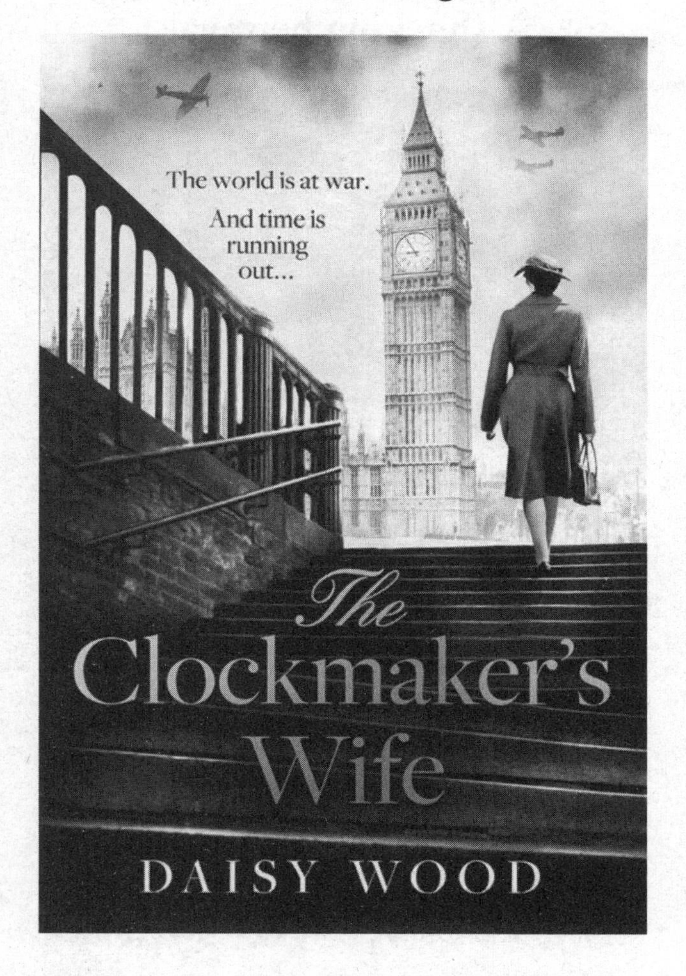


**A powerful and unforgettable tale of fierce love, impossible choices and a moment that changes the world forever.**

**A royal palace. A closed book.**
**A betrayal that will echo through generations . . .**

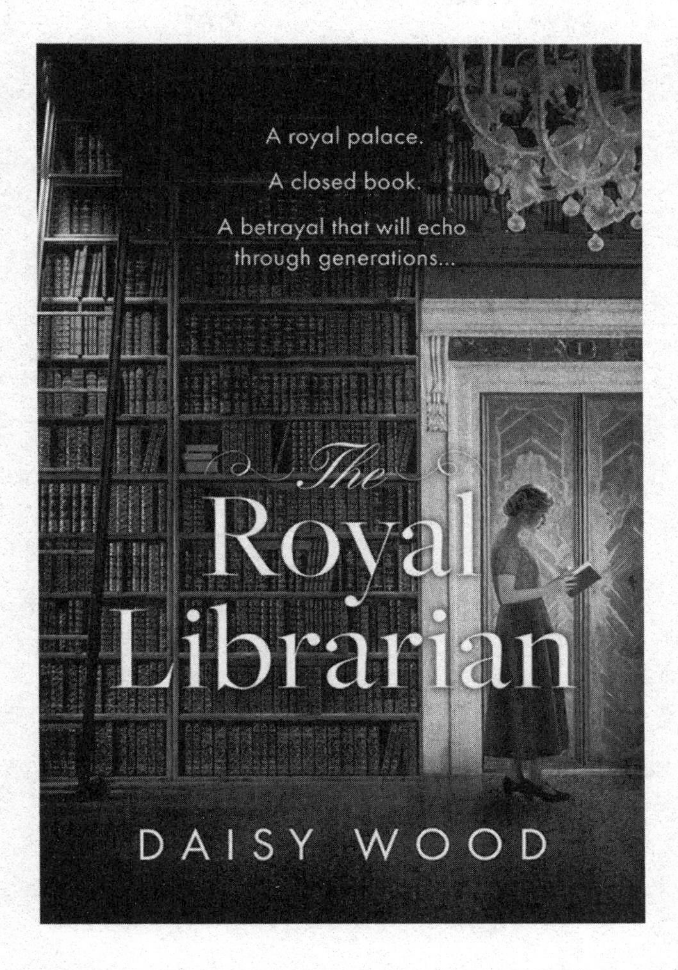


A sweeping time-slip novel, perfect for fans of Flora Harding and Madeline Martin.

For EU product safety concerns, contact us at Calle de José Abascal, 56–1°,
28003 Madrid, Spain or eugpsr@cambridge.org.

www.ingramcontent.com/pod-product-compliance
Ingram Content Group UK Ltd.
Pitfield, Milton Keynes, MK11 3LW, UK
UKHW012331130625
459647UK00009B/208

* 9 7 8 1 1 0 7 6 9 5 9 8 6 *